178

Blind Judgment

A Gideon Page Novel

Grif Stockley

SIMON & SCHUSTER

SIMON & SCHUSTER
Rockefeller Center
1230 Avenue of the Americas
New York, NY 10020

SIMON & SCHUSTER and colophon are registered trademarks
of Simon & Schuster Inc.

Designed by Deirdre C. Amthor

Manufactured in the United States of America

10   9   8   7   6   5   4   3   2   1

Library of Congress Cataloging-in-Publication Data
Stockley, Grif
Blind judgment: a Gideon Page novel / Grif Stockley
p.   cm.
1. Page, Gidgeon (Fictitious character)—Fiction.   I. Title.
PS3569.T612B58   1997
813'.54—dc21   97-16826
                                                   CIP

ISBN 0-684-81564-8

Prologue

"THE TYPICAL WHITE GUY who is moving to our town from the Delta does it . . . to get away from the Delta. Race enters into it about 100 percent of the time. But there are other things going on. That area is becoming too depressing for people. No one wants to be from one of those towns with all those problems." (Quote from an Arkansas businessman speaking on condition of anonymity to an *Arkansas Democrat-Gazette* reporter in a December 31, 1995, article on white flight from the Arkansas Delta.)

It appears only a matter of time before complete political control passes to the African-American racial majority in small Southern towns nourished by the Mississippi on its way to the sea. At the time of the Civil War, Arkansas, a diverse state geographically, with mountains to the north and west and rich bottom land to the east, was the second fastest-growing slave state in the Union (next to Texas). That legacy continues to haunt and obsess those of us who have been part of the landscape. This book is dedicated to those Arkansans, black and white, who remain and struggle in the Delta.

One

"ARE YOU GIDEON PAGE?"

I turn to my right and see an attractive looking black woman in her thirties seated in our waiting room. She is wearing jeans and a red cotton jersey sweater and tennis shoes. On the chair beside her is a faded cloth coat that can't be much protection in the raw February wind that is blowing fiercely outside the Layman Building.

"Yes, ma'am," I say, and look for Julia, our receptionist, who is probably already taking a break though it is only a quarter after nine. This woman isn't a scheduled client. I don't have an appointment until ten.

"I'm Latrice Bledsoe. I drove over from Bear Creek," she says, standing up. "My husband was charged with murder yesterday and needs a lawyer."

Bear Creek! My old hometown in the Arkansas Delta. A good two hours' drive away. I've never tried a case over there, nor have I ever wanted to. Too many skeletons rattling around in those cottonfields. I lay my briefcase on Julia's desk, covering up her latest issue of *Cosmopolitan,* and take off my overcoat. Thanksgiving weekend I had the delightful experience of confirming during a trip to Bear Creek with my twenty-year-old daughter Sarah that my paternal grandfather had impregnated a Negro girl in the 1930s. She couldn't have been more than six-teen at the time. He had been her mother's landlord. Still alive, Mrs. Washington, who lives there in a housing project for the elderly, was perhaps too circumspect to characterize the rela-tionship between them as rape. Since my grandfather went to her mother's shack every month to collect the rent, I'm not so sure. "Who was the victim?" I ask, wondering if I will recognize the name.

"Willie Ting, an old Chinese man who owned the meat-packing plant," Mrs. Bledsoe says, "where Doss worked."

I do know the name. Even though nobody else is in our wait-ing room, this is an inappropriate conversation to be having out here, and I invite Mrs. Bledsoe to follow me back to my office. Thirty years ago I had regularly played tennis with Willie Ting's son Tommy when I came home during the summers from Subi-aco Academy in western Arkansas. The Tings, like the three other Chinese families in town, had owned a grocery store in the black area of Bear Creek. Tommy, like his younger sister Connie, had been popular and an outstanding student. I won-der what became of him. I should try to find out even if I don't take this case, which I can't imagine I can afford to do. A meat-packing job in the state's poorest county can't pay for much of a defense.

After Mrs. Bledsoe sits down in my office and declines a cup of coffee, I ask, "What's the evidence against your husband?"

Mrs. Bledsoe says, her voice dropping to a whisper, "They say they found his butcher knife with the old man's blood on it, and Doss doesn't have an alibi when Mr. Ting was killed. He was home by himself." She paused to look hard at my face. "I know my husband, Mr. Page. He isn't a killer."

I begin to doodle on my notepad. Too bad she can't be on his jury. I glance at my watch. I've got some time to kill before my ten o'clock appointment. "What do the authorities think his motive was?" I ask, interested because of Tommy. God, he was a human backboard. The Arkansas Michael Chang. I could never beat him. His father I barely knew. I never saw him outside his crowded little convenience store. Mr. Ting's English was only fair, and he had a heavy accent. Sent by my mother to pick up a bar of soap or a box of salt, sometimes I'd see the whole family. Tommy would seem a little embarrassed, but maybe it was my imagination.

"Supposedly, he was hired," Mrs. Bledsoe says solemnly, "by Paul Taylor to kill him so he could buy the plant cheap."

"Paul Taylor?" I exclaim, my voice jumping high enough to shatter crystal. "A white man whose family owned half the county?" It can't be. Paul was an asshole, but he was too rich to have to commit murder.

"The very same," Mrs. Bledsoe confirms. "My husband hardly even knew him."

My stomach begins to knot up. I hated the Taylors. Oscar, Paul's father, had cheated my mother after my father died, and then years later as an adult, Paul had picked up eighty acres of her land at a tax sale. Because of them, Mother died in a shabby three-room apartment on the outskirts of town. Come to think of it, I still hate the Taylors.

"Now, tell me again why would he hire your husband?" I ask. In junior high, Paul and I had been best friends. Before my father's death, my parents would drive out to parties with other couples to Riverdale, the Taylor plantation on the banks of the Mississippi about fifteen miles from town. Many nights in those years, Paul would spend the night in town at our house. Six feet tall in the ninth grade, Paul had girls eating out of his hand while the rest of us were still borrowing our daddies' razors. After my father hanged himself in the state hospital, Paul never darkened our door again, and my mother never returned to Riverdale.

"He didn't!" Latrice Bledsoe says urgently. "Doss is being framed!"

"Who does he think is framing him?" I ask, paying more attention by the second. The memory of my mother's face when she learned that Oscar Taylor was foreclosing on the building my father had been buying registers in my brain like it was yesterday. Mother was trying to find a buyer for the pharmacy, but Oscar snatched the building away before she could sell it. It was the only time I ever heard her curse.

"He doesn't know; maybe one of the other workers," Mrs. Bledsoe says, her voice weary.

"Maybe it was Paul Taylor," I suggest, but unable to believe it. I can't imagine why he would do it. Not with all their money. "Couldn't he have planned with someone else to set up your husband?" I would love to prove that in a court of law.

Mrs. Bledsoe shrugs. She obviously hasn't made that leap yet. "We wanted to know," she says, her voice shy as she approaches the topic at hand, "how much you charge."

It has barely been two months since I regularly commuted to the northwest part of the state for a rape trial. Though the publicity was worth it, I lost money on that case with all the traveling and being away from the office. Though I think I know, I ask, "How did you find out about me?"

"You were the lawyer for Dade Cunningham, and you used to live in Bear Creek. Lucy Cunningham recommended you."

I nod, though I am a little surprised. Though Dade was acquitted, his mother wasn't all that happy with me by the end of the trial. Dade Cunningham was a wide receiver for the University of Arkansas who was accused of raping a white cheerleader. His mother, who lives in Hughes, a few miles east of Bear Creek, retained me to represent him, and I took his case hoping that if I got him acquitted I could negotiate his pro contract. It was hardly an accident she turned out to be the granddaughter of Mrs. Washington, whom my grandfather got pregnant some sixty years ago. I pretend to write some figures on my legal pad. "How much can you pay?" I ask, knowing I'd take the case for gas money. It surprises me to know how much I'd love to see Paul Taylor go to prison. "We've got seven thousand dollars in savings," Mrs. Bledsoe says, consulting a piece of paper she has taken from her purse. "We were going to use it to buy a house."

Mrs. Bledsoe somehow reminds me of the singer Keely Smith, a black singer from at least a generation ago whose

10

somber expression never seemed to change during a performance. I look past her out the window. Seven thousand for a
capital murder trial is a joke. I flip through my calendar and
note how full it is the next few months. Finally, after I've struggled as a solo practitioner the last few years, my mostly criminal defense practice has begun to build. I will be busy as hell,
but I think I can squeeze it in. Though it will mean endless
driving again, I vow that I will spend as much time in the office
as I possibly can. Pushing fifty, I've only been a lawyer for five
years, and so far I haven't managed to make up for lost time.
"That will do it," I say. "But I'll need all of it before I begin."

"Will you take a check?" Latrice Bledsoe asks calmly as if we
were discussing a parking ticket. I wonder if her husband has
been in trouble before. "I've got a thousand in cash."

Though I have been burned more than once taking checks
from clients, I say that I will, and watch her count out ten one
hundred bills and then also write on a green piece of paper that
obligates the Farmer's State Bank of Bear Creek to give me her
life savings. I make her a receipt, and we exchange paper. I will
have her husband sign a retainer agreement. It occurs to me that
it is not out of the realm of possibility that she is lying, and I,
like my client, am now on Paul Taylor's payroll. For that to
happen, though, Paul would have to be suffering from a major
case of amnesia, but the thought makes me nervous as does the
knowledge of how much time this case will take. I have recently
abandoned my neighborhood of over twenty-five years and am
moving into a new house. Add the new mortgage to Sarah's tuition and my other expenses and you have the equation for tight
money.

In the next thirty minutes I cover as much ground as I can but
don't find out anything that makes it seem less likely that Doss
Bledsoe is guilty of slitting his employer's throat. According to
his wife, the plant was in operation from six to two, and it was
her husband's habit to come home after work, fix himself some
lunch, drink a beer and take a nap. The time of death she thinks
is claimed to be between two and four in the afternoon, the time

when Willie's wife discovered his body. Bledsoe has no alibi, just his word.

In her haste to get over here this morning, she has forgotten to bring a copy of his charges and her information is sketchy at best. She has heard through a clerk in the courthouse that the prosecutor had been waiting for the DNA results from the FBI lab in Washington, D.C., before arresting Doss and Paul yesterday. Having exhausted her knowledge of the charges, I learn that Latrice now works the night shift in a 7-Eleven, but at the time of the murder back in September, she was working days. She and Doss, in their early thirties, and lifelong residents of Bear Creek, married four years ago. They have no children yet. Doss had been working at the plant for five years. He had liked Willie, although he didn't pay much. She adds dryly that eastern Arkansas was hardly union territory.

I think I'm going to like Latrice. She has convinced herself that her husband is innocent, and that alone is refreshing. My last client charged with murder had a wife who was itching to testify that she had no doubt her husband was guilty. We pleaded the case out to manslaughter. I look down at my calendar and tell her I can get over there this afternoon. If I leave after lunch, I can be at the jail by a little after three. Not that I'm going to be able to get Bledsoe out of jail. Unless he has a very rich uncle his wife hasn't told me about, he isn't going to be able to make bond even if I could persuade the judge to grant it. But at least I can visit with him and see if I want to change my mind about handling his case.

I get Latrice's address and phone number. She remembers to tell me that Doss is incarcerated at the new state-run detention facility near Brickeys, about thirteen miles outside of Bear Creek, and that I will need to call ahead in order to see him. My ten o'clock appointment, a rare probate case, is waiting for me, and I walk Latrice to the elevators, realizing I may be spending a lot of time in my old hometown. I'm not at all sure how I feel about that.

At 11:30 I get the number from information and call the jail to set up my meeting and then leave a message for my girlfriend, Amy, not to wait for dinner, when my friend Dan walks stiffly into my office holding his side. I haven't seen him since he won and took an all-expense-paid ski trip to Crested Butte, Colorado. "How was it?" I ask, glad to see him. Dan has been my best friend since I got an office here. He is a mess, but he makes me laugh, and that one quality covers up a multitude of sins.

"Well, I'm alive," he says, easing himself into the chair across from my desk.

"You look like somebody tried to hang some sheetrock down your spine. Is anything broken?"

Dan takes a deep breath and winces. "Only my eighth and ninth ribs. My instructor said I looked like I was trying to ski on the damn things."

Poor Dan. I try not to smile. As fat as he is, breaking a rib would be like trying to pop a balloon inside a bale of cotton. He must have fallen hard.

Dan's having a rough time. He got involved with a prostitute he once had represented; his wife kicked him out; and now he's hurt himself.

Dan fingers his rib cage. "The first two days I thought I was going to have a heart attack. When I'd fall, which was every five minutes, I couldn't get up. I'd flail around on the snow hyperventilating. It scared the hell out of the rest of the class. My instructor said that if I fell one more time, she'd leave me out in the snow to die. I've never worked so hard in my life just to stay upright!"

I don't want to laugh, but it's impossible not to. "Did you meet any women?" I ask, knowing they were the principal inducement. Years of beer commercials convinced him to take the trip despite his fears he was too old and fat. Maybe he would meet, if not snow bunnies, a bored housewife chaperoning a church group.

"Hell, no," he wheezes, "I was too achey and tired at the end of the day. The one night I made it to a bar I nodded off during the one conversation I had with a woman."

13

I cackle, knowing that I'd have been just as bad or worse. "When did you break your ribs?" I ask, realizing his injuries could be more serious than they sound. Guys our age can break a bone, develop pneumonia, and be dead within a week.

"Probably the second day, but everything else was hurting so bad by then, I thought the pain was normal. My thighs felt like somebody was coming in while I was asleep and hammering on them. My shoulders were almost as bad because of trying to get around using those damn poles. By the end of the week I was practically using them as crutches. Then some fancy clinic charges me four hundred dollars to take enough X-rays to sterilize a thousand-pound gorilla and then tells me to breathe deeply and cough a lot. I didn't even get a Band-Aid out of it."

I wince, knowing Dan doesn't have insurance. He was almost broke before he left and wouldn't have gone if it hadn't been a free trip.

Feeling sorry for him and guilty at the same time, I say, "I'll buy you lunch. I've got a case to run by you."

As I knew he would, Dan perks up at the mention of food. Gripping the armrests of the chair, he pushes himself up like an old man and looks around my office. "Where did you get those prints?" he asks respectfully. "They don't look too bad."

"Amy thought," I say, standing up, too, "my office needed sprucing up. I gave up on the plants since they insist on being watered."

"You gonna marry Gilchrist?" Dan asks as he follows me out. "You could do a lot worse."

"I have done a lot worse," I remind him, but not responding to his question. Amy, Dan, and I were classmates and friends together in night law school, and he knows about some of the women I dated after my wife Rosa's death. Actually, Amy and I are considering living together if I ever get heat in my shiny new house from hell.

At the front desk, Julia grins at Dan. "You couldn't look any stiffer if you were mounted on the wall."

It has taken me years to get used to Julia, a niece of the

owner, and I have needed every one of them. She has lifetime security in a job she despises. If that isn't a prescription for hell on earth, I don't know what is. As usual, Dan regresses in her presence. "Actually, my body is one long, stiff, hot poker," he says, leering at her.

Julia lets the skirt that Dan calls imitation cracked leather when she's not around ride up to within an inch of her panties. "If I had a dollar for every guy who believed that," she says, stretching her breast implants against today's tight wool sweater, "I could buy this dump from my Uncle Roy and turn it officially into the nursing home it's becoming. When are you guys gonna get some clients in here? It's like living in a morgue, it's so quiet."

"It's the cold," I say, knowing she is talking about Dan and some other lawyers on our floor. Dan is floundering, but then it seems he always is.

"If it was the summer," Julia challenges me, "you'd be saying it was the heat. Face it, you solo practitioners are dinosaurs. You don't know how to market yourselves. You charge too little or too much, and then don't collect half of what you bill. Half you guys on this floor are dead and don't even know it."

Dan grins. "Thanks for the pep talk, sweetie," he says, staring admiringly at Julia's chest. "You want me to bring you some pie from downstairs?"

"It wouldn't make it to the elevator." She smirks, staring back at Dan's stomach. Though she would sooner die than admit it, Julia has become quite protective of Dan. While he was going through his recent craziness, she worried about him like a mother hen. While Julia likes to pick on Dan, she becomes enraged when other people follow suit. Or putting Dan's own spin on it, to be such a competitive society, there is nothing we hate worse than competition.

Downstairs in the cafeteria, Dan blows through a plate of spaghetti in five minutes flat. "Have you ever noticed that the real pleasures in life," he says, wiping his mouth with a napkin at our table in the non-smoking section, "last no more than a

15

few minutes tops—fucking, eating, shitting, the few seconds right before you know you're finally going to sleep? All this civilized behavior just fills out the day. We're just animals, ole buddy. I'd just as soon drop over on all fours right now and quit kidding myself."

Poor Dan. He's never had a kid. Childish and silly, he would make a great father. The children of his divorce clients hang all over him. He plays with them as if he is their long-lost brother. "What's stopping you?" I egg him on. "Just get neckid and plop on down there. The country's looking for some honest-to-God leadership. If poor Bill tried to do it, half the country would say it was just a way to try to get a woman to go to bed with him."

Dan loosens his tie as he gazes out over the crowded tables of mostly office workers from inside the Layman Building, who, like us, are beginning to show symptoms of cabin fever after a long cold snap. How do people stand the north in the winter? Three weeks in a row of frigid air is all it takes for us to start talking crazy. Dan sips greasy coffee and then nags at me, "Have you thought any more about joining One-on-One? They've got a list of boys a mile long."

I roll my eyes and pretend to sigh. Dan has been bugging me to get involved in a buddy program for ghetto kids for the last month. "I know," I say, thinking of the fact sheet he left in my chair last week. "Let's make a deal. If you can keep quiet about it until after this case is over, I'll sign up, okay?" Despite Dan's cynicism, he has a bowl of mush where his heart ought to be. Actually, I've been feeling guilty for deciding to desert my old neighborhood. Rosa and I lived in a mixed area for years. Since her death I've felt increasingly detached from my black neighbors. At Dan's urging, I have thought of taking on a kid from one of the projects as a way of keeping a pledge to Rosa that I wouldn't try to become a Yuppie after her death. Fat chance with my income, but my new neighborbood will be lily-white, and maybe joining One-on-One will keep the guilt at a manageable level. Rosa would have been angry with me for leaving our neighborhood without a good reason.

Dan pretends to zip his mouth. "So go ahead and brag about your new case. I don't mind. I think I took a vow of poverty somewhere along the way and nobody told me about it."

I smile at the thought of Dan as St. Francis of Assisi. A monk he is not, even if he might be happier if he accepted his new solo status as permanent. Over a piece of pecan pie and a cup of coffee I don't need, I run through Latrice Bledsoe's visit and admit, "I had forgotten how much anger I've carried all those years at the Taylors. I thought I had gotten over it."

Dan burps into the fist of his right hand. "We never get over anything," he gasps, ever the philosopher.

I wonder if that is true. If I take this case because I think I can get back at the Taylors somehow, I will screw it up. Surely, I've got more sense than to pull a stunt like that. Though I have made more mistakes in the last five years than I care to remember, I have never betrayed a client or sacrificed his interest. Now is not the time to start. I look down at my watch. It's time to get on the road.

Two

I BEGIN THE DREARY TREK EAST on I-40 toward Bear Creek thinking how monotonous it would be to make this drive every day. The cold gray winter afternoon and unrelieved flatness of the Delta soil give me plenty of time to think. I know I am having a severe case of buyer's remorse, but it is hard not to second-guess my abrupt decision to move from a neighborhood I've lived in for the past twenty-five years. Yet, maybe I should have sold the house after Rosa's death seven years ago. It is only in the last few months that I've finally come to terms with the fact that my image of myself as an ex–sixties liberal no longer fits the facts. It was Rosa who had bonded with our neighbors, a mixture of mostly middle-class blacks and elderly whites who, for one reason or another, had decided they couldn't afford to sell when blacks had begun to be steered into the neighborhood.

The sixties (despite the excesses) had been such a hopeful time for me. I was helping to implement the legacy of Kennedy's Camelot and Johnson's "Great Society." Driven by the legislation of the period (the Civil Rights Act of 1964, Medicaid, Medicare, the Economic Opportunity Act, the Housing Act of 1968, etc.), America would wipe out its twin evils of racial discrimination and poverty, and I was doing my part. After my two-year stint in the Peace Corps, I worked briefly for a Blackwell County War on Poverty project until it finally dawned on me that it was a bureaucratic make-work project for blacks that rivaled any northern city's reputation for patronage, waste, and political intrigue. Damn, was I naive! After about a year of pushing paper I drifted into a social worker's job for the county, investigating child abuse, and stayed there until Rosa finally prodded me into night law school. And all the while, instead of becoming a model of peace, prosperity, and racial harmony, parts of Blackwell County, like much of the rest of the country, were becoming a battle zone for the gangs, drug dealers, and the underclass that seems to be growing daily.

As I angle south off I-40 before reaching Forrest City, I wonder why it took so long for me to realize I was no longer a soldier in a war that couldn't be won, not in my lifetime anyway. I didn't really need to solve the world's problems. It has been more than I can do to raise Sarah and keep myself out of trouble. Sarah. The thought of her makes me smile. Such a wonderful kid but a moralist as only the young can be. At various times in the past three years she's been a fundamentalist Christian, a dancer on the Razorbacks pom pom squad, a feminist. Now she's a caregiver to AIDS victims.

Always searching. I hope I haven't made her too insecure ever to be content with herself. Her mother's death from breast cancer when she was in junior high didn't help. How much did my father's schizophrenia and subsequent suicide when I was thirteen affect me? It is something I will always wonder about. Sarah has coped much better than I did.

I stop at a convenience store in Moro to use the bathroom. Middle age. If this is a precursor to what's ahead, I can't get too excited about it. Is it my imagination or do I really have to piss fifteen times a day? How do guys who work in factories cope with one fifteen-minute break in the morning? As I read the copy on the white condom boxes above the urinal, I realize I would need a catheter and a bottle the size of a water cooler strapped to my leg to hold a job in a plant.

On the road again with a cup of coffee, I can tell I am back

19

home in the Delta by the increasing number of beat-up old cars with blacks behind the wheel, many of them as ancient looking as their cars. Despite having been away, I can't escape the feeling that I know this area, and I know its people, better than I'll ever know any place else. There is something vaguely comforting about the past even if it was difficult. I think of the way I acted at thirteen after my father hanged himself on the state hospital grounds in Benton. As far as shitty adolescent behavior goes, I can't quite say I wrote the book. Walking out of class, talking back to teachers, sneaking beer out of neighbors' refrigerators, was small potatoes compared to the problems kids have today, but it was enough to make my mother think that she wasn't going to be able to handle me. She couldn't afford to send me to Subiaco, but, as Marty, my sister, has pointed out, at the time she couldn't afford not to. Fortunately, for me, society didn't have psychiatric institutions for kids who mainly needed a good kick in the butt every day.

At Subiaco I cried like the baby I was that first semester, but Mother had the sense not to let me come home. I resented it at the time, but she was right. Was she perhaps right also to discourage Rosa and me from returning to Bear Creek? Why did I want to go back, anyway? Rosa's presence would have been a constant reminder to the town that perhaps the rumors about my paternal grandfather's out-of-wedlock child were true, something that my mother had consistently denied. "It's in the Page blood," they would have said. "They're all nigger lovers."

Coming into the outskirts of Bear Creek on 79 I continue east toward Memphis, and I arrive at the state prison and county jail facility fifteen minutes later. I sign in at the reception desk and then have to get back in my car and drive around to a separate building to see my client, a hassle I'd like to avoid in the future.

Short, round, and balding in his bright orange jump suit, Bledsoe does not look like a killer. We sit across from each other in a visitation room in green plastic chairs separated from each other by a clear glass window and steel mesh, and I scribble notes while he talks. "I liked ole Willie," he says mildly. "I felt pretty bad when they told me someone cut him up. He was a hell of a good man. Hardly anybody would be workin' in Bear Creek at all if it wudn't for people like him."

"When did they first start acting like you were a suspect?" I ask, noting how easygoing Doss appears. I was afraid he was going to be some hulking monster who looked at home with a butcher knife. Instead, his hands are smaller than mine, and his receding hairline and a squint give him a mild, innocent expression that a jury can't help but notice.

"The best I figure now, the very next morning," Doss drawls, wiping his nose with his sleeve. "The plant's got these two meat inspectors, and one of them said he saw my knife wasn't put up exactly right, and they said there was some blood on it. I heard it turned out 'O' positive—same as ole Willie's. Of course, I didn't know all this was going on. They began questioning everybody on the kill floor that day and up front, too. Even though I'd been home that afternoon by myself, I never figured I had to worry."

"How'd they say Willie was killed?" I ask, realizing how much I have forgotten to ask his wife. "Was there a struggle?"

Doss shakes his head. "Naw, they said he didn't even put up a fight. That's why they knew right away it was somebody who worked in the plant. Whoever done it jus' walked right up behind him at his desk and cut his throat and then stepped back and watched him die. It wouldn't take long if you get that artery." Doss draws an imaginary line across his throat.

I feel a chill, and it isn't just from the cold. What a horrible moment it must have been for that old man when he realized what was happening to him. "So you were the only suspect?" I ask, thinking how tempting it would be to try to frame someone like him.

Doss shrugs. "They acted like we was all suspects for a while till that blood got checked. Then the sheriff wanted me to take a lie detector test, and I wouldn't. Hell, I don't trust that shit. Then they fired me, but nothing happened after that until yesterday when all hell broke loose." Somehow he is able to grin, though weakly, at the spectacle of himself being taken into custody.

"Your wife said she heard that the DNA analysis," I say, realizing he may not know, "showed conclusively that the blood on your knife was Willie's."

"I don't know about that," Doss demurs, scratching a sore on his ring finger. "Anybody could have got hold of my knife. We just kept 'em laid out in the back. Ever'body had his own spot."

I try to visualize the floor of a meat-packing plant and conjure up a scene of bloody, controlled carnage. I will have to get the judge to allow me a tour of the plant. The inside of my mouth begins to moisten at just the thought. This will be fun: I can't even see a dead weasel on the road without becoming a little queasy. "How do they tell them apart?"

"Most scratch a little mark on the handle," Doss explains. "I got my initials on mine."

It occurs to me that Doss misses his work. "What have you been doing since you got fired?" I ask, wondering how I'd handle months of idleness. I'd probably turn into an alcoholic after the first month.

"I've been helpin' out at my uncle's barbecue place in town for a while," Doss responds. "It's actually owned by Paul Taylor. I didn't even know that."

For the first time since I've been talking to him, I pick up a false note here. I haven't asked about his association with the Taylors. "What are you talking about?" I ask, watching his face carefully. If he is conning me, I'd like to find out earlier than later.

"They're sayin' he hired me," Doss says. "I hardly even know him."

I question him at length about Paul, and he admits that before he started at the plant he was a delivery man for an appliance store in town that Paul owned. Paul rarely came in the store, but when he did, he would make a point to speak to the help. "He was real friendly," Doss says. "We always got a ham at Christmas from him."

That sounds like Paul, the great benefactor of the underclass. He wouldn't pay minimum wage if there was any way he could avoid it, but he liked to play Santa Claus. "Have you seen him since you worked there?" I ask, afraid I see where this is heading.

"On the street every now and then," Doss says. "And then at Oldham's Barbecue some. See, like I say, it turned out he owned it, and my uncle just managed it for him."

Paul, it appears, has had Doss on the payroll for years. "So how long have you been working one way or another for Paul Taylor?"

"About eight years, I guess," Doss says, using his fingers to count.

It is easy to guess what has happened. While the prosecuting attorney was waiting for the results of the DNA analysis, he just sat back and watched Doss. I wouldn't be surprised if Mr. Old-ham was about to retire and Doss was going to join the entre-preneurial class, courtesy of Paul. On the other hand, it is not out of the realm of the possible it was a coincidence. Employers are few and far between in the Delta. "How much were you making?" I ask.

"More than I was making cutting meat," Doss admits. He sighs, knowing things don't look good for him.

I ask him directly, "Did Paul Taylor hire you to kill Willie?"

"Naw, sir!" Doss says, raising his voice for the first time. "I swear to God he didn't. I didn't murder ole Willie for nobody."

For some reason I think I believe him. Maybe I just want to do this case. We talk for a while longer and then I get a guard to let him come around to sign my retainer agreement. I don't make a practice of trying to milk the cow dry in one setting. I will have ample opportunity to find out Doss's story. I tell him that I will try to have his arraignment set as quickly as possible so we can get a trial date. I explain that since he has no money for a bond, he will have to remain in jail until the trial, which he accepts more stoically than I would. Paul, he tells me, has already made bond, which is hardly surprising.

I drive to the courthouse in Bear Creek and find the sheriff's office on the first floor. I want to pay a courtesy call on him before I go see the prosecuting attorney. If I do my job right on this case, the sheriff's job in this case is just beginning. As I walk into the building, I realize I haven't been here since I was a teenager and signed up for the draft. With the Vietnam War on, a heart murmur, which has never given me a moment's problem, probably saved my life. As I push open the door, I wonder why this case didn't make this morning's edition of the *Arkansas Democrat-Gazette*. I can understand that the arrest of a black plant worker in the rural Delta for the murder of a Chinese businessman would spark no great interest by the media, but Paul's arrest should be big news. At least it would have been twenty years ago. Maybe he isn't as rich as I thought.

I open the door and am greeted by a young black secretary behind a desk and a typewriter. "You lookin' for Sheriff Bonner? He just called and said he's on the way."

She has an old-fashioned bushy 'fro that I haven't seen in twenty years. Maybe eighteen at the most, she has an infectious smile that draws a smile from me. The last time I was in this building the only black face was behind a broom. "May I have a seat and wait for him?" I ask.

"You sure can," she says brightly. "Would you care for some coffee?"

I take off my overcoat and sit down across from her. I've drunk enough coffee today to float a battleship, but one more cup won't hurt. "With just a little milk or whitener in it," I say, pleased by the courtesy shown me. Could the sheriff be a black man? I realize I've got to find out what the hell has been going on for the last thirty years over here before I go too much further on this case.

"You must be a lawyer, but not from around here," my hostess says, pouring my coffee into a mug that has a replica of the design of the Pyramid office building and sports arena in Memphis. She's clad in a modest green jumper with a white blouse underneath; Julia's outfits, by comparison, look like the getups of a low-rent call girl. I realize how low my expectations are in the Delta. If you believe everything you read, you'd expect to find a girl this age at the welfare office with two children hanging on to her as she signs up for food stamps and AFDC.

"I'm Gideon Page," I say, holding out my hand for my coffee. She takes my hand and pumps it as if she were a politician seeking votes.

"I'm Yolanda Ford, Sheriff Bonner's secretary," she replies. "It's nice to meet you."

The door opens, and there is no mistaking the sheriff. Bonner is a compact black man in his early forties, in an olive and tan uniform. He measures no more than 5'9", and that may be stretching it because of the boots he is wearing. He sports a firm black mustache, and as he grins at Yolanda, I notice he has the whitest teeth of any black I've seen this side of Hollywood. The color of dark chocolate, Bonner is undeniably an attractive man. He smiles easily at me, but instead of introducing himself, he turns back to Yolanda and asks, "Who do we have here?"

By allowing her to make our introduction, I see he is training her, and I watch closely as Yolanda replies, "Sheriff Bonner, this is Mr. Gideon Page. He hasn't been here long enough to let us know what we can do for him."

Revealing his gun at his side as he takes off his leather jacket, Bonner offers his hand. "I'm Woodrow Bonner. How're you, Mr. Page?"

Such friendliness seems genuine enough, and with his firm handshake I begin to perceive why Bonner is surely the first black sheriff in Bear Creek since Reconstruction. He radiates a politician's affability. I tell him I am fine and that I am Doss Bledsoe's attorney.

"Yolanda, hold my calls," he says without changing his expression and leads me back through a door to his office behind her desk.

His office, though small, is very much like an up-and-coming politician's—on the walls is a picture of him with Bill Clinton and another with the once Surgeon General of the United States, Joycelyn Elders, who I recall as director of the Arkansas Department of Health helped start a controversial school-based clinic over here which made available birth control information. Directly behind his chair is a picture of him shaking hands with Jesse Jackson and Maynard Jackson, the former black mayor of Atlanta. This area of the state is heavily Democratic, and no serious candidate can afford to overlook it, despite the declining population. Beside the celebrities are framed certificates showing his participation in various law enforcement and community activities. On his desk is a picture of presumably his wife and his two children, both teenaged girls who look just like him. "I'm originally from Bear Creek," I say as I sit down, determined to make an ally of this man even though he surely must be convinced of my client's guilt. "But we didn't have many big names stopping by here thirty years ago. I remember Orval Faubus campaigning once at the square, but I doubt you would have had his picture up here."

Sheriff Bonner smiles politely, presumably blanching inwardly at the thought of the state's most famous segregationist schmoozing for votes in his office. "If the ugliest girl in town had the only car," he points out, "there comes a time when it's convenient to forget who used to ride around with her."

"I guess you're right," I say, not about to rub this man's face in whatever compromises he's needed to make to get where he is today.

Rubbing his chin, he asks, "Did your daddy own a pharmacy here a long time ago?"

I'll take whatever mileage I can get out of Page's Drugs. "On the square. You've got a good memory." My mind plays back summer Saturday evenings at closing time, when, locking the front door, my father, invariably dressed in muted slacks and short-sleeved shirts, would stare balefully across the square and shake his head in distaste at the gaudily dressed black males strutting like peacocks as they dipped in and out of the Busy Bee, a black café. I recall a liquor store and black movie theater adjacent to the restaurant.

"I used to go in there when I was a kid, and he'd shoo me out," Bonner says. "I'm pretty sure he thought I was stealing comic books."

"He thought everybody was," I say hastily. Though I don't remember my father as a rude man, I doubt if he was overly polite to the black kids who waited restlessly for their parents to decide what store-bought nostrums would ease their aches and pains. I try to picture Bonner as a ten year old and imagine him already picking up cues on how the world worked—slowly in our part of the state. I add, "You might not remember he became seriously mentally ill."

Bonner, to his credit, doesn't pretend sympathy he can't feel. "I had forgotten that," he says. "Well, what can I do for you, Mr. Page?"

I explain that I am merely trying to get oriented and haven't even seen the charges filed against my client. "Did your office handle the investigation," I ask politely, "or did the state police get involved?" Usually, small-town sheriffs need all the help they can get.

Bonner spins a small globe on his desk. "Do you know how many investigators there are on the state police force that are minorities? I'll give you a hint. Not many. As you probably know, Bear Creek is now seventy percent black. To maintain the credibility of law enforcement over here, I do all my own investigations."

And it keeps you in the public eye, I think to myself. In ten years I can see this man being the first black Congressman from the 1st District. He has that much charisma. "I can understand that," I say. "Though I'm just getting started, it seems to me that my client could easily have been set up. Weren't there other suspects besides him?"

Bonner puts his hand behind his head. "My policy is that once I've turned over a file to the prosecutor, I don't say anything about it until trial."

"So you don't have any doubts," I ask, "that my client was hired by Paul Taylor to murder Willie Ting?"

Instead of responding right away, Bonner rocks gently in his chair. Finally, he says, politely, "I think I just answered that question." He stands up, dismissing me. "Our prosecutor is upstairs. I'm sure he'll answer any questions for you."

I scramble to my feet. "If you received some information that Paul Taylor had hired someone else to kill Willie Ting," I say, "you'd investigate it before this case goes to trial?"

The sheriff shrugs. "Of course."

"I'll hold you to that," I say as if I already have something in mind. I don't. But it is never too early to begin the job of softening up the prosecutor. If law enforcement begins to have doubts about a case, you can be sure they will be passed along to the prosecutor. My advantage in this case is that I know Paul's track record.

I ask if he can arrange for me not to have to call ahead to the prison for an appointment each time I want to see Bledsoe. He says he can do that, but to call ahead if I can.

I smile and shake hands again with Bonner and head upstairs, not knowing how to ask if the prosecutor is also black. I should have asked Doss or his wife these questions. All I know is that the judge, Rufus Johnson, is a black man. The whites still left over here must be going nuts over this case. If Paul Taylor can be charged with murder, they have to feel nobody is safe.

I find the prosecuting attorney's office across from the top of the stairs. There is no secretary, but I can hear a black man's voice in an inner office. I go stand in the doorway and motion that I'll be sitting in the waiting room. On the telephone, he nods at me. In contrast to the sheriff's Hershey's Kisses color, the prosecutor is polished copper, and his eyes look yellowish from the distance of about ten feet. The sleeves of his white shirt are folded back at the cuffs, and his pink silk tie is flung back over his shoulder as if it has been getting in his way. He sounds agitated, but I can't make out what he is saying. He motions to me that he will be off the phone in a moment, and I go have a seat across from the secretary's desk. Unlike the sheriff's office, the walls in the prosecutor's office, as out here, are bare, and it occurs to me that his home base is probably either Forrest City to the north or Helena to the south. Both towns have been more prosperous than Bear Creek, but I remind myself prosperity is a relative term in the Delta these days. As I unsuccessfully try to eavesdrop, it occurs to me that I have deliberately avoided making inquiries about the case through the white community first. Why? The answer is obvious, now that I permit myself to think about it. I would have been pressured to turn down Bledsoe's case, and I might have done so. For the first time, I allow myself to guess who Paul has employed to represent him, but I know already that he must have hired Dick Dickerson, who is considered one of the best trial attorneys in the state. A graduate of Columbia Law School, Dick could have gone anywhere. For reasons I've never understood, he chose to come back to practice law in a place where ninety-nine percent of his clients couldn't have cared less where he went to school. He must be at least sixty. I wonder if he has any regrets. I may find out before this case is over.

Moments later, the prosecutor comes out and introduces himself. "Melvin Butterfield," he says, apologetically, extending his hand as if I have an appointment and he has forced me to wait.

"Gideon Page," I say, as we shake hands. "I'm representing Doss Bledsoe."

The prosecutor's mouth doesn't exactly drop open, but he is clearly surprised as he stares at me for a long moment. Perhaps he thought Doss would hire a black attorney. "How do you do?" he says. "Sorry, I was on the phone. Want to come on back?"

"Sure," I say and follow him back into the office. Butterfield is tall, perhaps 6′4″, and can't weigh more than one sixty.

"I know you," he says emphatically as he takes a seat behind his desk. "You're that guy who got off Dade Cunningham in that rape case up in Fayetteville. Damn. First, Taylor gets Dick Dickerson, whom I can't even beat on a parking ticket, and now Doss hires a hot-shot from Blackwell County." He grins, splitting his face from ear to ear. "Maybe we can plead this out to simple assault tomorrow, and I can go back to trying DWI's against the public defender."

I laugh out loud. Prosecuting attorneys invariably take themselves as seriously as God. This guy has a twinkle in his yellowish eyes. Compared to him, the sheriff was positively pompous. "That would be fine with me," I reply.

"Man, you're famous around here. How'd you get an acquittal in that case? There was only two blacks on that jury."

Flattered that he knows so much about me, I say modestly, "It probably helped that he had caught the pass that beat Alabama."

"Isn't that the truth?" he says breezily. "As long as they win, the Razorbacks can do no wrong."

Is this guy really the prosecutor? He seems pretty loosey-goosey. "Have you got a minute to talk? I just saw my client in the jail. I assume Paul Taylor is already out."

"You bet," Butterfield says. "Despite five-hundred-thousand-dollar bail Dick had him out before they could give Mr. Taylor a wiener for supper."

I smile, thinking how much I'd have liked to have seen Paul seated on his bunk eating a hot dog. "What kind of bond will you recommend for Doss?" I ask, knowing it doesn't matter.

"Same as Paul," the prosecutor says, "five hundred thousand."

"Can we get the hearing done this afternoon?" I ask, noting that Butterfield has only the slightest trace of a Delta accent. Maybe he went to school up north and they shamed it out of him.

"Can't do it," Butterfield says, turning around to check a large calendar on the wall behind him. "The judge is in Memphis for a funeral and won't be back until tomorrow afternoon. What about three o'clock? I'll call down and put it on the docket."

I have a hot-check case in municipal court tomorrow morning, but no more court appearances. "Sure, I can be back over here."

Butterfield pulls out a file from his desk drawer and pushes it over to me. As if we were on the same side of the case instead of opposing attorneys, he confides, "It'd be hard to believe these guys would try to get away with something like this until you see the evidence against them."

Normally, a prosecutor won't even talk to you until after the bond hearing and the arraignment, but Butterfield seems downright eager to discuss the case. I scan the formal charges, which don't tell me more than I already know. He points out the test results from the FBI concluding that it was Willie's blood on Bledsoe's knife and shows me a thick sheaf of statements taken from the other workers in the plant. "Everybody else we've talked to has an alibi during the time the old man was killed."

"What time was that?" I ask, wondering how airtight each of those alibis can be. Surely, one of the workers besides Doss was by himself that afternoon.

"Between two when the plant closed and four when his wife discovered his body and called the police. The medical examiner has confirmed the time," he says, flipping over to an autopsy.

"Is that all the evidence against my client?" I ask, knowing it must not be.

"Not hardly. We've documented where he lied about his contacts with Paul Taylor." I watch as Butterfield flips to the back of the file. He points to a statement by a woman named Darla Tate. "She's the secretary at the plant. She heard Bledsoe talking to someone on the phone in the plant office a couple of days after the murder. She was in the bathroom and he must have thought he was alone. She's signed a statement that she heard him saying, and I quote, 'I got the money.' She knew that we

31

had a tape of Taylor threatening Willie about a month before, and so she called the sheriff."

"You have a tape of Paul actually threatening Willie?" I ask, incredulous. It doesn't totally surprise me that Bledsoe would make that kind of phone call, but I can't imagine Paul being dumb enough to let himself be implicated on tape.

Butterfield pulls a tape from his desk drawer and places it in a pocket Olympus tape recorder. "This is a copy. The sheriff's got the original in his evidence room, and you can hear it anytime you want. The relevant part is only a few seconds long." He pushes a button, and I hear a click and then recognize Paul Taylor's rich, bass voice saying, "This place won't be worth a hundred thousand dollars after you die because you've got nobody here to run it."

"It sounds like you're threatening me," a soft Asian voice, not unlike Tommy's, responds.

"Willie, you can interpret it however you want, but one way or the other you're gonna die soon. . . ." I hear the sound of a telephone ringing, and the tape ends. Though I'm certainly not going to admit it to Butterfield, my reaction is one of deep satisfaction. There is no way in hell Paul can deny the tape. Though I've never done any research on this precise legal point, I'm certain the tape of this conversation could be admitted into evidence. I ask, "What was the deal? Was Paul trying to buy it and Willie wouldn't sell?"

"Exactly," Butterfield answers. "This was made about a month before he died. He gave this tape to his wife and told her that if anything happened to him to tell his son in Washington about it. He had told the secretary about it, too."

"Why didn't Willie take the tape to the sheriff the next day?" I ask. "He might still be alive."

Butterfield shrugs. "Who knows? Those folks have always been a mystery to me. All I know is that they're still sucking what little money there is right out of the black community with those dinky little stores they operate and never crack so much as a smile."

There is no mistaking the bitterness in the prosecutor's voice. It occurs to me that there is probably no love lost between the blacks and Asians in Bear Creek any more than there is in places like Los Angeles. "How many stores do they have left?"

"Three," the prosecutor says. "They're still hanging on, though there's not much left to get."

I file away his response. It may come in handy later. I wonder how he feels personally about Paul Taylor. Now is not the time to ask, but I would like to know. "Did Paul make an offer for the plant after Willie died?"

Butterfield presses down a creased place on one of the statements. "He waited about two months. Of course, we were working with the son in D.C., but Taylor didn't say anything more that incriminated himself. He offered a hundred thousand for the plant, but after a couple of meetings with the son, he withdrew the offer. The plant's being run by his cousin from Greenville. Obviously, you'll want to go out there."

The reason for all this chumminess and willingness to let me see the file before I've officially entered my appearance in court as Doss's attorney dawns on me as I realize there is no smoking gun linking Paul Taylor to Bledsoe. Butterfield has the one overheard conversation at the plant, but the secretary can't say whom he was talking to. I'd be willing to bet my fee in this case that at some point, perhaps very soon, Doss is going to be offered a deal he may not be able to refuse in order to get his testimony against Paul. If that's what this case comes down to, it will be fine with me.

Before I leave his office, I ask about the sheriff. "I see him running for a bigger office someday. The pictures on his walls are pretty impressive."

Butterfield gives me his only frown of the day. "Bonner's been running for something since the day he was born. He's a good sheriff," he adds quickly.

I resist asking the prosecutor what he will be running for next. I should have realized he and Bonner see themselves as natural competitors in this area of the state. With all the whites leaving, they have political opportunities they never dreamed possible when they were growing up. The phone rings, and when Butterfield gets off, he promises to get me a copy of the file tomorrow after the arraignment, and I leave his office understanding that Butterfield wants to convict Paul in the worst way. What better springboard to office than the murder conviction of the biggest planter in the county? He probably doesn't care about Bledsoe at all. Behind the courthouse I start up the Blazer. It is time to begin finding out about Paul Taylor.

Three

BEFORE IT GETS TOO DARK, I drive around Bear Creek's residential areas. Though I was here three months ago, I am struck this visit by my hometown's desolation on the eve of spring. The houses and businesses show the effects of years of neglect, a dismaying shabbiness I had not noticed earlier. In the summer the abundant honeysuckle vines, tiger lilies, and chinaberry trees framed by giant magnolia, pecan, and even persimmon trees hide the decay. As a child my favorite tree was the weeping willow. My friends and I stuffed the droopy branches down the backs of our britches and pretended we were horses.

On Sharp Street I drive slowly past our original family home. A wood two-story structure, it needs a paint job. Scott Nightingale, the town dentist whose work always required aspirin for days afterward, bought the house after Mother died, but he, too, is dead. Though there is a middle class and even some wealthy people still left in Bear Creek, many of the homes and yards seem shrunken. This area north of Hazelnut was my childhood universe. It occurs to me, for the first time in years, how much I loved it here. From morning to night Elmer Burton, Joe Hood, Hannah Carlton and I played "Army" in these yards, shooting each other and dying and rising to fight another day. The owners all knew us and our families intimately and

35

watched out for us. Two houses down from us lived the Carltons, my parents' closest friends. For years it seemed that I spent every rainy day playing with Hannah in their attic. She was a year younger but truly, in those prepuberty years, my best pal. A smiling, happy tomboy wise beyond her years, Hannah never cried or got mad no matter how many games of go fish, blackjack, or checkers she lost. To her, competition was merely an excuse for companionship. Winning was never the point; friendship was. To satisfy my curiosity one stormy Saturday morning we went in the bathroom, shut the door, and she pulled down her pants and showed me that bizarre, defenseless little crack between her legs. I reciprocated by exposing my equally exotic nub and its microscopic attachments. That done, we went back to our games.

As I cruise by the tennis courts at the old high school where Tommy and I competed against each other more than three decades ago, I marvel at our innocence in those days. It was a life so safe and secure it seems almost laughable now. No houses or cars were locked at night, much less during the day.

On Orchard Lane, I stop the Blazer in front of my old girlfriend's house, knowing she could be a major source of information if she feels like talking. Despite my status as a hometown boy, there are few, if any, people I feel I know well enough after all this time to trust completely or for them to feel like talking to me. Angela Marr is one of these few.

As I get out of the Blazer, I am reminded of the note she sent me last month after a case of mine was in the *Democrat-Gazette*. When I saw the return address, egotistical beyond all reason, I had assumed she was writing to congratulate me, when, in fact, she was letting me know that Dwight had died in December after a long battle with cancer. I had missed her husband's obituary in the paper.

The letter unleashed a flood of warm memories. Angela and I had started dating the summer after our senior year in high school. Both of us were almost strangers in Bear Creek that last summer before college. She had moved to town in January with

36

her father, the new manager of Bear Creek's one industry, a pants factory. I had been off at Subiaco all through high school. So when we met the first week in June at the public library, we hit it off immediately. For the rest of the summer we were inseparable.

Angela was the first liberal I had ever met, and before I was ever permitted to make love to her that summer in the back of my mother's '58 Fairlane, I had to endure an earful about the South. It was 1963, the year of the civil rights march on Washington and Martin Luther King's "I have a dream" speech. Segregation, with all its humiliations, was still in full flower in Bear Creek. Angela was appalled by our treatment of blacks and told me so at every opportunity, which was practically every night, since there was only one movie theater and nowhere to go except the Dairy Delight. When I confided to her how the Taylors had cheated my mother and then ostracized my family, it was simply confirmation of all she had read about our "morally bankrupt Southern way of life," as she used to delight in calling it. That summer she must have been so grateful I took her seriously that one night our necking on Spire Road outside of town got out of hand, and in time-honored fashion, we made love by the glow of the dashboard lights. What actually bonded us forever that night was less our lovemaking than our frantic but ultimately unsuccessful efforts to get a speck of Angela's virgin blood out of the seatcovers.

That fall I drove off to the University in Fayetteville in the '58 Fairlane, and Angela flew east to Goucher College in Baltimore, but each summer we resumed our romance in Bear Creek until I did my Peace Corps training the summer after I graduated. After I left, Angela began to date Dwight Marr, whose father had just died and left him and his brother a thousand-acre farm east of Bear Creek. When I came back that summer from Albuquerque after completing my training, Angela was engaged. She married Dwight that December. He was a super guy, the kind who wins the county "Farmer of the Year" award, and Angela, who originally had hated the South, became a farmer's wife. If she had been willing to wait on me, I am convinced we would have married, but it worked out for the best. In her December letter she called Dwight, a couple of years younger, as fine a man as she had ever known, and though I haven't kept up with Angela much over the years, I have never heard a word differently. And, in my own case, I was truly happy with Rosa, who, as the saying goes, melted my butter like nobody ever has before or since.

"I was afraid you'd be out digging ditches or whatever farmers do in winter," I say when Angela opens her front door to me.

After registering a look of total surprise, she smiles broadly, making me glad I decided to stop by. "You never did know a thing about farmers," she says, as if we were continuing a conversation we had begun earlier this morning. "You look cold. Come on in. I was about to heat up some vegetable soup."

As I come through the door, she steps forward and hugs me. "I got your letter," she sniffs, beginning to cry. "It was sweet."

I press her close to me, amazed at how familiar her body feels after thirty years. I had written her back and told her how sorry I was about Dwight. A great marriage is hard to find.

I stand back from her and take her in. She looks wonderful for a woman who, if memory serves, has just had her forty-eighth birthday. I notice a few crow's-feet around her brown eyes, and there is some gray in her once jet-black hair, but she is still petite despite the birth of two kids, twin boys whom I presume are in their second semester at Arkansas State in Jonesboro. As a teenager, Angela's most discussed physical feature among the boys was her perfectly rounded ass, but today, dressed in a roomy green and purple wind suit, the evidence of any damage done by thirty years of gravity is well camouflaged. "Are you doing okay?" I ask.

For an answer she wipes her eyes. What a stupid question. "Follow me to the kitchen. What are you doing here?" she asks over her shoulder as she leads me through a living room filled with furniture that has seen better days. "You've got that serious expression you used to get when you'd try to convert me to Catholicism. You want some coffee or a drink?"

Facing a two-hour drive, I say I'll take some coffee and sit at her kitchen table and marvel at how easy this feels, as if she has been patiently expecting my call for the last quarter of a century. She takes a sack of coffee beans and empties them into a clear plastic container and pushes a button. The noise prohibits an immediate response, and I look around her kitchen to keep from staring at her. Though spotless as I had expected, the appliances look ancient, and I remember a sentence from her letter that farming in eastern Arkansas has been very difficult in the past twenty years. In the driveway stands an '87 Mustang. There obviously hasn't been much replacing of big ticket items in the Marr household lately. "I know I mentioned my little epiphany the summer I met you," I say when the grinding stops, "but did I talk about it that much?"

"Night and day," she teases me, pouring water into her coffee maker. "You were such a zealot!"

"I was?" An agnostic now since Rosa's death, I find it hard to believe I ever proselytized anyone, especially Angela. "With all those hormones flowing," I ask, already comfortable bantering with her, "how did the subject of religion even come up?"

"You were such a talker," she says, smiling, "I was afraid you'd never shut up long enough to ever kiss me."

What different memories we have. "Sarah went through a period her senior year in high school of being a fundamentalist," I admit. "Maybe it's in the genes."

Angela sits down across from me to wait for the coffee to brew. "My boys couldn't find the inside of a church if they tried," she says, sounding regretful. "And after their grades this semester, I'm worried about them. But they can't come back here and farm. This place isn't going to be here."

So much for sex. Like a married couple, we substitute in its place talk of children and money. Angela's lower lip pooches out just a bit the way it did when she was upset three decades ago. "It's that bad, huh?" I say softly. "I'm really sorry."

Tears come again to Angela's eyes. She never knew how to hide anything. Maybe that was why I was attracted to her. In the South women were taught to play games. Angela didn't know how and was too honest to learn. "Dwight didn't really have anything to keep on living for. The farm has been going broke for years," she says softly, looking out her kitchen window. "And farming was all he ever wanted to do. He loved it. There aren't any jobs here anyway."

Behind his back, we made fun of Dwight. What a hick! A living teenage country legend. 4-H Club President. Won ribbons at the State Fair every October for pigs, for God's sake. Dwight wasn't cool. I pretended to be shocked when Angela told me after I returned from Peace Corps training that she and Dwight were getting married. I wasn't. Dwight had been in love with her for years, and finally she had the good sense to realize it. The only thing she asked of him was that they live in town. Never a fool, he bought a house in the city limits and commuted every day twenty minutes to his farm. "What are you going to do?" I ask, beginning to feel awkward.

"This isn't your problem," Angela apologizes, pouring coffee into two chipped mugs. "It's just that I've been dealing with the bank again this week. They keep telling me to rent out my land. Dwight's brother wants to buy me out and carry the mortgage, but I know he can't pay me."

I am taken aback by how much she is revealing to me, but I shouldn't be. For some reason we trusted each other from the moment we met. That first night on her front steps she had confided how upset she had been when she had learned her father was moving to Arkansas, of all places. Obviously, I had talked about the marvels of Catholicism. I stand up to take the cup she hands me. Her hand is shaking. Family businesses. They're messes, whatever the nationality. "What is Cecil like?" I ask, retrieving somehow the name of Dwight's brother. Odd what is in the memory bank. Cecil was two years younger, and since those kids worked all the time on the farm, I just barely knew him. "You're not obligated to sell to him."

Angela makes a face before sipping at her own coffee. I should know better, her expression says. "Of course I am," she says, her voice slightly bitter, as she sits down at the table across from me. "He's my husband's brother. What is Cecil like? He's like every younger brother. If Dwight had planted beans instead of cotton, if they had bought more land instead of renting . . . The last two years as things were going from bad to worse it got pretty tense between them. His wife, Nancy—you may not remember her since she was a lot younger—has been good to me and the boys, but it's been a strain on everybody."

I require some milk for my coffee, and, not wanting to make her get up again, I walk over to her ancient GE and open it. Damn. The top shelves are as bare as my own. Three cartons of Dannon fat-free plain yogurt, a quart of Carnation Coffee-mate Lite creamer, a quart of Minute Maid orange juice and four cans of Diet Coke. No wonder she's thin: she hasn't eaten solid food since high school. I flavor my brew, and wonder why I like instant better than the real thing. A character defect, undoubtedly. I like cheap bourbon better than the expensive stuff. It tastes better with Coke. Angela looks up at me and forces another smile. "How's Sarah?"

I nod, glad to talk about a more pleasant subject. My daughter has been the only thing between me and the nuthouse most of the time for the last seven years. I sit down again, making the oak chair squeak under my weight. Twenty years ago she must have had nice furniture in this room. Today, it could stand some glue. "She's great. First semester she became a raging feminist and quit junior varsity cheerleading because the costumes exploited women. I think she's calming down a little, but next year it'll be something else. She's very passionate, like her mother was."

Angela pushes back a lock of hair from her forehead. "Do you still miss Rosa?"

I take off my jacket and hang it on the back of the chair to give myself time to think. "Not consciously so much anymore," I say candidly. "But she was so alive that there's a big hole I've had to realize can't be filled. You really learn the hard way that people are unique and can't be replaced. She wasn't perfect, but she was good in a way I'm not. She cared about others past the point of just wanting to be liked herself. Do you know what I mean? You would have been friends."

Angela studies me carefully and strokes the left side of her face. "Do you have a picture of Sarah?"

From my right hip pocket I tug out my wallet, which as usual is too full of laundry slips, business cards, and ancient notes to myself to make a smooth exit. "This is Sarah last year," I say handing her the wallet. "She looks just like her mother when I met her in Colombia."

Angela examines the photograph and winks at me. "God, Gideon, no wonder you married Rosa. She's just stunning! I bet she has all the boys going crazy."

She doesn't know the half of it. "Let's see your boys," I say, taking my wallet back. To be so serious, Angela could be a real flirt. Though it was the first time for both of us, sex was, I seem to recall, her idea. I thought I was going to hell. Still, I can't say I needed much encouragement.

"Sure," she says, getting up. "I've got my favorite picture of them in the bedroom."

I watch her glide from the kitchen and wonder if she has begun to miss sex. Maybe she isn't missing it. Somehow, though, I don't think Angela is much of a date these days. She seems too emotional. Still, I can't deny that I'm interested in her.

When she returns, she hands me a framed picture. "They look just like my dad. This is Brad on the left and Curt on the right."

I study the photo and am reminded of her father's square jaw. He was a bear of a man, and I was scared to death of him. If he had known what his daughter was doing in my mother's '58 Fairlane all those summers, he would have killed me. A widower himself, he died from a massive heart attack, my mother wrote me in Colombia, while Angela and Dwight were on their honeymoon. "This is terrible to say, but when I heard he had died, I was a little relieved. I was scared shitless of him," I admit. "Even in South America I was afraid he would find out what we did those summers and come get me."

"I remember how you used to worry," Angela laughs, as she sits down across from me. "Either God or Dad was going to get you. It was just a matter of time."

There is a twinkle in her eye. I feel good, thinking this conversation must be providing some relief for her. Women allow themselves to grieve, and it is obvious to me that Dwight's death has affected her greatly. Still, she will have to make a living. She wrote in December that she had kept the books for the farm, but she had never worked in town. Who would hire a woman almost fifty with no skills? There were no jobs anyway. "It's not too late for God," I say, pretending to look out the window.

"Are you still religious?" she asks, getting up again to warm up the soup which is in a pot on the kitchen counter. "I'm more spiritual than formally religious, but Dwight went to the First Baptist Church every Sunday and Wednesday night until the month before he died. It didn't seem to accomplish much."

I watch as she takes two bowls from the cupboard above it and ladles soup into them. Angela seems to be swinging back and forth between bitterness and nostalgia. I know the feeling. Death is the ultimate thief. "Rosa's death cured me once and for all. I probably was looking for an excuse to give it up, and breast cancer was a real good one."

As Angela places one of the bowls into the microwave above her, she says brightly, "You must not have heard our big news. Paul Taylor was charged yesterday with murdering Tommy Ting's father. It's the most incredible story you can imagine. Paul was supposed to have hired a worker in his meat-packing plant to cut his throat. It's ridiculous!"

Angela's face has become red with indignation. I say, "I'm representing the plant worker."

"You are?" she says, surprise giving way to enthusiasm. "That's wonderful. You can help Dick get this case dismissed against Paul."

How strange! I realize now that I had unconsciously thought that I would get pressure from whites not to take Bledsoe's case. "How do you know Paul's not guilty?" I ask. "That summer we began going out, you regularly called the Taylors exhibit A of a bankrupt way of life."

A faraway look steals over Angela's face as she rearranges her mostly unused silverware on the mat. "I doubt if they were any worse than anybody else."

"They were, too!" I yelp, and tell her the story of Paul's buying at a tax sale my mother's eighty acres left to her by her father. I had lost contact with her during those years, and she probably never heard what had happened.

Angela had always liked my mother, and she murmurs sympathetically, "That was terrible, Gideon. Paul can be ruthless. I know that."

"Ruthless, hell!" I exclaim, thoroughly worked up now. "He threatened to kill that old man a month before he died," I say and relate to her what I have learned at the prosecutor's office. Angela will keep anything secret I ask her.

Angela holds her face in her hands while I talk and responds when I am finished, "Surely he wouldn't have someone murdered. Why would he do such a thing?"

"Greed!" I practically shout at her. "They've always been like that. You know they have. They're so damn rich they just have to have more and more."

Angela shakes her head. "Not as rich now. Like a lot of people, Oscar and Paul overextended in the eighties and lost quite a bit of their land. It's been really tough over here."

"Well, that explains his motive then," I say, understanding now why he was desperate enough to hire someone to kill to get his hands on the plant. God, I wish I had been around to see their faces when they realized what was happening to them. I still my right foot, which has been tapping the linoleum, and cross my legs. Where is this acid surge of venom pumping from? It is as if a volcano has been waiting to erupt, and now that it has started, it won't stop. I'm not sure I want it to. After all these years, it feels good.

Angela looks worried instead of indignant as I thought she would be. Maturity has made her cautious. "Gideon, you need to be careful about what you're getting into. Paul is still very powerful here. Taylor Realty probably still holds half the mortgages on the square even though they're not worth much because the economy's so depressed."

I am pleased by the concern in her voice. I think I like this older version better. She was so sure of herself as a teenager it used to bug me. "Tell me what he's been up to," I say, dredging up a spoonful of corn, green beans, onion, and beef from the bottom of the bowl. It has been almost thirty years since we have had an extended conversation, yet I sense I would have been comfortable if I had married this woman. Living with Rosa on a daily basis was sometimes like having a Roman candle go off daily in the house. Rain or shine, I could count on several bursts of heat and light. If I was within earshot, she could turn the job of scrubbing the sink into the Passion Play. For the most part, I loved it. Older now, I could enjoy somebody less wired.

"Until yesterday, Paul Taylor," Angela declares, pushing away her untouched bowl and dabbing needlessly at her mouth with a paper napkin, "could have been elected governor. He's got that much energy. He's smart, well-read, and interested in everything."

She smiles at some private memory, and, irrationally, I wonder just how well she knows him. Still, this is a small town. Bear Creek numbers barely six thousand people and more than half of them are black. Subtract them, the kids, old folks, and women, and there can't be too many men in her age group. They couldn't help being at least acquaintances even if they hated each other. "How's he holding up?" I ask. "His father put on some weight as he got older."

Angela glances up at a calendar on the GE. "He runs in the Dallas Marathon every year. He looks good. He stays in shape."

I finger the roll around my gut and decide against another bowl, though I could eat the whole crock pot. "It sounds like you keep up with him pretty good," I say, chagrined by the irritation I'm beginning to feel. God, I'm glad I don't live here anymore. I haven't been in Bear Creek two hours, and already my nose is out of joint.

"You know what it's like here," Angela says, cheerfully, not issuing a denial. "You can't hide anything in Bear Creek. He's been having an affair with Mae Terry off and on for years, and everybody in town knows it, including Jill."

"Mae Terry?" I exclaim, my memory kicking into overdrive. "She's been in a wheelchair since we were in high school!"

Angela takes my cup for a refill. "Paul is absolutely crazy about her. It obviously can't be the sex."

I study her face, thinking I detected a hint of protectiveness in her voice. For all I know, Angela had just climbed out of bed with him before I drove up. "Angela, he's an asshole!" I say, not even bothering to try to hide my hostility. Actually, I've kept up with Bear Creek more than I thought I had. Bits and pieces of gossip have made their way to me for years from eastern Arkansas, and I only pretended I wasn't paying attention. Though I haven't heard about Paul's sex life, I've known Jill and Mae forever. Both passed as small town beauty queens in high school until Mae was in an automobile accident her senior year that left her a paraplegic. She was, and is, I guess, the smartest person ever to come out of Bear Creek. Blessed or cursed with a photographic memory and supposedly an untestable IQ, until a decade ago she taught English at Duke, and then abruptly quit and came home to Bear Creek. I heard stories years ago she had been suspected of major plagiarism and cut a deal to retire with full benefits.

"Jill is cold as Christmas, Gideon. You remember how she was. She could divorce Paul in a second and clean his clock in the process," Angela says breezily. "But Sean is only twelve, and she's afraid he'd choose to go with his father and a judge would let him. Paul takes him practically everywhere with him. Actually, he's a wonderful father."

I wipe my mouth with a paper napkin. "Jesus, you make Paul sound like a role model."

Angela takes her bowl over to the sink and begins to rinse it out. "Paul obviously isn't a saint. I suspect you've probably got some woman hanging all over you, too."

"I do," I blurt, "but she's practically young enough to be my daughter."

Angela laughs at my admission, her voice booming all over her kitchen. "Poor Gideon. What a tragic figure you've become."

I smile. She is mocking me, but it takes me back thirty years when she used to tease me. "You know what I mean," I say, feeling this conversation about to turn even more awkward than it already is. "I'm sure you haven't started going out, but it's not easy to find somebody you're comfortable with."

"I don't expect to find a man," she says, her voice suddenly faltering. "Living with Dwight was so simple and easy it was like being in a different century. He was good to the boys, good to me, good to his brother and his family. He worked hard, believed in God, believed in helping others, he never cheated another man, never cheated on me. All he wanted to do was farm, but no matter how long and hard he worked, we rarely had a good year, especially in the last decade. I'm glad he died before he lost it. You know, there is something terribly wrong with this country if a man like Dwight can't make a living growing food."

There is a surprising amount of bitterness in her voice I have never heard before, but I suppose it is understandable. She's lived almost two generations through not much thick and a lot of thin. I feel a pang of jealousy toward St. Dwight. He probably never had a doubt in his life about anything, but what did it get him? Damn, the poor sucker's only been dead three months, and I'm ready to go drive a nail into his coffin to make sure he doesn't try to get out. "What they say about nice guys is undoubtedly true," I say, knowing any words of praise I could add would ring hollow. I ask again, "What do you think you'll do?"

"You want to buy a farm?" she asks, giving me a wintry smile.

What a ludicrous image that conjures up. I can't really see myself taking a tractor apart. The last light bulb I tried to unscrew somehow got stuck in the socket, so I just left it for the new owners. At least I left them with a working heating system. "Even if you don't sell to Cecil, will you be able to make enough," I ask, "to get your boys through school?"

From across the kitchen she eyes me suspiciously as if I'm some rich sugar daddy about to make her an offer she doesn't want to hear. "I'll be all right," she says, closing down suddenly. I feel I can trust her, but for good reason she obviously isn't ready to go too far with me.

"Does Paul really own half the town?" I ask, deciding to ratchet down this conversation a notch or two. Though I think I understand, it is safer for the moment to talk about the present than the past. Besides, I'm here to learn about the case, not take a trip down memory lane, aren't I?

My question pulls Angela back to the table. She wets her lips with her tongue and swallows like a child taking medicine that isn't as bad as she feared. "Maybe all of it," she says ruefully. "After the boycott by the blacks, people who had been here for decades began to leave Bear Creek. Oscar had brought Paul in with him by then, and they bought property downtown dirt cheap. Even though it's been almost twenty-five years a lot of it is still just sitting there. On the other hand, Paul doesn't seem desperate enough to kill anybody over another business. From the way he travels, he appears to have plenty of money."

I sip my coffee, now cold, wondering not for the first time today how much time has changed Angela. "Do other people admire Paul," I ask, "or are they just afraid of him?"

Angela hunches her shoulders. "To the white population he's

the air we breathe. He could raise the rents on his buildings, and close the doors on twenty businesses, black and white. The town would almost die completely, and it's not because we don't have some talented people here. But all the whites are, by necessity, in bed together. The blacks have unified whites like nothing else could. We've got the worst schools in the state, the highest rate of teen pregnancy, the highest infant mortality rate. And the blacks are not going to rest until they've taken over politically."

As she talks about the political gains made by blacks recently in Bear Creek, I remember again how idealistic she was as a teenager. At eighteen Angela said that if the whites in Bear Creek would be willing to compromise, everything would work out just fine. Doubtless, that was part of her attraction for me. She couldn't have been more different from the local girls if she had come from Mars. If I preached that summer to her about the virtues of Catholicism, her text was the evils of Southern racism. According to her, blacks had been the victims of slavery, rape, peonage, segregation, usury, in a word or two, total economic and political exploitation, but she hadn't even gotten warmed up. Separate wasn't equal, and all she had to do was point to the crumbling school and the gravel streets in the Negro sections of Bear Creek. It was the denial, Angela preached, of basic political rights in a so-called democracy that should shame me the most. Free speech, the right to vote, the right to hold office, these were just empty words in Bear Creek for over half the population. The only Negro in city hall, she pointed out, pushed a broom. We had treated Negroes worse than our dogs, and because it was coming from Angela, and not the NAACP, SNCC, SCLC, or some other civil rights group, I could see for the first time in my life that every word was true. By the time I left for the University of Arkansas I had become that rare animal—a Southern liberal. I didn't know then that things weren't exactly wonderful for blacks in the North. It took the TV images of Louise Day Hicks and South Boston years later before it sank in how segregated things were north of the

Mason-Dixon line. But no wonder we fell in love that summer! Who could have withstood all that sincerity?

"The county's now seventy percent black," she tells me as if she were some big-city ward politician. "It took that high a percentage before they could really begin to take over."

I try not to sound snide, but I can't help but comment, "You don't seem quite as sympathetic to blacks as you were that summer before we went off to college."

It is as if I have slapped her in the face. "You don't live here," she begins automatically, but already I see color in her cheeks. "It's changed; they're violent, they use drugs. . . ."

"Whites do, too," I bait her. "You can't have forgotten how you used to rake the South over the coals for keeping blacks down."

"You're absolutely right. I did," she says flatly. "I must seem like a terrible hypocrite, don't I?" She smiles, reminding me of how quickly she used to give in on the few occasions I convinced her that she was wrong. A delightful quality in anybody, but especially in a dogmatic eighteen-year-old from New Jersey. It made me respect her. "Thanks to you," I say, winking at her, "I went off to save the world. Talk about hubris!"

Her eyes shine with the memory of the power she had over me. "I really admired you for joining the Peace Corps. I would have written, but Dwight got jealous every time your name came up."

St. Dwight jealous? How nice! "I thought he was perfect," I say maliciously. What an advantage the living have over the dead! Short-term, of course, but even if all you have is the last word, it's still satisfying.

"Every jewel has a flaw or two," she says smugly. "He was pretty close to being a ten, though."

Every time she mentions how wonderful he was I want to puke. Why am I such a jerk? I had a good marriage. In the last few months though, thanks to a conversation with Sarah, I've begun to realize it wasn't as perfect as I liked to think it was, but it was a lot better than I deserved. Yet it's probably normal to idealize a dead spouse. It's a hell of a lot easier to get along with a memory than the reality of someone's day-to-day irritating habits. "Death's a pisser, isn't it?" I say, still feeling out of sorts. "What did Woody Allen say about it—that it was the hours that bothered him?" I laugh, knowing I am sounding needlessly cruel. "Who else is still around that I knew?" I ask, wondering if the entire town is in Paul's hip pocket.

"I've got my high school annual in the hall," she answers and rises to get it when I nod.

I look out the kitchen window into the backyard and notice the dark shapes of two magnificent trees, one pecan and the other a magnolia. How do people in places like west Texas and New Mexico stand to live without real trees? Nothing in nature is more satisfying. Could I live over here again? I don't know. Angela returns with a dark gold book and sitting down again across from me, slides it across the table. "I keep forgetting you're not in there."

"Thank goodness," I say, glad I don't have to be confronted with what thirty years has done to me.

"You were handsome!" Angela exclaims. "And you've hardly changed."

"That's silly," I say, turning to Angela's senior class. Actually, I am flattered beyond belief. I know she's lying, but maybe not too much. "Is Cary Holt still here?" I ask, looking at a picture of a boyhood friend who went through the University of Arkansas and then returned to Bear Creek to run his father's Ford dealership.

Angela shakes her head. "Almost a year ago he sold it and moved to Memphis to become an Oldsmobile dealer. The day they left, Martha told me Cary didn't want them to be the last white family in Bear Creek."

Damn. Cary's family had lived in Bear Creek since it was founded after the Civil War. When people like him begin to move, you know the town is in trouble. With the aid of the yearbook I ask about others I would have graduated with, and Angela helpfully provides a running commentary on their whereabouts. Surprisingly, several are still in or around Bear Creek. Despite the economy, a few whom I knew fairly well have flourished: Jeff Starnes is one of only two physicians in the county; Darby Nails has a CPA business that has offices all over the Arkansas Delta; John Upton farms and owns several businesses, including an insurance agency downtown. "If you had come to any of the class reunions," Angela reminds me, "you'd still know everybody."

I look at John's picture and wonder how much information he would give me. He and I had been inseparable in junior high before I got shipped off to Subiaco. Each year I would hang out with him during the summers, though our relationship never quite recaptured its adolescent intensity. "I always had ambivalent feelings about this place," I confess. "Rosa was so dark that I was afraid somebody would make a crack about her."

"If your daughter really looks anything like her, any remark would have been out of envy," Angela says, not denying the possibility. "Your mother was so proud of you when you joined the Peace Corps. She thought you were going to save the world, too."

I tell her, "She would have been delighted if you and I had gotten married even though you were a Yankee. Of course she didn't know what we were doing in the backseat of her car."

Angela laughs self-consciously, and suddenly I feel a sexual charge in the room. She shifts in her seat and studies the placemat in front of her. "I would have married you," she says solemnly, "but you never asked. Though it worked out for the best for us both, how come you never did?"

I look at the top of her head, now bent, and see a small but unruly patch of gray hairs. It has taken her more than a quarter of a century to ask this question, and I still don't know the answer. That last summer I loved her as much as I was capable of, but how much was that? My head obsessed with the sacrificial lives of the saints, and the rest of me one unrelenting sex hormone, there wasn't a lot of room left for single-minded devotion to one girl, however idealistic her mind and rounded her ass. "I was too young; you remember I was pretty callow back then."

She shrugs. "Do you realize you were the only person I ever preached to? I guess I felt safe with you."

Angela has begun to worry a spot on the mat with her ring finger. A modest diamond glints in the overhead kitchen light. At this moment an orange and black cat pushes through a tiny door by the kitchen window and leaps onto her lap. She strokes its back and coos, "This is Baby Dave."

"Hello, Baby Dave," I say, wondering what we do now. I'm not sure what Angela needs or even wants. For reasons I do not understand I am attracted to her again as much as I was when I was eighteen. Why? Is it simply nostalgia for lost innocence? Am I so middle-aged crazy that I think I can capture that again? In her passionate, arrogant way, Angela embodied ideals I had never encountered. But what is delicious about her now is that there is not even a trace of self-righteousness in her. I can only conclude she is what she seems: a complex, mature, enormously appealing woman my age, and one I can understand, given enough time.

Baby Dave leans back against his owner's diaphragm and begins to purr. "Gideon," Angela says, using my Christian name for the first time, "I'd very much like for us to be friends. I'm still half-crazy right now."

I know what she means. To get through the day, you have to repress. But sooner or later, the feelings and memories, bittersweet and painful, come at all hours of the day and night. "I understand," I say, truly sympathetic as she drops Baby Dave to the floor and begins to cry again.

I must not take advantage of her, but I don't stop myself from getting up from my chair. Awkwardly, I reach down and hug her while she sobs against me. Her face against my cheek is burning hot. Knowing I shouldn't, I kiss her.

For an unforgettable moment she begins to respond but almost immediately pulls back. "Will you leave now?" she asks, her voice barely a whisper. "I need you to do that for me."

"I'm sorry," I say, backing away from her. This isn't the time to admit that I would like nothing more than to take her back to the bedroom she shared with her husband for almost thirty years. Yet, what would be so wrong about that? I cared for her once, and already I've begun to do so again.

At this moment the phone in her kitchen rings. Watching me carefully as if I were a shoplifter about to walk out with a bag of cookies in a 7-Eleven, Angela picks up the phone, and her somber expression changes to a smile. "Hi, Mrs. Petty, how are you?"

How can that woman still be alive? If it is the same person I think it is, she was an old woman when Hannah and I were children picking up acorns in her yard. Now she apparently lives across the street. I hear Angela ask her if she remembers me. I am in town and stopped by to see her. As Angela talks, I look out the window and wonder if the old snoop has been trying to spy on us.

Small towns. I have forgotten what it was like. Every move I make here will be documented and recorded. After five minutes Angela shakes her head and more or less hangs up on her, explaining to me that she would be kept on the phone for hours. Of course, she remembers me. I was the Pages' only son who went off and married that nigger woman from Haiti or someplace.

"You know you can't hide anything here," Angela says, primly, not sitting down again. She still wants me to go. "I'm surprised that as soon as she noticed your car, she didn't try to stumble over here on her walker. She can't get up the porch, though. By the way I forgot to tell you she says she remembers you peeing in her backyard when you were five years old."

I laugh, not willing to leave just yet. "It must have been too regular an event for me to remember," I say, marveling at Angela's ability to kindle desire in me. Yet it shouldn't surprise me, for it was always like this between us. I try to read her expression, but I can't. "Would you like to go out sometime?" I ask, hoping I don't sound too plaintive.

"You need to go," she says firmly, coming over to me and taking me by the arm.

On her front porch with her yearbook under my arm I notice paint peeling above the door. The house could almost be considered shabby. I wonder if she'll have to take out another mortgage if she intends to stay in it. I hug my suit coat to me against a brisk cold wind that has arisen since I've been inside. "So what happens now?" I ask, not willing to pretend there was no chemistry between us.

Angela points with her chin past me. "I'll be answering a lot of questions about you."

I turn and look across the street to see movement behind a curtain. "This place is creepy," I say. "I can't believe you stayed." I wonder how many people know I was here for a couple of hours Thanksgiving weekend. Sarah and I didn't see anyone other than a black octogenarian female who lived in public housing for the elderly. Angela hasn't mentioned it, and with other things on my mind, I haven't either. If I asked her, I'm sure she wouldn't divulge the reason I was here.

"I need to figure out what just happened," she says dryly, "before I can begin to worry about the last thirty years."

"I know you do," I say, wondering if she feels anything for me at all. Angela could continue mourning for Dwight for months or even longer. Given my history, I couldn't complain if she did. "Obviously, I'd like to see you again," I say awkwardly, trying to forget how hurt Amy would be to hear these words coming from my mouth.

"But as friends, okay?" she says, warily, hugging herself in the cold.

I nod. "Then what about meeting an old friend for breakfast Saturday morning?" I ask, deciding to spend the night in Bear Creek tomorrow night instead of driving back home after the arraignment. We couldn't get more innocent than that.

Angela considers for a moment, visibly hesitates, but finally says, "Okay. I'll meet you at eight at the Cotton Boll. It's out on Highway 1 towards Helena."

"Where's a decent place to stay?" I ask. Her boys' rooms are vacant, but I doubt I'll get an invitation.

"The Bear Creek Inn on 79 toward Clarendon isn't supposed to be terrible," Angela says, not even pausing to consider inviting me.

As the afternoon gloom of the Delta fades into blackness and I begin to put miles between us, I wonder what I am doing. Can we really just pick up where we left off thirty years ago? Should we even try? Getting it wonderfully wrong, Rosa, exasperated by my stubbornness, used to scream, let sleeping dogs die. Maybe I should take her hint and try to keep the past buried. In the swampy soil of the Delta, however, six feet isn't always enough. Though it seems as if I have a good handle on my hometown, I have a momentary feeling there may be ghosts I don't want to see.

Four

TIRED BY THE DRIVE HOME, I glance at my watch. Nine o'clock. If my greyhound and I are going, we need to get out of here. "I think we'll just go on and sleep at the house tonight."

From the opposite end of her couch, my girlfriend exclaims, "You don't have any heat yet!"

"It's not too bad," I say. Actually, it is supposed to get down to thirty tonight. How could I buy a house whose heating system goes out the week after I signed the papers? It passed inspection, and the sale closed a week ago, but three days ago when I flipped the switch, it never even turned on, and the pilot light was blazing like the Tomb of the Unknown Soldier. "It's supposed to be fixed tomorrow."

"It'll be too cold for Jessie," Amy protests. "She doesn't have a coat for this weather."

I stare at my dog's powerful haunches. More like a lightweight brindle-colored jacket. I sigh. Guests wear their welcome out sooner than dead fish any day in my experience. The hitch is that Amy has long-term plans for us and seems willing to endure any indignity we can heap on her. Jessie has just taken a dump on her carpet. Maybe another night will cure that kind of talk. "This is what it would be like for us," I say, throwing in her face our fifteen years age difference. "Except in a few years it would be me instead of Jessie you'd be cleaning up for."

Amy wipes Jessie's nose, which is about to drip, on the sleeve of her warm-up as if she were the harried mother of a two-year-old. "I'd get you some diapers," she says, not cracking a smile. "And then I'd stick your butt in boiling water a couple of times. That'd help you remember."

I laugh, knowing Amy is okay about the carpet if she can joke with me. "See, Jessie," I say, leaning over to inspect a small raw spot on her leg, "there are ways to get your attention."

"Not hers," Amy says pointedly. "Yours."

I glance around her apartment and am reminded how little we have in common. Besides the age difference, Amy and I have radically different tastes. When she decorated my office she toned down the art she selected, but on display in her apartment, a two-bedroom in a gray brick structure just off the Wilbur Mills freeway, are drawings, paintings, and photographs, rarely, if ever, seen in a state where most of the inhabitants (myself included) are more at ease with art done by the numbers in Norman Rockwell style. Here, Amy has just redone her apartment by hanging life-size nudes on all the walls. A couple of men, too—one a guy with a penis the size of a boa constrictor that has just finished a good lunch. This new phase is weird and embarrassing. I look up at a photograph of a Marilyn Monroe lookalike on the opposite wall. She has a safety pin running through her left nipple. "What does it make you feel?" she asked me when I saw this particular photo for the first time. Nausea, I whispered, fascinated even as my scrotum tried to retract inside my body. I'm all for having my consciousness raised, but does it have to be a twenty-four-hour-a-day job?

"What does your mother think about this stuff?" I ask tonight. I can't imagine having friends over for dinner and having them try to pretend they aren't dying to get home so they can get on the phone and gossip about the horror show on Amy and Gideon's walls.

"She lasted about twenty minutes and then turned around

and left," Amy admits. Dressed in a green and blue warm-up suit that fits her like a glove, and with her hair pulled back in a ponytail, Amy looks like a teenager instead of a serious collector of sadomasochistic art. "My new stepfather thinks I've lost my mind. God knows what Daddy would have thought."

Poor Mr. Gilchrist. A retired factory worker from a paper mill in Pine Bluff who died only a year ago, he must be spinning in the hottest rung of hell for having allowed his only child to desert the South and accept a scholarship at a fancy school on the East Coast. First, his daughter wasted his hard-earned money on an art history degree at Princeton, and now she has the nerve to stain his memory by exhibiting the results on her walls. "Who was that guy, Mapplethorpe? Didn't he do some statue of a man pissing into another guy's mouth or something just totally beyond the pale? When is his exhibit getting up here?"

Amy rolls her eyes. I may not be educable. "I don't think he's in my budget for next month." She reaches over and pats my leg. "It's okay for art to make you uncomfortable, even scare you. It's how we grow."

I make a face. She sounds so damn condescending. I didn't just swing down out of the trees, and she knows it. On the other hand, if we got married or even lived together, it'd be my place, too. What would Sarah think of this? She's gotten a lot more liberal in the last year, but this stuff would embarrass her. She thinks Amy is too young for me, anyway. "I don't mind a little growth, but I think Mapplethorpe's stuff would prematurely age me."

Amy chucks Jessie under her chin. "I realize now who you named her after."

I get it. Jesse Helms, the right-wing senator from North Carolina who messed with the federal arts budget. "You artist types claim to be so open-minded," I point out, "but as soon as somebody disagrees with you about something, you start calling people names." Hardly role models for us hicks in the boonies.

"I just get so irritated with the attitude," Amy lectures, "that art is supposed to be immediately absorbed like some comic book. Do you realize that when somebody goes through a museum the average length of time spent on each exhibit is about eighteen seconds?"

I nod, more than happy to keep the conversation on this level. Some U.S. Supreme Court justice, hopelessly muddled, endeared himself to future generations of law students by confessing in a written opinion that maybe he didn't know what obscenity was, but he knew it when he saw it. "People know what they like," I say, knowing I sound hopelessly provincial. "They don't have to study it for a lifetime. You either respond or you don't."

Amy shakes her head. Trying to improve me is irresistible. "That's what you think," she says earnestly. "But it's like trying to judge a book when you don't understand half the words."

Is Amy like this with her clients? No wonder she isn't making any money. She is so damn earnest about it. "It's over my head is what you mean. I can live with that. But I don't have to have it in my house."

Jessie, sensing she is forgiven, raises her enormous muzzle and gazes at Amy with her big, beautiful brown eyes as if to say, this guy is full of it. Seeing that I am shifting the focus of the argument, Amy ignores my dog and says to me, "I wouldn't expect to have it out in the living room if it upset you."

Is every conversation we have these days about us? When I bought the house, I thought she got the message that I wasn't ready to get married. I take off Jessie's collar. The tinkling of her tags is driving me crazy. Despite our differences, Amy and I seem to be wearing invisible magnets that have each other's names embedded in them. How to explain it? Months ago she told me that I reminded her of her father. For her part she has Rosa's spunky personality and irrepressible good humor. Too, like some magical property that is essential to life but poorly understood, there is between us a steady sexual buzz, a ubiquitous all-purpose emotional SuperGlue that can temporarily seal every crack in the relationship. This strange attraction to my aging, soft-putty flesh is, to me, another sign of her kinkiness. But women are generally strange creatures. What drives them to seek solace in such a ridiculously unsubtle and ultimately woebegone-looking organ? This relentless, instinctive preference for the obvious proves they have no more intelligence or self-control than we do.

And tonight, like so many others, we end our discussion in her queen-sized bed, leaving Jessie in her crate in the kitchen, a decision naturally questioned by my girlfriend. However, this confinement, instead of being cruel, is an act of kindness. Used to a lifetime in tight spaces, Jessie feels secure in there. Freedom always sounds better than it is. I'm surprised Amy hasn't turned that argument on me. I haven't quite been honest with her, telling her that the reason I'm not hungry is that I was given a bowl of soup by an old friend whom I stopped by to visit in order to get information on the case. I don't mention that I kissed this old friend or that she responded. Amy, who used to be in the Blackwell County prosecuting attorney's office, has been fascinated by my account of the intrigues going on in Bear Creek and has listened in wide-eyed fascination at the description of my family's treatment at the hands of Oscar and Paul Taylor. Why should I tell her about Angela? I don't even know how I feel about her myself.

Amy's bedroom is even more bizarre than the rest of the apartment, probably because, in addition to nudes on the walls, she has pictures of her family on the nightstand by her bed. Her father's pinched face shows scarring on both sides, perhaps from acne as an adolescent. Bald, withered, he was already worn out at the time of this photograph, taken five years before his death from prostate cancer, but Amy assures me that emotionally, at least, he is still very much a force in her life. "Benign?" I ask, my arm around his daughter's bare shoulders. Her compact body is delightfully voluptuous as well as athletic. As I've come to know it, I've been confronted by the knowledge of how much work she puts into it. In the corner is one of those

NordicTracks, a fitness torture chamber whose very name suggests an uncompromisingly bleak and sunless existence. Waking up on occasion to my girlfriend trudging nowhere is unnerving. What if she were to give up exercise and start eating? She claims she weighs herself every day. I believe her, having seen her measure herself in ounces. Only five-two, she doesn't have any inches to give away to the never-ending battle of the twentieth century.

Light-years more comfortable naked than any woman I've ever known, Amy studies her father's grim likeness and answers my question. "Like you, not always," she says, putting her hand on my thigh. "I can feel his judgment even in my sleep. Actually, he tried hard to be tolerant, but his disapproval always found a way."

Later, as we lie in the darkness, it becomes clear what our discussion was all about: whether she admits it or not, Amy wants a father figure. Do I need another daughter? Surely not. Sarah is more than enough for me. Whatever the future holds, these few hours with Angela have made me wonder if I wouldn't be better off with a woman who shares my past. For better or worse, despite its past horrors and poverty, I have to acknowledge the Delta is still my emotional home. It is a generational thing: the visit with Angela has awakened feelings that I could never possibly have with Amy, who, growing up in the post–civil-rights era, understandably lives only in the present tense.

In the morning before we leave for our offices I talk almost compulsively about Bear Creek. Standing behind her in her bathroom and watching her put on her face, I explain about Bear Creek's Chinese families. "I never saw people work so hard. If they ever took vacations, I never knew it. And talk about family values: Their kids never got in trouble."

Amy, squinting in the glare of so much light (the frame of her mirror looks like the marquee of a Broadway musical), sniffs, "They must have felt really out of place."

Without her makeup, Amy looks pretty ordinary. Most women do, I guess. Rosa was one of the few women who could look good without it. Sarah has her coloring—an exotic blend of Negro, Indian, and Spanish blood and glossy curly hair and long lashes. In contrast, Amy begins each day pale as a premature baby and takes at least forty-five minutes to emerge from the bathroom as the more cute than pretty woman she presents to the public. I didn't know it took so much work until yesterday when I watched the whole process intently. Rosa never took more than ten minutes, and she was out the door to rave reviews. In the outside world Amy relies on her high-energy, almost manic personality, which, I realize, is as carefully manufactured as her face. Behind closed doors the smoke and mirrors vanish, and a cooler, more calculating persona emerges. "I think they must have liked it that way—at least the parents did," I acknowledge. "The old people probably thought being Chinese was better than being white, and maybe they were right. Some of them had worked for planters like the Taylor family. It didn't take them long to find out that the richest and presumably most educated whites in the South had only one thing in mind and that was to exploit them as laborers as thoroughly and as long as possible. It wouldn't surprise me to learn that the Taylors had Chinese working for them after the Civil War."

So painstakingly it makes my eyes twitch, Amy thickens her lashes. I'm surprised she doesn't blind herself with all that gook she puts on them. "I've never heard you obsess the way you have about this Taylor family," she says evenly. "You've never mentioned them before."

I lean back against the door sill and fold my arms against my chest. That may be true, but the resentment was always there. And until now, I had never been in a position to do anything about it. When I got back to sleep after having gotten up to go to the bathroom after two, I had dreamed about my mother for the first time in years. All I can remember now is that she had looked sad. "Out of sight, out of mind," I say, realizing how much I have traditionally tried to cope with parts of my past by minimizing its bleakness. However, with Sarah, now a history major at the University (this month anyway), becoming curious about the South and her ancestry, it is increasingly difficult to do. I realize I have never told my daughter how our family was treated by the county's leading citizens. Why? Embarrassment, I guess. We had seemed so weak and helpless. I didn't want her to think of her grandparents that way. When we had gone over to Bear Creek in November, she had wanted to know if they were racists. Of course, I had told her. In those times we all were. What I should have told her was that we were nothing like the Taylors. We hadn't owned slaves; we hadn't cheated people out of their property or land. We hadn't been hypocrites.

I notice Amy looking at me in the mirror. She says, "God, Gideon. You seemed to go into a trance."

Feeling foolish, I force a smile, but it looks weak as it comes back to me in the mirror. Am I really still handsome as Angela said? Except for the gut and my bald spot, I haven't aged too badly. I pooch out my bottom lip with my tongue, noticing the beginning of a fever blister on my lip. Damn. Why now in the middle of winter? If doctors got paid for what they actually cured, they'd go broke. "It was an interesting visit," I temporize.

"What were you thinking about?" Amy asks, coolly appraising her own face. She is performing this ritual nude. I wonder if Angela does. My mother would be horrified at this scene. She was almost laughably modest. Even my sister Marty said she had never seen our mother without clothes.

"Just the past," I say vaguely. Actually, I was thinking of the way Angela looked just before I kissed her.

"How can your client afford to pay you?" Amy asks, now blotting her lips. "Didn't you say he worked at a barbecue place?"

Without lipstick, her mouth is a hair too small. Painted, it looks bigger. Not Julia Roberts size, but wide enough.

"He and his wife had saved a few thousand for a house," I say. "I'll lose money on this case, but it's better than nothing."

"Anything is better than nothing." Sex is no problem between us, but I suspect money would be. From past comments I know Amy is struggling in her law practice. Domestic relations cases, her bread and butter, are usually a sinkhole unless your clients are rich. They eat up all your time and then don't pay, or you can't collect your fee. Dan is the expert in the divorce accounts receivable business. Women going through a divorce usually have less money than criminals. A former assistant prosecuting attorney, Amy, unfortunately, hates representing crooks. I get awfully fed up, too, but as a former public defender, defense work comes more naturally to me. It wouldn't entirely surprise me if Amy wanted to stay home and tend to a couple of yard apes. Her genetic clock is ticking down and that's probably where this pressure is coming from. Poor women. All this progress and they still can't figure out how to have it all. Men aren't much better off. After nearly half a century on this earth, I'm still paying for the one kid I've got.

Ten minutes later Amy and I kiss each other goodbye as if we were a longtime married couple parting to go to our respective jobs.

I start my day with a win when the plaintiff in my Municipal Court hearing is a no-show. When I hit the office, the mail has already arrived. There amid the collection of professional garbage I find an envelope with my daughter's handwriting, an event which usually signals some internal struggle being waged. I take it back to my office and close the door and sit down, prepared for the latest installment.

February 25

Dear Dad,

I sent this letter to the office, because I didn't know whether you were in your new house. I know you're thinking: Oh, God, what is wrong with her now, since I hardly ever write. Nothing really is, but I just wanted to describe to you some things that have been happening to me, and when I tell you on the phone sometimes I never can say what I'm trying to.

After I got back to school in January, I joined an AIDS Care team through one of the churches in Fayetteville. A friend of mine whose brother died of AIDS got me interested, and I went through the training on the Sunday before Martin Luther King's birthday. What we are is kind of a support group for people with AIDS, or PWAs as they are called. We do all kinds of stuff for the two assigned to our team, and some things I'm discovering I'm not very good at doing.

These guys really are dying, even though one of them is still doing okay. "Larry" (we're supposed to protect their anonymity) is sort of our healthy one. He was diagnosed two years ago and actually is able to work as a salesman for a computer company up here. We just kind of hang out together sometimes. I like him. He's funny and says the wildest things. He says he is most scared of going blind or getting Kaposi's Sarcoma which he says will make him look hideous. In lots of ways, he's a neat guy. He does a lot of things for guys who are sick even though he can be pretty hard on them. He has a real strong work ethic and tries to live a healthy lifestyle (he says some of these other people have given up and just do whatever they want—I guess I would, too). Even though he's gay, I couldn't tell it just by looking at him. I think he feels real ambivalent about his sexuality. Also, he's kind of religious. I don't really know him that well, but I'm getting to.

The other guy is "Luke," and he is sick. Right now he is in the hospital and may not make it much longer. My friend Barbara (the girl who got me interested) is really amazing. She just goes in the hospital room and takes over. She feeds Luke (he hardly eats anything), washes him, even brushes his teeth. I can't do that. I'm just too squeamish. I guess I'm afraid, too, even though I know I can't catch AIDS that way.

It really makes me respect what Mom did. I can't imagine being a nurse! Mom did all that stuff all day long until almost the month she died! I think something is wrong with me. I'm just too big a baby. Barbara says I'll get used to it, but I don't think so. All I'm good for is talking. Maybe I'll be a lawyer after all!

Mainly, when I visit Luke, I read to him though I don't know how much he listens. He likes me to read the paper, especially Dave Barry. He sort of goes in and out. Dad, he's only 27! I can't imagine how I would cope with knowing I was dying so young and in such a terrible way. Poor Mom. She wasn't even forty, was she? I know we've talked about this some, but didn't she feel terribly cheated? I know she wanted to see me grow up. You'd think I'd learn a lot from all this, but the only thing I've learned is to try to appreciate every moment, no matter how boring it seems. Of course, I don't!

I hope you don't mind too much me unloading about all of this. I know one of your best friends was gay. Didn't he move to Atlanta? I hope you are making sure Jessie is getting enough exercise. Say hello to Amy. Dad, is she even thirty?

Love, Sarah, Your Squishy-soft Daughter

I lean back in my chair and stare out my window. Sarah, a carbon copy of her mother, stays on high boil. But no wonder she can't go into that guy's room without her eyes watering: My mother used to say sarcastically that I wouldn't even drink after myself. Since I never washed a dish until I was married, it wasn't always said in good humor. I reread the letter. What a kid. Last semester she was a raging feminist; now, she's visiting the sick. A work in progress if there ever was one.

I pick up the phone and call her room. Amazingly, she is there. "Why aren't you in class?" I ask when she answers the phone.

"I'm just leaving," she says in the same breathless tone I'd hear when she was scurrying around at the last minute about to be late for high school. How did we cope in those years after her mother died? Between us, we had a hard time figuring out how to use the electric can opener. We managed, though. Despite some craziness on my part, those years forged a bond between us that will never be broken.

"I got your letter, babe," I say, knowing it won't do any good to preach. "I'm proud of you for doing this, but be careful. You're not around his blood or anything, are you?" I ask, wanting reassurance she is safe.

"Dad," she says, her voice impatient, "we're not nurses. Besides, I can't even thread a needle, much less give anyone a shot."

I laugh. Poor kid. What did I teach her? Not much. But I didn't ruin her either. "Are you sure this stuff isn't a little too heavy? College is supposed to be fun."

"Dad, it's so sad! They're either sick or terrified they're getting sick."

Sarah doesn't always listen to every word I say. I want to ask how these guys got AIDS, but I'm afraid I'd get more of a description than I want from my daughter. "Maybe it would be better if you were just doing this in the summer."

"Luke won't be here this summer," Sarah says coldly. "Dad, I'll have to call you. I'm late. Bye."

"Bye," I say before the phone clicks in my ear. I put the receiver down hoping she won't get too caught up in this latest obsession.

I go out to the front to go take a leak, and Julia tells me I have a walk-in. I check my watch and decide I can squeeze somebody in before I have to leave. I try to schedule appointments for everyone, but I've learned the hard way that some people would sooner eat broken glass for breakfast than agree to talk to me at my convenience. "Mr. Longley says he's got a personal injury case," Julia whispers respectfully as I nod at the big man in the corner who is already scrambling to his feet. "He says he has to talk to you immediately."

At the public defender's office we had the luxury of telling people they actually had to wait their turn. In private practice I can measure the month's take by what lengths I'll go to in order to accommodate a client. Usually, I won't risk asking a client to let me go to the bathroom first. He might be gone when I got out.

Eager as I am, he walks over to me and extends his hand. "Glenn Longley," he says. Is this a client or a life insurance salesman?

"Gideon Page," I say, sizing him up. If he was injured, he has made a nice recovery. The guy is undeniably handsome and looks in peak condition. About forty-five, he looks like the former pitcher Jim Palmer, though the only image I can now summon of that Baltimore great is the man in his underwear. What people won't do for money! The way things are going on TV, pretty soon we'll see Palmer slipping his briefs down to his knees and demonstrating how to put on a rubber.

"You got that Razorback football player off," he informs me. "That's how I got your name."

"The jury acquitted him," I say, politely.

In my office Longley gets right to the point. Neatly dressed in a suit patterned in slate and black mini-tooth that looks one hundred percent wool, he perches on the edge of the chair across from my desk and says, "My wife ran off with another man, and I want to sue the bastard."

I wince, explaining, "The Arkansas legislature abolished the suit of alienation of affection a few years ago. There's no cause of action in this state any longer."

Longley almost bounces out of his chair. "You mean a man can steal my wife," he thunders, "and I can't even get a dime?"

"I'm afraid not." Woman as property—obviously a concept still alive in our hearts if no longer on the books. Damn. On the witness stand, as good as Longley looks, this guy would have gotten some female juices flowing in the jury box. Still, I wonder what he did to run his wife off. In this day and age, women aren't exactly tied to a stake in the bedroom to await their husband's return. The longer I think about it, the more obnoxious the notion of a suit for alienation of affection becomes. The law, in its infinite wisdom, turned what should have been a consensual relationship between two people into a legal monopoly. Good for the legislature. It gets blamed for everything bad that happens in the state, but rarely gets credit for anything positive. But probably there was more to it than a mild outbreak of feminism. It's not unlikely that some of the members were afflicted by a "there but for the grace of God go I" mentality. I know the feeling. Less than a month after Rosa died I found myself being consoled in a motel by her best friend. This grief-induced madness could have, in theory, brought on a lawsuit by the innocent husband, but the real villain of the piece was the Grim Reaper, and, so far as I know, no lawyer has ever figured out a way to have the last word in that conversation.

Longley's face is mottled with rage. "I'll go to the prosecutor then and have the motherfucker put in jail."

I sigh. The only thing that is entirely predictable in human history is that the messenger always gets it in the neck. "Adultery," I tell him as gently as possible, "isn't a crime in Arkansas."

Longley shoots up out of his chair and looms over me. "What in the hell are you lawyers good for?"

I roll my chair back against the wall. Longley is too handsome to be a philosopher, but I have a weakness for purely rhetorical questions, myself. "The jury's still out on that one," I concede.

His chin high, Longley marches righteously to my door sill but once there smartly executes an about face. "Do you know what lawyers and sperm have in common?"

Actually, Julia, purporting to quote the wisdom of Rush Limbaugh, informed me yesterday, but feigned innocence may be the only way to get rid of Mr. Longley. "No, what?" I ask.

Mr. Longley's sickly expression convinces me that his wife made the right decision. "Only about one in a million," he shrieks, "ever grow to be a human being!"

Afraid to laugh for fear I may encourage him to launch into

a morning's worth of lawyer jokes, I stare reverently at his chin as if I were contemplating one of the great scientific discoveries of the century. God only knows what he thinks is really going through my brain, but after a brief silence, he wheels again and is gone. Nonplussed, I shrug. We lawyers are supposed to play the role of verbal hit men in our society. When the rules, in their quirkiness, forbid this part of licensed character assassins to us, it frustrates the hell out of Americans. Dan, who, after a couple of drinks, enjoys woolgathering on these matters, claims that TV violence, which includes pro sports like hockey, football, and basketball, provide surrogate physical expressions of our hostile national character, and attorneys are merely the intellectual equivalent of a generalized aggression. Thinking of Dan's boozy expression when he pontificates on these subjects, I suspect he accords the profession a little too much dignity. Rocket scientists, I think, trudging down the hall to the reception area to make sure Mr. Longley isn't harassing Julia, he and I ain't.

"What did you say to that man?" Julia says indignantly. "He was furious when he came by here."

I nod glumly. "That there's not a right for every wrong."

"He was so beautiful!" Julia wails. "Most of the people who come in here don't look any better than you and Dan. And you run him off in ten minutes. How can you make a living this way?"

I'm a lot better looking than Dan. I glance down at my stomach. At 5'11" I am battling a paunch, but Dan is obese. Gray as a fox, Dan, his hair thinning, looks older, too. "If you want to send him a bill," I say more snidely than Julia deserves, "be my guest." Hell, I would have done his divorce, but he didn't give me a chance.

Five minutes later I tell Julia I'm headed to Bear Creek and will see her Monday. She asks, "You're not going to get any lunch?"

I tell her I'll stop at the McDonald's in Brinkley, about an hour from now. She replies, "Get the salad bar, or you'll never lose that gut you're getting."

I suck in my stomach, thinking of Paul Taylor running the Dallas Marathon. "How would I do without you?"

"You probably don't do it very often," she says, still smarting over our loss of that jerk who was just in here.

"Little do you know, Julia," I say. "Little do you know."

Five

THE ONLY THING WORTHWHILE I have accomplished by five o'clock Friday is to obtain a copy of Bledsoe's file from the prosecutor. The bond hearing was a formality, since it wouldn't have made any difference if the judge had made it fifty thousand as I requested instead of the $500,000 we ended up with. The arraignment, where the defendant enters his formal plea, has been set for Monday afternoon, and I pull into the Bear Creek Inn thinking of the expression on my client's face as he was led out of the courtroom. I told him that I would come talk to him Monday. He had looked more resigned than sad. Despite the fact that the judge, sheriff, and prosecutor are all black, he must think that it is business as usual in Bear Creek. The white man is out of jail; the black man is in. No progress there. One other thing I have accomplished. Latrice's check is good. A trip by Farmer's Bank has removed that concern. Now, it is time to get to work.

The Bear Cre k Inn (an "e" appears to have been missing from the sign outside for some time) is a nine-unit motel almost across the road from the cemetery where my parents are buried. Though a willowy female clerk greets me warmly, I am relieved there is no hint of recognition by either of us. After my appearance at the bond hearing, already I feel as if I am being watched by half the town. She is a woman in her forties; her friendly smile cannot quite make me overlook her narrow, wedge-shaped face and brown eyes that are too close together. Still, her expansive manner makes me instantly forget her almost startling homeliness. When I was a boy, this place was called Horton's Motel. Alongside it was a restaurant by the same name, an early morning rendezvous for duck hunters. In answer to my question, Betty confides that the restaurant was destroyed by a fire set by the former owner in an unsuccessful attempt to collect the insurance. "It's the only way people can make any money these days. I got this place for a song."

I nod. Arson has always been a mainstay of the free enterprise system. She tells me to wait for a moment and disappears behind a curtain and soon returns with a small yellow cannister filled with ice cubes I decide not to inspect too closely. "The machine outside hasn't worked for years," she explains without apology. "Are you a salesman?"

It is probably pointless even to think about privacy. "I'm a lawyer involved in the murder case that was filed here a couple of days ago."

"You're that old boy who used to live here," she says excitedly, "who's come back to defend that nigger charged with killing that old Chinaman! You think that Paul Taylor would a hired somebody?"

Maybe I should drive on to Forrest City and stay at the Holiday Inn tonight. I don't know how much of Betty I can take. On the other hand, I better get used to people like her. "I don't know," I say, innocently. "What do you think?"

Happy to be asked, Betty smooths her hair down with her right hand, raising an ample breast in the process. "Hell, no. These niggers here are just power crazy—that's what I think. Yet I'm not so sure your guy is guilty either. It could of been that old man's wife. She's the one who found him. You don't really know what goes on between those old people. You never hardly saw them out together except in the store. The young ones are fine, pretty much like the rest of us."

"How long have you lived here, Betty?" I ask, wondering if there is any negative feeling about the Chinese in Bear Creek. When I was growing up, they were respected because the kids were likable and all of them worked so hard.

"Just five years," Betty says, "but this town is dead as a doornail. If I had any competition, I'd probably have to torch the place, too." She cackles merrily at the thought of it.

I smile and take the bucket from her, anxious to make some phone calls and then settle down with the file.

"If you need more ice, don't be shy about knocking on my door. I stay up real late," she says suggestively, handing my key to me with her left hand. She isn't wearing a ring.

This is one offer even I can turn down. "Thanks, I appreciate it." Afraid she'll volunteer to feed me, I decide not to ask her to recommend a restaurant.

In room number nine, which, logically enough, is on the end farthest from the office, I consider my surroundings. I have no desk to write on, but in the corner by an iron floor lamp there is a padded chair with big arms. I test the double bed, which proves to be a little hard, but better a firm mattress than one I need a rope to help climb out of in the morning. On top of a scarred brown dresser across from the bed rests a small color TV of indeterminate age and brand. I click it on and remember I am watching television beamed from Memphis, which lies across the Mississippi fifty miles to the east. I enter the bathroom and try out the plumbing, mentally lowering my expectations. Plumbing standards in this country seem to have undergone a decline in the last twenty years. However, I am pleasantly surprised to find that though it takes a while, the commode flushes, and though not exactly gleaming (I've seen too many commercials lately), it is cleaner than the commode the old owner in my new house left me. There is no tub, only a shower, and since except for my feet I won't be coming in contact with it, I decide not to worry about the walls too much. The color scheme, hospital scrubs green, is not my favorite, but if the heater works, it'll do. I try it and initially get as much noise as heat. Maybe, like Betty, it just needs to calm down. For twenty-five dollars I can't ask for much. I unpack and mix myself a bourbon and Coke in the one plastic cup (I must have the salesman suite) Betty has provided, and add a couple of ice cubes. I turn down the sound on the TV, and from a built-in shelf next to the bed, I take the phone and fulfill my promise to call Amy and let her know for certain I won't be coming back tonight.

"What happened?" she asks, her voice sounding fatigued. Like myself, Amy is a morning person, which may be the only thing we have in common.

I rehash the afternoon's events while staring at an animated and charming black female newscaster on Channel 5. It is amazing how much things have changed since I lived in this part of the state. "How's Jessie doing?" I ask, not wanting her to ask me too much about what I'll be doing tomorrow.

"She's so sweet!" Amy exclaims. "I hate that crate you make her stay in. It's terrible, isn't it sweetheart? Here, I'm putting the phone next to her ear. Say something nice. She misses you."

Hoping Betty isn't listening in, I say, "Jessie, don't shit on the floor again, okay?"

Jessie doesn't deign to respond, and Amy yelps, "That wasn't nice. She's done good today, haven't you sweetheart? I just took her out."

"I appreciate you taking care of her," I say sincerely. "I'll be by about this time tomorrow to pick her up."

There is silence on the other end. "Maybe we can go out to eat or something," I add.

"That'd be nice," Amy says promptly. She is still young enough to think of Saturday as "date night." "What are you doing tonight?" she asks, sounding more curious than suspicious.

How could she be? Even the most cynical girlfriend surely wouldn't expect me to bed down after an hour with a woman I haven't seen in a quarter of a century. "First, I'm going to call

Mrs. Ting and see if she'll talk to me. I want to arrange to get out to see the plant as soon as possible."

"Well, hurry back," she says, and adds, her voice suddenly insecure, "I miss you already."

"I miss you, too," I say. "We'll have fun tomorrow night." She knows something is wrong. I do, too.

After I get Amy off the phone, I look up Mrs. Ting's number and give her a call, but it is Connie, Tommy's younger sister, who answers. I haven't seen her since I moved away. My main memory is of a busty, ponytailed girl in a white T-shirt who practiced cheers on the sidewalk while Tommy and I played tennis. Cute as a ladybug, she was even smarter than her brother. She must have already heard the news that I'm representing Bledsoe, for there is an understandable lack of warmth in her voice as she explains that tonight would not be a good time to see her mother. She puts the phone down and then tells me that I can come by tomorrow morning about ten. "I'm really sorry about your father, Connie. I know he was a good man." She doesn't respond. I ask and get Tommy's number in Maryland before she practically hangs up on me. I wonder what she is doing now. Surely, she didn't stay in Bear Creek.

I put down the phone, feeling as if I am a salesman who is accustomed to regarding the rudeness of the human race as normal.

Disappointed that I have not been able to establish any rapport with Connie, I dial Tommy's number. When I go through that plant, I want the workers to open up and talk to me. If Doss has been set up by Paul, someone out there may know who did it. I recognize Tommy's voice as soon as he answers the phone. Even after all these years, and despite having been born in the United States, Tommy has never quite managed to sound like he was a Caucasian. There was always a slight burr in his speech, and that is what I hear now. "Tommy, this is Gideon Page," I announce. "I assume Connie's told you I've been retained to represent Doss Bledsoe."

There is silence on the other end while he absorbs the fact that he is getting a phone call from the attorney who represents his father's alleged murderer. Finally, he says, "She called me this morning."

I tell him that I am genuinely sorry that his father has been killed. "I had nothing but the profoundest respect for him. All of you worked so hard and did so well that I drew inspiration just knowing you. I can remember how persistent you were when we used to play tennis. You were Michael Chang before there even was one."

"Why are you calling me, Gideon?" he asks. "Shouldn't you be dealing with the prosecuting attorney?"

I watch as a gorgeous blonde flits all over the national weather map. What he wants to say, but is too polite, is, if you have such admiration for us, why are you taking the case of the man who murdered my father? "I am," I say. "But I know you want the right person to be convicted of your father's murder. If my client did it, the jury should convict him, but he swears he was set up, and I think that's a real possibility."

"Why?" Tommy asks, his voice unyielding. "My father's blood was on his knife. He has no alibi; I've heard he wouldn't take a polygraph test."

"I'm just starting to investigate this, Tommy," I say, watching the blonde draw squiggles over the Rockies, "but it's obvious that Paul could have hired any number of people in that plant to murder your father and pin it on Bledsoe, who seems like a decent man but probably isn't the brightest guy down there."

"So at least you're convinced Paul Taylor was behind this," Tommy says, his voice fading in and out, "because he thought he could buy the plant for a fraction of its worth."

"I've heard the tape," I say, watching the blonde flash her best Karen McGuiness smile, and return the program to the black newscaster. "I know you have. What do you think?"

"He threatened my father," Tommy says, his voice not at all confident, "but I don't know if there is enough to tie him to the murder."

"I don't know how well you knew Paul," I say, "but that entire family has spent a lifetime cheating people out of their land and property." I briefly tell Tommy about my family's financial dealings with the Taylors. "You may not be aware of this, but in the last several years they lost a lot of their land. He needed your father's business to maintain his lifestyle. I understand it was quite profitable."

Tommy responds, "What's your point?"

In the background I can hear a child's voice. I lost contact with him years ago and don't know if he is married, single, or working in an orphanage. "That Paul is slick as pig shit and if you let him, he will skate out of this just like he's done his whole life," I say crudely. "My guess is that he's guilty as hell and hired someone else to kill your father and set up Doss Bledsoe. So far his only mistake is that he didn't realize he was being taped. I know Paul. He plans to be laughing at all of us when this is over."

His voice sounding as if it is coming over string and a tin can instead of telephone wire, he asks, "What do you want from me?"

"Nothing, really," I say quickly. "I could get an order from the judge to let me go through the plant and inspect the murder scene, but what I'd like to do is to have as much cooperation from your workers as possible. I suspect they won't give me the time of day unless your family tells them that it is all right to be as candid as possible with me. If I don't get anything, then fine. But I'd hate to overlook some leads if it can be avoided. Once a prosecutor files charges, law enforcement gets hunkered down to prove the case, and it's hard to make them look elsewhere. If you could call your cousin and ask him to talk to your workers after I inspect the plant so that when I begin to interview them, they'll be more open with me, it would help."

The phone crackles and snaps in my hand like it is about to burst into flames. If I were paranoid, I would think the line was somehow tapped already. "Let me think about this," Tommy says finally. "I don't want to do anything that would jeopardize the case."

"They don't have a strong one against Paul," I say urgently, leafing through the file in my lap. "All they can show is Bledsoe has worked for him a long time. The only thing your secretary at the plant says is that she overheard Bledsoe say that he had gotten the money, but nobody knows what that was about. For all I know, he may have been stealing from the plant, but that doesn't mean he was the murderer. All they have on Paul is the tape, and Paul can explain it away in five minutes on the witness stand. It's ambiguous. He's going to walk away from all of this."

"What I have trouble understanding," Tommy says cautiously, "is why a man like that would risk so much."

I have trouble with that aspect, too, but I say, "I don't know how often you and Connie have been in Bear Creek recently, but I'm finding out it's changed a lot since I grew up here."

"It's changed, all right," Tommy says humorlessly.

Sensing that he is willing to talk, I ask him what he does for a living, and he tells me that he has a commercial real estate firm in D.C. It sounds as if he is doing quite well, which I don't doubt. He had the sort of mind that could make sense of the tax code but never tried to intimidate you with his intelligence. I ask what Connie does and learn that she is a physicist in Memphis who measures the amount of radiation given to cancer patients. She has been driving over on the weekends to stay with their mother, who has been ill for the last several years and whose health has not been improved by her husband's murder. I am sure he will be on the phone to them after this call.

Before I hang up, he asks, "Is there a trial date?"

I explain that Doss has to be formally arraigned first and tell him that despite the circumstances it was good to talk to him. We were friends once; maybe we can be again once this is all over. I place the phone on the table and lean back against the bed and watch Vanna swishing back and forth on the screen. How little it takes to entertain me. Before I can take a sip of bourbon, the phone rings, and I pick it up, hoping it's not Betty telling me she'll bring down some extra towels.

"Gideon," Paul Taylor begins, "damn, I'm glad you're in this case. Can you believe the shit I'm in?"

Who told him I was here? I stare at Vanna's backside while I try to absorb what he is saying. Can he still be this arrogant after all these years? Does he truly not know how I feel about him? Of course, he doesn't. Paul, I realize now, is the type who, regardless of what he does, can always rationalize his actions. "You're in some shit all right. Does Dick know you're calling me? I shouldn't be visiting with you without his okay."

"Hell, sure he does," he says casually. "We're on the same side of this, right?"

If Angela has talked to him, she didn't say how I feel about him. "Of course!" I say as if his charge is one huge mistake. "But what on earth did you do to piss off the new order, Paul? Unless somebody is playing a huge practical joke, I'd say somebody doesn't like you."

He laughs, but the sound coming through the phone is not a merry one. "This is the new order, all right! Can you believe we have niggers running Bear Creek? When we were kids, could you have ever imagined the sheriff, prosecuting attorney, and judge would have black faces when we got to be our parents' ages?"

Paul has some nerve mentioning my parents in the same breath with his. I realize I better take advantage of this moment while I can. "Paul, did you have some dealings with my client I don't know about?" I ask.

Paul's voice becomes intense. "What's he saying, Gideon?"

If I had known I was going to have this opportunity, I would have tried to figure out how to trap him. My mind races for a way to get him to admit that he hired Doss or someone else to kill Willie. "Well, of course, he can't very well deny once having worked for you, but I haven't had a chance to talk to him about the details. I just got hired yesterday. It sounds as if you had some contact with him after old Willie was killed. Is that right?"

"Why don't you come by the house for a drink after supper,

Gideon?" Paul asks, his voice polite. "I'll call Dick, and we can do a little brainstorming—unless you have plans tonight."

I wonder if something in my tone warned him away or he simply found out what he needed to know. I can't very well turn him down. "What time?" I ask, checking my watch. Hell, I wish he would invite me to eat. I'm getting hungry.

"About eight," he says. "You know where we live now?"

I confess I don't, and he says that he has moved into town. "We sold Riverdale years ago. We live in the old Yates house. You know where that is."

"I remember." Bear Creek's one mansion. What a piece of work this guy is. I'd love to ask about Mae, but I ask about Jill instead, and he tells me that she is "just wonderful" and abruptly gets off the phone. I put down the receiver without having gotten to ask how he knew I was at the Bear Creek Inn. All I can figure is that gossip travels the speed of light over here. For all I know, Betty may have called ten people since I checked in. I remind myself to be careful. If I don't watch myself, I'll be the one who will end up getting screwed.

I don't need to arrive at his house thinking that Paul was a great guy after all, and I pour out my bourbon and Coke in the sink. I decide to shower and get out of the clothes I'm wearing today. Friday night. Nobody in eastern Arkansas is wearing a suit unless he or she is getting married tonight or buried tomorrow. As I place the pants and jacket on a plastic hanger, I am reminded of Amy, who bought this suit as her Christmas present to me for my rape trial in Fayetteville. She is probably feeding Jessie about now. She is delightful and fundamentally a good person, but all those nudes! What is that about? Sex or art? If Sarah comes home for Easter in her Volkswagen with a trunk full of photographs of herself wearing just her birthday suit, what will I do? Shoot us both, probably. In the shower I look at my shrunken penis and marvel at its capacity to get me into trouble. Such an ignoble-looking piece of equipment, and, to my mind, visual refutation that humans are somehow endowed with some kind of special nobility among the animal kingdom.

Ten minutes later, wearing a pair of khakis that aren't too badly wrinkled, I ride into town and eat at Charlie's Pizza, an establishment whose most inviting feature, among all the computer games, is an old-fashioned pinball machine. I resist the urge to play it, preferring not to call any more attention to myself than I already have. Of course, I might as well be wearing a neon sign around my neck. Everyone in here, no more than twenty, and mostly teenagers, is obviously a regular. When I was a kid, Friday night in February meant basketball. I guess it still does, and with all the private schools in the Delta, sports are almost as segregated as they were when I was growing up. Integration was supposed to bring us together; arguably, nothing has driven us further apart.

Forty-five minutes later, after a cheese and sausage pizza that has burned the roof of my mouth, I make a turn onto Scott Street and realize I have missed the entrance to Paul's drive. Maybe I don't remember Bear Creek as well as I thought. I turn around and pull into a curved driveway that sits on a full acre of land, only two blocks from downtown Bear Creek. Three stories, brick, with a formal garden and a couple of birdbaths, this house doesn't look like it is owned by someone who has suffered from financial reverses. What I keep forgetting, however, is how depressed prices must be over here. Paul probably got this for a third of what he would have to pay for its equivalent in Blackwell County.

As I press the doorbell, I realize I am full of anxiety. My family must have been so inconsequential to the Taylors that Paul doesn't have the slightest idea of the impact he has had on the lives of my mother or me. I wonder what my sister Marty remembers about Paul. As big a pain in the butt as that conversation will be, I should call her and find out. Naturally, Jill comes to the door, though I was hoping I wouldn't have to see her. I always liked her, and feel awkward seeing her under these circumstances.

"Hello, Gideon," she says warmly, obviously thinking I am here to help her husband. She gives me a hug, touching me for the first time in our lives. Though once a high school beauty, now she is almost gaunt, and her once-lovely face is stretched tight against her skull, giving her the look of a middle-aged woman with an incurable disease. Living with Paul has obviously taken a toll.

"Hi, Jill," I say, and become immediately tongue-tied. I should have insisted on meeting Paul in his office. Though I never knew Jill as well as I would have liked, she was a caring, decent girl from a good background who just happened to be born with beautiful olive skin and the loveliest brown eyes in the entire Delta. I cannot help but wonder what her rival Mae Terry looks like after all these years in a wheelchair. Though she has never met her, Jill asks about Sarah as if I were their next-door neighbor who had just returned from a trip with his child to Disneyland. Sean, their son, is not in evidence, making me wonder if he has been hustled out of town to stay with Jill's parents until his father's life calms down a bit. What do you say to your child when you've been charged with murder? Sorry for making your life a nightmare, but mine is hell, too, so what about a little sympathy? Not if he's twelve. I can't help feeling a little sorry for Jill and Sean, but not sorry enough to resist sticking it to Paul if there is any way I can do it.

As she, chatting all the while, leads me through a formal dining room with a table that could seat twenty, it is apparent she has done her homework about me in the last twenty-four hours. Whatever her husband truly thinks of me, I am to be courted. She opens the door onto a den, and I see Dick Dickerson, who stands up as I enter the room. I haven't seen him in thirty years, but he is recognizable because of his uncanny resemblance to "ole Bullet Head," Gerald Ford, but unlike the former president with his reputation for ungainliness, Dick can do more than walk and chew gum at the same time. With the grace of a tiger, Dick meets me in the middle of the room and catches my hand before I can spread my fingers. "Good to see you, Gideon. You're doing some good legal work these days," he says, crunching my knuckles. "Your mother and daddy would be proud."

"Thank you, Dick," I say, flattered despite myself. "Coming from you, that's a real compliment. How are you?"

Behind me I hear Paul's voice, "Jill, can you get Gideon a drink?"

Jill smiles wanly at her husband, who has come in behind us. As Angela has said, he looks in great shape. His blond hair has gone sandy but there is still lots of it, and his stomach is enviably flat under a pair of faded button-up jeans. I wonder what it must be like for her as she visibly ages and he gets more handsome. She asks me, "What would you like?"

I notice that Dick has nothing on the table beside his chair, and say I'll take some decaf if she has some. Paul protests, but I shake my head. Something tells me that I am going to want to remember this conversation at least until this trial is over.

Before Paul allows me to sit down he pumps my hand vigorously and looks me in the eye. "I appreciate you coming by on short notice, Gideon. Dick and I both feel the sooner we start going down the same path the better."

"No problem," I say as I sit down on a black leather couch across from Dick and look around the room. On the walls are photographs of the whole family captured in activities that range from duck hunting to posing with Corliss Williamson, the former Razorback great. Jill smiles gamely in all of them as if to say, whose life goes as planned? Paul, clutching what appears to be scotch and water, takes a seat on the couch by me. I might need a drink too if I were charged with first-degree murder.

"Gideon, Paul says you haven't had much of a conversation with your client yet," Dick says, pulling up a yellow legal pad from the briefcase beside his Barcalounger. "Is he saying anything?"

They seem so eager to know if Bledsoe is going to implicate Paul that it is hard to avoid the feeling that both he and my client are guilty as hell. "Other than he didn't do it and that someone is framing him, not much."

"Does he have any ideas," Dick asks, taking notes, "who that might be?"

Jill returns with a steaming mug that has painted on it *Arkansas Razorbacks—National Champs '93–'94*. I wait until she leaves, since I'm not sure how much she is supposed to hear. It is difficult for me to gauge their relationship. Maybe his screwing around with Mae Terry is no threat to her. If your rival is confined to a wheelchair, it probably is easy to believe all you are missing when he goes out the door to her house is some good conversation. I answer, "He doesn't know. I don't get the impression that Bledsoe is working on a doctorate in nuclear physics."

Paul snickers appreciatively, but I detect some nervousness behind it. If he has a deal with Bledsoe to keep his mouth shut, so far, so good, but there is a long way to go.

"It could have been any of the workers at the plant," Dick suggests. "Or possibly someone who didn't even work there. I don't think it is out of the realm of possibility that Doris could have killed her husband and set up your client."

I cannot remember the last time I saw Mrs. Ting. It has to be at least thirty years ago and must have been in their store. Her English was not as good as her husband's, but she seemed to be there every time he was. Connie said her mother has been ill. I can't imagine she would kill her husband, but as a defense attorney I can't exclude anyone I can reasonably point a finger at. But I do not want to admit that I am seeing her tomorrow and have already been on the phone with Connie and Tommy. "Anything's possible," I say, knowing that Dick wants to tell me how to do this case.

Dick frowns at this lack of enthusiasm and says, "We know you have a primary duty to your client, but I think if we coordinate our defenses, it'll be in both our interests to do so."

The last thing Dick wants me to argue to the jury is that Paul may have hired someone else to kill Willie and is the one setting up Bledsoe. Why not pretend to cooperate as long as I can get away with it? It may be the only way I can get Paul. I respond, "I don't know why we can't do that. Bledsoe insists that he is innocent and that he didn't cook up any conspiracy with Paul."

After this exchange, Dick visibly relaxes. Paul has obviously professed his innocence, but until now, Dick couldn't be positive that Doss hasn't confessed to me that he murdered Willie and implicated Paul. For the next hour we talk generally about the case, and I use the opportunity to ask about the connections after the murder between Doss and Paul, who, as expected, minimizes them.

"Before he was arrested, I didn't even know Oldham had hired Doss," he says, "to help him with the restaurant. Talk to Oldham—he'll tell you. I own the restaurant, but I treat him like an independent contractor, so I won't have to worry with a bunch of niggers getting drunk out there and shooting each other and then suing the deep pocket. Oldham can hire anybody he wants. I guess I saw Doss out there a couple of times in the last few months but I don't remember if I even spoke to him or not. I didn't give a shit. Doss had worked for me years ago, and he had enough sense to deliver appliances and install them, so I figured he could make change and slice barbecue, and I didn't worry about it. My deal with Oldham was that he pay me five hundred dollars every month, and as long as he did that, I didn't care what he did."

Do Dick or I believe this? I doubt it. I try to remember what Butterfield told me: Bledsoe had claimed he didn't know Paul owned Oldham's. Dick explains that in the file there is a statement from Henry Oldham in which he denies being told by Paul to hire Doss, but Oldham admits that Paul made several trips to get barbecue during the time around the date of the murder.

Turning to face me on the couch Paul says, "That's no big deal. Henry makes the best barbecue in the best part of the state, and hell, yeah. I went out there—to pick up some free barbecue. I sure wasn't getting rich off of him."

It occurs to me that in my cursory examination of the file I haven't seen a statement by Paul and ask him if he gave one.

"I'd be crazy to talk to that sheriff!" he answers, looking at Dick for confirmation.

I ask Dick, bluntly, "Do you plan to call Paul?" Defendants who refuse to testify usually have a real good reason—they are guilty.

Dick, who has begun to massage the bridge of his nose, shrugs. "It's way too early to worry about that."

Paul snorts. "Of course I'll testify at the trial. I haven't got anything to hide."

His words hang in the air, though. Of course he does. Every person I know over the age of five has something in his past that can't stand the light of day.

Dick stands up and makes a show of stretching and says he is ready to call it a night. It has been a long week, he says, and we can get together next week. We both know he wants to shut up his client. He has found out what he needed to know tonight: Doss Bledsoe, if he has any beans to spill, hasn't done so yet. I ask Paul to take two minutes to explain about the tape. "You don't ordinarily buy a business from a man by telling him he's going to die soon," I say, pushing him just a bit.

Paul's smooth face becomes wrinkled as he frowns. "I wasn't threatening him. That old man wanted a fortune for that place. He was being absurd," he says scornfully. "Who was going to take over when he died? Connie's a physicist in Memphis; Tommy's a wheeler-dealer in Washington. All I was doing was pointing out the reality of the situation. Why in the hell would I have him killed just because he was being stubborn? I wasn't in any hurry."

Clearly, it pissed him off that old Willie wouldn't hand him over the keys to the plant. Whether he is acting or not, Paul cannot hide his arrogance. For a certain breed of Southerner the feeling that the world is his oyster only increases with age; for the rest of us, the certainty that it is not accelerates at a greater pace. "Since Clinton's been in the White House," Paul continues, "some Arkansans have had an inflated notion of the state's importance. We're talking Third World prices in the Delta. Southern Pride Meats doesn't quite abut 1600 Pennsylvania Avenue. I was probably being generous to offer a hundred thousand for it."

"You still want it, don't you?" I ask as Dick begins to jingle the change in his pocket. He doesn't trust me, I don't think.

"Not if I have to look like a murderer to do it," he says angrily. "You can't imagine how much this has hurt Jill and Sean and really the whole town. Things were bad enough between blacks and whites before. Now, it'll really be terrible."

I walk toward the door. As long as blacks stayed in their place, race relations were "good." Now that they are in control, I won't hear that cant again. How can Dick not gag when he hears Paul open his mouth? Surely he knows better. That old saying, I guess from the sixties, comes to mind: "If you want peace, work for justice." If I get my way, there'll be some justice, but Paul will get no peace—my clients tell me it is hard to sleep in prison. Dick tells me that he will walk over for the arraignment Monday afternoon, and we can get a trial date afterward. Our conversation is over, and moments later, I am let out the front door, knowing I have given away more than I have gotten.

I drive back to the Bear Creek Inn and sit on the bed while I work my way through the thick file Butterfield has had copied for me. I'm probably not fooling Paul and Dick at all. Yet who knows? To live over here, you have to wear blinders. Dick, who was raised by a wealthy uncle after his parents were killed in an automobile accident, has always been identified with the white power structure, but somehow seems apart from it. He will serve Paul well if Paul listens to him. In thinking about the evening, I doubt seriously if Paul consulted Dick before he called me this afternoon, but Dick would never let me know it. He would say something to Paul but not to me. I wonder what he thinks of Bear Creek. His children grown and gone, his wife dead, what keeps him here when all the other whites are beginning to leave in droves? Perhaps he finds something here that is comfortable. I cannot imagine what it is. He is a mystery to me. Perhaps I overestimate him.

From the nightstand I pick up the yearbook Angela has loaned me and find Tommy's picture first and then Connie's. She was cuter than ninety-five percent of the girls in her class. I realize that despite the obvious barriers, I was oblivious to their feelings about race. Why? I suppose in most ways we considered Tommy and Connie "white." During all her sermons to me about racial injustice in those years, I don't recall Angela ever mentioning the Chinese in Bear Creek. It never occurred to me to ask Tommy how he felt about us. He seemed to like us.

The phone rings. It is Angela. "How do you like the Bear Creek Inn?" she asks, her voice friendly.

I survey my surroundings. It is a bit unsettling that I am "home" but staying in a motel. "The owner is cheerful. I've already had a meeting with Paul and Dick."

"You did?" she asks. "You're certainly not wasting any time."

"Paul called me," I explain. "I got to see Jill. She's changed a little bit since she was a high school beauty." I flip through the yearbook as I look for Angela's picture. Suddenly, I realize she didn't move to town until after the class pictures were taken. When she arrived in Bear Creek, she had a terrible Yankee accent. Now, she sounds like us.

"Poor Jill," she says, perfunctorily. "This is terrible for her. Did you find out everything you needed to know?"

I don't hear a lot of sympathy in Angela's voice for Jill. Yet, who knows what slights Angela has endured in thirty years? Perhaps Paul's arrogance has rubbed off on his wife. Though Angela made Paul sound positively wonderful yesterday, maybe she's not as high on him as she sounded. The Taylors lose interest once you start slipping. Angela's voice is on automatic pilot. Jealousy? Perhaps. She has struggled and Jill never has. Jill was beautiful and married the richest man in town; Angela married a farmer who died broke. Paul's long-running affair with Mae and his current troubles may seem like simple justice to her. "I don't think I learned anything. Dick hasn't lost a step. He's sharp and doesn't give anything away free. Do you run into him much?"

Angela tells me that Dick is a workaholic and is usually out of town trying cases. Now that she is free, I wonder if he will hit on her. It doesn't sound like it. Unseen, I nod. Before we hang up, Angela tells me she is pushing back our breakfast half an hour. I realize that I was hoping she was going to invite me over tonight. I turn on the ten o'clock news and get another black newscaster out of Memphis. So much has changed, and yet nothing has.

Six

ON HIGHWAY 1 about a mile and a half from the center of downtown Bear Creek, I pull into the Cotton Boll Café parking lot. This place has surely seen better days. Yellow paint is peeling from the letters on the outside of the one-story wood structure, which has a definite tilt south. A gust of wind twenty miles an hour or better could give Cotton Boll patrons some anxious moments. With its wood floor and tables it would take about five minutes to burn the place to its foundation, assuming the builders included one. Almost deserted at half past eight on a Saturday morning, it is so lonely looking I have to wonder if I heard Angela correctly. A teenager in a ponytail behind a long green counter at the back of the room holds up a coffee cup as I take the seat nearest the window. I nod, uncertain whether she is taking my order or saluting her first customer in a month. Without a word, the girl, who is dressed in a clean, starched yellow waitress uniform, brings an oversized mug of coffee complete with a jar of real cream, an unexpected pleasure in an age where you usually get charged a buck for a thimble-sized cup accompanied by a plastic container of ground chalk. Solemnly, she places her pad and pencil on the table by the mug, and I wonder if she is seizing this moment to announce a work stoppage when it dawns on me that she is deaf. Uncertain whether she can read lips, I write that I am waiting for someone. She nods and leaves me to stare out the window across the street at the vacant lot where a small concrete block factory once stood. At the rate this town is going, twenty years from now, there may not even be a Bear Creek. Why doesn't capitalism work here? Is it racist to think that blacks don't take to free enterprise? Is it the need to dominate and control they lack? Even as black as Bear Creek is becoming, it appeared to me yesterday during my brief drive down Main Street that most all the stores are still owned either by whites, Chinese, or Jews. Yet that might not hold true much longer. Will Angela leave? She would if she's smart. There is no future for her here. I sip at my coffee, certain that her choice of meeting places reflects her ambivalence about seeing me again. How could any involvement with me do anything but hurt her? What did she say—Paul is the air we breathe?

As I begin to replay yesterday's visits and wonder how close we were to walking back to her bedroom, Angela bursts through the door, bundled up in a purple ski jacket and gray sweats. "I almost made it!" she says, pushing back her left sleeve to check her watch.

I stand up, my thoughts undoubtedly transparent. Her face is rosy from the cold. It is eight-forty. I doubt if she has ever been on time in her life. "A virtue of the dull, you used to tell me," I respond, helping her off with her coat. Why am I being such a gentleman? Amy would hit me if I tried to assist her. Yet, east Arkansas was part of the Old South. Manners were to be minded, whatever the circumstances. Forgotten habits have a way of reappearing.

"You used to believe everything I said," she says lightly.

The power of sex. I can't read Angela. Maybe she is not even conscious of the mixed signals I seem to be getting from her. "I still do," I admit. When she sits down, I ask, "Is the Cotton Boll the best Bear Creek can do these days, or are you trying to hide me?"

She smiles at our waitress who is approaching us with a mug

in one hand and a pot in the other. "Wait until you see who the owner and cook is," Angela murmurs, and says brightly, "Hi, McKenzie! How are you?"

Our waitress nods vigorously and says something unintelligible. She pours Angela a cup and refills my mug while Angela writes something on a napkin and hands it to her. She frowns, and Angela points to me.

"How do you do?" I say, thinking I am being introduced. What must it be like not to be able to hear and speak? Given my tendency to hear only what I want to and to put my foot in my mouth, I might be better off. Lately, in the press there has been a flurry of articles about a debate between those who want to bring the deaf into the mainstream and those who argue that the deaf have their own culture and should not be forced to adapt to the hearing world. Like religion, it is a useless argument for the true believers. Surely, it is academic in Bear Creek.

McKenzie smiles politely and points to the Cotton Boll's menu in front of me. It is an unadorned $8\frac{1}{2} \times 11$ pink piece of paper protected by plastic. "What's good?" I ask Angela.

Angela winks at me. "Everything that's bad for you. The biscuits and gravy with sausage are sublime."

How does anyone live past thirty over here? "I'll just take some toast," I say to McKenzie.

The girl knits her brow. Angela says, "You have to write it. She can't read lips any better than you can."

So she remembers, too. Embarrassed, I print out in block letters the words TOAST AND JELLY and push the paper over to Angela, who scribbles THE WORKS! and hands it to the girl.

McKenzie gives me a look that suggests I have insulted the honor of the Cotton Boll, but turns on her heel and marches back to the kitchen. Cautiously, I ask Angela, "How are you today?"

"I'm fine," Angela says, her voice neutral but friendly. "Mrs. Petty thinks you've come back to farm."

We both laugh at the same time. For someone who was raised in an environment so uniformly rural, I was remarkably ignorant of Bear Creek's lifeblood and still am. I stayed in town and cruised Main Street with my friends.

Out of the corner of my eye, I see Mr. Carpenter, my old junior high science teacher, doddering toward me. He must have been around my present age when he taught me, my last year in Bear Creek before I went to Subiaco. I loved ninth grade science. He made "the laws of nature," his term for the mathematical formulas he wrote on the board, seem real. Physics, three years later at Subiaco, was just a bunch of numbers I couldn't get to add up. Mr. Carpenter gave us the illusion the world could be comprehended if we just had the brains to do it. As an adult, I realized what a hoax he had played on us, but thanks to his passion, for years afterwards I retained a vague hope somebody would figure it out.

"Gideon Page," he says, his eyes twinkling as he comes up to us. "What an appreciative kid you were. You thought I was a magician, but then you were kind of dumb in science, weren't you?"

"Yes, sir," I say, getting to my feet, marveling that he remembers. He probably doesn't. Mediocrity is always a safe bet, and as a lifelong teacher, he knew the odds. "It's good to see you, Mr. Carpenter. You were the best teacher I ever had in nineteen years of going to school."

Rubbing his hands on a dirty apron, he beams as if I had just awarded him the Nobel Prize. Teachers have learned to be content with praise in Arkansas. "You know how much I liked your mother. A well-bred woman who deserved better luck. After your father died, she couldn't do a thing with you, though, until those Catholics scared the bejesus out of you. Are you still superstitious?" He offers his hand, and I take it.

Religious, I think he means. What a character he still is! Mr. Carpenter, a lifelong bachelor and, I suddenly realize, homosexual, lived two doors down from us. He used to quiz me about what the fathers and brothers were teaching me when I returned home for holidays and summers. He'd rail at me, "Those damn Papists were first class truth muzzlers! Coperni-

95

cus, Galileo, Descartes, anybody with a brain they scared shit-less."

"When did you open a restaurant, Mr. Carpenter?" I ask, as if I have been away at school. "I never knew you could cook."

The old man tugs at the St. Louis Cardinals cap that's perched atop his still formidable head of hair, which closely resembles cotton left too long in the fields, then tells Angela, "Gideon's grandfather on his mother's side knew some science. He couldn't cure anybody—they didn't have antibiotics then—but he was an intelligent man. Gideon got his gift for gab from his paternal grandfather. Now, there was a man who could rattle on for hours and never say a damn thing."

Odd what people remember about me. It is apparent I was known as a talker and not much else. Was that the reality? I can't remember, or maybe I don't want to. I glance at Angela, but she has no intent of rescuing me. "You've got a nice place here," I flounder. This old guy has me off balance. Maybe he felt sorry for me in junior high, but now that I'm an adult I'm supposed to be able to take it.

"It's a junk heap," Mr. Carpenter says calmly, inspecting a knife on the table as if he were running a four-star restaurant. He adds, "I heard last night you're here representing one of the Bledsoe boys in Willie Ting's murder case. Now, those Ting kids were students. Connie knew more physics when she was a junior in high school than the rest of Bear Creek put together. Tommy was good in math, but when she came along, Connie liked the experiments."

I sip at my coffee, curious about what it was like to have lived as a gay man in a small town. He must have felt like an animal in a cage. Always vague about his itinerary, he traveled during the summers. I know he lived with his mother at least until I went away to college. To keep his job, Mr. Carpenter had to repress his sexual urges nine months a year. Even at my age I have trouble going twenty-four hours. Why did he stay in this fishbowl, especially after his mother died? I can't imagine. Fortunately, we are saved by McKenzie. Mr. Carpenter raises an eyebrow at my meager order. "I would have cooked you a decent breakfast," he sniffs. "Come see me, Gideon. I'm closed Mondays, home during the middle of the afternoon and by nine every night. I still live where I always did."

"Yes, sir, I'll be sure to," I say, wondering if he must be lonely. From his point of view, it won't be for my intellectual stimulation. Maybe he wants to tell me who murdered Willie Ting. "I'll do that."

After McKenzie serves us and departs, Angela remarks, "He's always been thought of as a curmudgeon, but I think it has been a cover to hide the fact that he's gay."

I am pleased by her lack of prejudice (she must still be a liberal on some things), but I wonder if the obverse is true: Did Carpenter become a caustic old man because he was forced to suppress his sexuality? When I knew him, he displayed none of the characteristics I usually associate with homosexuality. I never thought of him as creative or artistic, and certainly he hasn't become so, judging by the decor of the Cotton Boll. As we are eating, a total of ten customers, including a family of five, enter the restaurant. Angela nods, but no one stops to talk. They are all younger by a decade. When I comment that she does not seem to know everyone, she acknowledges, "The older I get, the less curious about younger people I become. Unless they are my children or their friends, I'm not all that interested in them."

I feel the same way. As we age, we begin to let go. Generation X. So what? They seem boring and self-absorbed to me. But now that Sarah's gone, all I know about them is what is on the tube. It is hard not to feel a bond with this woman. She gets me to talk about Sarah again, which isn't hard to do. I tell her how hard it was on Sarah after Rosa died. "She was already insecure, and then I kind of went nuts and left her alone too much while I went prowling around for a while. I don't know how she survived it. Maybe I should have sent her away to a girls' boarding school, too."

Angela frowns from behind her coffee cup. "That's ridiculous, Gideon, and you know it. She sounds fine. You just want somebody to brag on her besides you. I'd love to meet her sometime. The next time she's home from college you ought to bring her back over here with you."

I smile at the thought. If Sarah is still in her morally indignant phase, as she was in November, she will denounce Angela as a racist. It occurs to me that Angela was much like Sarah when she was her age. "You might regret it," I kid her. "She can preach a sermon with the best of them."

I tell Angela about our visit to Bear Creek in November and how appalled Sarah had been by old Mrs. Washington's story. "Granted, what my grandfather did was terrible, but Sarah doesn't see the gray in history. It's all black and white to her."

Angela toys with her spoon. "I heard that you were over here."

I should have figured. Does nothing over here happen without the whole town knowing about it? "Why didn't you say something yesterday?"

Angela smiles sympathetically. "I assumed you would tell me if you wanted to talk about it. I think I heard it at a party over Christmas," she replies vaguely. "Mrs. Petty isn't the only one who likes to gossip."

I decide to let it go and am cheered by the fact that as much as people talk over here, at some point if Paul was involved in Willie's murder, somebody is bound to spill the beans on him.

The next hour whizzes by. Angela likes to talk about her boys as much as I like to talk about Sarah. I try to reassure her without much success that they will settle down and graduate. Yet, as soft as the economy is and as worthless as a B.A. degree has become, the only jobs they may be qualified for are as chicken pluckers at Tyson's.

Before we leave, Angela allows me to buy her "Deluxe" breakfast and nods approvingly as I leave a two-dollar tip for McKenzie. "I wonder if he hired her because he understands her isolation," she says as we walk out the door.

"Maybe," I say, thinking about my old friend Skip Hudson,

who is happily living out his life as a gay man in Atlanta. I wonder if Angela felt isolated all those years married to Dwight. I sense an undercurrent of bitterness in her that I don't understand. I remind myself that despite our two visits, Angela and I still know next to nothing about each other's lives in the last thirty years. Still, I want to know more. "Listen," I say, trying to sound casual, "I'm going to be over here again sometime next week. Is it all right if I call you?"

"Of course," she says, her face serious as she briefly touches my arm. "Thanks for breakfast."

Though her hand is gone in an instant, it is as if I have been given an electric shock. As I head north for my meeting at the Ting family home on Peach, I recall the pressure of her mouth on mine and wonder if our kiss meant anything at all to her. It did once, but three decades is a long time to try to jump-start a battery. I can't tell if we are starting a new relationship or resuming an old one. Though there is much that is familiar about Angela, she is not the same, but I can't put my finger on it. Perhaps, it is simply grief in addition to her uncertainty about the future that gives such an explosive feel to her personality. Though she was not emotional as she was yesterday, there was an edginess that I sensed beneath the surface. Time has given her a dimension that a younger woman can't match. Whatever it is, it's pulling at me.

As I near Tommy's old neighborhood, I think of how undeveloped this area of the town was when Willie and Doris Ting first built out here. I would occasionally give Tommy a ride home from the tennis courts and was always struck by how isolated they were. Though their house is literally on the edge of town, it is now in the most impressive residential area of Bear Creek, new houses having been built one by one until the development was full. Each brick home is on two lots and surrounded by magnificent shade trees. I pull into the circular drive wondering how much the home is worth.

Connie opens the door before I can ring the bell. "Come in, Gideon," she instructs me without any warmth in her voice.

Not that I expected her to fall all over me, but I was hoping that once she actually saw me, some of her natural friendliness would resurface. No such luck. "Hi, Connie," I chirp, knowing I sound insincere, "you look great!" In fact, she does not. Like most of us, she has put on some weight. Her face, once oval, is round as a volleyball, and her waist, so tiny as a girl, has thickened. She is not obese by any means, but beneath her loose blue trousers and matching tunic, which remind me of those grim documentaries on China before they embraced capitalism, it is clear that her once delightful figure has taken early retirement.

"I would have thought you'd be a professional cheerleader by now, but Tommy tells me you're just a physicist."

"I knew you'd become a lawyer," she says, at least interested enough to banter with me. She always had less of an accent than Tommy, who, now that I think about it, seemed more Chinese than she did.

It doesn't sound as if she is paying me a compliment. "Did I run my mouth that much when I was a teenager?" I ask, willing to make a fool of myself to draw her out.

"You always had an excuse," she says succinctly, "when Tommy beat you in tennis."

So she was paying attention. "Which was every time we played," I complain, good-naturedly. "Tommy didn't say much about how you've been doing. I've got a daughter in college. My wife died from breast cancer when Sarah was in junior high," I babble, hoping to make her talk.

"So I've heard."

So much for catching up on the life of Connie Ting. What is her problem? I liked the high school version better.

"Mother's puttering around in the kitchen," she says. "Why don't you follow me back there?"

Amy, bless her art historian's soul, would love this house: delicate vases, painted fans, teak furniture, jade, calligraphy, and paintings compose a veritable museum. All of it could be antiques, but, given my knowledge of art, for all I know this stuff may have been won at a carnival by turning a hand crank and dredging up junky trinkets. It looks expensive, but I'm easily fooled about these things.

Mrs. Ting (whom I wouldn't have recognized) is seated at a yellow kitchen table drinking what appears to be a cup of tea. She is wearing a wind suit which is startlingly similar to the one Angela had on yesterday. Her hair is snow white and pulled into a tight bun behind her head. Gold-rimmed spectacles magnify her eyes as she looks up at me. Connie asks, "Mother, do you remember Gideon Page? He'd like to visit with you for just a few minutes."

Connie isn't going to make this easy. Mrs. Ting gives me such a blank stare that I wonder if she is senile. "Hello, Mrs. Ting," I say loudly as if she were deaf, although Connie has spoken in a normal tone. "How are you? I used to play tennis during the summers with Tommy. He always beat me."

Mrs. Ting studies my face. "You look like your grandpa," she says, her thick accent making the years drop away. "He saved Willie's life. He made Willie go to Memphis to have his appendix out. No hospital around here. Willie almost died."

I blink, uncomfortable with the irony. My grandfather saved her husband's life; now, I'm trying to save the life of the man who is charged with killing him. But what did Mr. Carpenter say? My grandfather didn't cure anybody. Still, he knew enough to opine it wasn't a stomach ache caused by a bad bowl of rice. "I'm really sorry about Mr. Ting. I know what a shock it must have been to you."

I look at Connie, who is leaning back against the dishwasher by the stove. Like an umpire who has heard one too many players complain after taking a called third strike down the middle, she folds her arms tightly against her chest. One false move and I am out of here. Her mother says bluntly, "Willie didn't trust lawyers."

It sounds as if she has said, ". . . Trust rawyers." I'm glad I don't have to speak Chinese. Though I assume Tommy has said to her what I'm about to say, I tell her, "I can understand that, but I want you to know that though I represent the man accused of taking Mr. Ting's life, I'm interested in knowing the truth, and though I can't prove it yet, I strongly suspect someone else may have murdered your husband and has framed Doss."

Mrs. Ting looks at me blankly, while Connie interjects, "I thought a defense attorney's job was to defend his client and let the judge and jury worry about the truth."

I wish Connie would go shopping or something. "The way the system works," I say, repeating what I learned in law school, "is the truth emerges if everyone does their job well."

Connie rolls her eyes at me. "Gideon, do you actually think my mother believes that? Look at the O.J. trial. He got away with murder. If you get this Doss Bledsoe off, it doesn't mean you know what the truth is. It means you've manipulated the system. We're not idiots."

"The system didn't work in the O.J. trial!" I say with more urgency than conviction. "The police and forensics work in that case was terrible."

"Well, what do you think happened here?" Connie asks, hugging her arms tightly. She is full of anger, but I don't know why. As far as I could tell, Tommy wasn't.

"I don't know yet, but I think Paul Taylor could have been part of a plot to frame my client," I say candidly, and repeat what I told Tommy, though I've no doubt he has already given her that part of our conversation, too.

"I think that's crazy," Connie says, shaking her head when I am finished. "Paul didn't know he was being taped, so why should he go to the trouble of setting up somebody who wouldn't have had a motive? They didn't make it look like a robbery; no money was taken that I've heard. I haven't heard that Doss Bledsoe hated my father. By all accounts, he got along with him okay. He obviously killed him for the money that Paul Taylor must have paid him."

Or for the eventual ownership of Oldham's Barbecue, I think, but don't say. "I think it's a mistake to underestimate Paul Taylor," I say, not having an answer for her. "He's more devious than you think." She has a point. Why would somebody choose to set up Bledsoe? It occurs to me that maybe the person who did kill Willie hated Bledsoe for some reason and wanted to kill two birds with one stone, so to speak. If that's true, it doesn't eliminate Paul from the picture.

"I don't understand," Mrs. Ting says quietly, her arms resting on the table, "why anyone would kill my husband if it wasn't to get the plant. Everyone respected him."

I look at this frail, worn-out old woman and blanch at the thought of suggesting to a jury she killed her husband. I was her son's friend and I can remember the shy but friendly smile she gave me whenever I came into the store. I don't think I'll be seeing it again. "Paul's lawyer wants me to argue," I say, watching her face, "that you killed your husband, Mrs. Ting."

"My God!" Connie gasps as her mother bursts into tears and stumbles out of the kitchen. Connie runs after her, leaving me alone for a moment as I hear her wailing behind a closed door.

I regret having upset her, but don't feel I have any choice if I am to convince this family to cooperate with me. I am walking a fine line here, but no jury will believe for a moment that this frail, sick woman would have been able to murder her husband without some physical evidence of a struggle.

Connie returns and confronts me across the table. "Is that what you're going to do? If I had known this, I wouldn't have let you set foot in this house. How dare you come here and accuse my mother!"

I say quickly, "I haven't accused her of anything, Connie. This is Paul's strategy, not mine." I don't have the guts to say that I might have to argue this if I don't have anything better.

"So why are you here?" she says, her voice high with exasperation.

"Because I need your help," I say, wondering how I can convince her. "All I'm really asking for is not to be hindered in any conversations I have with Southern Pride's workers. I think Tommy understands this."

"Tommy doesn't understand anything," she says shortly.

I don't know what she means by this and don't want to anger her any more than I already have. "All I want is for you and Tommy to think about letting me really try to see if anyone else could have done this. Imagine how horrible you would feel if somebody else gets away with your father's murder."

"The sheriff has already conducted an investigation," she says, but the rage has already left her voice.

"I know," I say, "but what happens in these situations is that there is a lot of pressure in a high-profile case like this to get a conviction, especially if you have people who want to advance politically. Sometimes they make bad mistakes."

Connie is wavering, but finally says, "I'll talk to Tommy again."

"That's all I can ask," I say truthfully. I leave with a million questions, but this is not the time to ask them.

Despite Connie's dismissal of the possibility, I am curious about the other Chinese families in Bear Creek. I drive west for about a mile, take a right on Danner, and turn in at Guay's Grocery. Ting's Market was closer to where we lived, and now that I think about it, was not in such an obviously black part of town. I should have at least told Tommy I would visit them, but the truth is, like Connie, I can't begin to imagine that one of them was responsible. My assumption is that the Chinese, like blacks, stick together, though I personally don't recall any memory that would validate this feeling. Yet the old lady may know a lot more than she is telling. The trouble with this theory is that I never heard of any of the Chinese in Bear Creek even raising their voices, much less their hands. What is increasingly apparent to me is my lack of curiosity about anybody but the white families when I was growing up in Bear Creek. It was as if over half the town didn't even exist.

From the outside, Guay's Grocery is dilapidated and in need of a paint job, and the inside is not much better. Yet, my memory is that these stores were always marginal in appearance, perhaps deliberately, so as not to alert the dominant race that the proprietor was doing better than the consumers. Behind the counter is a Chinese man of indeterminate age in a brown cardigan sweater and gold-framed eyeglasses. He is taking change from a ten-year-old black kid, who is buying some hard candy. I look around the store to get an idea of the merchandise and marvel at how little stock he has, other than canned goods, some of which appear to be as old as he is. There is an old white man in overalls nursing a can of beer on a stool in the back, an activity that is surely illegal. Beside him is a totally bare meat case which has, judging by the rust stains on the white panel, been vacant awhile. I look over the top of the panel and see through the door to a room that has furniture in it. It occurs to me that I have probably erroneously assumed that the Chinese families in Bear Creek have homes separate from their stores. It looks lived in, but it is too dim inside to tell. Back up front, across from the counter in a corner, five middle-aged blacks gather in a semicircle around a Sony TV set watching the Razorback–LSU basketball game on ESPN. I can't understand a word they are saying. In front of me a black woman lays a sack of potato chips on the counter. Mr. Guay wordlessly changes a five-dollar bill, and I fall in behind her with a sack of plain M & M's I grab from a box. From what I am able to hear of his interaction with the woman ahead of him, he has a pronounced accent. After I pay for the M & M's, I say, extending my hand, "Sir, my name is Gideon Page. I'm a lawyer for the man accused of murdering Mr. Willie Ting. I'd like to come back and visit with you for a few minutes when your store's closed or you have some help."

Mr. Guay, or whoever he is, takes my hand, but says, "No business with them. No time to talk. Very busy."

Up close I can see the lines in the other man's face. Close to being contemporaries, if not approximately the same age, surely he and Willie had much in common. Business, their wives, children, whites, blacks. The way each was treated in the South. "This is about who killed Mr. Ting."

The old man murmurs again, "Very busy," and turns his back on me to fuss with his stock of cigarettes, which already seem adequately arranged. I have no talent for this business of figuring out who-done-it, but I am becoming curious about how these people coped all these years and the lies they had to tell themselves to survive.

I drive back to Blackwell County, wondering which generation of Chinese-Americans has felt the most comfortable in east Arkansas. Perhaps Willie's generation. They didn't have any choices and learned to be content by relying on each other. That couldn't be enough for Tommy and Connie, nor would it be expected to be enough. Who did want their father killed? I have no idea. I look out the window at the cold, muddy fields. A new planting season is just around the corner.

Seven

"YOU DON'T SEEM TO BE ENJOYING THIS," Amy calls from the other side of the net. "We don't have to play anymore."

"I'm fine," I say, forcing a grimace to become a smile as I stoop to pick up the ball that comes rolling back toward me. I have just hit my backhand into the same spot into the net for the third time in a row. In tennis, as in other aspects of my life, I have a way of perfecting my mistakes. "I'm just getting sick of being so consistent."

We meet at the bench where I sit down and grab my opponent's water bottle. I can't use the weather as an excuse: the temperature is a balmy 68 degrees, and the sun has stayed behind a mostly cloudy sky. Though it is only the first day of March, it looks like an early spring. "Why didn't you tell me you were this good?" I complain. "I could have prepared my ego for this little setback." Regardless of how liberated I tell myself I've become in the last twenty years, it is no fun being beaten by a woman. Amy, during warmups, casually informed me she is a legitimate 4.5 player under the United States Tennis Association rating system. Though in theory I can hit the ball harder and can cover the court more easily, my genetic head start has proved to be as useless as a long-range Arkansas weather forecast. Now, in the second set (I won two games in

107

the first) Amy zips around the court and is whacking the ball past me like some wind-up Steffi Graf doll.

Amy, who has barely worked up a sweat, straightens the strings on her racket. "You just need to practice. And to bend your knees on your backhand. You look like you're trying to putt a golf ball." She stands and imitates my swing.

Embarrassed by how ridiculous I must look, I nod and hand her the water bottle, noticing how supple her legs are under her blue tennis skirt. I wonder if she knows how sexy she looks. If she is wearing one of those bras that mash her breasts down, I can't tell it. Her white top swells out so nicely that it had the local pro in the clubhouse fumbling for her change for thirty seconds. Unlike almost every other woman I've ever played against, Amy can volley at the net. When I saw how well she hit from the baseline, I began hitting short and making her come in. No dice. It was like shooting fish in a barrel. Overheads, backhand volleys, even drop shots, her game is as complete as mine is limited. I can get some pace on a forehand if I have time to set up, but Amy won't let me do it. When I overplay the left side of the court, she runs me to death. If she controlled the rest of our relationship the way she does on the tennis court, all I'd need is Jessie's dog collar. "At my age," I crack, "they refuse to bend more than a couple of times a day."

She sips at the water and sternly shakes her head. "You could get in shape easy. There're several guys out here a lot older than you who can play all day."

Older than me? They must be playing in wheelchairs. Properly motivated, I stand up and head out to the north end of the court. I could get in shape. But it wouldn't be easy. "Let's get this beating going," I yell enthusiastically. "Time's a-wasting!"

As if in self-defense, early in the set, she drills the ball squarely into my chest the one time I am so foolish as to approach the net. At least she didn't blind me. "Sorry," she says, her voice concerned. "I wasn't aiming at you."

Unhappily, I think, *I'm not aiming at you either.* But it is the innocent who sometimes get hit. "I'll try to use my racket the next time," I say, glancing up at the group of bystanders who are watching from the top of the hill by the clubhouse. They seem to be enjoying the match. "I thought I'd get more bounce off my breastbone, but it's got too much padding."

Twenty minutes later the slaughter finally ends. I have won one game this set, a measure of pity that Amy couldn't resist. My teeth clenched in a pleasant smile, I hold out my hand as I come to the net at the end. When my old girlfriend Rainey used to thrash me at Ping-Pong, at least it was behind closed doors. I tell myself public humiliation is good for the soul. Amy grins and pats my shoulder like you see the winners do on TV at Wimbledon. "Nice workout."

"For me," I grumble. My shirt, underwear, and shorts are drenched with sweat. "Next time we won't play on court one," I say, looking at our fans, all men.

"Would you and Jessie like to come over to dinner tonight?" she asks, shoving her racket into her bag.

Maybe that's been my problem: I don't have a fancy nylon bag. "Sure," I say, rubbing my chest. "You and Jessie can finish what's left of me."

"Did I hurt you?" she asks innocently as we walk off the court.

"Just my pride," I grumble, fumbling with the latch at the gate. "You shouldn't have given me that one game. I'm not a child about to burst into tears because I lost."

"Oh, you're not?" Amy laughs, nudging me with her shoulder. "The way your lip was stuck out at the end I wasn't sure."

Ha. Ha. Ha. "You're so damn consistent."

"Just like Tommy Ting," Amy says, guiding me around the fence as if I were blind as well as old. "You make it all sound so fascinating. Maybe I can drive over to Bear Creek with you one of these days. I'd like to meet some of those people. The old ladies could tell me what you were like as a little boy. You were probably a crybaby then, too."

Great. She could meet Angela. That would be a delightful conversation. "Just very sensitive," I say. "If you're spoiled rotten, the least little thing upsets you."

She laughs, not knowing how pampered I was the first fourteen years of my life. The quintessential Southern male child. Waited on hand and foot. It's a wonder I learned how to change my clothes. Is the reality of the adult male too much to deal with? Until my father started going crazy when I was eleven, I had my mother's full attention. According to Marty, she might as well not have existed. As a child I'd come down the stairs into the kitchen and Mother would be waiting like my personal servant to cook my breakfast. The sports pages of *The Commercial Appeal* out of Memphis would be beside my plate, and she would pour me a cup of hot tea and watch me sweeten it with three teaspoons of sugar. Then she would vacuum my room and make my bed. No wonder I'm a crybaby. What male wouldn't be in perpetual mourning for that kind of worship?

I persuade Amy to cook over at my house, which doesn't take a lot of effort, now that I finally have heat. I suspect that she would prefer for Jessie to shit on my rug instead of her own. We stop off at Harvest Foods and I pay for some angel hair pasta and stuff for salad. In the store we must seem as married as any other couple, but last night during dinner and afterward I couldn't get Angela out of my mind and was too quiet. Despite two kids, a husband, and thirty years in the Arkansas Delta, Angela's basic personality hasn't changed. Circumstances and time have made her more conservative, but I put myself in the same category. I pretended I was preoccupied by the memories the trip had stirred up. My pretending didn't prevent me from making love to Amy last night and again this morning.

After dinner Jessie lies on the couch with her head in Amy's lap. Like her master, she knows a soft touch when she finds one. I click on *60 Minutes*. Mike Wallace looks older every week. According to Amy, her mother saw him on a trip to New York and complained that, in person, he was a wisp of a man, a virtual scarecrow. More power to him. I have begun to like old people on TV. Hugh Downs. Bring 'em all back.

Amy reaches over to the table and takes the remote and turns off the TV. "What's wrong?" she asks. "You've hardly said two words to me since you've come back from Bear Creek."

I would very much like to avoid this conversation, but I don't see any way around it. The trouble is, I don't know what I want or even what I want to say. I can rationalize all I want about the reasons why this May-December business won't work, but until I met Angela again it *was* working. There was a spark between Amy and me that was real. I care deeply about Amy, and I know she loves me. Somehow though, ever since I went to eastern Arkansas it is as if I am being drawn away from her, and I seem helpless to be able to do anything about it. Certainly, it is not that I know with utter certainty I have remet the love of my life. Though I can't put my finger on the reason, I do not feel entirely comfortable with Angela. What I do know is that it is terribly unfair to Amy to pretend everything is normal between us. "I should tell you I met my old girlfriend over there," I begin miserably. I am sitting in my recliner since Jessie is occupying my usual space on the couch.

Amy doesn't even raise her eyes as she strokes Jessie's head. "Goodness, that was quick. I knew something like that was going on. How long?"

She doesn't understand. "No!" I yelp. "I haven't talked to her in thirty years."

Amy looks up and gives me a brittle smile. "But she's divorced and wanted to talk about old times, huh?"

I rub the arm of the chair. "Her husband recently died. She's got two boys in college and now she's about to lose her farm. Things are pretty tough."

Amy strokes Jessie's muzzle with the knuckles of her right hand. "How long has he been dead? Two days?"

I laugh, despite myself. "Since November."

"What a nice consolation present you were," Amy says brightly, looking up at me. "Do you think you'll fit in over there now? It's been a long time. But I guess with your mocha-colored wife dead it's safe for you to go back home."

Damn! Amy's fingernails have grown an inch in an instant. She knows more about me than I do myself. Trying not to let this conversation get out of hand, I busy myself by picking up a dog hair from the arm of the chair. It is becoming obvious that Jessie uses the furniture more than I do. "It's not like what you think. She's very confused and bitter. I don't understand her," I confess.

"Oh, I bet you're trying real hard," Amy says, her voice strained with anger. "And to think I was feeling sorry for you—all alone in a tiny motel room. I'm glad I didn't drive over and surprise myself. What's it like after three decades? Is it like riding a bicycle? You remember a mole here, a scar there, what she liked, what you liked?"

Though I deserve this beating, I'm not ready to end my relationship with Amy. "I think you're going a little overboard," I say, not able to admit how attracted I am to Angela. "We've had a couple of meals together."

"Breakfast in bed?" my girlfriend asks, gently moving Jessie's muzzle off her lap and standing up. "Did you tell her about me?" she says, beginning to cry. "Your little young-enough-to-be-your-daughter fuck? I can hear you, Gideon. She's just a kid, but I can't drive her off with a stick. What's her name? I'd like to know her name."

Amy is little short of hysterical. She knows I haven't denied a word. "Angela. For God's sake, she's almost fifty years old," I stammer irrationally. "You don't understand."

"Angela! How divine for you! She's probably hornier than a March hare."

Madder, I think she means, but this isn't the time to correct her. Jessie has gotten down from the couch and stands beside Amy. I slap my leg for her to come to me. "Here, girl." In response, she pushes her muzzle against Amy's hand.

112

"Look, I'm going to take Jessie to live with me until this summer when Sarah comes home," Amy announces. "You're obviously going to be too busy to take care of her. I'll give her back
then, I promise. She and I can commiserate together."

"Don't act like this!" I plead. "I don't even know her."

"You will."

I rub my face as if to shake myself awake from a nightmare.
Will I ever know Angela? Not like I know Amy. "Don't leave!"
I plead, as Amy reaches for Jessie's leash on the floor beside her.
"You're not supposed to have pets in your apartment." I should
say that I love her, but I'm not sure I do.

"They don't care," Amy says, probably realizing I missed my
cue deliberately. "Other people have pets. The couple on the
first floor do."

This is ridiculous. She doesn't need a dog. Still, it would be a
help. I will be traveling so much to Bear Creek I really won't
have time to take care of an animal. My pragmatism at this
moment appalls me. I get to my feet. "You have to promise me
that as soon as you realize this isn't working out, you'll bring
her back."

Amy clips Jessie's leash to her collar. "I promise," she says,
"but you'll need to remember I'm pretty slow at figuring things
out."

I am, too. And what I need is time. Part of me wants to take
Amy into my arms and swear everything will be fine, but I can't
do that. "Let me get her dog food," I say, and go out to the
garage to get it. But when I return my dog and girlfriend are
gone. Sick at heart, I open a beer and wash the dishes, wishing
I had lied. Amy has been the best thing in my life for a long
time. Still, I feel a distant odd sense of relief.

At precisely three o'clock Monday with me standing by his side
and his wife and twenty onlookers in the spectator section,
Doss Bledsoe enters his formal plea of not guilty. After he sits
down, Dick Dickerson comes forward (Paul had his arraign-

ment last week), and Judge Johnson, over both our objections, sets the trial for the week of May 26. I complain that I won't have enough time to prepare my client's defense in a case like this, but Judge Johnson looks at me with a bemused air. Since he was just elected last year, he has no discernible track record. In private practice in Helena until he was elected, according to Dick, Johnson was by himself and like most small town practitioners, took everything that walked in the door. When I protest, he gives me a withering look. "You don't have the burden of proving your case, Mr. Page, do you, sir?" he says, with excessive courtesy. "Doesn't the prosecutor have the burden of proving his case, and you merely have to show reasonable doubt?"

I ignore his sarcasm and argue, "Of course, your honor, but the prosecution has worked on this case for six months. I'd like to have at least that long."

Beside me, Dick tells Johnson he has a heavy trial schedule in the next two months, and adds, "Judge, in order to do an adequate job of investigating this case, we'll have to track down everyone who was in the plant that day. It is my understanding not every one of the workers is still there."

Johnson, a small, gray-haired man in his fifties who seems entirely comfortable being the first black judge in the Delta, shrugs. "I would imagine Mr. Butterfield has whatever information there is available on the whereabouts of each worker in his file, which he is obligated to turn over to you. Since I have been judge in this district, I have observed that it is his practice to make his file available to the defense without a motion having to be filed. Do you anticipate problems in this regard?"

"Well, I don't know, your honor . . ." Dick begins, but the judge cuts him off.

"If you have problems locating witnesses, then you may file a motion closer to trial, but I warn you that I will not grant a continuance unless counsel has shown appropriate diligence and has shown he has complied with the criminal rules of procedure." He consults his calendar, sets what is known as an omnibus hearing for April 4 to hear any motions that may be pending at that time, and abruptly calls the next case.

As Dick and I walk out of the courtroom, which has all the charm of a bus station with its lime green seats, it is hard not to wonder if we were being picked on because we are white. There is no reason to schedule a trial with so many witnesses this quickly. I whisper to Dick, "Did you know he was going to be like this?"

Dick doesn't reply until we are out of the courthouse. When we are coming down the steps, he mutters, "He and Butterfield are old friends from Helena. Whatever he can do for him, he will. In civil cases he's reasonable most of the time. But if Butterfield ever makes it big in politics, which could easily happen now with all the whites pulling out, Johnson's chances of making it to the federal judiciary go way up. This area of the state has always been neglected when it comes to receiving our fair share of judgeships."

I realize that Dick is talking about himself. Despite his reputation, he has never had much political pull. He invites me over to his office across the street, but I tell him that I will have to call him later in the week. I have to drive back tonight to Blackwell County to get ready for a two-day child custody trial that I thought was going to be settled but has blown up over the weekend, and before I head back I promised Bledsoe I would come see him. With his practice primarily civil litigation, Dick understands settlements coming apart at the last moment, and says for me to call him when I get that behind me. As he crosses the square to go back to his office, I realize that he is still convinced that we are allies in this case, which is fine with me. After today's hearing, I suppose in some ways we are.

At the detention center Doss is not at all depressed with the judge's decision to set the trial the last week in May. "I jus' want to get it over with," he says, emphatically. "I'm sick of this place."

As bad as the old jail may have been, I doubt if it had this much security. Here, separated as we are, Bledsoe can't even shake hands with me, much less hug his wife. It is hard not to like this guy. As he tells me how much he has begun to miss La-trice, I think of a statistic I've read and wonder if it can possibly be true: a million black males locked up all over the United States. It is a mind-boggling number. Is this the only way blacks and whites can live together in this country? I wonder how many of them are innocent. Other than Willie's blood on his knife, there is no physical evidence linking Doss to the murder. If he had the money, I would hire a forensic expert to tell the jury why there were no hair, flesh, or clothing fibers found un-der Willie's fingernails. The only bloody footprints leading away from the spot where he died were Doris Ting's, apparently made when she discovered the body. I'd also like to get an in-vestigator to do a thorough background check on each of the individuals who worked at the plant. One of them could easily have something in his or her past that could be useful to us. Here, as in too much of life, you get what you pay for and no more.

We talk at length about the events of the day of the murder, which occurred on a Tuesday, September 21, but it is painfully obvious that Doss has no memories of that afternoon that can help him. Though I don't know if it will cut any ice with But-terfield at this point, I urge him to consider taking a polygraph, but he is disturbingly adamant on the subject. "Like I already said, I don't trust 'em," he says, his voice more stubborn than I've ever heard it.

"In a case like yours," I explain, "the defendant they really want is the one who arranged the murder."

Doss pushes his hands inside his pockets. "I'm not gonna take no test."

My heart sinks a little at his intransigence. The last time a de-fendant of mine refused to take a polygraph test it turned out he was lying. It sounds as if Doss has already talked to a lawyer long before he ever contacted me. I ask him if he consulted any-one else, but he claims he has not.

He insists that he never had a conversation with anyone over the telephone from the plant office about having received some money. "If I'd a killed ole Willie, I'd have to be dumb to call someone from there," Doss argues, staring hard at the concrete floor.

"Not necessarily," I respond. "You would have had to think that nobody was around." Actually, I agree with him. Criminals do amazingly stupid things all the time, and that's why some of you get caught, I think, my frustration growing. "Why would the bookkeeper make up a story like that?" I ask, flipping through the file to find her statement.

"I don't know," Doss says, his voice getting more stubborn by the moment. "Maybe she killed Willie, but I doubt it. She's all right."

I make the speech I make to all my criminal defendants—that I can't help them if they lie to me—but it is water rolling off a duck's back. I ask him if he has ever stolen from the plant or anyone in the plant. He denies that he has. Surely in five years he would have had the opportunity to smuggle out a ham for his birthday, but he insists he hasn't. So much for an explanation for his conversation over the phone in the plant.

I work the discussion around to the other employees in the plant, and finally get Doss to think of at least one person who had it in for Willie. He knows someone, he says almost sheepishly, who was fired by Willie about a month before he was killed. Vic Worthy had come in drunk and had nearly cut his little finger off one morning while shaving the hair off pigs' feet. Willie had driven him to the hospital but wouldn't let him come back to work after he got his finger sewed up. "'Bout three times a year, he'd drive across the bridge and gamble his paycheck away," Doss says. "He'd drink all the way home, and then come to work skunked, and I guess Willie finally figured that it shouldn't be on his time."

Doss sneezes into his hand. He has caught a major cold. "So he was pissed off because he got canned?"

Doss looks up at me, his face a study in disapproval. "He'd be drinkin' and talk about how he'd like to kill Willie for firin' him. See, he wudn't the only one to ever come to work fucked up."

It's about time Doss got around to this story, but I'm beginning to learn Doss doesn't do anything in a hurry. I write furiously and ask for as many details as he knows, which aren't much. Doss had ridden over to Tunica with him to gamble on the riverboats a couple of times, but they had never pulled an all-nighter together. Since Doss always took his car when they went together, he could control the time they came home. He had seen him downtown hanging around the square a time or two after Willie had let him go. Usually, Vic was half lit. He was more than half lit the time he'd made the remark about killing Willie. Nobody was with them at the time, and Doss had forgotten about it until last night when he had been thinking about the other workers in the plant like I had asked him. I ask if he has seen Vic around town recently, and he says a time or two and tells me where Vic lives.

I tell him I will try to see him later in the week, and walk out to the Blazer, feeling only slightly better about the case. I drive back into Bear Creek and cruise by Angela's but am disappointed to see that her car isn't there. I go up to the door and leave a card and write on the back that I'm sorry I missed her. I look back across the street at Mrs. Petty's to see if she is watching. Sure enough, I see the venetian blinds move in her front window. I wonder if when I leave she will hobble up the stairs to read what I have written.

At ten, tired by the trip home, I collapse into bed, and fall immediately into a hard sleep but am awakened by Angela at eleven. At first I am so groggy that I don't realize that it is she, but her voice, warm and confiding, is a shot of adrenaline, and I come instantly awake. How like a teenaged boy she makes me feel! Lust but more than that. How can that be? Was our history together as good as I imagine? It seems to me that it was. Whatever the truth is, I seem programmed to respond to this woman, who surprises me by saying she has been given two tickets to the Razorback game with Memphis Saturday afternoon at the Pyramid. Since the game will be shown on ESPN, I think I would rather watch it from her couch under a blanket in her living room, but I tell her that sounds like fun. We arrange a time for me to come by. It's still too early to be thinking about making love to this woman, but this will be a real date, which is a starting point. Maybe her off-again on-again attitude is normal. As I lie in the dark, I try to remember what it was like making love to her. I find I can't actually recall the moment of an orgasm, but my failure of memory does not stop me from imagining what it would be like now.

Later, sinking back into sleep, I think there may be just an awful lot I don't remember about Angela. Maybe we'd be better off not knowing everything. Is everyone's life as messy as my own? I turn onto my stomach, wishing futilely, like most people I know, I could undo some things.

Eight

WEDNESDAY AFTERNOON I receive a call at my office from Tommy, who confides to me in a less than confident voice that his family has decided to allow him to instruct his cousin Eddie to encourage his workers in the plant to talk with me. Buoyed by the miracle of my client's finally realizing just how stupid it was to allow a third party to make a decision about the future of his children and accepting the agreement we'd hammered out a week ago, I try to think of how to keep Tommy from suddenly changing his mind. I begin by asking if he has been made aware that a former employee named Vic Worthy had threatened his father less than a month before he died. When he says he hasn't, I add, "He probably wasn't the only person angry at your father, either. There's never been a person who didn't overestimate his charms as a boss."

Perhaps pausing to consider that I could be right, Tommy finally asks, "How does Bledsoe explain the phone call he made from the plant?"

Tommy isn't going to forget anything and neither will a jury. "He swears he didn't do it. Maybe she misunderstood him," I say. "Maybe it wasn't him she heard. I just want to be able to open up some communication with people like her." For all I know, she killed Willie and is framing Doss; however, women don't usually commit premeditated murder with a knife.

"Gideon, promise me you won't manipulate anyone into saying something they don't know," Tommy instructs me, "or honestly believe."

"I'm an advocate," I assure him, "but I'm also an officer of the court. I wouldn't do that."

"My father didn't trust lawyers," Tommy says, repeating an earlier comment from last week. "I wouldn't be doing this if we hadn't grown up over there together. We were both kind of outsiders."

Actually, I've never thought of us quite like that, but now is not the time to quibble with him. "I appreciate this, Tommy. I won't abuse the situation. You can count on that."

I can't ask Tommy to keep our conversations a secret from the prosecutor or Paul's attorney, and will have to assume he is sophisticated enough not to volunteer them. It is inevitable that sooner or later, Paul and Dick will find out that I am actively working against them, but by then I hope it will be too late. I suggest that he not talk to Eddie about encouraging the workers to talk to me until I have had an official tour of the crime scene, which will probably be made with Paul's attorney. In order to get this out of the way, I will have to call Butterfield, who could require me to jump through the hoops and file a motion with the court, but I don't suspect he will.

Friday morning I follow Tommy's directions and take Highway 79 to the plant, which is only a mile from the city limits. This visit to the crime scene has turned into a full-scale production. Not only is Dick to meet me out here but the sheriff will be here, too. Since the plant is in operation, there can no longer be any crime scene to tamper with, but Sheriff Bonner, I'm learning, goes by the book. Off the highway a good fifty yards and shielded by a stand of trees, the plant is bigger than I imagined, almost as long as a football field from end to end. I turn into the parking lot, which is full of old junkers and trucks. As depressed as the economy is over here, I suspect most of the workers don't receive much more than minimum wage. Some of these people are obviously skilled butchers, but I doubt if old Willie had much of a profit-sharing plan.

Inside the plant office I ask a white male, who looks like Willie Nelson with a full white beard, for Eddie Ting. Apparently, neither Dick nor the sheriff has arrived.

"Darla, is Eddie in the can?" he says, scowling at a woman who must be Darla Tate, the woman who claims she overheard Doss. A tall, big-framed woman in her late forties toiling behind a computer screen, Darla smiles, making up for her colleague's lack of candle power. There is something familiar about her, but I can't place her. "Either that or he's vanished into thin air," she says to me. "He'll be out in a minute."

Her questioner frowns. If this is actually Willie Nelson hiding out in a meat-packing plant in east Arkansas, he doesn't look very happy about it. Yet, in my coat and tie, I probably look like I'm from the IRS. I glance around the room. If this is the entire front office of Southern Pride Meats, no one can accuse Eddie of wasting the profits on furnishings. Three scarred desks, beat-up chairs, metal filing cabinets, and a hat tree constitute the furniture. They all look as if they were stolen from a Goodwill warehouse. None of the desks is separated from the other by more than a couple of feet. The five essentials of modern office life—coffee maker, copier, calculator, computer, and fax machine—give the room a busy look. Maybe Eddie has an office somewhere in the back. Then I notice the desk directly across from the woman. I realize I am looking at the exact place where Willie Ting was murdered.

"Are you the lawyer?" the Willie Nelson lookalike asks. "Eddie said Bledsoe's lawyer would be coming by today," he says to Darla. It is more a question than a statement. Dressed in jeans, cowboy boots, and a green John Deere cap, Willie doesn't give me the impression he spends a lot of time getting briefed in corporate meetings.

"Gideon Page," I say, nodding and holding out my hand.

"Cy Scoggins," the other man says, reaching across the desk and giving my hand a tentative squeeze which communicates the feeling that lawyers have never scored highly on his personal hit parade.

"I'm Darla Tate," the female says. "I'm the secretary and bookkeeper, and Cy runs the back. Would you like some coffee? The sheriff and Mr. Dickerson should be here any minute," she says politely.

Before I can answer, a stocky individual with Asian features appears from around the corner wiping his hands on faded khaki pants. "You must be Mr. Page," he says, his voice more Southern than my own. "I'm Eddie Ting. Did you meet Cy and Darla?"

"Sure did," I say, looking for a family resemblance and finding one in the nose and mouth. His face is more fleshy than I remember Tommy's, but he has the same serious expression. We shake hands, and Eddie looks me squarely in the face. We must be equally curious about each other.

I turn back to Darla and tell her I'll take a cup of coffee, but when she gets up, the door opens and in walk Woodrow Bonner and Dickerson. Given Paul's earlier outburst about blacks taking over the town, I doubt seriously that they rode together. Bonner gives me a suspicious look, and I assure him that I arrived only moments ago and that I was about to have a cup of coffee.

Bonner, all business, shakes his head and says that if we want to look around the plant we should get started. "I guess we need hats and coats," he says to Darla. It is obvious that Bonner has spent some time out here. "Mr. Ting, can your foreman or you show us around back?"

Though his manner is polite, there is no doubt who is the boss. I don't know what I expected from a black sheriff, but this guy seems comfortable enough in his job.

"Cy will give you a tour," Eddie says to Bonner and then nods at the banty rooster across from me.

I wonder how Cy and Darla like taking orders from an Asian twenty years their junior and a black sheriff. Assuming they are from this part of the state, neither they nor I was raised with the expectation that anyone other than white males would ever sign our paychecks or tell us what to do.

Darla has moved with surprising grace from her chair and disappeared around the corner. With her fingernails painted a bright red and artificial pearls over her lavender sweater, there is something almost touchingly feminine about her in this oppressively male bastion. She probably was never pretty, but she still doesn't mind trying to raise the flag.

With the crime scene photographs in mind, I point to the desk across from me. "I take it this is where your uncle was sitting," I say to Eddie while we wait for Darla.

Eddie looks at Bonner. "That's what I was told."

Dick, obviously coming from his office and dressed in a three-piece suit, crowds in by me. He has been content to sit back and watch this exchange. Like me, he is probably thinking east Arkansas will never be the same again.

Bonner nods, but doesn't say anything else, and I marvel at the contrast between the sheriff and the prosecuting attorney. Bonner won't give anything away and the prosecutor won't shut his mouth. One is a professional, and the other is a professional politician. I'm not sure which is which, though. We all stare at the desk and chair as if we expect them to start talking to us. Too bad they can't. Willie didn't even have an individual cubicle for himself. If he picked his nose, Darla could just not look. I say, "There must have been a lot of blood here. I'm surprised the floor isn't stained."

Cy grunts, "We're used to cleaning up blood around here."

I imagine so, thinking what must be going on behind us. Squeamish, I'm not looking forward to Cy's show and tell. Darla returns with three white coats and caps. As we put them on, Cy volunteers, "They figure he had his back to whoever done it. The person had to know him just to come up behind him and slit his throat. It was bound to be an employee," he says, putting on the soft white coat that had been lying on his chair.

I tug at my sleeves. "The coat and hat are for the inspectors," Eddie explains, ignoring his foreman's comments. "I didn't know this until I came, but you can't legally operate the plant without them being here. The public has no idea how safe their meat is. They're here at six and leave when we shut down at two. You'll see them back there," he says, nodding at the wall.

Damn. No wonder this country runs a deficit. "How many are there?" I ask.

"Two," answers Darla. "At the big plants, they probably have their own softball team."

I look down at Darla's desk. She has a picture of two teenaged boys within stroking distance in an 8×10 frame. I wonder if she took the polygraph. She doesn't seem like the murdering type, though.

Cy nods. "All this stuff here," he says, pointing to the desk and chair, "is new."

Darla says dryly, "That's a relative term here."

Cy reaches into a cabinet and extracts a wicked-looking knife with a blade about five inches long. He hands me the brown-handled knife, and I press the tip against my thumb. As sharp as it is, it wouldn't take much work to reach bone. "These babies come from Germany," Cy says. "Koch butcher knives. Five inches of the finest cutting steel in the world. If you put this under a microscope, you'd see it has a bunch of teeth. This is what the murderer used. Only fifteen people in this plant had knives like this, and all of their stories were rock solid. Doss, he claims he was home by hisself. If he came around here, he'd have hisself a little accident, I expect."

Cy motions us to follow and pushes through a door in front of me into a hall and then through another door to the left. "This is the kill floor," he says over the squealing of pigs, men's voices, and machine noise. In front of us about twenty feet

125

away a black guy dressed in knee boots touches what looks like a cattle prod behind the ear of a huge hog and immediately the animal collapses on the concrete floor of an oversized shower stall. Beside him another hog watches impassively. "Does that kill him?" I ask Cy.

"Naa, that's just a little stunner. It's only got two hundred and forty volts. Knocks him woozy for about a minute," the manager yells into my ear. "Now watch what happens."

From his side the black guy pulls out a knife and bends over the hog, and quickly there is blood spewing onto the floor. The hog beside him sniffs the twitching carcass but otherwise makes no move to flee. I thought pigs were supposed to be smart. This one acts as if his buddy were merely suffering from a major mosquito bite. If I were him, I'd be looking for the back door. "If Archie doesn't get him killed," Cy yells, above the din, "they'll get back up."

As dumb as these animals are, they probably think they've just been out in the sun too long. Archie reaches down and hooks the dead animal's back legs and pushes a button on a machine beside him. I watch as the pig is hoisted up and moved over to a vat of water and then dipped. "That water is one hundred and fifty degrees," Cy says. "It helps remove the hair."

After more than a minute, the dead animal reappears and is placed on a machine that rolls the body back and forth in a vigorous beating motion. Cy, who has moved ahead of me, motions me over. "The hair comes right off," he says, pointing to the carcass.

Indeed, the pig is practically nude within a few moments as wisps of hog hair fall away through the metal rods on which it is bouncing. Finally, it is pink all over, looking like a cartoon pig—Porky or Petunia, minus their clothes—and again it is hoisted up and sent along its way. Cy directs us to a new station only a few feet from us, and I watch as a skinny white guy who looks to be in his early thirties moves in on the animal and scrapes at the remaining hair. Every few moments he stops to sharpen his knife. "He'd wear himself out, and it'd take forever, if he doesn't keep the blade razor-sharp," Cy responds when I ask him about this incessant and deliberate process. "What is happening if you could see it is the teeth of the knife get lined up again. Still, these guys go through a knife about every month. We give 'em the first one, and they have to buy 'em after that. Before we did that, they'd go through one every couple of days."

Damn. A plant where the workers have to pay for their own tools! At the next station the toenails and more hair on the feet area are removed, and then the actual cutting begins. "Watch Tolly rip," Cy says, with obvious pride in his voice. "I taught him myself ten years ago, I've never seen anybody work with less wasted motion." Tolly is a middle-aged black man with sloping shoulders and arms as long as Scottie Pippen's, also an Arkansas product. First, he splits the hog, still hanging from the grappling hook, lengthwise. As Tolly works, Cy explains that at Southern Pride (unlike many other plants), they do not save the lungs, ears, or intestines, because Willie demonstrated to his own satisfaction long ago it wasn't economical. Tolly tosses these items into a bag that makes me nauseated to look at. Then, as the head comes off, I find myself listening more than watching.

"Some people come direct to the plant and buy hogs' heads for five and a half bucks, and we sell 'em to stores. They cook up what we call souse out of it. We make it up ourselves, and you can buy it over the counter. Spreads good on crackers. I'll give y'all some before you leave."

For the first time Dick, standing beside me, grins. It is a promise neither of us would be brokenhearted to see go unfulfilled. Almost directly in front of me is a guy squinting hard at various pig parts. He looks as if he dropped a contact lens into them. "Who's that guy?" I ask, noting that the sheriff has grown even more tight-lipped than usual though he is watching everything like a hawk. I realize that "some people" means blacks.

"Harrison—one of the federal inspectors," Cy says. "He's

still kind of an asshole, but it was him that noticed that Doss's knife was out of place the next morning. If it wasn't for him, it might not have been checked."

Dick asks, "What's he doing?" Dressed like everybody else in a white coat and cap, Harrison looks as if he is about to lose his cookies, too.

Cy points at the pig hanging above us and then to a metal table to our left where four men are busy cutting meat. "Before the hog makes it to the table, the inspector checks each one's parts for abscesses, tumors, signs of disease in general. They've already checked them in the lot before they go into the plant."

Dick suggests that we visit with Harrison, and we walk over to him. Cy introduces us, and it is clear that despite who we are, he is eager to talk. "Since they gotta buy their knives in this plant, each man puts his mark on his so nobody will run off with it," he says in answer to my question about how Doss Bledsoe was fingered so quickly. "Every afternoon when this plant closes down, I know exactly where every piece of equipment, including knives, is, because I've inspected them to make sure it's all clean. The next morning the sheriff here had me walk with him over every inch of this place. I noticed that Doss—he was the best meat cutter Willie had working—had moved his knife just a little from the night before. Want me to show y'all where it was?"

"I'd appreciate it," I say, looking down at Clarence Harrison, who can't be more than 5′4″. Beaming as if he had solved the murder of John F. Kennedy, he looks in the face exactly like James Carville, the President's celebrated political guru. We follow him across the floor, and he stops in front of the east wall and points to a small wooden table. "Doss nearly always kept his knife overnight in a sheath on the center of this table just like so," he says, pressing the knuckles of his left hand against the wood. "When I came through the next morning," he says, flipping his hand over, "it was upside down and a little over to the side. As soon as I remarked on this, Sheriff, you remember you had a man take pictures of all the knives, where they were and everything."

Bonner merely nods. Despite his redneck look, Harrison, it seems clear, respects the sheriff, now that criminal charges have finally been brought. It dawns on me that Harrison expects to be considered the hero in this case and testify as the star witness. I doubt seriously he will be willing to harbor any doubts that anyone other than Doss was the killer. If that is true, it will be unfortunate. He is in an ideal position to observe the social dynamics within the plant. I'll get back to him later, but I am not hopeful I will get anything.

Dick asks, "How well did you know Doss?"

"Well, we didn't socialize, if that's what you're getting at," Harrison says and laughs. "Doss had a mouth on him, I'll guarantee you. He was good for one thing—cutting meat and throats. I'll give him that."

We move on and Cy points out the men who are doing various cuts of meat: hams, bacon, ribs, chops. Their knives flashing, they work quickly and steadily. This part of the job doesn't seem as gross as what I've just been witnessing. The hog, alive a few minutes ago, now looks more like what I see in the store. Of course, humans can get used to anything.

He leads us through a door, and in the hall we see large containers of presumably inedible hog parts. "These are hauled off to the rendering plant near Memphis," Cy says, his voice conversational now that he doesn't have to shout. "They boil this down and make dog food and stuff out of it." He bends down and picks up a bottle. "Before it's taken off, it has to be denatured, so nobody'll be tempted to try to sell it for human food." He unscrews the cap and pours a green liquid over the offal. I feel my gorge rise. "I guess some people," he says, chuckling, "ain't got out of the habit of eating this shit."

I burp into my hands. If it were warm in here, I'd be throwing up. Fortunately, Cy opens a door and leads us into a cooler. The frigid air feels good despite the fact that I was not at all warm. "It's ten below in here. One of the many things we don't have a handle on since Willie died is maintenance. Costs are beginning to eat this plant alive. Willie had it figured out, but we sure as hell don't. There're not a lot of people who know the refrigeration business around here, and I think we're getting ripped off. According to Darla, we're paying a lot more for things now that Willie's dead."

I look around the room and see giant slabs of pork that look like frozen monoliths. Though there is plenty of space, I feel claustrophobic. Perhaps, it is the knowledge that it wouldn't take long to die in here. "Do you think Eddie is running things okay?" I ask, curious to see Dick's reaction.

Cy folds his arms against his chest. "I guess so," he mumbles. Cy may be a redneck, but he, too, knows that it is the messenger who gets shot. He wants to keep his job. Since he is part of management, criticizing it won't help him.

We go out and into another room, and see our first female employees in the actual operation of the plant. Not unexpectedly, they look a little rough, but one woman, about my age, catches my eye and grins. "Fresh meat," she says, nudging her coworker, a woman at least ten years younger.

Cy ignores her and explains, "We vacuum pack our sausage. The profit's back here. You can't hardly find butchers in supermarkets these days. More and more all the grocery stores do is stick it out on the meat racks. This business is changing all the time."

Clearly, it is beyond him. The kill floor he can manage, but Cy probably isn't much help to Eddie on the business end. We follow Cy around the rest of the plant and soon I am hopelessly lost as he shows us more cookers, smokers, a spice room, a kitchen, and the break room. Willie's killer could have tried to hide his body in a dozen places. But obviously, it would have been found immediately, so why bother? Standing on the lip of the loading dock he points out the trucks and then spits harshly on the concrete. I ask, "Couldn't his killer have been someone who had never seen the plant? All he needed to know was that Willie often worked there by himself after closing time."

Though he should be used to it, Cy hugs himself in the damp February air. "It had to be somebody who knew the plant," he says, shaking his head.

"I've been looking for you!"

We turn and see a woman standing at the door with a clipboard waving at Cy. She, too, is in a white coat and is wearing a cap. Cy takes a long drag on his cigarette and turns his back on her before saying under his breath, "Frieda—she's the other one. She's not so bad, anymore."

Government inspector, he must mean. Since Cy isn't budging, she walks toward us, impervious to Cy's studied indifference. A tall, awkward woman with bad teeth, she is probably used to men being rude to her and affects a professional cheerfulness. "You can run, but you can't hide." When Cy deigns to turn and glare at her, she hands him her clipboard.

Barely glancing at the paper he is signing, he says, "These are some lawyers, and I guess you know the sheriff by now."

Dick nods, and I introduce myself, wondering if Cy remembers my name. He is not what I would call a people person.

"Frieda Blakey," she says, smiling again. "I've got an uncle who's a lawyer. He's in prison."

There is no malice in her tone. Perhaps this is how she bonds with other humans. "Great place to find clients," I say, deciding to humor her. Given her reception by Cy, she must have a lonely job.

"I've been telling Kip to keep 'em spaced," she says apologetically to Cy. "He just blows it off."

"I know," Cy says, handing her the clipboard back. "I'll talk to him."

Frieda stands a little closer than absolutely necessary and says, "You know the difference between a dead lawyer in the road and a dead skunk in the road?"

"No, what?" I respond, thinking I had heard every lawyer joke told in the last ten years.

"There are skid marks in front of the skunk!" she cackles.

Dick and I laugh politely. Frieda wants desperately to be liked, and I'll do my best when I contact her later on.

Our tour is at an end, and since neither of us is going to interview witnesses with the sheriff breathing down our necks, we return to the office to say goodbye to Eddie. I ask to use the bathroom, and sure enough, I can hear the talk in the office through the thin plywood door as plain as day. The secretary could have easily overheard Doss on the phone. Dick thanks Eddie for the use of Cy's time, and we head for the parking lot. Dick tells me that he will buy me a cup of coffee at the Delta Star restaurant two doors down by his office, and I follow his Mercedes back into town, wondering what I have learned. Probably nothing other than that if I lose my law license, I don't want to work in a meat packing plant. I could stand around for an hour at the crime scene and not pick up a damn thing.

At the Delta Star restaurant next to his office downtown Dick makes me feel better by confessing, "The only thing I learned was that Willie must have felt very comfortable with the person who killed him. What you need to find out is how often someone like Doss came up to the front office. Did they come up to use the telephone? If somebody was in the bathroom in the back, could they come up and use the one in the office? What I don't understand is, if the plant closed at two, how is Butterfield going to explain to the jury what Doss was doing hanging around after hours? If he had come up front after the plant was shut down instead of going home, wouldn't that have made Willie suspicious? You need to talk to that Darla Tate if you can get anything out of her. She's probably wedded to her story, though."

The Delta Star is nicer than the Cotton Boll but not by much. The downtown area is thin, indeed. There are few retail establishments and even fewer people on the streets. Though it is half past eleven, there are only two other customers in this café. I ask, "Are you going to interview all the workers?"

Dick tastes his coffee and winces at its bitter flavor. "Not if you're going to. I have such a heavy trial schedule between now and June I don't see how I can. You'll share it with me if you learn anything that can help Paul, won't you?"

Their arrogance shouldn't surprise me now. "Sure," I say. Dick expects me to do his work for him because he doesn't have time. I'll be happy to oblige him. We talk for a few more minutes, and then I am back on the road to Blackwell County for a deposition in one of my two personal injury cases. I will turn right around and be back over here tomorrow to pick up Angela and drive to the ball game. What will Dick think about me when he learns I have lied to him? Gunning the Blazer up to seventy-five, I pretend I don't really care.

Nine

THE NEXT MORNING I get to Angela's a little before noon, but as usual she is running behind and comes to the door with a tube of lipstick in her hand. "Come on in," she says, smiling. "I'll be ready in a few minutes." Even without her face completely made up, she looks good. She is wearing black stockings and a tight gray skirt, and I feel a stab of desire slash through me like a sudden twinge of heartburn. Goodness. Does she know what she is stirring up in me? I tell myself to calm down. She is entitled to dress up without me thinking about what she looks like naked. I stand in the kitchen and to still myself contemplate the oak tree just outside her window. I spot two squirrels chasing each other on a branch that almost touches her roof. Probably a male chasing a female. Damn, if that's what she wants, I don't have a chance.

Driving over the desolate flatness of the Delta, we are soon chattering as if we were a pair of old biddies heading out for an afternoon's shopping in the big city for our grandchildren instead of two healthy heterosexuals enclosed in a small space with a long erotic history between us. As she talks her skirt creeps up an inch on her thigh. A scent that reminds me ever so slightly of honeysuckle permeates the space between us in the front seat of the Blazer. As children, my best friend Hannah and

I used to pretend we were hummingbirds, rapidly waving our arms and biting off the ends of the flowers on the bush in old Mrs. Speight's yard to try to siphon off the almost imaginary amount of nectar contained inside. Of course, we had to use our hands to remove the stems to get at the juice, but the image of Hannah's pixieish face as she waggled her palms up and down beside her head remains an indelible memory. I have never been that innocent in the company of a female again.

Angela wants to know everything about the case, and I tell her, beginning with my visit with Connie and her mother last Saturday morning after breakfast and ending with my cup of coffee with Dick yesterday. "Dick acts like I'm on their payroll," I say, not without satisfaction. "Neither of them has a clue how I feel about Paul."

Angela, who has been listening and asking questions with the devoted fascination of a true trial junkie, comments, "Maybe they don't remember the past exactly the way you do."

I swerve to avoid the remains of a possum. "Are you saying the Taylors never cheated us, or that Paul never bought up our land at a tax sale?" I exclaim, irritated by her dispassionate tone.

Angela reaches over and pats my leg. "I wasn't there, Gideon. If you say it happened, I believe you."

Though her comment reassures me, I begin to wish my memories of the actual events were more concrete. But I was only a kid when my father died, and I was in the Peace Corps when my mother lost her land. It was only when she died that I discovered there were no eighty acres to inherit.

When I do not respond, Angela says, "There is already so much gossip about us that half the town will be disappointed if we don't come back married."

I chuckle at the thought of it, but the fact that she is willing to tease is proof that she has been thinking about me. "I've stirred the pot pretty good, huh?"

"You don't know the half of it," she says cryptically, and then adds, "At least this will take some pressure off me. As soon as your husband dies or divorces you, and the pity wears off, a woman, unless she's old, becomes a pariah in a small town. You're viewed with fear and loathing by the women and the men suddenly think you're white trash."

This outburst and the vehemence with which it is said is straight from the heart. I now understand better my mother's words after the funeral that she should have just jumped in the grave with my father. She wasn't just grieving for the past; she was thinking of her future. "Unless you're old, it must be terrible being a single woman in Bear Creek," I say, sympathetically.

Angela shrugs. "Maybe it's the futility of the situation over here that gets us down. East Arkansas is probably more like South Africa than anyone cares to admit, but we don't have a Nelson Mandela to save us."

Again, the hyperbole. Yet, in Memphis, less than an hour's drive east, it is hard to get away from the feeling that racial problems in the Delta are as permanent as the land itself. At the Pyramid, just across the Mississippi River, the coaches and players are almost all black while the crowd is overwhelmingly white. Dan and I have just this week been to see *Hoop Dreams,* a documentary that follows two black Chicago youths through their high school basketball careers to college. One kid, the less talented of the two, ended up at Arkansas State after graduating from a junior college. I left the movie more convinced than ever that big time university athletic programs are poorly disguised professional sports businesses that should pay corporate income taxes. Both the Memphis and Arkansas coaches have recently complained loudly and publicly of racism directed against them. Their bitterness stems from some commentators' past contentions that as coaches they are better recruiters than tacticians. White coaches such as Bobby Knight and Eddie Sutton get praised for their game plans. The implication, the black coaches contend, is that they are too dumb to be astute tacticians. Angela, chewing contentedly on a hot dog before the game begins, asks, "How hard can it be anyway? I've never known any coach who I wanted to do brain surgery on me."

I laugh, glad I am here with her. Angela is an enthusiastic fan, calling the Hogs with the cheerleaders as if she had been one herself. Our seats are a mile from the court, but Angela over-rules the referees' decisions with the confidence of the con-firmed sports couch potato. "That was a charge!" she screams, as the game winds down, punching my arm for emphasis. "He had position! Didn't you see it?"

How? From this height, the players look like ants to me. It is easy to forget some of these guys are seven feet tall and weigh more than 250 pounds. "They ought to give him a couple of foul shots just out of sympathy," I agree. "I wouldn't stand still and let one of these rhinos run over me unless I were wearing a full suit of armor."

Angela nudges me with her shoulder. "You would if that's what it took to win."

When I ran track in high school, I was never sure if I com-peted so hard because of a desire to win or the risk of being hu-miliated. The race I remember most is the Meet of Champions race in which I finished last, not the state "A" finals, the week before, which I won.

The buzzer sounds. The Razorbacks are victorious by seven points. Though I never quite got into the game, Angela gives me a high five, irritating some Tiger fans sitting next to us. To hell with them. The next time they win they will be just as obnox-ious. Angela is grinning as if she had scored the decisive points. She likes to win, too. I wonder what motivates her. As Hog fans celebrate around us, I lean over and kiss her quickly on the lips. Though she doesn't respond, she doesn't chastise me either, and even this chaste contact has made my blood thicken.

After the game we park near the Peabody Hotel and walk around in the damp chill on Beale Street, a historic black area because of its musicians that has been revitalized to attract tourists—one of Memphis's many efforts over the years to pre-serve its downtown. We stop at the King's Palace restaurant and have a couple of beers and talk over a jukebox that seems mainly devoted to the blues. The game has left her in a good mood and she lets me kid her about her devotion to the Razor-backs. "When they beat Duke for the national championship, you probably danced down Main Street wearing nothing but a Hog hat."

"If I thought it would have helped them win, I might have," she says, sipping a Killian's. "Honestly, if I'd had a dream when I was sixteen years old that I would marry a farmer and live in rural Arkansas until I was almost fifty, I would have woken up screaming I'd had the worst nightmare in history. It shows humans can get used to anything, I guess. Until Dwight died, a few people, obviously traitors, had almost begun to think of me as a native."

I smile, knowing how Southerners are about people who move in from north of the Mason-Dixon line. From our perspective, it takes a couple of generations for them to fit in. "You should consider moving toward the center of the state," I say, serious but still hoping to keep the conversation light. "We're more civilized over there."

Angela places the bottle carefully on the mat in front of her. "It looks as if I'll be moving somewhere," she says, her voice suddenly harsh. "I decided to go on and sell to Cecil and Nancy. We had the papers drawn up this week and got them signed."

Her eyes look so sad I reach across and touch her hand. This is what has been bothering her. "Is that going to work? What will you do?" I ask, remembering her comment last week that Cecil wouldn't be able to make the payments.

"It doesn't matter," Angela says brusquely, and pushes back from the table. "You've never seen the farm, have you?"

"No," I admit, not at all eager to see it now. I was hoping we could stay in Memphis, go out to eat and who knows what? There are plenty of motels between here and Bear Creek.

"I'd like to show it to you," she says, standing up. "You might never see it."

"Sure," I say, reaching for my wallet. The expression on her face is so determined there is no point in arguing with her. There are obviously some things she needs to work out before she gets around to me. I need to take my time. But, damn, she is an attractive woman. She has combed her hair forward, making her look younger. Her breasts swell nicely under her black sweater. I wish we were staying right here. The way I feel now I wouldn't care if she were seventy. On the jukebox is some song about a man whose woman has betrayed him with "Backdoor Jack" after he left for work at a hospital in the early morning hours. I can relate to that. What better time than the freshest part of the day?

On the drive back, she waxes nostalgic about her father who had brought her south with him at the last moment. "I was going to stay with my older sister in Buffalo. Gwen was married, but Dad was afraid her husband would seduce me, or one of his brothers would. They were Irish, and every one of them was extremely good-looking. Dad didn't trust them."

Oddly, despite all the confidences we shared, Angela never told me this story. Muddy, barren fields skip by in a blur as I gun the Blazer up to seventy-five. When I was a child there was only one crop. The soil yielded year after year the "white gold." Cotton was still king and admitted no rivals. Now, after a love affair with soybeans, it has come back. "Why did he think he could trust me?"

"He knew your mother had shipped you off to Subiaco, and I told him how religious you were. I think he figured you were too eaten up with guilt to seduce me."

"I almost was," I admit. Yet did I seduce her—or was it the other way around? We drive in companionable silence as I think back on that first summer I knew Angela. Mr. Butler, a stern agnostic, did seem to approve, as I recall, of my own religious fervor. I ask, "Do you think your father ever knew what was going on?"

Angela shakes her head at the psyche's long-term capacity for denial. "He would have had to have been in a coma not to. You radiated guilt like an atomic bomb. Typically, I convinced him that you were merely having impure thoughts. Poor Daddy. To be such a smart man, he could be such an idiot."

Typically? Was I not the first? "What about the blood?" I ask, forlornly, more than thirty years later. "I thought you were a virgin!"

Angela reaches over and pats my hand, which is on the steering wheel. "Menstrual," she confesses. "I was just starting my period that night. It came in handy for a change."

"Damn!" I say, speeding up. My speed has dropped to forty miles an hour. "All these years I played this tape in my head that it was the first time for both of us. How many had there been before me?"

"Eight," she says, solemnly.

"Really?" I ask, horrified.

"Men," Angela says benignly. "You were the second, for God's sake! I had dated the same boy for two whole years."

I keep my eyes on the road, knowing anything I say will sound foolish. What difference does it make whether I was the first or the second or even the eighth so long as she did not give me a disease? Ego. The male ego. On TV the other night I saw a news clip showing how some very religious teenagers were being given gold rings by their parents for agreeing to stay virgins until they married. Guilt used to be enough, but now it takes heavy metal.

Soon Angela points to a dirt road bisecting a muddy field to my right. "Our land, mine and the boys', starts here on the east side of the highway. When Dwight's father died, his will divided the property in half. Dwight was given the land nearest Bear Creek, except the house, which was left to him and Cecil jointly. When Dwight built the house in town, he sold his interest in the one out here to Cecil. Despite the division, they continued to farm as if it were still all one piece of land. I wish now Dwight could have bought Cecil out. He's not cut out to be a farmer. He's okay with machines and a hard worker, but you have to be a business person today to farm, and Cecil's not. Dwight got a degree in agriculture at Mississippi State, and Cecil barely got out of high school."

A blast of wind hits the Blazer as a semi passes us from the opposite direction. A college degree apparently didn't keep the farm out of trouble. As she looks out over the bare fields, Angela falls silent. Land. Since I've never owned anything but a single lot, I've never understood the attachment. Maybe Angela is thinking of Dwight and all the work he put into it. The truth is, I don't know why she brought me out here or what she is thinking. All I see is mud.

"Slow down and turn in to the left by that mailbox," Angela commands, pointing almost a hundred yards up the highway.

I do as I'm told, and the road becomes gravel instead of goo, as I feared. Soon a one-story faded redbrick house behind a grove of trees comes into view. It can't be more than twelve hundred square feet and is almost boxlike in design. Are we visiting Cecil or what? "Ugly, isn't it?" Angela says, a brittle tone to her voice, which is a comment that needs no corroboration. "I can't imagine why anyone would want it."

By a butane tank behind a nearby barn I spot a GM truck, whose rusty bed makes me think of those ads on TV showing the number of trucks still on the road with two hundred thousand miles on them, but there is no sign of life around the house. "This is the old homestead, right?" I ask, assuming that Angela will tell me the purpose of this visit.

"Cecil and Nancy are in Birmingham with their children at a funeral for a couple of days," she says, her voice betraying a hint of what sounds like contemptuousness. "You want to go in for a while?" The expression on her face is brutally frank. We won't be going in just to use the bathroom.

Whew! This is bizarre, but Angela apparently is not ready for me to make love at her house, and isn't comfortable going to a motel. All I can do right now is imagine what the gossip will be if Cecil and the family show up unexpectedly an hour from now. Yet, didn't I hope something like this would happen? "Sure," I say before she can change her mind, though in truth that doesn't seem to be something I need to worry about.

I follow her into the house, astonished by her boldness. Cecil's kitchen table is covered up with a year's accumulation of bank statements, receipts, IRS forms and two pocket calculators. I feel ill at ease even though Angela apparently has no qualms about using her brother-in-law's home as a trysting place. Still, the smile on Angela's face is enough to overcome my scruples, and within two minutes we are rolling around naked in Cecil and Nancy's bed as if it were our own. I needn't have worried about rubbers. Angela makes me laugh by withdrawing a fistful from her purse and placing them on the nightstand by the bed. "Don't you think that might be about four more than we need?" I ask, more than a little intimidated by the prospect of at least seven orgasms.

The expression on my face makes her burst out laughing. "I just grabbed up a handful from a box in the boys' room. I'm not expecting company."

"Good," I say, relieved. I was beginning to think Dwight died from something other than cancer.

Her body is amazing; I run my hand over her right hip and am delighted by its suppleness. "You don't mind betraying your eighteen-year-old girlfriend?" she asks.

Rising to the bait, I answer, "She's almost thirty. Actually, we broke up last week." Aroused by long-forgotten memories and the sight of her flesh, I add, "It wasn't that big a deal."

Angela buries her face into my neck. "I bet she would disagree."

"She might," I allow, not wanting to argue. Angela's hands and mouth feel spookily familiar. Can I really remember after so many years? "You're still so sexy."

She raises her head and pretends to roll her eyes back in mock disbelief and then kisses me hard on the mouth. Yet because I am in another man's house and bed, I am uneasy. "I doubt if Cecil and Nancy would be too happy to see me right now," I say.

"I called them yesterday," Angela says, stroking my thigh with her hand. "They won't get back until late tonight."

"If they knew, they'd die, wouldn't they?" I ask. Instead of answering, Angela kisses me again and puts her hand between my legs.

An hour later, with Angela resting in the crook of my arm, I look across the room at the far wall, which contains a collection of family photographs. I can identify Dwight standing next to Cecil in one of them. Dwight, in addition to being brighter and better educated, was, as well, by far the better looking of the two. This picture, probably taken when they were in high school, shows a pockfaced boy whose unstraightened teeth and unruly hair were too much in evidence, as if someone hadn't bothered to take any trouble with him. Dwight, on the other hand, is, as I remember him, a boy with a strong chin and piercing blue eyes, his hair neatly combed as he smiles serenely into the camera's eye. To the right, another photograph, perhaps a quarter of a century later, of the same individuals, confirms my suspicions that life wasn't going to get any better for Cecil, who, instead of a farmer, looks like a middle-aged hippie with his long, untamable hair and acne-scarred face concealed by a beard. Judging by the set of his mouth, teeth still shoot in all directions behind unsmiling lips. Dwight's weathered face gives the impression he is older than his chronological age. Perhaps disease had begun to alter his appearance even before it began to destroy his ability to breathe. Certainly, toward the end, Rosa's lovely features were fast-forwarded by her pain. Still, he is handsome, with his Paul Newman eyes still undimmed.

"Nancy's not bad looking, is she?" Angela asks, looking up at me and then twisting her neck back to follow my gaze to the next picture. "Why she married an ass like Cecil, I'll never know. If his mouth were open, he would even look like a donkey."

I stroke her flank thinking that her bitterness seems all out of proportion to what she has told me about him. As someone whose sympathies usually lie with the underdog, I have begun to feel sorry for Cecil. I was never unhappy I didn't have an older brother to torment me emotionally or physically. Perhaps preoccupied by her own teenage demons, Marty rarely abused me unless I asked for it. "Is he as sorry as all that?" I ask, now curious about him. Until now Angela has made him seem slightly pathetic but not mean. Bad people have always been more interesting to me than good. Maybe that's why I have so many clients who won't pay me.

"Yes!" she says, her voice an angry hiss, but instead of saying why, she turns and grinds her pelvis into mine. Once more I am made to understand that pent-up lust in a sexually mature woman, despite the twaddle to the contrary, is the most exciting kind.

An hour later, as we ride through the now dark town toward her house, Angela asks, "If you were given evidence that convinced you that Paul wasn't guilty, would you tell him?"

I look over at her. In the dark I can't see her expression. Now that we are out of another man's house, I am again filled with desire. I would love nothing better than to be invited inside to supper. "Sure," I say, wondering if I would. "But my primary job is to represent Doss Bledsoe."

As we stop in front of her house, Angela becomes slightly distant. She reaches over and covers my hand on the steering wheel. "Listen, I know you'd like to come in, but I need some time to assimilate this afternoon. Do you mind?"

Buyer's remorse already. "I understand," I say, trying not to have my feelings hurt. Yet maybe I should be more charitable. Maybe she feels as if she has somehow betrayed Dwight.

"I like you very much, Gideon," she says, squeezing my hand. "I just need some time. I'll call you next week."

I nod, and in an instant she is walking quickly into her house. A little pissed that she won't even let me walk her to her door, I drive westward in the cold night air, telling myself that Angela's guilt is normal. She was married almost thirty years to one man. I hold the Blazer on sixty-five, deciding not to risk a ticket. I will be back over here many times. If I don't rush things, this could have a happy ending.

Ten

AT 4:30 MONDAY I receive a fax from Eddie that says he has "talked to the employees per Tommy's request." Included is an up-to-date list of the plant employees' addresses and home phone numbers. Tommy has kept his word. The first call I make is to Darla Tate at her home. I ask if there is a time when she would be willing to talk to me. Though it would make just as much sense to start the interviews with someone like the foreman or one of the meat inspectors, Darla's testimony of what she overheard Doss say on the phone will be an important part of the prosecution's case, and I want to find out how solid it is.

"Eddie told us that we should feel okay talking to you about his uncle's murder," Darla says, a Jimmy Buffett song in the background. "For some reason, he didn't say why, the family isn't convinced that Willie's murderer has been charged."

Leaning back in my chair with my feet propped on my desk, I notice I have written Angela's name on the pad in front of me as if I were a lovesick punk in junior high. To my relief, this woman doesn't sound defensive, merely curious. "I think they believe it would have been easy for someone to have set up Doss," I say earnestly, "and since I've known the family for a

145

long time, they trust me enough to talk to the people in the plant who worked with him."

She, or someone in her house, turns the music down, before she says, "Mr. Page, I think I've figured out who you are. Your father used to extend credit to my mother at his drugstore. She said she couldn't have made it without that."

Score a point for Page Drugs. All anyone, including myself, remembers is my father's drinking and schizophrenia. It is easy to forget what a decent guy he was. "That's nice to hear. Did you live out in the county?" I ask, searching for anything to build a connection with this woman. If she eventually can be persuaded to back off her story, I'll be more than happy to make it easier for her.

"Moro," she says. "We rode the bus in. School consolidation was hard on a lot of people, but it was worth it for me. I never would have gotten to take physics or calculus."

What did she need them for if she ended up a bookkeeper for a meat packing plant? On the other hand, what did I need them for either? If someone could have taken that time to teach me to balance my checkbook, I would have been better off. "I admired y'all," I say sincerely. "It couldn't have been any fun." For kids out in the county, it was like being black in the early days of desegregation. They were the ones to have to give up their schools and teachers.

"Lots of kids in town were snobs," she says. "That didn't make it any easier."

"I got shipped off to Subiaco for high school," I say, making it clear I wasn't one of them before maneuvering the conversation around to a date when I can come see her. She tells me tomorrow after work will be a good time for her. As bookkeeper her hours are normally from eight to five. I look down at the statement she gave the sheriff. At the time of the murder she was volunteering at her kids' school, which I assume is the private segregationist academy in Bear Creek. Her alibi has been corroborated by the principal's secretary and the log kept by the school. Obviously, Willie's murderer knew her schedule. I get her address and thank her for agreeing to talk with me. I hang up, knowing she doesn't realize how hard I will have to go after her on cross-examination unless she changes her story.

As soon as I put the phone down, Dan lumbers into my office and sits unnaturally erect in the chair across from me. Still in pain from his skiing debacle, he has a nervous sheepdog look on his face that tells me he is up to something. The chair creaks under his bulk. I thought now that he is eating his own cooking he would lose some weight. No such luck. He must be up to two hundred fifty, maybe more. I hope Brenda will leave him alone now that she's kicked him out. They didn't have kids, and he didn't have any money. "What's going on?" I ask.

"I guess," he mutters, "I have a date tonight."

A date! No wonder he looks so miserable. "Are you sure you're up to it?" I ask solemnly. "Women nowadays have all these weird positions they want you to try. You could really hurt yourself if she gets going."

"Are you serious?" he asks, alarmed. "I'm too fat and sore to do anything but stare up at the ceiling. I was hoping we could go to Luby's in the Mall and then watch a little TV."

From the top drawer of my desk I take out a paper clip and straighten one end of it but resist the temptation to stick it in my ear. "No way. As soon as she gets a sexual history, out come the creams, the oil, the leather—you name it."

Dan slumps in his chair. "You gotta be shitting me. For God sakes, this girl teaches the third grade and likes bird watching. She can't be like that."

I lean back in my chair. "Teachers are the worst. They love the discipline. She'll have you in a harness swinging from the ceiling before the night's over."

Dan grimaces at the thought. "As fat as I am, it'd have to be from the bridge," he says, nodding in the direction of the river, "and that might not even hold me."

"Seriously, though, you gotta do better than Luby's on the first date," I instruct him. Then grinning I say, "That's married food. She'll want some raw meat. Lots of protein. She's got a long night ahead of her."

Dan takes off his new bifocals and squints at a spot on the right lens I can see from across my desk. He rubs a tissue over the lenses, smearing them. The glasses now look as if his dog, a mutt he found limping down the street in front of his apartment, has sneezed on them. "Maybe I should have just shot myself," he says, his voice morose, "instead of letting Brenda file for divorce."

I relent. He sounds too serious. "It won't be all that bad," I say. "Tell me about her. If she's in her seventies, you'll probably be pretty safe."

He gives up on the glasses and massages the back of his neck while he considers his answer. "She says she's forty." He reaches into his wallet and hands me a picture. A brunette, the woman isn't bad looking at all, and actually looks a lot younger than any forty-year-old I know. "How'd you meet her?" I ask.

Dan leans forward and reclaims the photograph. "Well, actually I haven't yet," he mumbles. "This is through one of those computerized dating services."

"Tell me you're not serious," I beg, amazed he would spend what little money he has on a blind date. Yet we both know Dan doesn't do well with women he finds on his own. Brenda was a ballbuster from hell, and a few months ago the hooker client he was in love with allegedly abused her kid by holding her down in a tub of hot water. As a favor to Dan I represented her in juvenile court and got her off, but whether she did it, I'll never know.

"She sounds pretty nice on the phone," Dan says defensively. "I think we have a lot in common. She likes to eat, watch movies on TV. Besides, if this doesn't work out, they guarantee ten more dates."

Ten? I grit my teeth to keep from saying something sarcastic. "How much does all this cost?" I ask, trying not to laugh out loud. Knowing Dan's tastes, I wonder if this woman is a blind mud wrestler. His divorce won't be final for a while, and here he is trying to get involved with someone else. Yet, how in the hell can I say anything? I'm more obsessed with women than Dan will ever be. I even called Amy last Sunday to check on Jessie and ended up spending a half hour on the phone with her.

"Lemme see, a total of almost a thousand bucks," Dan says, studying his checkbook, which he has tugged from the inside of his suit coat. "I finally settled the one personal injury case I've had for a couple of years. I should be saving the money to pay some taxes, but it's hard to make myself put any aside."

"Tell me about it," I say, more than happy to agree on this subject. The government can't come within hundreds of billions of dollars of balancing its budget and yet it has the nerve to demand that people like Dan and I try to pay as we go. "Does she get a picture of you?" I ask.

Dan chuckles. "Not a recent one," he says. "I didn't want her to think I was trying to get out of the nursing home for a night on the town. I kind of fudged and said I was divorced, too. If this works out, I hope she doesn't read the paper much." He pats his rib and says solemnly, "Anyway, she can't be into anything too bizarre. She said she can see my dimples in the picture they sent her and that she likes them."

It's not love that makes the world go round; it's lies. "You're in big trouble, then," I kid him, wondering if any of the information they've exchanged is true. Dimples? Why not? Women have loved men for far worse reasons. I haven't seen Dan's dimples in a while. He hasn't had much to smile about. Maybe this will turn out to be the love of his life. Brenda certainly wasn't.

"The woman I'm interested in," Dan says, rubbing his sore ribs, "is the old girlfriend in Bear Creek. Now, there's a hot mama. Did you do any good with her this weekend?"

I nod, knowing Angela fascinates him almost as much as she does me. One day last week I gave him a line-by-line account. To be such a screw-up himself, Dan is a good listener and fairly shrewd when he's not talking about himself. Omitting the more graphic details, I bring him up to date. He comments when I come to a stopping place, "If Angel baby had a happy marriage to that pig farmer, then I'm Judge Crater."

I have begun to think the same thing. Angela talks about how great Dwight was, but she doesn't talk about how much fun they had. "He may have been so sick the last few years that's all she remembers," I say, happy to defend her dead husband now that his memory doesn't seem like such a threat.

Dan leers at me. "Well, she's starting to make up for lost time now."

"I don't think she knows what she's doing," I say, thinking how odd Saturday was. Angela made up her brother-in-law's bed, but she didn't bother to wash the sheets. "But she looked so damn good I couldn't have resisted her if I had wanted to."

"You should get her over here," Dan advises. "It sounds like she prefers somebody else's bed to her own."

I take out a rubber band from my drawer and pop it against the desk. "She's gonna have to do something. For some reason she feels obligated to sell out to his brother, but she doubts if he can pay her. I can't help but feel bad for her."

Dan snorts and wags a finger at me. "Who you ought to feel bad about is Amy. If she put out a contract on you, I wouldn't come to your funeral."

Amy, Dan, and I were all friends in night law school. He is rightfully protective of her. "I wouldn't blame you," I say, contritely. "I called her the other day to see how Jessie is doing. She sounded okay."

"Don't you fuck her over anymore!" Dan orders, and pushes himself up out of the chair. "If you're through with her, leave her alone! Damn it, she's crazy about you and this is killing her! The stupid little fool."

"I won't," I say quickly. Dan's face is flushed, and he's actually panting. With a look of disgust on his face, he huffs out of my office and slams the door. I give him five minutes to get over it. One of Dan's problems is that he can't stay mad at anybody any more than he can lose five pounds.

Dan's right. I shouldn't have called her. It's just that this is an unsettling time in my life. Taking this case in Bear Creek probably wasn't a good idea. There is too much unhappiness over there, and I feel as though I am becoming sucked in by it. Still, things could work out for me and Angela. All she needs is time. My problem is that slowing down is not something I do well. Apparently, neither does Angela.

At four o'clock I get a rare business client, a young man who told me on the phone last week he wanted to come in to see me about a zoning problem. Len Chumley, a kid who can't be much out of college, follows me back to my office, telling me that he knew Sarah his last year at the University. "She was just a freshman," he says respectfully as he sits down across from me, "but you could tell she was going to be special."

"She's doing fine." Special in what way, I wonder, as I try to size up Chumley. This guy looks a little slick, but I have no handle on males his age. Only a couple years out of college, he probably doesn't have a lot of money, but he doesn't mind putting it into the clothes on his back. He has on a black and white herringbone sportscoat that looks to be silk and a dandy purple handkerchief poking out of the pocket. "What kind of problem do you have?" I ask, deciding not to inquire about my daughter. He probably wouldn't tell me the truth anyway.

"I'm primarily in the condom delivery business," he says, not batting an eye. He whips out a business card and slides it across my desk. I put on my reading glasses. In old English script it gives Chumley's telephone number and an address that I recognize as only a couple of blocks from an exclusive area of town. In the center it says: CHUMLEY'S CONDOMS DELIVERED TO YOUR DOOR. Then below it: WE COME BEFORE YOU DO.

"A business for the nineties," I concede, thinking this kid will probably be a millionaire someday. Chumley is short, maybe no more than 5'6", and already a bit thin on top, but he has the salesman's way of using what assets he has to his advantage.

"They have a condom store in Fayetteville," Chumley reminds me, "but for every person who isn't embarrassed buying their rubbers in front of their neighbors, there are fifty in Arkansas who would prefer to have a conservatively dressed salesperson come to their house and show them a variety of products including condoms, sex toys, and videos."

Maybe their neighbors will mistake them for Mormons. "Sex videos, huh?" I ask. "So it's not just condoms?"

"Related products. In my marketing course at the University, I was always fascinated by surveys which show how difficult it is for the customer to say what it is he or she would really like to buy. Even though the interactive video is revolutionizing the art of merchandizing, there will always be a place for the Fuller Brush man and the Avon lady."

I would hardly place French ticklers, dildos, vibrators, and porno movies such as *Sore Throat* and *Full Speed Ahead* in the same category as cosmetics, but maybe I'm out of touch. I can picture Sarah's reaction when my picture shows up on the front page of the *Democrat-Gazette* defending the First Amendment rights of this little hustler. I ask, "Specifically, what is your problem?"

"They want me to take my 'We Come Before You Do' sign out of my front yard," he says, his voice registering high with indignation. "I work out of the house my parents left me." He hands me a letter from the city warning me that he is in violation of city ordinance #1437. "All I'm doing is advertising a legitimate business."

"Where do you live?" I ask, wondering who on the floor has a set of municipal ordinances. We have more laws in this country than ants. It's hard to believe that we need every single one of them.

"On the corner of Riverview and Dayton," he says. "Even though it's zoned residential, there's a lot of traffic by there in the day. You'd be surprised how many people see it."

I don't doubt that. I suspect that it hadn't been up fifteen minutes before someone called city hall. This case is a loser, and I tell him so. "There're all kinds of eloquent arguments that can be made on behalf of free speech and the free enterprise system, but I suspect it would be so much pissing in the wind. You could wind up spending a fortune trying to get a variance and falling flat on your face."

The kid gives me a sly smile. "I was thinking maybe you'd barter your fees."

I groan inwardly, thinking this is what my law practice has come to. "Follow me," I say, standing up and heading for the door. Dan, I think, have I got a client for you!

At home Tuesday night Angela calls to tell me that she has been invited to Atlanta to spend a week with an an old college roommate. She is driving down Thursday morning. I wonder if she is trying to avoid me, but she sounds friendly enough. I want to talk about Saturday, but I manage to restrain myself. The quickest way to make her back off is to crowd her, especially when she has asked me not to do so. I tell her what is going on in the case and that I will be back in Bear Creek Thursday. She is keenly interested in the details and reads to me an article in the *Bear Creek Times* about the case. For the only source of news in Bear Creek, it is amazingly succinct and reports only the barest outline of the case. My recollection of the news media in Bear Creek is that its primary business was advertising revenue, and distinctly not investigative journalism or crusades of any kind. Since most of the stores that must advertise in the *Times* are probably in some way associated with Paul, I shouldn't be surprised. Angela at eighteen would have been indignant at this article and charged a conspiracy between the media and the business community, but today she says that she is grateful no one is trying to exploit the already tense race relations in town. If Angela has changed, so have I.

If anyone had told me I would make love to Angela in her brother-in-law's bed thirty years after I left Bear Creek, I would have doubted his sanity. She promises to call me when she returns and hangs up. I go to bed and dream that we are making love in her house in Bear Creek. Someone was watching, but when I wake up, I can't remember who it was.

Darla Tate's house is the first one on the right on Kentucky Avenue, less than a mile from Jefferson Academy, where she sends her sons. It is in a development that was relatively new when I was growing up, but like everything else here, it seems much smaller. The homes are modest A-frames with tiny yards. Darla's house has siding, however, and is distinguished by a large pecan tree in front. Driving over, I have realized this woman can be a gold mine of information if I don't make her defensive. Outside of his family, probably nobody spent more time with Willie. What I'm afraid I'll find out, though, is that Willie, being Chinese, rarely confided in anyone except his wife.

Darla Tate comes to the door in a pair of baggy brown slacks. Now that I get a good look at her, I realize she is almost as tall as I am. Her oval face is partially obscured by long, straight hair of a hue that seems to have gone through several changes and is now the color of winter wheat. As I follow into her living room, she offers me a beer, which I regretfully decline. I don't want this to turn into a party. "My boys are still at basketball practice," she says. "They both play, but they can't jump more than two inches between them."

I laugh, remembering that I would have liked to have played basketball at Subiaco, but I, too, had a vertical leap of an inch. What furniture she has is old, and a little worn. A couch, coffee table, TV and VCR, and recliner more than fill the room. Pictures of her boys in their football uniforms are on the walls. I sit on the couch while she plops down in the recliner and picks up a can of Bud Light by her feet. "They're good-looking kids," I say sincerely, wondering what the future holds for white adolescents. I think of Angela's comments about her two sons. These two boys could easily end up at the plant like their mother.

"They're a handful," she says, "especially without a father around."

Without any prompting, Darla explains that she waited until she was almost twenty-five to get married, and then her carefully chosen husband took off after just three years, leaving her to struggle through one marginal job after another until Southern Pride Meats came into existence five years ago. "That old man," she volunteers fervently, referring to Willie, "was the most decent human being I've ever known. Even when he'd cut down on the number of hogs, he still kept our workers on the clock so they'd get a full paycheck. Two years ago, I was sick a whole winter, and he kept my check coming. That's just how he was. There aren't many white men who'd do that around here as far as I'm concerned."

I ask her if she minds if I take some notes, and begin to scribble furiously on my legal pad. Perhaps I can make her seem so blindly loyal to Willie that she would do anything to incriminate his killer. Unfortunately, she doesn't seem like someone who would tell a lie when the truth is less convenient. Instead, she simply comes across as what she portrays herself to be: a profoundly grateful woman who needed a decent job to support her children. "He must have trusted you a lot," I say, "or he wouldn't have told you about the tape between him and Paul Taylor."

Darla winces as if I have struck her. "If I had known what was on the tape, he might still be alive today, but there was always a line I wasn't permitted to cross. He just said to make sure Doris played a tape he had given her if anything mysterious happened to him. When I asked about it, he just gave me this look, and so I shut up."

Darla is a talker and requires no urging to gossip about the personnel in the plant, thus relieving me of the fear that she was so wedded to the idea that Doss was the killer that she wouldn't be willing to discuss anyone but him. "Harrison, one of the meat inspectors, hated Willie," she says in response to a question about who, other than Bledsoe, could have killed her employer. "And, frankly, Willie hated him. Willie wrote to his boss and tried to get him fired. He was nitpicking us to death."

I ask about the other inspector, Frieda, who seemed that day in the plant almost apologetic about having to write up somebody. It was Harrison who noticed that Bledsoe's knife was slightly out of place the day before. "Surely you've had this conversation with the sheriff or an investigator," I say, delighted with this information.

"It's not in my statement, but I mentioned it the same morning the sheriff went through the plant with Harrison," Darla says, gulping at her beer, "but the problem is that he's got a pretty good alibi. See, he and Frieda commute all the way from Memphis every day. He couldn't have made it back after the plant closed before Doris found Willie's body."

I tap my pen against my pad. Some alibis are only as good as the amount of time it takes to understand what they're built on. "Maybe Harrison has some kind of hold on Frieda. You think they could have been sleeping together?"

Darla laughs out loud. "That little bitty peckerwood? Frieda's no prize, but I sincerely doubt if she's that desperate. She knows on a daily basis what an asshole Harrison is. I'm not gonna say it'd be impossible, but a woman's got to draw the line somewhere."

In an ideal world maybe—but from what I've seen of Frieda, it's not hard for me to make that leap. While I write, Darla gets up to get another beer. "Are you sure you won't have one?"

I nod, having decided one won't wipe me out, and a moment later take the Budweiser she hands me. If beer helps her keep talking, I'm not going to discourage her. "You ought to try to check out that illegal alien who ran off after the murder," she says, snapping the top off her second can of Miller Lite in less than twenty minutes. "Now, if Doss didn't do it, that boy could have. But I'll bet you a dollar to a doughnut he's in Mexico, and nobody will ever find him. They haven't got a clue."

I reach down into my briefcase and flip through to the back of the file where I find a copy of his work permit. Jorge Arrazola. I study his picture. In his early twenties, he is a nice enough looking kid but basically indistinguishable from a million of his countrymen. Dark, lots of hair and a mustache. Darla gets up from her chair, stands by the arm of the couch, and looks over my shoulder. "This is an obvious fake, if you study it. Who knows what his name really is? But it doesn't pay employers to study their identification papers too closely. Willie liked Mexicans and hired them whenever he had the chance. Typically, they're the best workers in the plant. Jorge hardly spoke a word of English, and so we relied on Alvaro Ruiz to tell him what to do."

That name rings a bell, and I rummage through the file to find his statement. As I do, I ask, "Who is he?"

"He's worked for Willie ever since the plant opened and is like a godfather to the Mexicans who come through here. A real steady and sweet old guy. Jorge lived with him before he took off. I'd go talk to Alvaro if I were you."

I've scanned his statement once before and do so again. Darla adds, "Alvaro had another part-time job he went to after he got off at the plant. He worked as a butcher for Bear Creek's one supermarket, so he was never a suspect."

In his statement Alvaro says that their usual arrangement after work was for Jorge to drop him off at Jenner's Foodsaver and then come pick him up at six. That day Jorge had told him he was going fishing. Two days after the murder he put a battery and tires on an old truck he had in his front yard and was gone. "Did the sheriff really consider him a suspect?" I ask, squinting at the papers in the poor light.

Darla returns to the couch. "I've heard they think he was just scared and took off. That's what Alvaro figures, anyway. Since there was no robbery, it's hard to figure his motive."

I sip at my beer. "Not unless somebody like Paul Taylor hired him to murder Willie," I speculate. "He'd make a perfect hit man. A faceless Mexican who sticks around just long enough to collect his money, and within twenty-four hours has slipped back across the border never to be seen again."

Darla smiles. "You guys are something," she says, a hint of admiration in her voice. "I can hear your closing argument right now."

It is never as easy as this, of course. "Tell me what you thought about Bledsoe. Did he seem like he was capable of murdering Willie to you?"

Darla strokes the arm of the couch. She has a ring on her right hand, but the stone is a modest opal. "Frankly, no," she says carefully. "Willie really liked Doss. He wasn't one of these wild-ass blacks who drives off to the Lady Luck a couple of times a week to throw away his paycheck and come in half drunk the next day. He was an excellent worker and could do anything you asked him. Always on time. Neat, clean, careful. Never cut himself. A model employee if you want to put it like that. If he did it, I don't know why he did it."

If he did it. I ask, trying to sound offhand about it, "When you were in the bathroom and heard him on the telephone, could it have been someone else who just sounded like him?"

"I know his voice," Darla says, but her tone isn't stubborn. "We worked together five years."

"Is it possible," I ask, looking down at my pen, "that it could have been someone who sounded like him?"

She is quiet for a moment. "I doubt it," she says finally, "but I haven't really tried to compare his voice to others. I just assumed it was Doss because that's who it sounded like."

"Obviously, that could be real important," I say, beginning to hope she will help me. "I assume occasionally the workers come up to the front for things like to use the phone or something?"

Darla takes another sip of her beer. "They come up to get their checks, sign forms, use the phone, stuff like that."

I'm reluctant to press her further right now. This won't be my only visit, and the better she gets to know me and like me, the more likely she will be willing to say that it could have been someone else's voice. I ask her if she knew Paul Taylor. She shrugs. "How could anybody not know him? When I was growing up, and, I guess, you, too, the Taylors were supposed to be one of the richest families in the state."

The front door flies open, and her two sons saunter in. They are lean, good-looking kids, tanned and lean with no stomachs. Dressed in jeans, flannel shirts but no jackets, and tennis shoes, they look from their mother to me and back to her.

"Is this guy the lawyer?" the taller of the two asks, his voice protective.

"This is Mr. Page," Darla introduces me.

I stand up. The boys eye me suspiciously, but politely introduce themselves as Arlen and Walker. Arlen, stockier and shorter, and whose upper lip hints at a thin mustache or maybe is just dirty, says anxiously to his mother, "You're not getting fired, are you, Mom?"

Darla laughs and makes a show of rolling her eyes. "No, for heaven's sake. Listen, you two get back in the car and go get yourselves a pizza. Bring me back a couple of slices of pepperoni and sausage." She reaches down into her purse, pulls out a twenty, and hands it to Walker, who jams it into his front pants pocket. "And I want all the change back, too."

Pleased by their good fortune, they both grin and are out the door. When she hears the door slam, she says quickly, "The plant's losing money under Eddie. That hasn't happened in years. It was a gold mine with old Willie running it."

She must be scared to death of losing her job. "They seem like real nice kids."

"They are," she says, and tears suddenly fill her eyes. "It's not easy alone."

"It must be hard raising boys," I say, thinking about Angela. "I have a daughter a little older than your two, and we've been alone a long time, so I know what you mean. If it's not one thing, it's another. She's a great kid, but if she told me tomorrow she'd shaved her head, it wouldn't surprise me."

Darla is able to smile at this, and I return the conversation to the Taylors. "What was your take on Paul?" I ask. "I have to confess I've never been a big fan of him or Oscar."

159

Darla drains the last of her beer and seems to be thinking about getting up for another one. "I've got mixed emotions since he's given work to my boys for the last two summers. Paul's reputation is that if he wants something, he's used to getting it," she says, her voice bitter. "You've probably already heard that until a couple of years ago, he was the major stockholder of Farmer's State Bank here. That's how he was able to keep as much land as he did after they got in trouble. A lot of people who used to farm but don't now, including my father, thanks to Paul, hate his guts for cutting off their loans when things got bad. Of course he didn't cut off his own. He played favorites and a lot of people still despise him for it. For one thing, he knew how much Willie was making, because four years ago when he expanded the plant he borrowed some money from Farmer's and paid it back a year ahead of schedule. I think Paul's been wanting the plant for years."

Damn. Why didn't Angela tell me this? Like a dumb student finally catching on in school, it hits me that Dwight and Angela were among his favorites. I finally understand her reluctance to criticize him. But now that he's no longer involved, the bank won't loan her any more money. "What happened?" I ask.

"It got bought out last year," Darla explains, "by an out-of-state bank, but they've kept the name. All this is common knowledge or gossip, depending on who you talk to."

It shouldn't be hard to find out. Now I understand, too, where Paul got the money to try to buy Willie's operation. Instead of getting back into the farming business on a large scale, Paul wanted a cash cow to milk, but Willie refused to sell, and being a Taylor, Paul wasn't going to stand for that. My respect for Darla Tate grows by the second. Though she may still be country as all get out, she knows how things work in Bear Creek. And though she may not be willing to say it yet, I'm convinced she suspects Bledsoe may have been set up, and with a little massaging, may well say so, even if it means coming off her story that she heard his voice. We talk for a while longer, and she suggests the names of a couple of other workers she believes might have something to tell me. When her boys come back I thank her and say I'll be in touch.

She walks me out to the Blazer and hugging herself in the cold, says, "I hope this was helpful. I thought the world of that old man. If I think of anything else, I'll let you know."

I assure her it was and drive away, congratulating myself on having the sense to start my investigation with Darla Tate. Women like her—homely, dependable, and completely country—are always ignored in small towns. Truth be told, they're the ones who don't miss a trick. I wasn't a snob and never underestimated the kids who came in from the country. They may not have had the social graces we did, but they were always watching what we did and obviously were keeping score. Darla was, anyway.

Eleven

SATURDAY MORNING, I get up early and drive to Bear Creek to pay a surprise visit to Alvaro Ruiz and three other workers who have agreed to talk to me today. By making it a point to encourage me to talk to Ruiz, I assume Darla suspects he could know more than he is telling about this murder and is simply scared he will end up getting deported if he talks too much. If he would be willing to say that Jorge Arrazola had acted suspiciously before he took off, it would help enormously. Of course, what I would like for him to say is that he suddenly remembers he saw Paul Taylor stuffing hundred-dollar bills into Jorge's hands the night before he took off, but that is a bit much to expect. It is at least worth a try. Somehow, even though I can't remember where I put down my reading glasses half the time, I remember some Spanish from my Peace Corps days and perhaps can establish a rapport with this guy that will loosen him up a little.

I pull into town and stop for some toast at the Cotton Boll, where McKenzie greets me with a smile and old Mr. Carpenter comes out of the kitchen to remind me to come by to visit him. He seems lonely and I promise that I will. I then head east through town toward the river, resisting the temptation to drive by Angela's on the off chance she changed her mind and didn't

162

go to Atlanta. I go nearly thirty years without seeing her and now she is on my mind every day. As I fumble on the seat for the list of workers Eddie faxed to me, it occurs to me this visit won't entirely be a surprise to Ruiz, since presumably he was around when Eddie announced that it was okay to talk to me.

In the cold morning light I squint at the address I have for him. All it says is "The Landing," but I remember enough to get me close. Lasker Huber, a kid in my sixth grade class, caught his foot under a submerged tree limb at the Landing and drowned. For weeks afterward, I had nightmares of being caught by a branch and struggling unsuccessfully to free myself. Even now it is the first thing I think about when anyone mentions the L'Anguille River.

Lasker's family was basically white trash. River rats, we called them. I liked Lasker. He hadn't lived long enough to have a chip on his shoulder like the rest of his family. Unless it has changed, the Landing is a boat dock behind a defunct lumber company. A road the city fathers never bothered to name leads down to it. There were some shacks down by the dock, which I doubt have become mansions since I last saw them thirty years ago.

As I suspected, the Landing hasn't changed much. Though it has been fixed up, I think I recognize Bobby Don Hyslip's old shack and wonder what happened to him. One hot summer's night parked in the gravel outside the Dairy Delite—where our most sophisticated joke was to send a younger sibling to ask for "colored water" and laugh hysterically as the help sent him or her around to the drinking fountain for blacks—Bobby Don had taunted me with the hoary gossip of my paternal grandfather's own sexual escapades. He had infuriated me by calling me a "nigger lover." My mother had never allowed me to say "nigger," not out of some passion for equal rights, but because our family was above that sort of thing. The daughter of a physician, she had no intention of doing anything that would allow her, or anyone under her control, to be equated with the Bobby Don Hyslips of the world. She vehemently denied any allegation of sexual misconduct on the part of her father-in-law. As it turned out, Bobby Don was right.

The L'Anguille River, a tributary of a tributary on the way to the Mississippi, was once said to be good for fishing, and may be still, though I never caught any. As I look into the cold greenish water, a pleasant boyhood memory surfaces of a Sunday afternoon outing with my father. We had borrowed or rented a boat and small outboard motor at the dock, and while we were out a fish literally jumped into the boat with us. It was before he had become delusional, but it was hard not to regard the event as an omen that we would be successful if we took up fishing. We did and never caught a single fish. That summer, bonded by bad luck or simply incompetence, we were closer than we would ever be again. I walk up to the door and am astounded when Bobby Don, now a carbon copy of his own father, answers my knock.

He doesn't quite know me. Balder than I am, fatter, too, he squints at me as if he should recognize me but doesn't. "Yeah, who you lookin' for?"

I try to look into the room behind him, but he fills the door like a bear protecting his den. I get a whiff of cooking odors, onion and grease, and perhaps fish. Talk about white trash: Bobby Don is still writing the book. "You know where an Alvaro Ruiz lives around here?" I ask, hoping he won't recognize me.

"Who are you?" Bobby Don demands, staring hard at my face.

"Gideon Page," I say and then add, hoping my lying is not ridiculously apparent, "You look real familiar." I feel a curious mixture of distaste, superiority, and shame. Somehow, this man, by his resentment and boldness as a teenager, has a hold over me after all these years.

"I'm Bobby Don, Gideon. You remember me," he says, his upper lip curling in a sneer that is familiar after three decades.

"Hell, yeah," I say, pretending his face is coming back to me. "You've changed a little," I throw in, beating him to the punch. "You look like your father."

To his credit, Bobby Don doesn't deny it or make a comment about my own. "What the shit are you doin' over here?" he asks, offering his right arm, which is covered by a faded red corduroy shirt that stops short of his wrist by a good inch. His jeans look as old as he is. Of course, he wasn't expecting company either.

Taken aback by this display of friendliness, I nevertheless extend my hand. His palm, as I expected, is rough and hard. Bobby Don must be the only person in Bear Creek not to know already why I'm here. "I'm a lawyer in Blackwell County, but I've got a case here and I'm interviewing some people who might know something about it."

"Who is it, Donny?" a female voice calls from somewhere in the back. Whoever, wife or girlfriend, she sounds slightly hung over, too. I hear no children.

"An old friend of mine from when I was a kid," he calls over his shoulder without a trace of irony.

Friend. He's got to be kidding! I feel my cheeks begin to burn, but try to say amiably, "I need to find this Ruiz guy. You know where he lives?"

Bobby Don must see something in my face, for his old expression of disdain returns to his own. "He lives a couple of houses that way," he grunts, pointing to my left. "So you're a lawyer, huh? I should have figured that."

I know: a gift for gab, though I suspect I know what word Bobby Don would use. "So, what are you doing these days, Bobby Don?" I say in my snottiest tone.

"Fishing," he says, giving his answer as much dignity as possible. He gives me a hard stare and shuts the door in my face.

I walk down off his wooden porch and return to the Blazer and back out of his yard. People don't change, I decide. Yet if Bobby Don knew that my purpose was to get Paul Taylor, I suspect he would approve. He's spent his life envying people like Paul.

Alvaro Ruiz's shack is on higher ground than Bobby Don's, but I wonder whether it has ever been flooded. Maybe it only seems that hundred-year floods come every ten years these days. I know I'm glad I haven't lived on this bank for the last thirty years. In summer the mosquitoes must be like dive bombers. From the outside the structure looks about a thousand square feet, but unlike Bobby Don's it has been painted in the last few years. I wonder why he doesn't live better, but I wouldn't be surprised if he sends most of his money back to Mexico.

I knock at the door, and wait a full minute before a gray-haired Hispanic with long sideburns and a mustache cautiously sticks his head out. I introduce myself, and at the mention of Eddie's name, the door opens wide to reveal a short but power-fully built man of about sixty in a red cotton jersey and jeans whose cuffs are folded several times at the bottom, revealing a pair of unpolished Army boots. "Are you Mr. Ruiz?"

"Yes, I am," he says, his voice heavily accented. "You want to come inside?"

"Thanks," I say and offer my hand to him. His jaws relax into an unforced smile, and he shakes my arm so vigorously I could be a long-lost relative. I walk past him into a room that shows few signs, if any, of a feminine touch. An ugly green couch, two folding chairs, a scarred unpainted coffee table, and an old 17-inch Motorola TV make up all the furnishings I take in on first glance.

He politely offers me a cup of coffee, and though I already need to piss after two cups at the Cotton Boll, it would seem rude to refuse. He leaves me alone in the room to take off my jacket and to stare at the blank TV screen and contrast this hos-pitable beginning with my exchange with Bobby Don. Alvaro may think he has no choice but to appease me. Whatever the differences, I already like this guy more in ten seconds than I ever did Bobby Don. In the moments before he returns I notice on the table a snapshot of a younger woman and four children. His daughter and grandchildren? Wife and kids? Though I spent two years in Colombia, I am basically ignorant about Central America in general and Mexico in particular. I know the African slave trade flourished in South America, but have no idea if it was a part of the Mexican economic system. My host returns with a tea tray, which though not laden with strawberries and cream, contains a carton of milk, a bowl of sugar, a spoon, and a mug of coffee. Maybe there is a woman in the kitchen after all. This seems oddly elaborate in such spare surroundings, but Alvaro, from outward appearances, appears not at all surprised to be entertaining an uninvited stranger who has shown up at his house unannounced before nine o'clock on a Saturday morning. He seats himself in a folding chair across from me and sips at his own coffee, taken black, while I explain that I just want to ask him a few questions about Jorge Arrazola. "I'm trying to find out if he did anything while he was here," I say, "to make you think he might have had something to do with Mr. Ting's murder."

"No," Ruiz says, "he is a good boy. A hard worker. He has trouble with the English, but he is learning a little."

"Are you a citizen of this country, Mr. Ruiz?"

His eyes widen slightly. "No, but I have papers. Do you want to see them?"

"Not at all," I say, hastily. "What I meant by that question is that you may not realize that you can't get into trouble if he had told you something that made you suspicious he was involved in Mr. Ting's death."

The other man studies the floor. "So someone tell you I know where he is?" he asks, his fists clenched on his knees. "I already speak to the sheriff and say I don't know where Jorge go. They say it isn't even his real name."

"I realize that," I say, "but my understanding is that you were very helpful to this boy. Maybe he said some things that would help give you an idea of where he went or where he was actually from. He might have gone back home. His family might know where he is."

Mr. Ruiz looks past me out the window to the other side of the river. "I know he say he is born in Juárez, but that isn't going to help you much. He won't go there. He breaks the law by having a false ID. But he don't kill Mr. Ting. I know him. He just need to make some money to help his mother and don't have no green card. That's not so bad."

I can't help but think this man knows more than he is telling. There is too much emotion in his voice. "Not at all," I say, taking another tack. "The problem is that if he doesn't come back and clear his name, the Tings might have a problem with hiring any more Hispanics at the plant. It's too bad. Eddie said y'all are the best workers they ever had. Maybe he left behind something that could help find him."

Ruiz cuts his eyes back at me. Clearly, he feels he is being coerced, however subtle it appears. "He live with me and sleep on this couch," he admits. "But when we find out the next morning Willie is murdered and they think it's somebody in the plant, he get scared and leave two days later without a word to me. He don't have nothing here to see."

I look down at the couch as if I might be looking for an address between the cushions. It's possible that this kid was Willie's murderer and Ruiz was in on it. Nobody needs money more than these people. Paul could have easily made a deal with this man, who was too smart to do it himself. So Ruiz hired a fellow countryman and showed him how to frame Doss. Why the hell not? "Did he steal your truck?"

Ruiz shakes his head. "I give it to Jorge for his birthday last July and he fix it the day after the murder. All it need is a battery and two tires. He take it."

A murder charge would motivate me to get some transportation, too. "Mr. Ruiz, how do you know he didn't kill Mr. Ting?" I ask, making my voice firm.

Ruiz seems more guarded now, but it could just be my imagination. He avoids my eyes and looks out the window again. "He don't act no different. He say he take the boat and go fishing the day Mr. Ting killed. He go fishing a lot."

"Do you know Paul Taylor?" I ask, sipping my coffee.

Ruiz gives me a quizzical look. "I see him downtown, but I don't talk to him."

I take a sip of my coffee. "Did Jorge ever mention him or did he ever come out here?"

"No," he says emphatically. "Mr. Taylor don't ever come out here to fish."

Getting nowhere fast, I ask, "Do you think Doss Bledsoe killed Mr. Ting?"

Ruiz looks down at his own coffee, which he hasn't touched. "I been knowing Doss for a long time. I don't think he kill anybody."

I look down at the photograph. Despite his defensiveness, I feel a grudging respect for Ruiz. He has come to a foreign country, learned another language, gotten an honest job, and has helped others. "Who do you think did?" I ask, certain I won't get an answer, and I don't. He shrugs but doesn't respond, too circumspect to point fingers at anybody.

"My wife was from Colombia," I tell him. "The day she became a United States citizen was one of the proudest days of her life. She always said people who are born in this country never appreciate it enough."

"You have work here," he says, his voice heartfelt. "In Mexico, there is never enough. If this plant closes, I can go somewhere else in the state and work in the chicken plants. Here, I send money to my family every month. In Mexico many barely have enough to eat." He smiles and says in Spanish, "Su esposa es de Colombia, sí?"

Embarrassed by my pitifully accented Spanish, I reply in English, "She died seven years ago from cancer, but we had a daughter who looks just like her." I pull out my wallet and show him Sarah's picture.

He nods appreciatively. "Qué hermosa!"

I tell him that she is a student at the University of Arkansas and ask about the picture on the table. He picks it up and says in Spanish that his first wife died, too. I make out, or think I do, that three of the children in the picture are by his first wife and the boy is from his second. He is speaking too rapidly for me to follow every word, and I ask him to speak English. "Comprende bien, no?" he says, but with his typical deference switches back to a language in which he can only express himself in the present tense. He tells me his first wife died in childbirth twenty years ago. Yet he chose to marry again and begin another family. I can't imagine having that kind of hope in a country that promises its people so little security. Only one of his adult children has a full-time job and that as a taxi driver in Mexico City. As I often did in the Peace Corps, I think about how lucky I was to have been born a white male in this country.

We are interrupted by someone at the door, and when Jorge opens it, I have a partial view of a man in hunting clothes who is carrying a shotgun in his right hand. It looks like a .20 gauge, which was the size my father and I used to hunt rabbits before my mother, in her growing terror of his paranoia, gave away his guns. I stand up to get a better view and see Jorge's caller is a wormy, sallow-faced white guy in his early twenties. I wonder if he is one of Bobby Don's sons. He says irritably, "Where the hell you been?"

Jorge mutters an apology to him, but I pick up my coat and go to the door with a card in my hand, and say that I will be back in contact with him. With characteristic politeness, he introduces me to his friend, but I do not catch more than his first name of Mickey. Possibly hung over with his red eyes and vacant stare, Mickey eyes me suspiciously and does not offer to shake hands, which is fine with me. I drive off, wondering how hard Ruiz was questioned by the sheriff.

The rest of the day is one dry hole after another. Though each of the three men I talk to is more or less willing to discuss the case (they don't want to lose their jobs, I assume), all, despite being encouraged to talk, are understandably suspicious of me. Obviously, if Bledsoe is not Willie's killer, one of them might be. Still, I have no choice but to begin the process of visiting each one and satisfying myself that not only are their alibis airtight, they don't have any information that could point to other suspects. The most irritating of the three is Cy Scoggins, who, away from the plant, has no doubt who killed Willie.

"For a nigger, Doss was okay at his job," Cy admits as he slides underneath his truck to tinker with something. "Sooner or later, though, they all revert to type, and will kill you just as soon as look at you. Name me a family where one of them doesn't have somebody in jail."

Squatting on my heels to talk to Cy since he isn't going to interrupt his work, I resist arguing with him. All it will do is piss him off, and that won't help me. I ask if he remembers Vic Worthy, the man whom Doss claimed he heard threaten Willie. This launches him into a diatribe against blacks. "A perfect example of what I'm talking about. He came to work drunk, got his ass fired, and then had the nerve to file for unemployment compensation. Hell, yeah, he hated me and Willie, but he couldn't a done it, though, 'cause Willie wouldn't let him get near the plant. He would a noticed a nigger like Worthy trying to slip up on him."

He discounts Darla's theory that Harrison, the male meat inspector, could have framed Doss and killed Willie. He gestures at me with the wrench. "Name me a meat inspector anybody likes. They're assholes, but that's why they're meat inspectors. Harrison didn't give a shit that Willie hated his guts and was trying to fire him. If Willie had liked him, Harrison would have thought he wasn't doing his job."

I drive off, thinking how much Cy resents blacks. Maybe he framed Doss, and Darla is afraid to say so or is fooled. Yet I doubt it. Cy's alibi is rock solid. According to the statements gathered by the sheriff, three junkyard employees are willing to come to court to testify he was at a salvage yard during the time Willie was murdered. I'm glad he isn't my client. It can be a pain in the butt to defend someone you instinctively dislike as much as Cy. His implacable racism makes me glad I didn't come back here. The problem with Bear Creek is its hothouse atmosphere. In Blackwell County you can escape the subject of race occasionally, but here it controls everything.

From a pay phone at a Fina station, I call the jail to arrange a visit with my client, but when I get out there Bledsoe has come down with the flu. Shaking, his teeth chattering, and complaining of a savage headache, he says he has a fever that is going through the roof. He is too sick to talk, and I tell him I'll come back next week. The jailer assures me he will be taken to the medical center in Little Rock if he gets much worse, and I head back into town and decide to drop in on my old friend John Upton. Driving through town earlier, I had noticed a light on in the office of the insurance company he owns. A Cadillac was out in front of it, and I doubt if it was his secretary's. I have been meaning to talk to John since I went through the yearbook with Angela. He remained a friend even after my father went crazy, and the one thing I know for sure is that I need help understanding what is going on over here.

I drive the Blazer along Main Street and then turn right on Apple and pull up behind the Cadillac. If he's willing, John can surely give me a perspective on Paul Taylor no one else can. At one time, John's family had more money than anyone in the county except Oscar Taylor. Outside John's storefront, I buy a copy of the *Bear Creek Times* and scan the paper before I go in. This issue doesn't even mention the case, and, in fact, seems to have changed little since I was a boy. All the stories on the front page are about whites. I wonder if African-Americans buy any advertising. The longest story on the cover is about a man named Buck Canner who is moving to Harrison to work in an electrical business. Family by family whites are leaving. An article on the back page says that farmers are required to buy crop insurance by the end of next week in order to be eligible for price supports and loans by the Farmers Home Administration. In the center of Bear Creek it is easy to forget this area is dominated by agriculture, and how little I know about it. I suppose if Angela was going to sell her land to Cecil, she had to do it now. Planting season is just around the corner. I fold up the paper, put it under my arm, push open the door, and hear John on the phone in his office. I take a seat and wait for him to hang up.

John's father was a farmer, and though John has always dabbled with other businesses, it is the land that has kept him here. I hear John hang up, and I go in to find him sitting behind a large clean desk with a computer on it. He looks damn good. Though he is my age, there is just a tinge of gray in his sideburns, and I realize he is one of those people whose faces age well while the rest of us grow bigger ears, noses, and warts. Smarter than the other kids I ran around with, John, thinking as a kid he would leave east Arkansas, went to the trouble of becoming a civil engineer before ending up back home in Bear Creek. As far as I can tell, all he has to show for a difficult college major are aerial photographs in his office of enormous bridges and dams. He stands up and gives me a warm smile. "The man with the silver tongue," he says. "Come back to terrorize his old hometown."

I laugh and reach across his desk to shake his hand. Slim (he was chubby and pimply all the way through high school), he is better looking now than he was as a boy. "You were always the best shit shoveler," I accuse him. It was true. John could talk his way out of trouble better than anybody I ever knew.

He grins and gestures for me to sit down across from him. "At least I didn't go and make a profession out of it," he says enthusiastically. "How the hell are you, Gideon? I've missed you. Are you moving back here? That's one story I've heard."

God, this place! "How do you stand it, John?" I ask, sincerely curious. "I can't take a crap here without the whole town wanting to see how much toilet paper I use."

On his desk he has pictures of his family. As I recall, while in the army at Fort Knox John married a divorcée whose family roots were deeply embedded in the pungent soil of Kentucky Democratic politics. I pick up a photograph of his wife, who hasn't aged as well as John, but he says proudly, "Our anniversary was yesterday. Twenty-seven years. Can you believe that Beverly and I are pushing fifty?"

If her photograph is any guide, I can believe Beverly is, but I don't say so. Like Paul, John could have made it anywhere, but he chose to come home and be a big fish in a pond that's been going dry for years. Yet what if I had married Angela and settled down in Bear Creek after college? Had it not been for having to run into the Taylors, I tell myself, I would have enjoyed it. I have missed seeing people like John, whom I have known since the morning we met in old Mrs. Blount's kindergarten class, then a private school in her house. And I have missed knowing the parents and grandparents of my friends. For better or worse, we knew who we were, where we had come from. Perhaps, too, Angela and I could have helped to make a difference before such bitterness set in on both sides of the racial issue. Surely Bear Creek didn't have to be the tragedy it turned into.

We talk about his four boys, all out of state now, I note. I tell him about Sarah and show him the picture in my wallet. He whistles. "My boys would like to meet her."

Not if they were still living in Bear Creek. I finger a photograph of John, Jr., now an electrical engineer for the state of Oregon, his father tells me. He looks like a carbon copy of John. "I wouldn't let them within a hundred yards of her," I kid him, remembering John's deserved reputation, even in junior high, for mischief. "Remember the time you shot an arrow at your sister? You should have been prosecuted for attempted murder."

Even a third of a century later, John blushes. "I wasn't really trying to hit her," he says, and begins to giggle. "Jesus, we must have been nuts."

I lean back in my chair, remembering how, bored on a hot summer's day on Danver's Hill, he had asked his sister Cynthia, who couldn't have been twelve, if he could try to shoot at her with his new bow and arrow set. Setting a new standard for sibling stupidity, Cynthia asked only for a twenty-second lead. As I began to count, she began to run, zigzagging through the tall grass like some escaping POW. The arrow embedded itself into a tree a foot behind her. Naturally, she couldn't wait to tell their mother, and John talked me into taking him on as my first client. With a straight face I told Mrs. Upton, who was hysterical, that John wasn't even going to release the arrow from the bow and certainly hadn't been aiming at his sister, and that the arrow had landed ten feet from her, not twelve inches. The bow and remaining arrows were confiscated, but John, as usual, escaped without further punishment. "You were nuts," I correct him.

John says, "I've been wondering when you were going to come by. Can you believe they've charged Paul with murder? This place is crazy now."

His initial reaction is no different from Angela's or perhaps any white person's over here. Now that John has raised the subject, I ask, "Do you think Paul could possibly be dumb enough to hire somebody to kill an old Chinese man for a meat-packing plant?"

John points with his chin over my head. "Look behind you."

I turn and see a dozen photographs on the back wall and get up to inspect them. The pictures go all the way back to 1950. From left to right they show John's uncle, who began a Ford dealership in Bear Creek with a "grand opening" surrounded by fifteen employees. The last picture, taken two years ago, is of his uncle with five other people. "Is that all he has now?" I ask.

"The bookkeeper isn't even full time anymore," he says. "We own some other businesses and some investments in town, but Bear Creek isn't the place it was when my father was alive. The Taylors aren't the only ones who got hurt."

I study the photographs. It's like looking at pictures of reunions of those "last man clubs" from World War II. There are fewer returnees almost every year. I realize that despite my conversations with Angela I have been looking at Bear Creek from the perspective of a visitor. But it is not only a matter of the town looking shabby; John's point is that it is disappearing economically. Not only blacks have been losing their land; whites have, too. The agricultural base that supported them no longer exists to the same degree as it did fifty years ago.

"Things are that bad, huh?" I ask.

"Well, there's still the one factory," John says loyally, "and we have some retail stores, but they're not here on the square anymore. When Paul lost a big chunk of their land, they didn't have any choice but to look some other place to make money. It wouldn't be easy for anybody. But whether Paul would go so far as to kill somebody, that's a hell of a big step."

I come back and sit down. "That's kind of Angela's position, too." I have decided not to let John know my feelings about Paul. Though the Uptons never had the cutthroat reputation that the Taylors had, Angela's reaction has made me cautious.

John's blue eyes twinkle. "I had heard through the grapevine that you've already called on the widow Marr. You've got to hand it to Angela: She looks pretty damn good after all these years. This case seems like an opportunity for you to combine business with pleasure." He leers at me in a familiar way. John knows my history with Angela as well as anybody.

"Angela's still got a lot of grieving to do," I say, "before she'll be ready for a relationship with anybody." I know I sound ridiculous (especially if Angela is ready for us to start going out), but I'm not ready to confess my growing obsession with "the widow Marr." When we were kids, once he got on a subject, John would never let up.

"What happened to us, John?" I ask, wanting to change the subject from Angela. "When we were growing up, there weren't any murders; we weren't afraid. Were blacks under such control that none of what goes on today was even conceivable back then?"

John opens a drawer and pulls out a half-empty bottle of Jack Daniel's. I put my coffee down, and he pours me a couple of fingers in a paper cup and hands it to me. He says sternly, "It's drugs. They're killing the black community. You remember those billboards forty years ago that used to say, 'Impeach Earl Warren'? You wouldn't have crack cocaine within a hundred miles of Bear Creek if Eisenhower hadn't been such an ignorant fool and appointed Earl Warren. It was his court's decisions on search and seizure and interrogation that have made people want to buy an arsenal to protect their homes when fifty years ago there wasn't a locked car or house in the whole town. Hell, you don't think the cops don't know who brings drugs into this town? Sure they do! But you lawyers have taken the cops' handcuffs and shackled them to their desks and told the drug dealers they have carte blanche. And when you take away a society's power to protect itself against the bad guys, individuals will arm themselves."

I sip at the liquor in my cup and remember just how conservative this area of the state is. Until this moment, I didn't know John had ever had a political thought in his life. As an adolescent, he was as much a rebel as a future civil engineering student could be, which, granted, wasn't much, but he didn't sound like a future charter member of the Rush Limbaugh fan club.

John pauses and catches himself. Despite this sermon, he isn't a preacher. "Are you eating at Angela's?" he asks, a grin returning to his face.

I try to hide my irritation at his assumption that Angela and I are already involved and say, "If you're inviting me to dinner, I accept." I can drive home later.

He picks up the phone and dials his wife, saying, "Beverly'll be glad to see somebody else. I'm too tame for her these days."

I'm not sure what this means, but five minutes later with a drink in my hand I follow John to his farm, which is north of Bear Creek about five miles out of town. Two brick stories with four columns in front, his house, a mansion really, is set back from the highway a good hundred yards. Two horses stand at a white fence staring into my headlights. Built right after World War II, John's home is still one of the largest in the area.

Beverly greets us at the door, and I am immediately struck by the affection between her and my old friend. Instead of just a dry peck on the mouth, she kisses him hard on the lips as if they haven't seen each other in months. Since I was already gone when John brought her back with him, I never knew Beverly. Unlike Angela, she was born in the South. Afterwards she sizes me up like some quarter horse she might be interested in buy-ing. "So you're the great Gideon, huh?" she says, her crinkled gray eyes magnified by gold-rimmed bifocals.

Taller than her husband and more muscular through the shoulders, her wrinkled face appears, despite her husband's opinion, closer to sixty than fifty. I can smell burnt tobacco and spot a package of Camels in the front pocket of her blue work shirt, which hangs down outside a pair of baggy rust-colored pants. Though definitely not a sight for sore eyes, she exudes the warmth of a potbellied stove going full blast. "Your hus-band's former partner in crime is probably a better way to get a handle on me," I say, already liking this woman.

"My husband's a boy among boys, and so are you," she says, punching me on the shoulder lightly. "I'm cooking. Y'all follow me," she orders, taking my coat from me and tossing it care-lessly on a small table by the door. Though the house is huge, and I am curious about it, I just get a glimpse of the combina-tion living and dining room as we proceed directly down a hall lined with books and family pictures.

We emerge into a kitchen that would service a small restau-rant. A wooden chopping table sits in the middle of a brick floor. Against the far wall on either side of a stove hang enough pots, pans, and knives to feed all of the white population of Bear Creek. She tells John to fix us all a drink while she is cook-ing, and, needing no urging, he heads to a pantry at the far end of the room. Beverly points to chairs on the other side of the chopping table. "So you defend people accused of committing crimes," she says, winking at me as she begins to sprinkle flour on some kind of meat, I'm not sure what.

I take a seat and lean wearily against the table, already feel-ing defensive. If she is as conservative as her husband, it will be a long night. I look over at John, who is holding up another bottle of Jack Daniel's. I hold up a thumb to indicate my ap-proval and say to Beverly, "And others who haven't gotten caught."

She laughs, and scratches the end of her nose, turning it

white. "Criminals are the price of a free society; John is such a wuss that he'd be more than happy to turn this country into a worse police state than it already is. He's scared to death some escapee from Brickeys will someday stop in and rob and kill us."

I take a glass from John and watch him drop an ounce of liquor into it. "Like the poor, they'll always be with us, huh?" I ask, afraid I am about to hear another diatribe against the federal government.

John, however, steers the conversation around to more personal topics, and instead of talking about her own boys, over venison, mashed potatoes and vegetables served in the kitchen on the chopping block, she asks me about Sarah, and I come to life, glad to talk about a subject that to me, at least, is inexhaustibly rich. During my description of her personality, I let slip her latest crusade, which, I fear, is a mistake, given their conservatism; yet Beverly is more supportive than I could have hoped, telling me that she is convinced no one chooses to be gay. Why would anyone be that masochistic? "She must be a wonderfully compassionate young woman. Most kids her age can't think about anyone but themselves for more than a minute. You must be very proud of her."

"I am," I gush, noting that John hasn't said anything. Because of the way we were raised over here, I can guess his attitude. "She's a lot like Rosa."

John instructs me to bring out Sarah's picture, and Beverly, like her husband, is properly impressed. "She's gorgeous! I'm glad we didn't have a girl. I would have been jealous from the day this child was born!"

The conversation moves from her boys (she doesn't want any of the four of them coming back to east Arkansas) to the topic I've wanted to discuss since I walked in the door, Willie Ting's murder. "This thing has stunk since day one," Beverly declares, slicing off a piece of sourdough bread and offering it to me. "Believe you me, the fix is in all the way round on this one. Johnson and Butterfield have been paid off big time. This is a capital murder case, and Paul is walking around town like he was given a parking ticket. It doesn't matter what color the law is. It's still business as usual around here."

I take the bread and tear off a corner to sop up some gravy. How does someone like Beverly become so totally disillusioned that the only explanation for events is that the system is totally and unredeemably crooked? I'm willing to concede that a year ago, with white officeholders in power, Paul perhaps wouldn't have been charged based on the evidence so far, but the mere fact that the prosecutor recommended bail and the judge accepted his recommendation doesn't automatically mean they were bought off. Yet it is consistent with her survivalist mentality.

While I eat, Beverly and John argue whether Paul was involved. Beverly has no doubt, and John concedes that he could be, though he thinks that the charges against Paul could simply be a payback for his family's long history of domination over here. "Hell, Beverly, his family owned slaves," he says, a little drunk since he has forgotten to eat. "For all you know, Oscar Taylor's grandfather used to whip Butterfield's grandfather twenty times a day. They may say they're not interested in revenge, but that's bullshit."

Beverly helps herself to more wine. "Your family owned slaves, too," she reminds her husband. "If Butterfield hated him so much, why did he recommend any bond at all?"

"John's family wasn't mean like the Taylors," I interject, interested in both points of view.

"You don't know," Beverly says. "They couldn't have been too wonderful, or they wouldn't have owned slaves at all."

The truth is, I don't know, but I do know the Taylors. "It wasn't just the way they treated blacks; it's how they treated everybody." For her benefit I explain about the two incidents involving my family, concluding, "Paul and Oscar were cutthroat in everything they did over there. It's finally caught up with Paul."

John gives me a quizzical look. "I never knew that stuff or I had forgotten it."

"Shit, yes!" I exclaim. "Not only did Oscar foreclose on the pharmacy when he didn't have to, Paul got my mother's farm she inherited from my grandfather."

Instead of agreeing with me as I expected, John looks puzzled as if he doesn't know what I'm talking about. It pisses me that he doesn't remember, but maybe I expect too much. If it had happened to the Uptons, he damn well would have recalled all of this. Meanwhile, Beverly continues to argue with him. "Niggers have been taking money from whites so long over here they probably didn't even blink when Paul offered them a bundle."

"Beverly's more cynical than me," John says amiably. "I've known Butterfield's people for years, and remember when he used to climb poles in this area for Southwestern Bell, when there was such a thing. He's an ambitious nigger, I'll give him that. I could see him stealing an election like any other politician, but I'll be damned if I think he cares about the money."

Beverly, across the table from him, rolls her eyes at her husband. "Because his family used to have some money, John forgets that ninety-nine percent of the human race can be bought. Bonner and Butterfield aren't the Kennedys, honey. They're just high-pocketed country niggers on the make."

John chews patiently but gives me a wink as if to say his wife can't help but believe that nothing is as it seems. Every murder involves a giant conspiracy that, if she but had enough time to unravel, would implicate Pope John, Boris Yeltsin, and Madonna. "Don't patronize me, buddy boy," Beverly warns her husband. "I know that little smirk. You think you know all these people because you grew up with them. You have no idea what's going on."

John shrugs, apparently not wanting to incur his wife's ire. Beverly looks as if she could be a mean drunk. "That's for damn sure," he says, his tone still friendly.

"Do you really think Paul is involved in this?" I encourage

Beverly, who is chewing vigorously on a piece of meat she has cut for herself. The deer tastes disappointingly like chicken. It doesn't have the gamy distinct flavor that I remember from my childhood. Maybe it is the way it has been cooked.

"Of course he is!" Beverly says. "Everyone's heard about the tape. Why else did Willie tape him if he wasn't afraid of Paul? Just like you say, nobody's ever crossed the Taylors. And when they started going down economically, Paul couldn't stand the fact that an old Chinese man had, outside our one factory, the only decent business in town. He had him killed and now he's bought off a nigger sheriff, judge, and prosecutor, the way people have been buying them off for years. What else is new?"

Beverly's face is flushed, but I'm not sure whether it is from liquor or from anger. Hell may have no fury like a woman scorned, but the way she looks I doubt if she was ever in the running for Paul's affections. Perhaps she has been jealous for her husband's sake. The Taylors have been top dogs here for years, and Beverly, for one, is glad to see them get their due.

Perhaps to change the subject, John turns to his wife. "I've heard that Gideon here has been calling on the widow Marr. She would have married him, but he broke her heart by joining the Peace Corps."

Beverly rolls her eyes at her husband. "John's told me that at least twice, but since it's usually after a pint of bourbon he never remembers. I admire Angela, and I'm sorry I've never gotten to know her as much as I would have liked. For all those years she was so involved with their farm. What is she going to do?"

"I don't know," I say too quickly, but not wanting to betray what I think was told to me in confidence. For all I know, she may have told the entire town that Cecil wants to buy her half of the farm, but she seemed too angry about it for me to feel comfortable enough to gossip about it. "Angela and I are just friends," I add, hoping I'm not blushing. If my face is as florid as Beverly's, I look like as big a fool as I sound.

John leans his elbows on the table and snickers, "And I'm the ghost of John Lennon."

Beverly laughs, but defends me. "Dwight's body isn't even cold," she scolds her husband. "You just know how a man would react, not a woman. Men can barely wait for the funeral to be over before they're trying to get in another woman's pants."

Knowing me too well, John scoffs, "It's cold enough. He was sick for years."

I say nothing. If I start talking about Angela, I may not be able to shut up. There is much I want to know about the past thirty years, but Rome wasn't built in a day, and I like both John and Beverly too much to let them think I accepted this invitation just to grill them for more information about the principals in the case. There will be plenty of time for that, I hope. I switch to coffee, hoping to sober up for the drive home. Beverly pumps me for anecdotes about John. She doesn't even know he tried to shoot his sister, and I delight her with stories he either has forgotten or told her so long ago neither of them remember. One Halloween John broke into the nursing home and hid all the bedpans that weren't in use. "I thought he was going to jail for that."

Far from being apologetic for the implicit cruelty in his behavior, John concludes the evening with a joke. Licking at his glass for the last drop of the amaretto Beverly produced and I couldn't resist, he tells the story about the old man in the nursing home who went around on his birthday asking his fellow residents to guess how old he was. "'You're seventy-three,' says the first man he asks. 'No, I'm seventy-eight!' the old man cackles. Then he hobbles a little further down the hall and asks an old woman in a wheelchair, 'It's my birthday. Guess how old I am.' The old woman peers over her bifocals at him and tells him to unzip his pants. He does, and she takes his old shriveled penis into her hands and begins to rub it as she looks from his member to his face and back again. 'Seventy-eight!' she says finally. 'How did you know?' the old man marvels." Delighted that we haven't yelled out the punch line, John grins at us and says in an old woman's voice, "'Well, I heard you tell that old man down there.'"

I stand up, and take my leave, dimly aware that there is a moral here somewhere. Women, I think the message is, know what they're doing.

Instead of trying to drive all the way back to Blackwell County, I head for the Bear Creek Inn and check in. I'll drive home tomorrow morning. Poor women. They never quit trying to change us. When they do, that's when we'll need to worry. Betty gives me a wistful look as she takes my money, but the last thing I need is to accept her invitation to watch television. Inside room number nine, I begin to think about Angela and wish there was a way to call her. I feel as if I have a crowbar in my pants, but it is probably because I have to piss so bad. I go to bed with the room spinning, my last thought that once again I am in a motel room in my hometown.

Twelve

Hung over, I arrive home at ten the next morning and find an urgent-sounding message on my machine from Tommy Ting. I sit down in my recliner in the living room and dial his number, wishing I'd had more sense than to keep drinking with John last night.

"Connie is worried," Tommy says, without preliminaries, "that you're going to argue that our mother killed our father!"

I look across the street into the park where I was going to walk Jessie. Damn, I wish Amy would bring her back. I miss her. "No jury would buy that for two seconds," I say, not really answering the question. "Anybody just looking at her will know how ludicrous that is. She's so frail she can hardly lift a tea cup. Now, I can't take responsibility for what Dickerson might do."

"Will you talk to him and convince him not to make that argument?" Tommy presses me. "It would kill her!"

Tommy doesn't know what he is asking, but I don't want to piss him off. On the whole, I am getting some good information from the workers at the plant. At least Darla Tate was helpful. "Sure, I'll talk about it with him. Dickerson is too smart to insult a jury's intelligence."

185

He seems mollified, and I tell him what I have found so far. "I'm not at all convinced that the Mexican worker didn't kill your father," I tell him, thinking of the dignified expression on Alvaro Ruiz's weathered face.

"The sheriff doesn't seem to consider him a suspect," Tommy reminds me.

"It'd be a mistake at this stage," I insist, "to eliminate anyone." Perhaps Tommy unconsciously is worried that I will try to pin the murder on another defenseless minority. "Anyone could have set up Doss Bledsoe. Hell, Ruiz could have gotten someone to do the job for him. Doss was a sitting duck."

We talk for a few more minutes and by the time we are finished, Tommy seems calmed down. Unlike his sister, he wants to trust me.

Tuesday afternoon I hurry home to see Sarah, who is home for spring break. She has stayed in Fayetteville with a friend for the first three days, so I am anxious to see her. When I turn in the drive, there is a Subaru behind Sarah's ancient Beetle. Perhaps one of her friends from Fayetteville has dropped by. These girls look so young to me that I wonder how any of them are taken seriously when they apply for jobs. As I go in the back door, I hope Sarah has picked up a little. College hasn't made her a better housekeeper. Though I can tell she has matured in the last couple of years, she comes home and sometimes regresses into an adolescent who might not make it out of junior high.

In the living room Sarah is sitting on the couch with a guy who is much too old for her. Though not bad looking in the face, this man even has a receding hairline and looks kind of flashy in a sports jacket that reminds me of the coat the Masters golf champion is presented after he wins.

"Hi, Dad!" Sarah says brightly. "This is my friend Larry. He's down here for a meeting for his company and I invited him to come by."

The AIDS patient! He jumps to his feet and offers his hand. "Larry Burdette, Mr. Page," he says, giving me a firm grip and looking me straight in the eye like every other salesman I've known. "Your daughter talks about you all the time. It's a pleasure to meet you."

"Nice to meet you," I murmur, noticing he looks pretty good for someone on his last legs. Though I know all the literature says you can't get AIDS except by sexual contact or through contact with their blood, I feel uneasy. A plastic glass full of water sits on the table by his chair. I need to try to remember to wash it thoroughly. I wonder if the guy has used the bathroom.

"Dad, you want a beer?" Sarah asks, her voice too loud, since she is standing right beside me. I feel in a daze. I wasn't expecting this guy.

"Yeah," I manage. "That'd be good." I need something.

"Have a seat," I say to Larry, who is appraising me coolly. I watch Sarah disappear into the kitchen and wish she had warned me about this visit.

When he sits back down, I take in the chair opposite him. "Sarah says you sell computers. I can hardly turn one on, much less do anything with it. A friend of mine down the hall has one, but it just sits on his desk like a pet rock."

He crosses his legs. "In ten years they'll be as simple to learn as driving a car."

"Given some of the drivers I see around here," I say, "I don't know if that'll help much." He doesn't even look gay to me.

He smiles as my daughter walks into the room and hands me a Miller Lite. "Would you like one?" I ask, wondering if Sarah has already offered.

"I haven't had a drink in five years," he says, moving back his legs to let Sarah by. "I'm in AA."

Damn. AIDS. An alcoholic. If I were this guy, I'd be climbing the walls, but he seems pretty laid back. Maybe he's on drugs. "After a couple of drinks," I say, watching Sarah's face, "alcohol has never done me any favors."

187

"Or solved a single one of my problems," he responds amiably.

"Which are not inconsiderable, Sarah tells me," I say, taking a long swallow.

"Dad!" Sarah shrieks. I wonder if she was expecting him to come by. She is wearing old baggy jeans and a faded Razorback sweatshirt.

"Larry is the guy you've been writing me about, isn't he?" I ask innocently.

"It's okay, Sarah," Larry says. "I don't expect to live in a vacuum. The more people get to know us, the less afraid they'll be."

Out of politeness I nod, but I wonder if the reverse is true. I've been nervous ever since I found out who he was. "How long since you've been diagnosed?" I ask, not really wanting to talk about this, but morbidly curious.

"Two years," he says. "It's been quite an adjustment, but the support people like Sarah have given me has made all the difference in the world. You've got some daughter."

For an instant I feel as if I am going to cry. This poor sucker is dying, and he credits my child with helping him want to live. "I couldn't agree with you more," I say, watching Sarah blush. "Has she told you about her personal odyssey the last few years? She's quite the seeker."

"No," he says, turning to Sarah. "I'm afraid I've done most of the talking."

Sarah gives me a look but answers, "Oh, I just went through a period in high school when I was real religious and went to a fundamentalist church, and then last semester I got kind of caught up in a feminist movement on campus."

Larry runs his arm down the back of the sofa. "So I'm part of the quest, huh?" he asks, gently.

"No!" Sarah says, her face suddenly agonized. "I just got involved with RAIN because it seemed the right thing to do. Everybody in school is so self-centered. All they talk about is themselves and parties and dating and the Razorbacks. It feels good to be a part of something more important than who got drunk last week at the Sigma Nu house."

By the expression on her face I know Sarah is mad at me. So be it. I am not particularly pleased with her for having set this visit up without talking to me first. I suggest that we invite Larry to go out to eat with us, and though he says he needs to work for a while, Sarah easily persuades him to come with us. At my suggestion we drive out to the Breadbox in western Blackwell County for Mexican food. I have eaten out here with Amy, and not only is it cheap, I am not likely to run into anybody I know. It is not that I think this guy will suddenly start bleeding on the dishes, but I feel uncomfortable with him. Yet, for all I know, half the staff at the Breadbox has AIDS.

Larry proves to be an entertaining dinner date. Open and talkative, it is easy to see why Sarah responds to him. "I had no clear understanding something was different about me," he says over bread pudding and coffee after polishing off a full chicken enchilada dinner, "until I was in junior high. And then I spent the rest of high school and college trying to pretend I was normal and feeling incredibly lonely. I was like a bad magician telling a ridiculous joke while doing sleight-of-hand tricks, hoping nobody would notice what was actually going on."

His parents had been stalwarts of a nondenominational Bible church in Texarkana, and the minister ranked homosexuality with mass murder on the top ten sin chart. Not to fear, however. Homosexuals could be saved through prayer and rigorous counseling. When I ask whether he let them try, he responded quickly, "I wouldn't have confessed to being gay in that church if they had put me on the rack."

As he talks, I think of old Mr. Carpenter and resolve to go by to see him when I return to Bear Creek. He has asked me every time I have seen him.

"What was scary was that by the time I was seventeen I had gone from simple loneliness to thinking I might be some kind of monster. The day I graduated from high school I took off for

San Francisco. I've never been back home for more than a couple of weeks."

His brave talk earlier of educating people that AIDS victims are just plain folks has disappeared. Yet who does not regress to childhood in front of their parents?

"How'd you wind up in Fayetteville?" I ask, curious. There are gay hangouts up there, but it's hardly San Francisco.

While he explains that it was cheaper to go to school in Arkansas and pay in-state tuition, I glance at my daughter's face. She has doubtlessly heard this story before, but she is hanging on his every word. Her mother was the same way. She was a sucker for victims. Yet, to this guy's credit, he isn't whining. This was how his life was.

Over a final cup of coffee, he brings up his alcoholism and says that it has nothing to do with him being gay. "Like most people, I've got a hundred excuses, and none of them has ever stopped me from opening a bottle. The only thing that's ever helped me is the twelve-step program. I'm a big believer in it. I go to an AA meeting once a week."

Damn. This guy lets it all hang out. These recovery groups are all the rage. The paper is full of them. Hi, I'm Gideon. I'm a human being. Still, if they work, who can knock them? If they work. Dan went to an overeaters anonymous group and said a couple of the guys stood out on the steps of the church during a break and ate a box of Snickers, proof that you can lie to yourself anywhere. I've done it every place but in the kitchen sink. I wonder if I am lying to myself about what things were like in Bear Creek. I have begun to have the feeling that my memories don't jibe with what other people remember. The other night John looked at me as if I were making things up about the way the Taylors had treated my family. Yet the problem with Angela and John is that they have lived in Bear Creek so long that they probably have come to accept the Paul Taylors of this world as normal.

Back at the house Larry declines Sarah's invitation to come in and says he needs to get back to his hotel. I wonder if he is go-

190

ing out to one of Blackwell County's drag shows. Sarah would probably like to go check it out with him, but he doesn't ask. Probably she has already been to something similar in Fayetteville with him and wants to spare my feelings. I'm all for that.

Inside, I putter around the house, straightening up a bit. I am not used to having Sarah home, and her habit of not taking anything back to the kitchen is already getting on my nerves. She gets the hint and folds up the pages of the *Arkansas Democrat-Gazette* she has spread out all over the kitchen table. "Dad," she says, watching me load the dishwasher, "Larry made you nervous while he was in the house, didn't he?"

I turn on the hot water and wash the glass he used by hand. "It just seemed weird," I say, irritably. "Nobody understands the disease. How can you be too careful?"

Sarah stacks the paper on top of the refrigerator. She can't fold up a newspaper any better than I can. "I know how you feel," she says. "I felt funny around him at first, but less and less as time goes on. With all his problems, he's still a neat guy. I think he thought you were okay."

"I liked him," I admit. "I don't see how he's sane, but he seems as normal as I do." I have noticed that since she has been home, Sarah has been less obsessed with her own personal problems, and as a consequence, she has been in my face less. I had expected an entire lecture from her and was ready to give as good as I got. Yet the old confrontational Sarah has disappeared, or at least didn't make the trip. Maybe she is growing up.

"How is Amy?" she asks when we sit down in the living room. "You haven't mentioned her since you told me Jessie was going to stay with her while you worked on the case in Bear Creek."

I lean back in the chair and listen as my stomach tries in vain to digest my dinner. I shouldn't have tried to fit in the bread pudding. I realize I haven't mentioned Amy because I feel guilty about her, and so I haven't said anything about Angela either. Sarah has always accused me of using the women I have been involved with to help me on my cases. "You'll be happy to know it looks as if Amy and I are probably history," I say, thinking of the best spin I can put on this. "You always complained she was too young for me, anyway."

Sarah tucks her legs up beneath her on the couch. "I liked her because I know how much she cared about you. That made up for the age difference."

I don't want to think about Amy. "Well, I'm dating a woman exactly my own age, and one I've known for over thirty years."

"Dad!" Sarah exclaims. "Who is she?"

I feel a mild explosion in my stomach. I need to quit eating so much at night. I had enough chips and cheese dip before they brought out the food to feed an army. "My first girlfriend," I say, and tell her the story of how I met Angela at the library in Bear Creek.

She is entranced and quizzes me for the better part of thirty minutes. I omit a few things, including how we first made love in my mother's Fairlane and recently in her brother-in-law's bed. Nor do I tell her how much desire I feel when I am around Angela. I suspect that one of the reasons my daughter does not want me to date younger women is that she, understandably, does not want to be confronted with my sexuality, nor do I have any desire to be confronted by hers. I'm all for Sarah's getting to know me as adult to adult, but there is a limit to how far I want us to be pals. Maybe when I'm old and less of a sexual being we'll sit around in our bathrobes and tell war stories, but not quite yet.

"She's been through a lot," I tell Sarah, wondering whether they'll like each other, "but at one time she had more influence on me than anyone I've ever met."

"She sounds neat, Dad," Sarah says. "I hope it works out if that's what you want."

Do I? I pick up a dog hair from the arm of the chair, a legacy of Jessie's that seems perpetual, and drop it into the trash can beside me. "We've really gone out only a couple of times," I demur. "She's still got a lot of grieving to do." As I say this, I wonder. Angela, I'm coming to realize, is more of a mystery than I like to admit.

The phone rings. Naturally, it is for Sarah, who tells me moments later her old friend Donna Redding is coming by to pick her up at ten and she needs to change clothes. They are going "out." I am strangely comforted by this act of normalcy. I know better than to ask where but do anyway.

"I don't know," she says, standing up. "Dad, have you been by to see Dade's grandmother?"

I find another hair and realize it is one of Woogie's, not Jessie's. Damn. I miss Woogie, exiled to my sister's over a year ago after an alleged kitten-eating episode. Have we ever cleaned anything in this house? I knew this question was coming. It was at Sarah's insistence that we drove over to Bear Creek to try to confirm the story that my grandfather had fathered a child by a black woman.

"Dad, she might appreciate it if you went by."

"Well, I might," I say, "I just haven't had time."

Sarah leans back against the wall. For once she doesn't argue with me. "I'm proud of you for representing a black man over there," Sarah says. "I bet you're getting some criticism for doing it."

I realize that Sarah has no idea, despite our visit, what my old hometown is like. "It's not as if I'm suing the town on a race discrimination suit. White attorneys have always represented blacks in Bear Creek."

Sarah nods absently, perhaps thinking about her coming evening, and leaves the room. I lean back in the chair and allow myself to remember how delicious my lovemaking with Angela was the last time we were together. How could I tell Sarah what that feeling is like for me? That is the last thing either of us wants to discuss. We don't always want the truth, just a level of comfort. Is that so bad? About ninety percent of the time truth is an overrated virtue.

. . .

Wednesday night Angela calls to tell me that she has made it back, and I am pleased to hear a warmth in her voice that wasn't there when she left. "I've been doing a lot of thinking," she says after we tell each other about our past week, "and I think I'm ready to have a relationship if you're interested. But I'd like to go slow."

Taking her call in the living room, I hear Sarah in the kitchen, and I whisper into the phone that this is good news indeed, and that I completely understand her feelings. She asks when I will be coming back and I tell her Saturday. Shyly, she invites me to dinner Saturday night, and I waste no time in accepting. After I hang up I stare out the window. It is amazing how some things come together after so long a time. Sarah comes in and tells me that I am smiling. I am.

Thirteen

THE THURSDAY MORNING after April Fools' Day, I get a call from Melvin Butterfield that may be Doss's only chance. In the last few weeks I have interviewed several more workers from Southern Pride and checked their alibis. If someone is framing Bledsoe, I can't find out who it is.

"I think it's time for us to have a chat about some things," he says, his voice booming in my ear as if he were in the room with me.

Though I am busy in the office this week and had not planned to drive over until Saturday to meet with Doss and have dinner with Angela, if Butterfield's ready to offer Doss a deal, I don't want to give him time to change his mind. Though I have a new client coming in this afternoon, Julia can try to reschedule it for tomorrow. I've had the feeling all along that Bledsoe won't implicate Paul until he gets a concrete offer of a reduced sentence. "Actually, I was planning to come over this afternoon if I could get away," I lie glibly.

He asks if I can be there at four. I say that I can and hang up feeling a little hope for the first time since I took the case. Granted there are many more witnesses to interview, but the law of diminishing returns has already begun to kick in: the more people I talk with, the less I get out of them.

195

Moments later Dan charges into my office, muttering loudly, "I've never been so insulted in all my life."

"What's happened?" I say, looking up at my friend, whose face is even glummer than usual. Over a beer last week after losing a case in Municipal Court to a near-deaf nursing home resident who represented herself from a wheelchair, Dan waxed philosophical, describing the life of the bad lawyer as one long humiliation, with death the final but not inappropriate indignity. First you lose, and then you die.

"One of the women I went out with complained to the Attorney General's office that the dating service had misrepresented me," he says, collapsing opposite me into one of my chairs, which trembles from the impact. "This assistant A.G. from the Consumer Protection Division just barged her way into my office and called me part of the biggest fraud in Arkansas consumer history," he huffs, his double chin beginning to jiggle. "I couldn't believe it. This little miniskirted girl who couldn't be more than twenty-five flashed her badge at me like she was Eliot Ness about to close up half of Chicago and said if I wouldn't agree to testify she could practically guarantee my picture on the feature page of the *Democrat-Gazette* as part of her investigation. The nerve some people have. If she hadn't been such a babe, I would have thrown her out of my office!"

Glad to take a break, I push the papers in front of me aside and put my feet up on my desk. "I thought you were the victim in this dating service business," I say, remembering his last complaint about the woman who couldn't keep her eyes open past nine o'clock.

Dan pats his beefy cheeks with a folded handkerchief, which this humid morning looks like a sponge. Did this woman make him cry? "I'm a victim," he whines, "but this A.G. says that each of the four women I've been out with has complained that I lied about too many details. Hell, everybody puffs their 'pif' a little.

"Personal information form," he adds when I raise my eyebrows.

"A little!" I exclaim. "You put down that you're single."

"It's the weight thing that bothers most of them," Dan says, fluttering the fingers on his right hand as if he were a famous music conductor dismissing a critic's carping about a few bad notes. "They believe you when you say your divorce is just a matter of time. It's when you show up at their door at two fifty instead of one fifty that pisses 'em off."

I whistle. That's quite a stretch. "I bet you haven't weighed one fifty since you were in junior high," I guess, amazed at his gall.

"Sixth grade," Dan corrects me. "Trixie—that's this girl's name—says her office wants these matchmaking companies held to some kind of minimum truth-in-packaging standard so that singles can get their money back if they've been ripped off. She wants me and the women to testify at a legislative subcommittee meeting that's coming up next month."

He's got to be kidding. Matchmakers Who Lie Too Much. Surely, it's already been done, but we could have our own redneck version of Oprah: That ol' boy lied like a dog on his "pif." Ah'd a dated him if he'd jus' been a little bald, but he didn't have a hair on his haid! Fearing the worst, I ask, "Do you really want that kind of publicity?"

"No," Dan admits. "But it'd be a good way to get to know Trixie better," he says. "She's cute as a button, and she wasn't wearing a ring."

The species' capacity for self-delusion knows no bounds. Dan would fall in love with a boa constrictor if it were wearing a skirt. "Don't you think she's getting to know you a little too well? You won't exactly be coming off as Washingtonian in this story."

Dan looks hurt. "She could do a lot worse," he points out. "At least I haven't served any time yet. Besides, there're some women who don't mind fat men."

Or men who are married, broke, desperate, or liars. "Go for it," I advise. "This may be the love of your life. She sounds like a female Geraldo. You could be on daytime TV together."

A gleam comes into Dan's eyes. "If her skirts get any shorter," he predicts, "she'll have to be on the Playboy Channel. She uncrossed her legs once and I swear I thought I was looking at Sharon Stone."

So much for Janet Reno being the next role model for our female attorneys. "You haven't been sued by one of these women?" I ask suspiciously. Every few months Dan requires some kind of major rescue job. I had thought a failed marriage would slow him down, but it seems only to have speeded up his self-destruct button.

"Hell, no," Dan assures me. "They know I'm just a pawn. This last woman told me kind of wistfully that if I had a tummy tuck, she'd consider going out with me again."

I eye Dan's stomach over the desk. It's going to take more than a tuck. To get rid of that much blubber, the surgeon would have to go in there with a backhoe. "Are you sure this Trixie character is for real? She sounds a little eager to me."

Dan nods solemnly. "Consumer protection is big business. It's how state attorney generals go on to being governors. It's not just old folks who go to the polls. Half the country is divorced and miserable, and the other half is thinking about joining them. Singles like myself are a vulnerable part of the population and tend to vote if given a decent reason."

I think of one of the comic strips that Dan substitutes for artwork in his office and laugh out loud. As Pogo said, "We have met the enemy, and he is us."

At 4:15 I walk into Melvin Butterfield's office on the second floor of the courthouse in Bear Creek, deliberately a few minutes late, but if he is annoyed, I can't tell it. He smiles and shakes my hand and invites me to have coffee, which I decline. As chatty as last time, he gossips about the Razorbacks as if we had been teammates ourselves, telling me that the reason the Hogs will lose in the NCAA tournament this year is that this team has too many JuCo players who won't stay focused enough to play defense for an entire game. His hands parked behind his head, Butterfield proclaims, "Corliss Williamson was ready for every game. These guys play only when they feel like it."

I ask him how come he doesn't have a framed, autographed picture of Nolan Richardson on the wall like the sheriff, and Butterfield laughs and puts his feet up on his desk, saying one is in his filing cabinet. "Woodrow has threatened to arrest me if I try to put mine up."

I nod, appreciating his willingness to acknowledge the rivalry between him and the sheriff. From what I've seen of Bonner, he doesn't have enough of a sense of humor to joke about it. Without missing a beat, Butterfield says casually, "If your client is willing to testify at the trial that Paul Taylor hired him to murder Willie Ting, I'll knock his charge down to second-degree murder."

Butterfield hasn't changed expression. This is no time for me to be cute. Though the maximum sentence is twenty years for second-degree murder, Doss could be eligible for parole in five years. I reply bluntly, "I'll talk to him. When do you need an answer?"

Butterfield, who seems the type to dress for the occasion, whatever it is, fingers the vest of his three-piece gray pinstriped suit. "No later than this time next week," he says, his voice going flat and betraying an intensity I haven't seen before.

Suddenly I realize that behind his almost folksy, deferential manner, Butterfield knows exactly what he is doing. This friendliness is just his way of dealing with white folks. Wanting to know if he has his own reasons for prosecuting Paul, I ask, "Did you know the Taylors once were the richest planters in this part of the state?"

Butterfield again retreats behind a smile and makes a show of stretching his long frame as if he is tired. "I know lots of things about east Arkansas. Some good, some bad."

I wonder what he knows about my history over here. "It's easy to make a case that the bad ole days were pretty bad," I say, hoping to encourage him to talk.

Instead, he says, his voice bland, "That's all in the past. Better to get along. Y'all didn't like the bad ole days much either. They were hard on everybody."

I think to myself this guy must be a pretty smooth campaigner among whites. What good does it do to throw the past up to somebody if you want his vote? If Butterfield is one of the blacks who wants to take over completely, he isn't admitting it. "Getting along isn't so easy," I say. "Bear Creek is living proof of that."

Butterfield holds up his right hand and wiggles his fingers. "But we're stuck with each other. I tell my campaign audiences to try to move their index fingers while keeping the ones on each side still. You can't do it. That's how we are in east Arkansas."

I smile politely. One of the flies in Butterfield's metaphorical ointment is the rate at which whites are leaving places like Bear Creek. This guy isn't going to give away shit. If he weren't running for office, he might tell me what he really thinks about the Arkansas Delta, but all I will get now are platitudes.

I get to my feet and tell him that I'll be in touch as soon as I can but no later than Thursday. He says he'll be in Helena and gives me his office number there. I leave the courthouse, pleased with this conversation. Second-degree murder is quite a leap from capital murder. Bledsoe may say he is innocent, but a few years in Cummins Prison compared to death row will cause him to reconsider. For whatever reason, Butterfield wants Paul in the worst way. If I have anything to do with it, he will get him.

I speed the thirteen miles to Brickeys. Bledsoe is healthy again and surprised but glad to see me. I waste no time in telling him about my conversation with Butterfield. "He needs your testimony to convict Paul Taylor," I explain, after I tell him the offer. "That's why he is willing to give you a reduced sentence."

Bledsoe, who has begun to lose some weight, shakes his head. "I can't say nothin' that will help," he mutters, "'cause he didn't hire me, and I didn't do it."

I squint at him as if the truth might become clearer if I could bring him into focus better. What does he have to gain by lying? Maybe much more than I know. I say, hastily, "I don't want you to tell me right now what you want to do. You think about this offer. If I could guarantee you an acquittal, I would have told Butterfield where he could go with his offer. I can't do that. There're innocent men who have been murdered by the state. If you insist on a trial, I can't sit here and promise you that won't happen to you."

"More than a dozen people could have framed me," he says, his voice choking into a whisper. "Aren't you gonna show that in court?"

I nod. "I'll do my best, Doss, but there's a big difference between telling a jury you might have been framed and proving that you actually were. Juries hear alibis all the time, and frankly one of the weakest and most ineffective is that a suspect was framed, unless there's some real evidence to support it. So far, I haven't been able to find any, or anyone or anything that proves you were home between two and four that afternoon. We still have a couple of months before the trial, and something may turn up, but things don't look good."

Doss sighs heavily. "What about Vic Worthy?"

"I still haven't talked to him," I admit, "but you know as well as I do that Willie wouldn't have let him within five yards of him if he had shown up at the plant. Whoever killed him was somebody he knew and at least halfway trusted."

His despair changes to anger, "You think it was me!"

Admittedly, my faith in him was stronger three weeks ago, but I say, "Personally, I don't think it was you, but you know as well as I do, it's not what I think but what the jury thinks, and so far all the evidence is going to show is that the only fingerprints on the knife that killed Doss were yours, and you're the only worker in the plant who can't show you didn't have an opportunity to kill Doss. Now that may change, but that's the way it is now."

Doss shakes me by asking, "If I plead guilty, will you give some of the money back we paid you? Latrice can't support her and the baby on what she gets from that store."

I shake my head. I can't let him make a decision based on money. "If you take this deal, and, in fact, it's only a recommendation by the prosecutor, you have to tell the judge you're pleading guilty because you are guilty, not just saying you are." As soon as I recite this familiar phrase, "pleading guilty because you are guilty," I realize how hypocritical the criminal law is. The judge is essentially telling a defendant he must stand trial if he believes he is innocent. But what innocent person in his right mind would risk a trial where the penalty could be death and the evidence appears overwhelming?

Doss, clearly puzzled, scratches his head. I have confused him. He asks, "Can't I plead guilty, no matter what?"

"You're not supposed to, because you are lying to the court if you say you're guilty when you're not. On the other hand, I don't see how justice is served if an innocent man can't avoid a death sentence by pleading guilty and getting a reduced sentence. In other words, I'm telling you, if I were in a situation where I was innocent and was offered a reduced sentence but was pretty certain I'd get the death penalty if I went to trial, I'd say I was guilty."

He looks down at his feet. "And you think I'll be convicted?" Butterfield is testing me by making this early offer. It's a smart move, but he doesn't know how smart. "It's too early to say. There may be evidence by the time we get to the trial that exonerates you."

"But it's my decision, isn't it?" Doss asks.

"Yeah, it's your decision," I say.

"I'll think about it," Doss says, dismissing me.

I drive back to Blackwell County, resisting the urge to call Angela. She wants to go slow. I can do that.

202

. . .

Saturday afternoon spring is definitely in the air. It has made it all the way to 78 this afternoon. Even as unobservant as I am, I notice the trees beginning to bud and some daffodils blooming in the yards on Orchard Lane. Bear Creek before the mosquitoes arrive can be a nice place. As a kid here, my memory seems stuck in the sweltering summers of the Delta.

In Angela's yard there is a FOR SALE sign. I wonder how much her house is worth. With so many others leaving, undoubtedly not as much as she wants. Angela greets me at the door with a warm smile. She is wearing a pair of shorts and a sleeveless blue T and nothing on her feet. "Well, you look comfortable," she says, giving me the once over. I am wearing a pair of jeans and a pullover short-sleeved shirt that Sarah gave me for Christmas.

And you look sexy, I think, but don't say. I glance over my shoulder across the street. The house is dark, but Mrs. Petty must be in there somewhere peering out at us. As gorgeous as today is, I would have thought she would have been outside puttering in the flower bed around her house. "Do you think Mrs. Petty approves of you entertaining in short pants?"

The smile on Angela's face disappears. "She died in her sleep while I was in Atlanta. Her sister found her. I wasn't here to go to her funeral."

I try not to stare at Angela's legs. They look great. "She probably died of boredom," I comment, "because you weren't here for her to spy on."

Angela laughs. "You're terrible. We're all snoops here. You know that."

I turn my head away and stare at the sign in her yard. "Bad timing, wasn't it? Now her house goes on the market at the same time."

Angela says dryly, "I can tell you're really broken up over this."

Death. It's seldom convenient. "You don't seem all that upset either," I observe.

"She had a long life," Angela says. "Not everybody does."

Since it is too pleasant to stay inside, we end up in her backyard drinking margaritas. I must have passed some test for Angela to show me off this way. In the next hour before it grows dark from the small brick patio she waves casually to her neighbors on both sides. I don't know them, though doubtless with a couple of phone calls they can find out who I am if they don't already know. Whatever the reason, Angela seems more relaxed. She admits to feeling better now that she's made the decision to leave Bear Creek. "When the house sells, I'm going to move. I thought the boys would be angry, but they weren't."

"They're probably relieved," I say, licking salt from the rim of the glass. "Farming sounds like hard work. Where are you moving?" I ask, not having anticipated this decision so quickly.

Angela picks at a spot on the arm of the deck chair. "Maybe Atlanta, maybe Memphis. The problem is, I haven't seen a lot of job ads for farmers' wives."

So that is why she went to visit her old college roommate. "Have you thought about Little Rock?" I ask, trying to see her eyes for a clue to what she is thinking. "Now that your boys are in college, you don't have to worry about the schools. It's the center of the state. Granted, there are bad areas, but there are plenty of safe neighborhoods, too. You could easily get a job as a bookkeeper."

She looks up at me, her face solemn as an owl's. "I have thought about it," she says. "But I don't want you to think I'm chasing you, Gideon."

I laugh at the thought. "If our relationship so far is your idea of a chase, I figure I'm safe until the turn of the century."

Instead of smiling, her eyes fill with tears. "I'm so scared. I know it's stupid, but I've lived here thirty years. It hasn't been easy, but we made it. Now, all I do is lie awake thinking: What if I can't sell the house? What if Cecil and Nancy can't even pay me the first year? Who wants to hire a fifty-year-old woman from the Arkansas Delta who never held a job in her life?"

I reach over and pat her right hand, which has a death grip

on her chair. "It's going to be okay," I say, not understanding until this moment how little self-confidence Angela has had. Maybe for good reason. Her life with Dwight wasn't a bowl of cherries, and as good as she looks, most employers would rather have a perky twenty-two-year-old who is already a whiz with spreadsheets than a widow trying to support two kids in college.

Over a delicious dinner of pasta and salad, Angela pumps me about the case. I tell her what I've been doing the last week, but feel I shouldn't reveal to her that Butterfield has offered Doss a deal. It is not that I don't trust her, but even I have my limits of violating client confidentiality.

She sips from a glass of the California zinfandel I brought along and then asks, her voice wistful, "Isn't there a chance that the case against Paul could be dropped? If they don't have any evidence other than the tape?"

I eye my empty glass and decide against another one. "I have no idea," I say cautiously, but as usual made slightly irritable by her concern for Paul. "Why do you care so much?"

"Even if he is found innocent, his family will be tarred by this for the rest of their lives," Angela says passionately. "I may be leaving here soon, but some people won't. It isn't right!" Again, she breaks into tears, and this time I am allowed to lead her into her sons' bedroom. She turns on a light between the twin beds and turns to me, her face mostly in shadow. "Are you sure you want to do this?" I ask, wondering if she will be upset to-morrow.

For an answer, she kisses me and pulls me down on the bed on top of her. For once, we do not talk about Bear Creek or the lawsuit. Sober, I leave about eleven and make the two-hour drive back to Blackwell County. Even though Mrs. Petty is dead, her ghost may be watching.

Fourteen

WEDNESDAY MORNING Doss finally tells me he has decided to reject Butterfield's offer. "I don't want to do that now," he says vaguely, rubbing his eyes as he stares at me through the glass. He has been complaining he can't sleep more than a couple of hours a night.

My reaction is mixed, to say the least. I'd love to get Paul, but I don't want to spend the rest of my life wondering if my client perjured himself. "Even if Butterfield tells me this is the only offer he will make, I don't necessarily believe it," I say. "It depends on how bad he wants to get Paul Taylor. If he does, he'll call me right before the trial."

Bledsoe leans back in his chair and folds his arms. He wants me to get out of here and get to work.

Twenty minutes later at the courthouse in Bear Creek, Butterfield takes my news calmly. "I'll just have to manage without him," he says, the tone of his voice as amiable as ever.

I hem and haw around, but I can't get him to give me any indication that this rejection closes the door permanently. Poker-faced, Butterfield stands and shakes my hand, dismissing me.

"It'll be an interesting trial. Did you hear what happened in Helena yesterday?"

I nod, feeling a little weak. Butterfield got a first-degree murder charge to stick against a black woman accused of murdering her husband. Usually, that kind of charge is knocked way down by the time the jury comes back. "It sounds like you did a good job."

"I get lucky every now and then," he says, escorting me out of his office. If he is upset, I can't tell it.

I head over to Dickerson's office and find him alone behind a computer modifying jury instructions for a civil trial beginning next week in Blytheville, in the northeast corner of the state. I wonder if he has ever come to his office without wearing a tie. Dick is definitely from the old school, which holds that an attorney's name in bold type in the yellow pages is a betrayal of the ideals of the profession.

"I wanted to let you know that Doss turned down a deal to testify against Paul," I say, sitting down in a comfortable chair across from his desk. "He still insists he's not guilty and that Paul never approached him about anything."

Dickerson leans back in his chair and flexes his fingers like a concert pianist about to rip into the Warsaw Concerto. "Of course he did," he says. "Butterfield has absolutely nothing on Paul except one tape of him and Willie that one time. It's an abomination that Paul was ever charged. I knew this is what the legal system would come to with them in charge."

I study Dick's diploma from Columbia. Beside it is proof that he took his undergraduate degree from Washington and Lee. It is hard not to be impressed. Dick can probably lecture for a week without notes on the history of Southern efforts to block integration. "When you get some time after this trial," I say, watching his fingers fly over the keys, "I'll go over with you what I've found so far. Paul's not hurt any, but I can't say I've found anything to help Doss."

Dick gives me a distracted smile. "I appreciate it, Gideon. I know you're busy, too. Call me next week and we'll get together. I know you're doing all the work right now."

"It's all right," I assure him. "I've enjoyed being back over here."

"I hear you're seeing Miss Angela," he says, glancing at me and smiling. "She's struggled like a lot of people over here, and I'm sorry she's selling her house. It's people like her we can't afford to lose."

I admit that we have gone out a time or two, but as I have with John, I minimize the relationship. Dick is both too polite to say more and anxious to get back to work, so I let him. As I walk back to the parking lot at the courthouse where I left the Blazer, I marvel at Dick's capacity for self-delusion. What does he expect to happen over here? Does he think whites will suddenly stop moving out and come to terms with the black political domination that is sure to come in every area? Two members of the city council are white; the county judge, Terry Keith, is white, but unless there is some kind of major turnaround about to take place, the handwriting is on the wall. And what would he think of my relationship with Angela thus far? Dick sees himself as honorably old-fashioned and surely would be shocked if he knew that Angela had taken me to her brother-in-law's bed with a fistful of rubbers in her purse.

During the rest of April I have occasion to see Dick several times as I plow through the list of plant workers and check and double-check their alibis. Some, despite Eddie Ting's entreaties, have no interest in talking to me or, when they have, express the view that Doss is guilty. Whatever their views or attitudes, time after time their alibis check out. Though his schedule is busier than my own, as the trial approaches, Dick, when he can, begins to take an active role in the investigation. But between us, we uncover very little that suggests that Woodrow Bonner has not done a thorough job in meticulously documenting the whereabouts of each worker in the plant the day of the murder.

So long as Bledsoe continues to stick to his story, Dick has little to worry about. As we continue to meet together on a weekly basis to compare notes, he seems mainly interested in keeping tabs on what I am doing, and for good reason. If I can't come up with another suspect and Doss testifies as expected, Paul has nothing to worry about.

What keeps the month of April from seeming like a complete waste of time is my steadily growing relationship with Angela. Though I do not spend a night at her house and am wearing out myself and the Blazer commuting, I see her two and sometimes three times a week and have taken to stopping at Bear Creek's one supermarket, where occasionally I see Alvaro Ruiz in the meat department setting out cuts of beef and pork. One rainy, unforgettable Saturday we drive to Memphis and spend almost the entire day in a motel. Depending on her mood, she can be aggressive, and I glimpse the passionate girl I knew thirty years ago and experienced that bizarre afternoon in her brother-in-law's bed. Other times she becomes moody and depressed, which I relate to Dwight's death and her fears about the future. Though she has had no offers on the house, she has begun to work on it, and more than once has come to her door with eggshell white paint on her face and hands. Having gotten a full-price offer from a middle-class black couple on my house (with no fixing up) after it had been listed for only a week, I am sympathetic to her plight but have no suggestions about how to move it. Bear Creek is hardly a seller's market.

I have met her boys, who have been home for a weekend. Although neither is as mature as Sarah, they seem like good kids and both are closer to her than I would have thought. I caught Brad wiping away a tear as he hugged Angela when they were going back to school a couple of Sundays ago. Distressed by their mother's plans to sell the farm and further disrupt their lives by moving, they have begun to privately pressure her to stay in Bear Creek. Like many Delta-raised children, their manners are so good they can get on your nerves. Accordingly, both boys have been polite and courteous to me but are naturally suspicious since lately I seem to be at their mother's house every time they call. At first, Angela maintained the fiction that I was "just an old friend" but has begun to admit that we are going out. Since the Blazer is over here all the time, they could easily discover the truth simply by asking the neighbors how their mother is doing. The Saturday night they were home, Angela instructed me to show them Sarah's picture, and they were suitably impressed. I guess they figure that if I have a daughter that beautiful I can't be too bad. Angela has encouraged them to look for summer jobs in Jonesboro since if she gets an offer she could close on the house within a matter of weeks.

Having so much time to think during the long two-hour drives back and forth, I have begun to admit to myself that I am falling in love with her. Despite a certain amount of baggage, she seems to be getting used to the idea that I am serious about her. She has let me know that I nearly blew it by kissing her that first day, and I realize now how unsettling it was for her. Would I act differently if I had the chance to do it over again? I tell myself that I would, but hardly from the purest of motives. There is an undeniable sexual attraction between us, something that time hasn't dimmed. Both of us will be relieved when the trial is over because we are on opposite sides there. She believes that Paul is innocent while I am convinced he is not, despite the fact that I have no more proof of that than the day I took this case over. I try to convince her that a year from now we won't even remember the case, but she knows that's garbage. If he is found innocent, it will simply be viewed by the whites as another battle in the never-ending racial conflict, but if a jury convicts him, it will be etched in the memory of everyone who ever lived here.

On May 3, I get a call at my office from Darla Tate, who, to her credit, has continued to be helpful by furnishing me updated addresses and telephone numbers of plant employees. In the past week or two I have fudged the truth a bit by suggesting that I fully expect Doss to be acquitted, hoping probably futilely that this news will have the effect of convincing her she should decide to climb aboard his freedom train and testify that it could have been some other employee's voice she heard that day she was in the bathroom. Today there is an excitement in her voice that I haven't heard before, but it is hard to take her too seriously. While everybody has a theory in this case, the only evidence still points at Doss. In an earlier conversation, I told her that I haven't found out much that wasn't already in the prosecutor's file. And she knows that I am still checking out alibis. She says she has something to show me and asks when I am coming back to Bear Creek. Since I am about to walk over to the prosecutor's office to try to plead out a cocaine posses- sion case, I check my calendar, tell her the fifth, and head out the door. As I walk, I realize that I am beginning to distance my- self from the outcome of this case, a tendency I have always had to fight against when I get frustrated.

When I arrive at the plant Thursday morning, Darla hands me a cup of coffee and seats me behind Eddie's desk, explaining that he's over in Greenville on family business. She makes small talk until Cy, who has been goofing off up front, heads back to the kill floor. When he leaves, Darla reaches into a drawer and pulls out a box of receipts and spreads them out on her desk. "Eddie said I could tell you about this. I honestly don't know if it has a bit of significance to your case, but I knew the salesman involved, and I wouldn't put it past 'Muddy' Jessup to have murdered Willie."

I notice a bit of lipstick on the lip of the mug and rotate it a half a turn. Neither of the two salesmen/truck drivers, to my knowledge, has seriously ever been considered suspects since they were out on the road selling meat the day Willie was killed. I look down at the notes I have made on every employee I've talked with, and realize that Jessup is not on my list. On the other hand, I have dutifully talked on the phone to grocery store employees in Memphis, Earle, Marion, West Memphis, and a couple of towns in Arkansas I don't remember, who have confirmed through their receipts that meat was delivered to them that day by Jessup. I remember now that Darla's updated list shows that a couple of employees, Jessup one of them and Jorge Arrazola the other, no longer can be found in Bear Creek. Since the sheriff got a statement from him before he left town and his alibi seemed solid, I haven't worried that the new updated West Memphis address for him hasn't been checked out. "What's the deal on this guy?" I watch as Darla arranges the papers side by side on her desk.

"Let me explain what Eddie and I think he did," she says, "and then I'll tell you what I know about him." She points with her pen to a sheet in front of her. "The first thing you need to know is that we give every salesman a price list each time they leave here to take with them to call on customers. Eddie works on the list constantly, because every time we buy a load of hogs there's a price change. For the last couple of weeks Eddie and I have gone back through everything, trying to figure out why the plant's been losing money, and we even went back through stuff from when Willie was still alive to see what he was doing different. Well, in going through all the receipts we developed a suspicion that Muddy was cheating the stores in his territory. Come over here, and I'll show you."

With my coffee cup in hand, I get up and walk over behind and look over her shoulder. She puts her finger on a sheet in front of her and says, "This is our price list from June of last year."

I look down at a sheet that has the name "Southern Pride Meats" in white against a blue border. Below it are three rows of products ranging from pork tenderloin at $5.15 a pound to fresh pork jowls at sixty-five cents a pound. "What we think Muddy was doing," Darla says, "was marking up some of the prices after he left the office. You'd be surprised how few store owners even look at the price lists. The salesmen know which ones do, and we think Muddy would just tell them what the cost was that day and they'd ring it up and pay cash. If you look closely, you can tell on some of the tickets that the figures have been altered."

Darla points to a smudged spot on a ticket she has marked as the plant copy. "In other words, when Muddy came back to the plant, he'd turn in a doctored ticket that matched the price list that we'd given him and keep the difference. Actually, he was cheating the customer, but, of course, it was cheating Southern Pride, too, because it was raising our prices against our competition. Sooner or later, we'd lose their business. But in the short run, unless the customer checked the price list, he wouldn't know he had been cheated."

I put on my reading glasses and pick up the ticket. Darla runs her index finger down the middle column of the price list. "For example, on June fifth, we were supposed to be selling sausage patties for a dollar thirty-five. On the ticket copy the customer retains, we now know Muddy made the three into an eight and was charging a dollar eighty-five for sausage patties. On the plant copy he turned in, you can see he changed it back into a three so it would match our price list."

I squint at the numbers. True, it is slightly smudged, but it seems inconclusive to me. "Why did you take so long to find this out?" I ask.

"Carelessness on my part," Darla admits. "The price lists change so fast that I didn't pay any attention. The customer wasn't complaining, so I didn't pick it up. But we know now, because last week after we suspected something had been going on, we called some of the stores in his old territory, and were able to verify that he had cheated at least two of them. It wasn't easy, because most stores had thrown out their receipts, but a couple hadn't. They're letting us give them a discount for a while."

I peer down at the papers, not sure what to make of this. Just because this guy was a thief doesn't make him a murderer. "Did he not get along with Willie or what?" I ask, leaning back against Cy's desk.

"Muddy's a son of a bitch," Darla says, bitterly. "I've known him for years. Marla, his wife, went around town for years with two black eyes. The thing that you ought to know is that

Muddy can use a knife. He was on the kill floor for years before he persuaded Willie to let him try out as a salesman."

I realize I've watched a truck or two being loaded, but I've never paid attention to the men who drive them. When I ask what happened to him, Darla explains that Muddy quit a couple of weeks after the murder, saying he was taking a job at a meat-packing plant outside of West Memphis. "What would be his motive?" I ask, sitting back down behind Eddie's desk.

Darla stacks the papers on her desk into a neat pile. "Maybe Willie was suspicious and told him he wanted to talk to him. The salesmen come in and out of the office all the time to turn in their receipts and get the price lists."

"Wouldn't Willie have talked to you first?" I ask, not at all impressed with this theory. Willie was killed at his desk with his back turned to his assailant. There was no confrontation, no struggle that indicated a fight.

Darla opens a drawer and places the tickets inside. "At some point he would have. Maybe he was going to, and just hadn't gotten around to it. I have a theory about what happened. You want to hear it?"

"Sure," I say. Darla is watching me carefully as if she is afraid I may not be interested in what she is about to tell me.

She leans forward and almost whispers, "Well, it's pretty much an accepted fact that one of the stores that Muddy sold to is controlled by the Memphis Mafia. It's a legitimate store but it probably washes a lot of money for them. What I figure is that they found out Muddy was cheating them and made an offer he couldn't refuse."

I am getting a sty on my right eye and rub it. I didn't sleep well last night and must be too slow for this conversation. "I don't get it."

"Southern Pride does a cash business," she says, her voice animated. "Those guys are constantly looking for places to launder their money and get into legitimate businesses. My guess is they assumed incorrectly that they could pick up the plant cheap if the owner was bumped off. And now I doubt if it was any coincidence that since Willie died, the Tings have gotten a couple of offers for the plant, one out of Memphis. If I were in your shoes, I'd be looking for Muddy Jessup."

I stare at Darla, thinking she has been watching too many cop shows set on the east coast. Organized crime isn't exactly a stranger in the South, but you don't hear much about it. Still, I have heard of the "Dixie Mafia." "So you now think Paul Taylor didn't have anything to do with it?" I ask, wondering if she is onto something.

"Maybe he didn't," Darla says, arching her back as she stretches against her chair. She is wearing a tight sweater and skirt that is too young for her, but it is hard to fault her for making an effort. "It's probably more likely that Muddy could have thought that Willie was going to get him sent to prison when he found out he was stealing. The salesmen sometimes came back to the plant after it was shut down. Willie wouldn't have thought anything about Muddy's being in the office."

This seems more plausible to me. "But what about all the people who said he was selling meat to them that day?"

Darla shrugs. "He could have delivered early and come back or come here first and gone to his stores late. Hell, he could have bribed a couple. Somebody could have owed him a favor. He could have been slipping an employee of one of those stores free meat for years."

I nod at her. It is worth checking out if for no other reason than I've about worked my way to the end of the list of plant employees. "Do you have any idea where Muddy went?"

Darla shakes her head. "He didn't leave a forwarding address, and I checked at the plant he was working at in West Memphis. He just didn't show up one day. They're still checking to see if he stole any money."

I smile at her. "You should have been a cop."

She doodles on a pad in front of her. "Hardly. I was just trying to help you out."

"Thanks," I say, pushing up from my chair. It dawns on me that Darla is probably hoping that I might ask her out. We're about the same age, and I doubt if there have been too many guys lining up to ask her for a date. "Have you told the sheriff about the theft?"

"I wanted to let you know first," she says. "Bonner kind of plays things close to the vest, in case you haven't noticed."

"I have," I say. I wonder when Bonner would have gotten around to telling me. If nothing else, I will be able to argue, for what it's worth, that a thieving salesman and an undocumented alien got the hell out of town after the boss was murdered.

"Are you still friends with Muddy's wife?" I ask, thinking she might keep up with her ex-husband. Some women never let go, no matter how badly they've been abused.

"More or less," Darla says, reaching for the phone book. "She lives outside of town."

I ask her to give Mrs. Jessup a call and see if she has any idea where Muddy is. She says she will, and I leave, relieved that at least one person is actively helping me on this case. I'd be at ground zero if it weren't for this woman. What is her motivation? If I am honest with myself, it can't only be that she's attracted to me. I suspect that, outside of his family, Darla may be the person who misses Willie the most.

Fifteen

SHERIFF BONNER SITS IN HIS OFFICE and looks at me with an expression that says I'm not very bright. "I would have told you where Mr. Jessup was if you had asked. We found him a couple of weeks ago. He's living in Nashville working for another plant."

I feel like an idiot. For the last two weeks I have been wasting my time trying to find him and nailing down his alibi which today is even tighter than it was before I began to try to track him down. Feeling dumber by the minute, I ask Bonner if he has checked out whether Mike's Super Bargain store in Memphis is Mafia controlled.

He does his best not to smile. "We've checked every lead we've been given," he says. "If they're fronting for anybody, we haven't been able to find it out."

For some reason I feel a little better. At least he investigated it. I tell myself not to be too hard on Darla Tate. Hell, she made as much sense as anybody else. "Will you bring him back for the trial?"

The sheriff picks off a piece of lint from his uniform, which is as pressed and starched as the day I met him in February. The only difference is that he is wearing a short-sleeved shirt. The third week in May, it is already warm enough for air condition-

217

ing, though Bonner hasn't turned it on in his office. "Not unless you offer any evidence during your defense that he killed Willie Ting. As you probably know by now if you've retraced his route, more people saw him that day than claim they've seen Elvis."

I laugh for the first time in a month. After weeks of going through the records, Darla has told me that they can't even find enough theft by Muddy to charge him with a felony. This was a complete waste of time. To get in at least one jab against him, I ask, "So, Sheriff, what do you think the odds are that a jury will convict Paul Taylor?"

Bonner's professional mask descends once again. He says easily, "Go see Mr. Butterfield. He's the lawyer, not me."

That's as close as Bonner will come to "dissing" his rival. I leave his office, and drive out to Brickeys to see Doss, realizing how much I have underestimated Bonner and Butterfield. I thought by this time there would be enough honest-to-God suspects that Bledsoe would be a cinch to walk. Now it looks as if I will have to depend on the blacks on the jury to distrust the system so much that I can get a hung jury. Unfortunately for Doss, instead of a racist detective from the L.A. police department, the star witness against Doss will be an African-American sheriff who, thus far, has been as competent and professional as any person I've met so far in law enforcement.

Bledsoe, who has lost at least fifteen pounds in the two and a half months he's been in jail, looks more depressed than ever when I sit down with him. "There's hardly anybody I haven't talked to," I say, feeling dejected myself. "I'll argue that anybody could have framed you, but damn it, I don't have any evidence."

In response, Bledsoe begins to cough and sneeze. Some guys take to jails and prisons as if they were their summer homes; Doss is not one of them. He's been sick almost since the day he got here. Jails are not great places to be sick. Just last week an asthma patient died in the Blackwell County jail.

His congestion finally settling for a moment, Doss sputters,

"I'm ready to take that deal Butterfield offered me. I did it. You think you can get him to make it again?"

I watch Bledsoe wipe his face with his sleeve. Has he really been conning me all this time? "Doss, does this mean you're changing your story? And this time you're telling me the truth? I can't be a part of anything that railroads an innocent man." Sure I can. This is what I've wanted to happen ever since I realized Butterfield needed Doss to get Paul. Yet, if Doss tells me he is lying to save himself from execution, I can't let him do it.

Doss covers his mouth and begins to cough again. When the spasm subsides, he says, "It's like this. Taylor promised me the barbecue place after Oldham retires next year. Then I'd take it over and in a couple of years Taylor was supposed to give me the deed to the place. It'd be like I was buying it from him. We figured the Mexican would get scared and take off and then get blamed. I suspected his papers were forged."

"When did you and Paul plan this?" I ask, watching his face carefully. His eyes are rheumy, but he looks straight back at me while he talks.

"About two weeks before I did it," he says stolidly. "When I'd be out working for Oldham, Taylor would come out. That's when we talked."

I drop my voice to a whisper. "How could you kill Willie?" I ask, realizing I've always been lulled by his passive demeanor. "Everybody said he liked you and that you liked him. You even said you did."

Bledsoe gives me a cold look. "What makes you think we gonna tell you the truth unless we have to?"

I put my face close to the window to try to get his attention. "You don't act like any murderer that I've ever represented, Doss. Not somebody who'd kill in cold blood."

"It was a lot easier than killin' a pig," he says, his voice cold and hard. "I jus' slipped behind that old dude when I was walking by him to git some pills I said I left in the bathroom. He gave a little grunt—didn't even holler."

A change has come over Bledsoe, but whether he is acting I

219

can't tell. There definitely is another side to him. For the first time I can see he can get mean in a hurry when he wants to. "How'd you slip up on him?" I ask, not as skeptical as I was.

"That place clears out right at two, 'cause he didn't pay a dime after that, and I circled the block and came back. I picked a day when the secretary was gone and then came back and went in the front door and told Willie I had to come back and get some medicine I had left in the bathroom. He wudn't paying no attention, and when I come out, I jus' slipped up and cut him and stepped back and watched him die. It didn't take but a minute or two."

In the time it has taken him to tell me this, I have deep-sixed any thought that Doss couldn't have killed Willie. Gone is the affable, almost teddy bear–like man I first met, and in his place is a cold son of a bitch I wouldn't want to meet in a dark alley. "What'd you do then?" I ask, transfixed by his story.

"I had me a rag and a paper bag in my pocket and I wiped off my knife with it and took it back and laid it where I always did, but I guess all the blood didn't come off. I didn't know my nerves would get to me like they did. I wanted to get the hell out of there. I stopped and burned the bag on the way home."

"Why didn't you go somewhere so you'd have an alibi?"

"Me and Taylor talked about that," he says, nodding, "but he said it would look suspicious if I did something different than I usually did. He figured someone would notice my car and think I got home when I always did. See, I got home just fifteen minutes later than usual. It only took five minutes to kill him and put my knife up. But it turns out nobody noticed nothin'."

I nod, knowing I have been to every residence in his neighborhood and along the route he took from the plant to his house in a futile effort to find someone who might confirm that he went home the day of the murder at his usual time. The sheriff's office already covered much the same territory six months earlier and found nothing, and neither did I. In his haste or nervousness, he acted too fast. Assuming he is telling the truth. I ask, "So, Darla Tate did hear you that day in the bath-room?"

"I reckon," he says and shrugs. "Taylor had left a couple hundred in cash in my truck for me the next night, and I called him that week to let him know I got it. I didn't see nobody around and figured the secretary had gone home."

Nobody has claimed Doss was a genius, and clearly, that was the dumbest call he ever made. We talk for a few minutes longer, and he asks if I think that Butterfield would go for a shorter sentence than twenty years. "See if I can do less time," he instructs me, his voice bereft of emotion now that he has got-ten through his story.

I am not ready to do anything yet, and I stall for time by telling him that the best time to approach Butterfield will be two or three days before the trial begins. Today is the nine-teenth, and the trial begins on the twenty-sixth. "If you're lying, I can't be a part of it."

"I ain't lying," he says stubbornly, "but I ain't gonna take the fall for Taylor. See, we knew he was a suspect less than a day af-ter I killed Willie. Somebody couldn't keep their mouth shut about that tape, and Taylor was real cautious after that and didn't do nothing where they would link him up with me. He's knowed all along they was after him."

I lean back in my chair now, understanding why no evidence has turned up against Paul. No wonder he didn't give a state-ment. Though I pump him for more details, Doss, still hacking and wheezing, doesn't have much more to say. He had seen Paul at Oldham's a few times, where Paul had slipped him small amounts of cash, never more than a couple of hundred. Any large sums of money he would have had to have withdrawn from a bank and could have been traced and used as evidence against him. No wonder Dickerson was so relieved when I told him that Doss hadn't implicated Paul. "Does Paul's lawyer know you and Paul planned this?"

Nonplussed, Doss mumbles, "I don't know." He looks at me

as if the question hasn't ever occurred to him. Clients, he obviously believes, don't confess to their lawyers unless they think it will help them. What he won't accept is that it is always in a client's interest to tell his lawyer the truth.

Shaken, and wondering what the truth is, I drive away from the jail, having promised to return no later than forty-eight hours. Despite what he has told me, clearly he wants to believe that I will discover a crack in the case against him. The only moment he lost his composure was right before I left when I asked him if Latrice knew he had killed Willie. Distressed, he said that she didn't. For the first time, a look of agony replaced the hardness on his face. He can do the time; he isn't sure that Latrice can.

I drive back into town, my head spinning with the conversation I've just had with Doss. I had told Angela I would come by for a glass of iced tea before heading for home to get ready for a DWI jury trial tomorrow. I have to win this one because it's my client's fourth trip down this road. If I lose he automatically goes to prison. The noise from her Lawn Boy tells me Angela is in her backyard cutting the grass. I walk around to the back, where she gives me a wave and continues mowing a small rectangle in the center. Through with the jobs she can perform herself on her house, she spends more and more time with her garden. She still has had no offers on the house and has only shown it twice. Though cutting the grass is a chore her boys would normally do, they, as she hoped, have gotten jobs in Jonesboro this summer, Curt working as a desk clerk for a motel, and Brad making sandwiches for Subway.

As I watch her, I wish I could tell her about the conversation I had with Doss, but disclosing what he has just told me would be the ultimate violation of client confidentiality. Still, if it would help to talk to anyone about what Doss has just told me, it would be Angela. She would serve as the perfect devil's advocate, since she has never believed that Paul was involved in the murder. On the other hand, if she thought Doss were telling the truth, it would go a long way in convincing me, too. Dressed in short shorts, sandals, and a T-shirt that advertises the King Biscuit October Blues festival in Helena, she makes me wish this case were safely behind us. Though it has not been an easy time for her, she seems to trust me more each time I am with her. I go through the back door of her house into the kitchen and find a pitcher of iced tea already made up in the refrigerator. I'd rather have a beer for the trip home, but if I had one, I'd want two, and would wind up wanting to do something else. When I come back out with two glasses full of tea, she is done, and we sit on the patio under the shade of her pecan tree.

"What's wrong?" she says immediately. "Something's happened."

"Nothing," I say, realizing I should have called her from a service station and told her I had to get back.

"Did you come by to dump me," she asks lightly, "just as I was starting to feel comfortable with you?" She is smiling, but her voice is tense.

"No!" I exclaim. "It's the case. I really can't tell you. I should have just driven on back home."

She wipes sweat from her upper lip, reminding me of Doss wiping his nose with the back of his hand. "Doss has confessed to you, hasn't he?" she guesses. She knew I was going to see him.

I know I have been talking too much to her. Angela has pumped me for details on a regular basis. "Let's talk about something else," I say, unable to look at her. She has always been able to read me like a book.

Angela reaches over and grips my arm. "He's not trying to say that Paul is involved, is he?"

I stand up abruptly and pour my tea out on the ground. This was a terrible idea. "I can't talk about it. I need to get home."

"Paul didn't do it," she says. "I know he didn't!"

Angela is practically shouting at me. I look around to see who is listening. "How could you possibly know for sure?"

She shakes her head, and begins to cry. "Let's go inside. I can't talk out here."

She runs into the house, and I follow, now prepared for her to tell me she doesn't want to see me anymore. She sits down at the kitchen table and motions for me to do the same. When I do, she wipes her eyes with a tissue and says, "Gideon, I'm absolutely certain that Paul didn't kill Willie. I haven't told you this, but Paul said to me the day after Willie died, and this is an exact quote: 'If somebody hadn't killed the old son of a bitch, I might have done it myself.'"

"Are you serious?" I say, leaning across the table toward her. I am dumbfounded that she hasn't told me this before now.

Angela nods. "But don't you see? He was joking! I know it makes him look bad, but it proves he didn't kill him. When I told him how horrible he sounded, he said he wouldn't have harmed a hair on his head."

"Why didn't you say something before now?" I demand. "That doesn't prove he didn't have Willie murdered. He was giving himself a cover in case something backfired down the line. Something must have scared him, and he started constructing an escape hatch."

Angela shakes her head furiously. "That's the craziest thing I've ever heard you say! That's not what he meant at all!"

"Listen to me," I say, excitedly. "I've got to call you as a witness. A jury has to hear this. Where were you? Had he taken you out to lunch?"

"No," she says, her voice now frigid. "We were in bed at the Peabody Hotel. Paul and I had been lovers for over a year."

I collapse against the back of my chair, my face tingling as if she has just slapped me. Damn it, why didn't I figure this out? She has talked about him nonstop for three months. "Why didn't you tell me?" I gasp. I'm suddenly lightheaded, as if the blood in my brain has thinned into water.

She puts both hands to her face and begins to cry. "I didn't want to lose you! But Gideon, I know Paul. He would never have somebody killed. You've got to believe that."

I clench my fists, which have become the color of mayonnaise. "You couldn't wait," I cry, "until your husband died to

224

crawl into bed with him?" At the time Willie was murdered, Dwight had just two months to live.

Angela begins to sob, but I don't give a damn. I fight back a wave of nausea before yelling, "Why did you do it? Is Paul that great in the sack?"

Angela stares at a spot to the right of my head and forces out the words, "I got involved with him originally so we'd get our loan. But it became more than that."

More than that. I look at this woman. Thirty years ago she was the most idealistic person I'd ever known. I can't believe what I'm hearing. "Was Dwight in on this little plan?" I ask sarcastically, opening my hands and watching blood rushing into my fingers. I feel my face go beet red as the shock of what she has told me transforms into rage.

Angela puts her head down on her arms as her body is racked by spasms. I am tempted to grab her by the hair and shake her. Why has she done this to me? "Though he would have, Dwight didn't actually die from the cancer," she says in a tiny voice. "Cecil suspected I was involved with Paul and told him. After Dwight confronted me, and I admitted Paul and I were lovers, he took an overdose of pills that night and never woke up."

"Oh, shit!" I gasp, feeling my breath coming in short bursts. The guilt she must feel! Despite my own rapidly growing feeling that Angela is like an old-fashioned grifter and I am the gullible dupe in some ancient con game, I can't help but have some sympathy for her. I force myself to take a calming breath and wonder if this is for real or part of an act that involves Paul. If she would betray her husband of thirty years, surely she would betray me.

When she can speak again, she says, "Cecil knows how Dwight died, but I begged him not to tell the boys. They'd never forgive me."

I feel a numbness creeping up my chest, my body unable to keep up with all I am hearing. "Cecil's blackmailing you, isn't he? He's forcing you to sell him the land."

Angela clears her throat and sighs heavily. "Yes."

Now I comprehend why we rode out to Cecil's and screwed in his bed. "You hate him, don't you?"

She nods but doesn't speak. If I make her testify, everything will come out, including my own conduct. My mind races as I review my options. Damn it! I feel like some wild animal caught in a trap that can't escape unless it gnaws off a leg. It is too late to try to withdraw. Johnson wouldn't let me. "When did it end with Paul," I ask, my own voice tight. "Or has it ended?"

"We were never together again after Paul said that," she says, her eyes searching mine. "Dwight was getting sicker, and I felt terrible. It's only been since I met you again that I've begun to admit to myself how deprived I felt all those years. I've finally admitted to myself what a sham of a marriage I had."

I stare at her in amazement. "What are you talking about?" I ask, incredulously. "You said Dwight was as close to a saint as any man you ever knew."

Angela stares past me at the diplomas on my wall. "A plastic one," she says, her voice bitter. "Dwight never let himself entertain a real doubt in his life. He had this image of the way our lives were supposed to go, and no matter how ridiculous the reality, nothing interfered with it. Yet, by most standards, he was considered a wonderful man. He worked hard, went to church, loved his children, and kept every emotion he'd ever had bottled inside twenty-four hours a day. I think now that he was scared to death of life the whole time we were married, but his defense mechanisms were so strong he never admitted it. When I finally got through my head you weren't going to propose, instead of going back east, I went after Dwight because he seemed to be the nicest guy around. I probably did it to spite you. I didn't know I'd never get closer to him than I am to my cat. True enough, Paul is a womanizing son of a bitch, but I found out he was wonderfully human, and I was starving for somebody real. It wasn't until after I got involved with him that I even had an inkling of how much I had allowed myself to miss in life."

My emotions begin to whirl around me like a dust storm. Put

side by side with Paul, Dwight, to ninety-five percent of the population, sounds like a bargain, but something in me is stirred by Angela's story. Her confession makes me realize how I, too, have always tried to idealize women, making them either Madonnas or whores. I should be repulsed by what Angela has told me, but I'm not sure what I feel. "It sounds to me like you're still in love with Paul."

Angela brushes her hair back from her face and gives me a grim smile. "I know this sounds terribly callous, but he was just a wake-up call. I can do much better than Paul Taylor. I love you, Gideon."

Angela's intensity forces me to drop my eyes. I've been waiting to hear these words for two months, but given the moment, I'd be a fool to believe them right now. The problem is, I'm in love with her. I stand up, and say, "I need to go home and think about all of this, Angela."

She stares at me and nods. "I know."

I leave her sitting at the table and let myself out of the house, thinking I am a damn fool. How could I get myself in such a mess?

Sixteen

My phone is ringing when I walk through the door in my house. It is Dickerson, who wastes no time in getting to the point. "Angela called Paul. According to him, she says that Doss is going to make a deal and testify against him."

"You better talk to Angela," I say, stalling, "and get the facts. I didn't tell her that. She's just worried that her friend Paul is going down." I have no idea how much Dick knows about their relationship. I doubt if Paul has told him the truth, but maybe he has by now.

"What I want to know, Gideon," Dick says harshly, "is whether your client is going to testify against Paul. Either he is or he isn't."

"I don't know," I reply, "and that's the truth. He may feel he has no alternative."

"He'll be perjuring himself," Dick says fiercely. "Paul may be many things, but he's not a murderer."

I have heard that too many times. "How in the fuck do you know, Dick?" I blast into the phone. "Unless I'm a total idiot, Paul has lied to you already about this case, so I wouldn't be so damn sure if I were you."

"What in the hell are you talking about?" he sputters.

I can't imagine that Paul hasn't admitted to him by now that he was having an affair with Angela. On the other hand, perhaps he has, and Dick merely wants to see if Angela's confession matches Dick's. Well, I'm not going to give him that satisfaction. He can talk to Angela if he wants. I've been humiliated enough already. "Dick," I say, knowing I am enraging him, "it's not up to me to figure out this case for you."

There is a deadly silence on the other end. "If you are suborning perjury in this case," Dick finally says, "I will spend the rest of my life seeing that you never practice law again. And if I hear of you talking to Paul again without my permission, you can be sure you'll be reported to the committee on professional conduct."

I feel my forehead grow warm. If Bledsoe goes through with his plan to implicate Paul and then a year from now begins to suffer from a guilty conscience, I know one person who will take him seriously. I wonder how close I have come to encouraging Doss to lie. A good lawyer could argue that I put the idea in his head because I wanted revenge against Paul. And Dick is definitely a good lawyer. "I think I'd spend some time on this case if I were you, Dick."

Dick sputters into the phone that I better tell him what Bledsoe is going to do. For the first time since I have known him, there is a sound of desperation in his voice. He knows that he didn't have time to take this case. He knows now that he will have to prepare for the worst, regardless of what I say. Finally, he concludes by saying, "Your mother would be ashamed of you, Gideon. I'm glad she's not here to watch how you're handling yourself."

I'm glad she isn't either, but I'm not about to admit it and give Dick that kind of satisfaction. He's such a holier-than-thou prick he makes me want to puke. Abruptly, I tell him I have to get off the phone and do some work, and hang up. To hell with the old fart.

At three o'clock the next afternoon I'm on the road to Bear

Creek. Judge Greer, who has a history of heart trouble, became sick on the bench and abruptly declared a mistrial, freeing me to focus on Doss's case. I'm headed straight for Oldham's Barbecue. I was out there a month ago and got nothing out of him, but maybe I didn't ask the right question. Henry Oldham is nothing like his nephew. A tall, light-colored elderly man with short white hair, he was a high school math teacher who, according to Doss, lost his job when the schools were first desegregated and then was hired back when blacks got control of the school board. He retired from teaching three years ago and worked out his arrangement with Paul. On my way to his restaurant, I pass the Cotton Boll, and suddenly it hits me that the one person who may put some things in perspective for me is an old gay man who never had much respect for my abilities. I have been out of synch for most of this case, and I don't know why. My recollection of what went on in Bear Creek when I was growing up doesn't seem to jibe with what others remember. Maybe Mr. Carpenter, who has spent his life on the outside looking in, can clue me in. I will stop by here as soon as I finish with Oldham.

Oldham's Barbecue is a nondescript whitish concrete block house out Highway 1 just inside Bear Creek's city limits. There are five vehicles parked in the gravel out front, and I realize I have arrived at the worst possible time to talk to him. Inside there are only six plain vanilla tables and metal chairs on a concrete floor. Most of Oldham's business is carry-out. Like last time, a black girl who surely isn't out of high school is at the counter handing over Styrofoam containers to a black customer, with two behind him. I remember that before Oldham was out back tending his cookers. I retrace my steps, go around the north side of the building, and almost run into Oldham, who is leaning up against the wall smoking a cigarette. The smell of barbecue is delicious. I tell him I realize he can't talk but a minute or two, but that it is important to his nephew's case. He gives me a look of scandalized distaste. Clearly, the last

thing he wants to do is be called as a witness. Throwing his cigarette into the grass beside him, he says, "I told you everything
I know last time."

Knowing I won't get much out of him, I ask the most important question first. "Mr. Oldham, all I want to know is whether
Paul Taylor had talked to you about retiring at any time or giving up your arrangement with him, either before or after Willie
Ting was murdered."

"Why do you want to know?" he grunts, irritably.

"All I can tell you is that it's important to your nephew's
case."

"Well, I don't remember right now," he says cagily.

I want to throttle the old man. "Doss can easily end up on
death row if you don't tell me what you know."

Mr. Oldham gives me a skeptical look. "You tell me why you
need this."

"I can't do that right now," I insist. "You know that I represent your nephew. All I'm looking for is the truth." This last
sentence comes out sounding hollow and trite. What am I looking for? I have felt so conflicted about this case I don't even
know.

As if the odor of hypocrisy is overpowering the smell of the
cooking meat, the older man frowns. "I gotta go help inside,"
he says abruptly, and wheels to his left inside a back door into
the building.

Frustrated, I stomp around to the front, get back in the
Blazer, and drive back toward the Cotton Boll, where I pull in
and give McKenzie an order for chicken fried steak, lima beans,
cole slaw, mashed potatoes, corn bread, and iced tea. Maybe I
will have a heart attack and die so I won't have to try this case.
I dawdle over my food and order coffee and a piece of pecan pie
for dessert. By 7:30 the last of his few customers has cleared
out, and Mr. Carpenter himself brings out a pot of coffee to
pour me a refill. "Gideon, you've never come by," he re-
proaches me, wiping his hands on a mostly clean apron.

I cut through the syrupy crust. It is wonderfully sweet and perfect with coffee. "I'd like to come by tonight," I say, watching him refill my cup, "if you're not too tired."

He gets up from the table. "I'll start locking up now," he says gloomily. "I won't have any more business tonight."

I had forgotten how early people in small towns eat at night. Fifteen minutes later I follow him to his house and realize I could almost close my eyes and get there, so familiar is my old neighborhood. Nothing in my memory is more vivid than a few select moments in my childhood. On nights like this if our homework was done, we played kick the can until bedtime. Though I can't see the honeysuckle, I can smell it. Inside he flips on lights, and tells me to have a seat while he disappears down a hall, presumably toward the bathroom.

I look around the room, curious about what I will find. I can't ever remember being here. Mother must have suspected he was homosexual and discouraged me from coming here. Since I was such a flop as a science student, he probably wasn't interested in me anyway. On his walls are reproductions of what I call "trick art." It looks like a bunch of white ducks flying one way, but if you stare at it long enough you realize a flock of black ducks is headed in the opposite direction. Only the baskets and stands of fresh flowers around the room indicate a sensibility that fits my idea of a gay man. His furniture is, I realize, probably a collection of antiques, though I'm not knowledgeable enough to know if any of the desks, tables, and chairs are simply junk or fine pieces of furniture. Knowing Mr. Carpenter, they're the real thing. "You want a beer?" he asks from the doorway. Even without his apron he still looks like a baker or delivery man in white pants and shirt. I nod, and he heads into his kitchen, leaving me to wonder again why he has stayed in Bear Creek. Surely he would feel more comfortable around others who are like him. But as soon as I think this, I realize (not for the first time in my life) that assumptions have always been my worst enemy.

When he returns with a beer for me, and a glass of what smells like sherry for himself, I ask him why he is still here. He sits down on a love seat across from me and takes off his shoes. "Too much standing for an old man," he says apologetically, before adding, "I was seventy-three when mother died at the age of ninety-five in the room behind you, and then it didn't seem to matter anymore." He points with his thumb over his shoulder. "I never was out of her sight except for two weeks every summer, but for some reason I couldn't stand being away from her. Don't ask me what that was all about," he says, warning me away from psychoanalyzing him. "It's too late for me to worry about. Most humans aren't capable of any more than playing out the hand genetics and our upbringing have dealt us. Look at the blacks around here. You wonder how they get out of bed. What could be more disheartening than knowing the people around you consider you genetically inferior? Did you read *The Bell Curve?*" he demands, his voice harsh and accusing as if he were back in the classroom.

I shift in my chair, trying to get comfortable. Too many buttons sticking into my rear. "I just remember reading something about it," I say. "It didn't really say anything new about I.Q., did it?"

Mr. Carpenter gives me a look that takes me back to my junior high days when I gave him an answer that revealed how limited my potential for understanding science was. "And nothing new will be said until they can quantify what goes on in a person's brain," he says in an imperious tone. "What is worthwhile is the authors' opinion about what this country is going to look like in the future. There's going to be a technological elite, and then a giant black underclass that's going to make the current racial situation look like a minor irritant. Nobody wants to face it. In my opinion, the Delta has already returned to pre–Civil War days, but without the slavery. The whites here who can afford it have their own schools, their own culture and entertainment, basically their own society. If they had their way, they'd close down the federal government except for an army that wouldn't venture off American territory. You think things are bad now? I'm glad I won't be alive to see what's coming."

I nod, thinking of Beverly's tirade. I'm afraid he'll go on all night on this subject if I let him. I ask how well he knew my physician grandfather. Without missing a beat, Mr. Carpenter assures me, as he did the morning Angela and I had breakfast at the Cotton Boll, that he was an intelligent man. "My mother was the one who really knew him. A fine man who worked himself to death. She said he was one of the leaders of the Klan around here after the First World War. Did you know that?"

I squint at this old man, who is beginning to seem crazier by the minute. "That can't possibly be right," I say, wondering if he is kidding me or even has my grandfathers confused. "He wasn't that type of person at all." Granddaddy Page may have been susceptible to that kind of racial violence, but my mother's father most certainly could not have been.

Mr. Carpenter grins broadly and slaps the back of the couch. "Don't get your nose too out of joint. If you knew your history after the First World War, you'd realize the Klan back in those days wasn't a redneck organization. They had thousands of members and elected their own people to the Legislature. Some of the best men in Arkansas were members. Lawyers, doctors, businessmen, planters. It was probably as much a reaction to the war as anything. Besides blacks, they were against Catholics, foreigners, and for keeping the country lily white and isolationist. Pat Buchanan would have fit right in."

"How do you know for sure my grandfather was a member?" I ask, furious at this information. He doesn't mention homosexuals, but I suspect they were on the enemy list, too. Clearly, this old man enjoys unsettling me. "Like I say, my mother was a great admirer of his. I can't prove he was, but look in a college yearbook from the times and you'll see it wasn't something a man was ashamed of."

He brings his mouth to his glass, but hardly touches the liquor in it. "You knew my mother pretty well, didn't you?" I ask, realizing now they were almost the same age.

He nods vigorously. "A Southern lady if there ever was one," he pronounces. "She shouldn't have ever married your father. She should have found someone with money who would have taken care of her all her life. That's what she expected to do."

This comment pisses me: my father couldn't help his mental illness. I don't want to shut him up, however. I ask, "What do you mean?"

Mr. Carpenter takes a tiny sip of sherry. "She never coped a single day after he died. She wasn't trained to make a living. If your daddy had left her rich, she could have managed, but the way I remember it," he says, slightly embarrassed, "she kind of went to pieces after he died."

I shift uneasily in my chair. I don't remember it that way at all. I was the one who had problems and ultimately had to be shipped off to Subiaco to get straightened out. "People took advantage of her," I contend. "Oscar Taylor foreclosed on the pharmacy."

Mr. Carpenter winces the way he did when I would give a wrong answer in class. "Well, I think he carried her for almost a year before he did anything. And then all I think he did was let her sign it back to him and didn't actually foreclose and go after any deficiency. That building stood vacant for a couple of years before he got anybody in there."

"I think you're wrong," I say, shaking my head. "She called him a son of a bitch when she got the letter telling her he was foreclosing."

Mr. Carpenter studies the reddish liquid in his glass. "See, I remember all that because your mother and I were friends. I liked her, but she kind of felt people owed her special treatment because her daddy was a doctor. The way I remember it, all she got was a letter from Oscar saying that since she couldn't sell it and was a whole year behind on the payments to sign it back over to him. She was angry, but I thought he had gone the extra mile. He didn't want to humiliate her by filing suit. Finally, she signed it back over, but she stayed mad at him."

It will be easy enough to check this out through John's abstract company. "Well, I remember the Taylors pretty much ostracizing us after my father died," I say. "I guess that's the reason."

The old man closes his eyes as if the sight of me hinders his memory. "It was a hard time for her, but she kind of did that to herself. She got real bitter. I think she felt like everybody was supposed to ignore her debts and got mad when they didn't. I was about the only friend she had left, and sometimes I think that was because she didn't owe me anything. She was in debt to people while she sent you off to Subiaco. That hacked some people off, too."

Though it is cool inside his house, I feel sweat dripping down my sides. Have I really misremembered so much of the past that none of it makes sense to me? What is making me feel out of synch is that I am realizing that I don't understand what I do remember about it. This old man has no ax to grind. "Were you around when Paul Taylor got my grandfather's remaining property by paying her taxes?"

Mr. Carpenter bobs his head up and down like a sparrow drinking from a pond. "I couldn't believe she would be so negligent. She showed me the notices afterward. She just couldn't believe anybody would do that to her. But if it hadn't been Paul, it would have been somebody else. She was kind of a lost soul by then. See, my theory is, your grandfather had overprotected her. It would have been okay if your dad had stayed healthy."

My mother, a lost soul? I feel guilt seeping into the room like carbon monoxide. I never thought of her that way. Now, I see that my father, until his drinking and schizophrenia destroyed him, was the stronger of the two. After he died, she hid her weaknesses behind a naive belief that nobody would dare hold her accountable for her life after all she had been through. Where was I? Where was Marty? She was off being a hippie, rebelling against the world, while I was off saving it in the Peace Corps. Were we so selfish we didn't see what was happening to her? "For some reason I always thought of my mother," I admit, almost dazed by these revelations, "as tough, even feisty."

"An act," Mr. Carpenter says, almost apologetically, as if he can smell my guilt. "She was scared to death beneath all that sarcasm."

"Did she begin to drink too much?" I ask, knowing the answer.

"More than she should have," he says, and actually sighs. "I should have helped her on that. Too many of us did drink too much, of course, and still do."

And certainly a fault that has carried over to her son. I put down the empty can, noticing that I have made small dents in it with my fingertips. I realize I came over here secretly hoping that he would tell me how wonderful my mother was, and how badly the Taylors exploited her. Instead, for the first time I realize how badly I neglected her.

As if he were back in class giving me time to answer, the silence fills the room as he waits for an explanation of my seeming inability to get a single detail right from my past in Bear Creek. Why should he be surprised? I've had thirty years to get it wrong. Sensing my humiliation, Mr. Carpenter asks, "How's the case going? I still can't believe Paul would be involved in a murder. But maybe so. Getting old doesn't make you get better."

"Is it true that he and Mae Terry are good friends?" I ask, ignoring his question as I put the beer can down on the coffee table in front of me.

A sardonic smile comes to Mr. Carpenter's face. "I think they are, but Mae is a lesbian. You knew that, didn't you?"

I squint hard at the old man in the dim light, wondering if he is pulling my leg. "You're kidding!"

Mr. Carpenter finally takes a healthy sip of his sherry. "The girl who moved here from North Carolina and has taken care of Mae is her friend," he says discreetly. "There's no doubt about that in my mind."

What a dupe I've been. So Angela constructed that scenario to keep me from suspecting she had an affair with Paul. My undershirt feels clammy, and I wonder whether Mr. Carpenter can smell my fear and embarrassment. What else has she been lying to me about? The chair I'm sitting in has begun to pinch every part of my hips. "I need to get on the road, Mr. Carpenter," I say, and get to my feet. "I appreciate the beer."

The old man looks crushed. Yet what does he expect? "Your mother was a fine woman. The circumstances were just too much for her. Women are better prepared today to take care of themselves."

"I'm not upset," I lie, edging toward the door. "I just need to get on the road. We'll get together again."

I head out into the soft spring air, thinking that tomorrow I will call my sister for a long overdue chat. Marty has long warned me away from eastern Arkansas. I used to think it had to do with my grandfather's liaison with a black woman. Now I'm not so sure. If I'm not capable of understanding my past, what chance do I have to understand what is going on over here now? I look at my watch. It is only 9:30, and desperate to do something that will help my client, I drive by Darla Tate's house and see the glow of her television through the window.

Darla is Doss's last hope, and I go up to the door and boldly knock on her door as if I am a late-arriving dinner guest.

Barefoot and in a pair of brown shorts, she opens the door with a can of Miller Lite in her hand. I apologize for not calling, but she invites me in with a shy smile that suggests to me that she hopes I might be staying for a while. If she knew that inside my shirt I was wringing wet, she might not be so eager.

Embarrassed anew by her obvious hopefulness, I sit down (there is no evidence of her boys), decline a beer, and get right to the point. "Now that you've had time to think about it, is it possible you might have mistaken," I ask, trying not to sound as if I am too desperate, "someone else's voice for Doss's that day when you were in the bathroom?"

The sad little smile on her face is not reassuring. "I've been reconstructing that moment and comparing others' voices with his," she says, carefully, "and now I'm more convinced than ever it was Doss. I'm really sorry."

Shit! I feel depression clamping down like a fist on my will to think. "You're absolutely sure?" I ask.

"Don't be mad at me, Gideon," she says, her tone becoming anxious. "You wouldn't want me to lie, would you?"

"No," I say, telling myself not to be angry at her. "I just thought you weren't so sure." Why should I be pissed? She is merely confirming what Doss has admitted. Of course, Doss may have been calling someone else, not Paul.

"I didn't want to," she says, her voice wistful. You don't score points with a man you would like to ask you out by convicting his client.

"It's okay," I say. "If that's what you think, you have to say it."

Her eyes follow mine to her muscular legs, and she awkwardly covers her thighs with her large, rough hands. "Are you absolutely sure Muddy didn't drive back over and murder Willie?" she asks. "I thought I had solved the case for you." There is self-mockery in her voice. She knows I'm not interested in her as a woman; yet I know the feeling. False hopes are among the last things we give up.

My heart no longer in it, I ask how the plant is doing, and she says that Eddie appears finally to be getting a grip on the costs that were eating the plant up. Once the trial is over, things should settle down and get back to normal. Life goes on, her manner suggests. I leave after a few more minutes, thinking that is easy for Darla to believe. She isn't going to have to cross-examine her lover about her affair with a murder defendant. Knowing this case is going down the tubes, I drive back to Blackwell County. Riding through the interminable blackness, I wonder why I thought I knew what I was doing when I took this case. A simple matter of hubris? But arising from what? Was it that Southern white male arrogance that kicked in the moment my mother gazed on me at birth and assumed she would die happy? As I swerve unsuccessfully to avoid the remains of a skunk, it occurs to me that Paul Taylor and I may not be much different.

Seventeen

THE NEXT DAY I drive out to Hutto, on the western edge of Blackwell County, to pay a visit to my sister's clothing consignment store, which she, deaf to pleas of political correctness, has named the Wigwam. Hutto, a small town growing bigger almost daily due to white flight from the county's metropolitan areas, is so unlike Bear Creek it is hard to imagine they are in the same country. With its multiple car dealerships, real estate offices, and bustling retail downtown area, Hutto displays a business vitality any chamber of commerce president would be proud to pitch to a visiting Yankee industrialist seeking to squeeze labor costs.

A former sixties hippie turned nineties entrepreneur, my sister has cashed in on the conservation movement in clothing: I understand it's thought smart now in some circles to wear a second-hand skirt. Our mother must be turning over in her grave. Marty, I'm told by a clerk who accepts my word that I'm her brother, is in the back, and I'm pointed to a door in the rear of the store marked PRIVATE. I knock, and hear my older sister's voice commanding me to come in.

I open the door and find her behind a desk hunched over a computer, wearing dollar-store reading glasses identical to my own and an old-fashioned eyeshade that makes her look like a clerk out of a Charles Dickens novel. Surrounded by papers and what I figure are boxes of clothes, her work area is as messy as Dan's. "Gideon, aren't you doing your Christmas shopping," she asks, without missing a beat, "a little early this year?"

I smile, never having been known as much of a shopper. Despite pledges to get together more often, we haven't seen each other since Christmas. "How's Woogie?" I answer, inquiring about my old dog who was exiled to Hutto. With Sarah due home for the summer in a day or so, and with me living in a new neighborhood, Woogie can make a fresh start. It doesn't appear that Amy is anxious to return Jessie, despite her promise to do so.

"King of the road," my sister says, leaning back in her chair. "He's a roamer, but that's okay. You want him back?"

"Not today," I say. "You got a minute?"

Not too long ago, Marty would have rolled her eyes and groaned aloud at this imposition. Now, happily married for the first time in four or possibly five tries, she has mellowed just a bit. "Love trouble, job trouble, or Sarah?" she asks. We never seem to talk unless I have a problem.

"Just more family history," I say, taking a seat on a metal folding chair she points out for me.

"Not another nigger in the woodpile?" she says, grimacing. Last year she had counseled me unsuccessfully to ignore the allegations concerning our paternal grandfather's sexual exploits.

"Not yet," I say, knowing if I wanted to aggravate her I could tell her Mr. Carpenter's story about our maternal grandfather being in the KKK. Not that it would really bother Marty, whose contractor husband is so right-wing he thinks Phil Gramm is another Fidel Castro. "What do you remember about the Taylors when we were growing up?"

Marty pushes up the sleeves of her gray sweatshirt. A true native of the Delta, it is never warm enough for her. "That I would have liked to have gotten in Paul's pants if he had been a little older," she says, smirking at me. "He was a cutie. Remember when he used to stay at our house. I kept hoping he would come try to crawl in bed with me. Of course I was so fat back then he couldn't have gotten in my bed with me if he had wanted to."

My sister will say anything, and I laugh, despite myself. Since her marriage, Marty has slimmed down for the first time in her life. She has claimed she was a virgin against her will until she was twenty. "After Daddy died," I ask, trying to sound nonchalant, "didn't the Taylors drop Mother socially? Paul quit coming over; she didn't go out to Riverdale."

Marty frowns and shakes her head. "Don't you remember? After Daddy died, she went to hell," she says, "which was understandable for a while. But Mother thought she was a Southern belle. When things got tough, instead of climbing down off her high horse, and figuring out how to survive like the rest of the human race, she stayed in her bedroom and felt sorry for herself. It didn't do any of us any good: If Oscar hadn't loaned her the money to send you to Subiaco, which she never paid back, you would have turned into a little thug. I was a mess, too, but that was mostly my own fault."

I can't believe my ears. "The Taylors paid for me to go to Subiaco?" I yelp. "How come you knew and I didn't?"

"You probably did, but you wouldn't be a lawyer if you didn't believe your own shit smelled good. But maybe you didn't. You were spoiled rotten from the word go. Mother always acted like somebody had told her that you were supposed to be the next Jesus Christ," Marty needles me. "She was bitter as hell in those days. She went into a snit that lasted the rest of her life when Oscar finally wanted the building back. When he offered to lend her the money to send you off to a private school, she acted as if it was the least he could do."

Like a balky window being wrenched open an inch to try to catch a breeze, my brain yields a fragment of a conversation with Mother about how Oscar was probably going to charge her interest. Until now all I have allowed myself to remember was her resentment, which became my own. Why have I had such a need to rearrange our past? I no longer really trust anything I think I know. "You remember Paul got granddaddy's land just by paying off the taxes?" I ask, hoping to confirm at least one fact.

"Sure," Marty says, pushing a button on her computer. "But that was only fair. They had gotten fed up with Mother by then. She really let things go after Daddy died. If you recall, I was off in San Francisco part of that time being Bear Creek's only contribution to the drug and macrame industry. I suspect the Taylors felt they were entitled to something by then. I'd be surprised if Mother ever paid a penny back on the loan."

I feel dazed by what I am learning and shift uneasily in the hard chair. Am I so out of touch with reality that I don't even know the difference between right and wrong? "You don't remember the Taylors as being predators?"

My sister laughs. "Who have you been talking to, Gideon? Are you going to give me a sermon on slavery? Sure, they owned slaves, and when the Civil War was over, they exploited the blacks and the white sharecroppers. Then, when they couldn't do that any longer, they kicked them both off the land and farmed with machines. While the rest of the country was slaughtering Indians and herding them onto reservations, Southerners were doing their thing with blacks. But if it weren't for people like the Taylors, you wouldn't have the United States.

"Anybody with drive in this country is eventually seen as evil by people like you because humanity doesn't come in equal little packets like Sweet'n Low. Fortunately, this country doesn't reward the weak, stupid, or lazy. It protects them too much, but the truth is, we're talking about subsistence when we're talking about welfare, so it's a silly debate as far as I'm concerned. If a welfare system is the price of free enterprise, I don't really care. Just keep giving people like me and my husband a chance to compete economically, and the United States can afford people like you."

Her face is flushed, and I'm glad there isn't an American flag in the room, or she would probably stand up and salute it. Though she has been on this kick for a couple of years now, it is hard to believe this is my old anti-establishment "give peace a chance" sister talking. "Who are people like me?" I ask, my blood beginning to boil. This right-wing drivel makes me sick.

"Give it a rest, Gideon," my sister says, her voice suddenly weary. "You know you're a lot like Mother. It's been seven years now, but you never made yourself get over Rosa's death. She was supposed to live forever or at least until you keeled over at the age of a hundred with her at your bedside drooling over you. Since she died, about half the time you've gone around acting like an arrogant shit because somebody cut off your lifetime happiness guarantee."

I feel my scalp on fire. The truth of what she is saying radiates through my brain. Maybe this is why I have gotten things so wrong in Bear Creek. Everything I thought I remembered has been filtered through my own self-pity. Poor me, poor Mother. Death busted both our bubbles. But I'll be damned if I'll give Marty the satisfaction of knowing she is right. "Speaking of people like me," I say, maliciously, "did you know Paul Taylor has been charged with capital felony murder in Bear Creek and goes on trial week after next?"

My sister's eyes widen. "Paul killed somebody? Are you his lawyer?"

"Not in a million years." I should have called Marty two months ago, but I see now I didn't want to have this conversation. I wanted to believe we were victims. We may never talk about it, but Marty and I both know we could have looked after our mother better. Instead, we both got the hell out of Dodge. I realize now that guilt is one of the reasons I've worked so hard to scapegoat the Taylors. I demonized Paul because I didn't want to have to deal with the fact that things were a mess at home, and I coped with them, as I always have, by leaving.

For the next twenty minutes I give Marty a sanitized version of my participation in the events in our old hometown for the last two months, omitting my own motives and Angela's confessions and my involvement with her. Even without them, there is plenty of juice to the story, and, as I knew she would be, Marty is fascinated. "Why didn't you call me?" she demands when one of her clerks interrupts us to say it is time for her break.

"You've been too busy making money," I say, getting in a final jab. Despite my attitude, she wants me to come out for dinner so I can fill in the details, but I'm not ready for the third degree. Marty can smell a rat as well as anybody, and I'm not ready to spill my guts to her. "I'm too busy now. I'll come out after the trial," I say, standing up, "and tell you all about it."

"You don't think Paul did it, do you?" she asks, darkening the screen on her computer.

"I wouldn't be too sure," I say, still smarting from her speech. Actually, right now I don't, but I'm too irritated with this entire conversation to make her feel better. "Paul isn't exactly a knight in shining armor."

"Neither are you," my sister says dryly, "but I doubt if you've turned into a killer."

Knowing I'm better off letting Marty have the last word, I leave. She would skewer me for my behavior in this case if she had the chance. If we talk more today, we will end up fighting.

At home all I can think about is how badly I've screwed up Doss's defense. I have no idea what is going on in Bear Creek and haven't since the moment I took the case. Sitting in the living room and staring out the window, I feel self-hatred begin to eat at me like an ulcer. Lawyers like me are a danger to the profession. This entire attempt to go home again has been a disaster, and I have only myself to blame. At least now I know why.

In desperation I dial Mrs. Ting's number to see if she will let me talk to her again. Surely, knowing Willie best, she knows more than she has told any of the investigators. My call, however, is answered by Connie, who is as cold as she was when I first went out there. "Gideon, what is going on? Tommy says you haven't found anything. Are you going to argue that my mother murdered my father or not?"

Every couple of weeks I've called Tommy and reported to

him. Each conversation is shorter than the last. "I can't imagine even suggesting it to a jury," I say, not quite answering her. "As frail as she is, it would be ludicrous."

"Nobody cares about my mother or what this is doing to our family," Connie says, angrily.

"That's not true," I say. But it is. The Tings have been forgotten.

"Bullshit! My mother spent her whole life watching my father walking a tightrope between whites and blacks and look what it got him! You must think we are idiots! I know my father wasn't respected and neither was my mother."

"I don't agree, Connie," I say, trying to mollify her. "We all knew how hard your family worked. People did respect y'all."

Connie ignores me. "They weren't treated the same. And you know why! They weren't white. I don't care how much Tommy pretends things were different. No matter how much we achieved, we were never really a part of Bear Creek. Nobody treated them or Tommy and me as social equals. I never had a date. Neither did Tommy. Not that they would have let us go, but we weren't asked either. My parents weren't invited to any white person's parties. To their credit, they wanted to be Chinese, while Tommy and I wanted to be white. It didn't work for us, whatever Tommy says."

This torrent of emotion is as unexpected as her coldness had been. I never saw her or Tommy angry. I ask, "Didn't you marry a white guy?"

"And it didn't work," Connie says. "Once his family figured out what our status was in Bear Creek—they were from Memphis—I was never accepted. I remember my future mother-in-law's expression the first time she saw Ting's Market. She nearly fainted. In retrospect I'm amazed Alan had the nerve to go through with the wedding. He never had any courage after that."

I slump against the wall in the living room, wondering frantically how to salvage this conversation. "Weren't you a physicist by then?" I ask.

"I could have been the Empress of China at that point, and it wouldn't have mattered," she says sarcastically. "His family had old Memphis money, and their son had scandalized them. My parents weren't happy with my choice either. I was expected to marry a nice Chinese boy from Mississippi."

Connie and I were in the same boat. "Rosa, my wife," I say, "was about a quarter black. As soon as people figured that out, she didn't have a chance."

"I remember the gossip," Connie says, her voice less heated. "You were kind of a hero to me when you came back from the Peace Corps."

I had no idea. "You must have still been in college," I say, trying to remember when the last time was I saw her.

"I had just graduated and was home for a couple of weeks," she says. "You were the talk of the town. Of course, she was described to me as being a lot darker than she was."

Back then Connie must have viewed my marriage to Rosa as a hopeful sign that things were changing. And, in fact, they have, to a point. "My sister told me later that one of the rumors going around was that I had married a pygmy from a Brazilian rain forest."

Connie laughs for the first time. "Bear Creek would have accepted a pygmy as long as she could pass for white."

I look out my window into the park across the road. I've understood almost nothing until the last few days. I had an image of my family and I filtered out any memories of Bear Creek in a way that didn't agree with that image. Tommy has been wearing blinders, too. "It must have been harder for your parents than it was for you and Tommy."

"It's all relative," Connie instructs me. "They made money here and saved almost every penny. It allowed us kids to escape."

I'm curious to know what her life is like now, but I'm afraid to ask. Though she doesn't seem quite as hostile as she did when we first began talking, there is still an edge to her voice that she doesn't bother to hide. Blacks, not whites, have been the majority in each place she lived. Though for years they have been saying they were invisible to us, I've never admitted to what extent both races were merely background noise. "If your mother can think of anything that could help find who your father's murderer is," I plead with her, "let me know, please. The only person at the plant who's really been cooperative is the secretary, Darla Tate. Though she hasn't actually helped his case any, she says your father liked Doss, and he liked your father."

"That doesn't prove anything," Connie says. "I'll talk to Mother if you'll promise not to accuse her of my father's murder."

It hardly seems as if I'm giving anything away—or getting anything, for that matter. Bonner has never considered her a suspect, and he went all through the house the night of the murder. "I promise," I say, knowing Dick will suggest it to the jury if I don't.

Connie hangs up, and I curse myself, knowing how badly I have served my client in this case. I should never have taken it. I couldn't have screwed up any more than if I had stayed drunk for the last couple of months. The only thing I'm convinced of is that Doss is simply trying to save his skin, and I haven't given him any reason to act otherwise.

"You can't let Doss plead guilty," I tell Latrice Bledsoe four days before her husband's trial begins. She has warily invited me into her house as if I were an investigator instead of her husband's defense attorney. She is seated on a brown tattered couch across from me. "You know he didn't kill Willie."

"He's saying now he did," she says, holding a two-year-old on her lap. With no income coming in, she babysits during the day before she works the evening shift at the 7-Eleven. The child's eyes are enormous brown pools. She leans back against Latrice and stares at me as if I am the first white person she has ever seen.

"I don't really believe that and neither do you," I say urgently. "Almost the first words out of your mouth when I met

249

you were something like, 'I know my husband and he's not a killer.'"

"I don't want him to die," she says, keeping her voice even, but unable to keep tears from sliding down her cheeks.

I lean forward on my knees and argue, "Take away his explanation that Paul Taylor was going to give him Oldham's Barbecue and there is absolutely no motive. Half a dozen witnesses, including Mrs. Ting, will have to testify that Willie liked Doss, and Doss liked Willie. Without Doss's testimony there is hardly any evidence of any plan for Doss to be paid to kill him."

The child, whose name is Tisha, is perhaps frightened by my tone, and puts her thumb in her mouth while Latrice reminds me, "Doss says you told him once a jury doesn't need a motive to convict."

I, of course, have not been honest with Latrice or her husband about why I took this case. I am responsible for Doss winding up in this position. Whether I've actually said the words or not, I've wanted him to do exactly what he is doing. "You have to convince Doss that he simply has to trust the system," I argue. "I think he can persuade a jury he didn't kill Willie. This isn't going to be a lynch mob. There'll be blacks on the jury, and no Chinese."

Latrice pats Tisha for comfort. "How do you know he didn't kill him?" she whispers. "You can't be for sure. And neither can a jury. There's gonna be a black sheriff and a black prosecutor sayin' he did, and there're a lot of black people who are ready to believe the worst about ourselves if it's black people doing the accusing."

I watch Tisha as she begins to fidget on Latrice's lap. "Before he can be convicted, twelve people have to believe that Doss is capable of killing someone. If he can convince people he came here, and stayed, he won't be convicted. No one is going to testify they saw him. I believed him the first time he told me he didn't do it. Your marriage won't survive him going to prison, no matter what you think now. You're selling him short."

I can see Latrice wavering. "He won't do me any good dead," she says, but there is no conviction in her voice. "Can you promise you'll get him off?"

"Even if he is convicted," I temporize, "I can't imagine any jury will give Doss the death penalty unless they think he was a paid killer." But even as I say this, I remember that Darla Tate, despite her testimony that there was a good relationship between Willie and Doss, will make a strong, if reluctant, witness, for the prosecution. If the jury wants to, they can simply believe he was hired by someone else.

"You haven't answered my question," Latrice says.

I feel my face flush with shame. Under the circumstances, I can't conceal my own bad motives any longer and admit, "Initially, the reason I took your husband's case was that I wanted to see Paul Taylor convicted. Because of some things I thought he did to my family years ago, I wasn't at all surprised he was charged, and my thinking was originally that Doss might be guilty, and if he could plead to a lesser charge in exchange for his testimony, I would have done my job and gotten to see Paul Taylor paid back at the same time. But now I think the only reason Doss wants to implicate Paul is that he's afraid."

Latrice gives me a hard stare. "So you were ready to sell him out?"

I feel like a moth being pinned to the wall. "Not sell him out," I say, unable to meet her gaze. "I just started off with a different agenda." Is that what it was? What words we lawyers use! It was a vendetta, pure and simple.

"Lucy Cunningham said you were pretty much like nearly every other white man she had met—out for yourself," Latrice says, her voice resigned, "but that you'd probably do a good job eventually."

I shrug, not having the heart any longer to defend myself. I've managed to accomplish nothing here while I waited, hoping Paul would shoot himself in the foot sooner or later. And somewhere in the back of my mind, I've assumed my client's testimony could make it happen if need be. "I'll do my best," I say, not about to use the past tense.

Latrice draws air into her lungs and then exhales, rocking the child gently against her. "I'll talk to Doss," she agrees finally. "He's okay until he gets to feeling pressure, then he sometimes panics."

Welcome to the club, I think but don't say. I thank her and leave before she can change her mind. I want to get out of this place in a hurry.

Eighteen

"LADIES AND GENTLEMEN," Melvin Butterfield, resplendent in dark blue pinstripes, begins his opening statement to the jury, "the state of Arkansas will prove that on last September twenty-third, between the hours of two and four P.M., Mr. Willie Ting, owner of Southern Pride Meats, was murdered in cold blood at his plant by the defendant Doss Bledsoe. Further, the state will show that Doss Bledsoe, who worked in Mr. Ting's plant, was hired to commit this murder by the defendant Paul Taylor. . . ."

What Latrice said to convince her husband to go to trial, I may never know. As I listen to Butterfield, I lean back in my seat and watch the faces of the jury. Six blacks and six whites. Dick struck blacks as fast as he could, and I struck whites, unable to shed my belief that blacks will be less likely to convict Doss. The whites on the jury, each over forty, are from all over the county; only two are actually from Bear Creek. None of the individuals selected admit to knowing Paul Taylor other than casually. On voir dire Dick asked prospective jurors if anyone had applied for loans during the years Paul was on Farmer's State Bank's board of directors. When one old man from Rondo raised his hand, Dick didn't run the risk of asking him if he got the loan, but struck him after conferring with Paul, who has been whispering in his ear all morning. Yet if whites or blacks on the jury harbor any buried resentments toward his wealth, no one has admitted it. Judge Johnson, far from tilting in favor of Butterfield, allowed both Dick and me latitude in our questioning of prospective jurors. From the way Johnson has handled the proceedings and our pretrial motions, he seems pissed at Butterfield, as if a promise somewhere along the line has not been fulfilled. I glance up at the judge, and he has his nose stuck up in the air like a man avoiding a bad smell.

I look over at Dick, who is doodling on a pad as he listens to Butterfield. Knowing now he can't trust me, Dick hasn't spoken to me in a week except to call me to discuss the order of our opening statements. Having already decided to say as little as possible, I have agreed to go second. If I were absolutely sure that Butterfield wouldn't offer Doss a new deal in the middle of the trial and equally certain that Doss wouldn't take it, I would have no qualms about telling the jury that Doss was going to deny there had been a conspiracy between him and Paul, but at this point I'm going to play things as close to the vest as possible.

While Butterfield briefly explains what the testimony of the FBI chemist will involve, I allow myself to think of the look on Angela's face while she was being sworn in and led off to the witness room. She had the sad, resigned expression of someone who knows her world is about to come crashing down on her head and knows there's nothing she can do about it. She never even looked in my direction. How can I love a woman I don't fully trust? Easy. Just watching the back of her head while she raised her right hand to take the oath made me wonder if romantic love between two people is programmed into the genes just like eye color.

After finishing his summary of the case against Doss, Butterfield then turns from the lectern and faces Paul, whom Dick has seated to his right so the jury can watch him. "Now, the state doesn't believe for a moment that Doss Bledsoe acted alone; we believe Bledsoe was hired by Paul Taylor," Butterfield says, pointing his finger at Paul, and his voice rising, "because he wanted to buy Southern Pride Meats from Willie Ting and got turned down because Mr. Ting didn't want to sell his very profitable business to someone who wasn't Chinese. And when Willie Ting refused for the second time, the defendant Paul Taylor threatened to kill him." A silence of perhaps ten seconds elapses as Butterfield stares hard at Paul, finally turns back to the jury, and continues. "How do we know Paul Taylor threatened to kill him? Well, the fact is, Mr. Ting was so frightened by Paul Taylor that he made a tape of the conversation, and you will hear it for yourselves. Now, those of us in the criminal justice system fervently wish that Mr. Ting had given us this tape as soon as the threat was made—because if he had, he just might be alive today."

Butterfield's voice drops as if he is truly experiencing regret. He looks down at his hands gripping the sides of the podium and resumes forcefully, "But that wasn't his way. His widow, Mrs. Doris Ting, will tell you that her husband always preferred to keep a low profile in the community and spend his free time with his family. He did tell her, however, that if anything happened to him she should tell her son Tommy about the tape. Well, after Mrs. Ting found her husband's body in the plant that horrific afternoon, she, as instructed, told Tommy Ting, who lives in Washington, D.C., about the tape, and he immediately called the sheriff, and as I have said, you will hear it in the course of the trial. . . ."

Doss, who has been provided a cheap black suit by Latrice that doesn't take into account his recent weight loss, stirs restlessly beside me. He knows as well as I do that the jury is eating this stuff up. What I fear is that even if the jury doesn't think there is enough evidence to link Paul, Butterfield will have established a motive by the time he is finished. When Butterfield tells the jury that Darla Tate will testify she overheard Doss talking to someone about money, it is clear he is laying the groundwork for his closing argument that even if the jury doesn't convict Paul, it doesn't mean they have to come back empty-handed.

As expected, Butterfield has a harder time talking about Paul's involvement once he gets past the tape. "You will learn that Paul Taylor employed Doss Bledsoe for years as a delivery man at one of his stores . . ." he says, explaining the arrangement Paul had with Henry Oldham, who will testify that in August of last year, one month before the murder, Paul had told him he thought he should retire in another year. Butterfield also tells the jury he will prove that Doss has lied about how many times he was seen talking to Paul, a discrepancy that I, and surely Dick, will attribute to nothing more than lapses in memory. Even a jury made up entirely of former prosecutors would have to conclude that without Doss's testimony, there is no compelling evidence that Paul hired him to murder Willie. As the evidence comes in against Doss, the pressure will mount, and I won't be entirely surprised if by this time tomorrow, Doss will be wanting to sing a song I have heard once before.

I get up to make my opening argument, uncertain about the best place to begin. Butterfield has been talking close to an hour, and I don't want to be up here nearly that long, but I want to do more than just wave to the jury and then sit down. "The evidence will show, ladies and gentlemen," I say, when I reach the podium, "that anyone working in Southern Pride Meats that day knew, or could easily have found out, where Doss stored his knife on the kill floor every night. And the evidence will show that everyone in the plant knew or could easily have known that it was his habit to go straight home after work, fix himself lunch, drink a beer, and then take a nap. Everyone in the plant knew or could easily have known that Latrice, his wife, was at that time working the day shift at the 7-Eleven in Bear Creek, because at the plant everybody knew everybody else's business. You see, ladies and gentlemen," I say, coming around the lectern to the front of the jury rail, "the testimony will be that Doss Bledsoe was the type of employee who never missed a day's work and gave a hundred percent on the job he had held for the last five years. You're going to hear at least six plant employees say that Doss Bledsoe genuinely respected Willie Ting as a boss, and Darla Tate, the plant secretary, will testify that Willie Ting thought Doss Bledsoe was a model employee because he came to work every single day and did his job as well as it could be done. What the evidence is going to show is that Doss Bledsoe," I say, and turn and point to him, "was as predictable as a Timex watch. He did the same things, at the same time, in the same way every day for five years. The fact is, there will be no physical evidence at all linking him to Willie Ting. Absolutely nothing! No hair or fiber, no trace of skin or fingernails, no bloody clothing. At the end of this trial there will be nothing that links Doss Bledsoe to this murder except his knife, and everybody in the plant knew or could have known exactly where he kept it."

I turn back to the jury and focus on Emma Parsons, an attractive black schoolteacher in her thirties, whom Doss has said might be sympathetic to him. "And every person who testifies in this trial will say they know Doss either by reputation or personally as a family man who was as stable, reliable, and dependable as any man or woman in Bear Creek."

I walk back around to the podium, not at all satisfied by the cold expression on Emma Parsons's face. If she is sympathetic to Doss, she has a funny way of showing it. "You see, obviously my theory is that someone in the plant framed Doss Bledsoe because he or she knew that he wouldn't have an alibi. That person or persons knew he was going to be by himself between the hours of two and four; that person or persons knew every worker's routine, what they did after getting off work and who they did it with, so Doss was the perfect setup, because he isn't going to be able to produce a single person to say where he was between two and four in the afternoon on September twenty-third. He will tell you that he was at home by himself as he always was."

I come back around the podium and place my hands in the center of the rail, wondering how many of these jurors already have their minds made up. Four of the whites on the jury and three of the blacks have their arms tightly folded across their chests, not a good sign. They are waiting for me to name a suspect. It is time to oblige them. "So who could have done it? Well, the undisputed evidence will be that an undocumented alien from Mexico with forged papers by the name of Jorge Arrazola, who had been working at the plant for six months, fled Bear Creek two days after Mr. Ting's murder and hasn't been seen since. The sheriff is going to admit to you that nobody in law enforcement, despite all the fancy communication systems and cooperative agreements among law enforcement agencies on a local, national, and international level, has a clue where Jorge Arrazola disappeared to. Mr. Alvaro Ruiz, who works at the plant and whom Jorge Arrazola lived with, will tell you that Jorge Arrazola dropped him off that afternoon at his second job after they left the plant at two and said he was going fishing. Mr. Ruiz will tell you he didn't see Jorge Arrazola again until six that night, when he picked him up after work. Then two days later Arrazola fixed up a truck Mr. Ruiz had given him and took off without a word to him. Folks, I think by the time the trial is over, the evidence will suggest to you that Mr. Ting's murderer is long gone from Bear Creek."

I step back a few inches from the railing and put my hands in my pockets, telling myself not to jiggle my change, a bad habit I've gotten into lately. To keep the possibility of a deal alive during the trial, I don't tell the jury that there is nothing but the most marginal circumstantial evidence of a conspiracy between Doss and Paul. Dick will hammer that home better than I can. Focusing on a black retired farmer in his sixties, I say, "If we're looking for a motive for Jorge Arrazola, ladies and gentlemen, forty-eight hours is about forty-seven more than he needed to collect payment from whomever may have wanted Mr. Ting dead. . . ."

I wind up by telling the jury that even if there were no other suspects in the case, they can decide the case on the issue of the credibility of Doss Bledsoe. I walk over to the witness chair and point at it. "When the time comes for us to present our defense, Doss Bledsoe is going to sit right here and look you in the eye and tell you he left the plant when everyone else did and didn't leave his house again that afternoon. Regardless of what Mr. Butterfield said or didn't say about the evidence in this case, Mr. Bledsoe's testimony is evidence, too. If you believe him, you must acquit him."

I sit down, having no idea what effect I have had on this jury. At no time did I get a feel that I was getting through to a soul. I fear that Woodrow Bonner's reputation for competence and integrity will decide this case. If he thinks Doss did it, that might well be good enough.

Dick practically sprints to the jury rail. Practically on top of the jury as he leans into the railing, he lectures them sternly, "Ladies and gentlemen, let's get one thing clear: If Mr. Butterfield doesn't introduce this tape he has talked about, you can be sure I will, because the tape you will hear in this trial no more makes Paul Taylor out to be a potential murderer than the man in the moon. In fact, the tape to be introduced in this courtroom will simply show that Paul Taylor, a farmer and businessman who has lived in this county his entire life, wanted to buy a meat-packing plant that he knew was a profitable business and made what he considered was a fair offer for it. Far from being a threat, the tape will show he merely pointed out that Willie Ting wasn't going to be around forever, with the implication being he ought to sell now to someone with a realistic offer."

When he has said this, he cups his right fist and taps it against his chin. "Mr. Taylor is hardly going to deny that years ago he hired Doss Bledsoe as a deliveryman in one of his stores; he will gladly admit that he talked to Henry Oldham about when he was going to retire; he will happily confess that he may have talked to Doss Bledsoe a few times when he went out to Oldham's to buy some barbecue and to see how his business was going. But Mr. Butterfield has virtually admitted there's not going to be a shred of direct evidence that Paul Taylor hired anyone, including Doss Bledsoe, to murder Willie Ting; there will

be no evidence of a conversation, no evidence of money changing hands, no evidence of a promise made."

Like a preacher at a revival, Dick spreads his hands and then
slowly brings them together as he says, "The evidence, ladies
and gentlemen, consists of an ambiguous tape and a few coinci-
dental and harmless meetings. I could call this so-called evidence a lot of things," Dick thunders, "and, believe me, I will at
the end of this trial when I am permitted to argue the case, but
whatever it is, it isn't enough to put a man in jail for five minutes. . . ."

As Butterfield jumps to his feet and has his objection sus-
tained that Paul has already begun to argue, I realize that Dick
has not told the jury that Paul will take the stand and deny that
he paid to have Willie killed. For the first time in a week I consider the possibility that Paul is guilty, and that Doss was telling
the truth. If Paul has confessed to Dick, he can't knowingly let
Paul commit perjury, and Dick, despite what I think of him, has
too much integrity to let him. And minutes later, when Dick sits
down, I have no idea whether Paul, who surely wants to pro-
claim his innocence, will do so from the witness box.

After lunch, Butterfield begins to put on his case with the FBI
expert, who testifies first because she must leave immediately
for another trial in Phoenix. As she explains why there is no
doubt in her mind that the blood on Doss's knife is Willie's, it's
hard not to be impressed. This same agent, a Ph.D. chemist—
and a coolly attractive blonde—testified in a murder trial in Little Rock a couple of years ago, and better lawyers than I am
couldn't lay a glove on her. I am content on cross-examination
to emphasize the obvious when she is through: no tests she has
performed prove that it was Doss who used the knife to kill
Willie. It is, of course, a dumb question to ask her, but it gets my
point across.

The rest of the day is taken up by testimony from personnel
from the state medical examiner's office and the sheriff's office,
whom Butterfield puts through their paces as if they have been
preparing for this trial for a lifetime. They leave little to quibble

about: The crime scene was properly secured, preserved until the investigation was completed; no gaps exist in the chain of custody of the blood and knife; the victim may have lived for as little as two minutes after his throat was slashed from left to right two inches in width. The wound on his neck is consistent with the Koch blade which, as the plant foreman told us, actually cuts like a pair of scissors. The only fingerprints on the handle are my client's. Butterfield, with Johnson's permission, passes the knife to the jury and not a single member can resist touching the blade to test its sharpness.

Butterfield produces the tape for Bonner to identify and is allowed to introduce it into evidence. Though this moment has been long anticipated, it is something of an anticlimax when Bonner plays it for the jury. Perhaps I have heard it too many times by now, and while the members of the jury all seem interested, some raise their eyebrows when it is finished as if they are wondering what the fuss has been all about.

Bonner tells the jury that he investigated every employee's whereabouts between two and four and that the only suspect is Doss Bledsoe. By the time he describes what he has done, it is five o'clock, and we are through for the day. The spectators, about equally divided between blacks and whites, clear the courtroom rapidly. Outside, it is a perfect spring day and anybody in his right mind wants to get outside. The tension has risen each hour, and everyone seems eager to get away from each other. Before he is led off to be taken back to Brickeys, Doss whispers, "It looks bad, don't it?"

I glance across at Butterfield, who smiles as Woodrow Bonner says something to him. "The first part of any criminal trial is always the worst."

"They'll let Taylor go," Doss says, his voice doleful, "but not me."

Tonight will be the hardest time for Doss to keep from changing his mind and telling me to try to make a deal with Butterfield, who can't be feeling too good about his chances of getting a conviction against Paul. Anybody who wasn't impressed by

Dick's opening statement had to have been asleep, and I didn't see any eyes closed. "Tomorrow I'll get to cross-examine Bonner," I say. "It'll be better," I promise.

A hopeless expression on his face, Doss shrugs as Amos Broadstreet, Bonner's elderly black deputy, who weighs at least three hundred pounds, comes over to the table to handcuff him and put him in leg chains. He has gotten to like Doss and has waited an extra moment to pick him up.

I look behind me and see Tommy Ting behind the spectator railing waiting to speak to me. Connie had told me he wouldn't be getting into Bear Creek until late last night, and though I got a glimpse of him in the courtroom, this is the first time I have had a good look at him. He is wearing a tailored olive-colored suit that must have cost him a thousand dollars and is easily the best-dressed man in the room. His face is fleshier but still recognizable, his cheeks pushed up in a smile I remember after thirty years. His hair is much longer, of course. Boys in eastern Arkansas in the early sixties didn't know what long hair was or if we did, we didn't care. Now, Tommy's salt and pepper hair comes to his collar in the back, making him look even more Asian than I remembered.

Once Doss leaves, I motion for him to come forward, and we shake hands by the counsel table as if he were a rich corporate client chatting with his high-priced legal counsel during a civil trial. "How's it going?" Tommy asks softly, his slight accent more pronounced now that we are face to face.

I know he means the trial, and suddenly I have an impulse to tell him how wrong I've probably been about everything I've thought and remembered about Bear Creek, including our friendship which, now that I force myself to think about it, was as superficial as most male bonding is. Like myself, Tommy has been operating out of denial, but instead of thinking that people were worse than they were, he has misremembered them as better, more caring. I reply bluntly, "I honestly don't know who killed your father. I don't know that anyone will ever know the truth either except the person or persons who did it."

Incredibly, he seems surprised, as if by giving the plant employees the green light to talk to me, the answer would become obvious. "Do you think Paul was involved?" he whispers.

I look over at the other table, now empty. If Paul wanted to shake hands with Tommy and say how sorry he was, he isn't going to risk doing it in public since he and Dick are already making their way out of the courtroom. "I don't know, Tommy. I swear to God I really don't know who killed your father."

As if I have said something profound, he nods and walks away, presumably to find his sister and mother. A few moments later, depressed, I leave too, and check into the Bear Creek Inn to prepare for tomorrow. Betty, dressed in red shorts and a T-shirt advertising her business, asks, "Not going too good, huh?"

I try to smile but fail. "It's going okay," I lie.

Betty places the key to number nine in my hand and presses her palm flat against mine. "It's got to be tough representing a nigger. He's probably scared to death and not much help."

Glad Betty isn't on the jury, I ignore her comment and ask if she knows if Charlie's Pizza delivers. Right now I don't have the energy to find out. She replies that people will do anything for money, and says she'll call up a kid to run get me whatever I want. I tell her fine and carry my bag into my room, wondering if the case is, after all, that simple.

Nineteen

WHEN DOSS IS BROUGHT into the courtroom the next morning thirty minutes before the trial starts up again, I watch for signs that he will tell me to try to make a deal with Butterfield. He looks terrible, and I ask him after the deputy moves off, "Did you get any sleep?"

He rubs his face. "Not much," he says. "I've been thinking about my chances." His bloodshot eyes blink rapidly in the glare of the courtroom.

How does anyone stand to live in a steel cage, whether they are guilty or not? "It's going to come down to a matter of your credibility, Doss," I say, trying to cut him off. "If they believe you, you'll walk out of here a free man." As I say this, I realize I'm putting on his shoulders the entire responsibility for his acquittal.

"Are you gonna argue that the old lady could have done it?" he says. "She says she found his body."

"Depending on how she looks and acts," I hedge, "but it might piss off the jury. If all they see is a sick old woman who can hardly lift a fly swatter, it'll insult their intelligence, and they might take it out on you." I can't tell him I promised not to make this argument.

"What're you gonna do, then?" he asks, a plaintive tone in his voice. "Just say it was the Mexican?"

I watch as the deputies open the doors to allow spectators into the courtroom. "I'll do more than that," I whisper. "But that'll be part of it."

"He couldn't speak hardly a word of English," Doss says, shaking his head. "He didn't seem like the type who could have done it."

"He could have known a lot more English than he let on," I explain. "All we need is to get them thinking he might have done it. We don't have to prove he did."

Doss sees Latrice and gives her a little wave. She has convinced him to trust me. The corners of his mouth turn up in a brief smile, and for an instant I am permitted to see what his face must have been like before he was charged. If I don't get him off, I hope he doesn't hate her. I know he will hate me.

Woodrow Bonner climbs back into the witness chair and smiles at me. I waste no time in asking him about Jorge Arrazola, not caring how much he repeats himself from yesterday. By the end of this trial I want the jury to have the name burned into their brains. Bonner has no choice but to admit that he has continued to look for him right up until the trial. "I would have liked to talk to him," Bonner says, in response to one of my questions, "just as a matter of routine investigative work, but I don't consider him a suspect."

I come around to the side of the podium and bellow, "You're telling this jury that this man is not a suspect because he was in this country illegally and might have been afraid he'd be found out?"

Bonner is sitting ramrod straight and his metal badge positively gleams. "My guess is that he was afraid and that's why he took off," he says casually, "but that's not why I don't consider him a suspect."

"Well, tell the jury why not," I say sarcastically, not remembering anything in his notes or files that would make me afraid to ask this question.

"Well, you see, Mr. Page, Jorge Arrazola was left-handed," Bonner says, "and you heard what Dr. Miller testified about the knife wound."

What in the hell have I been doing the last three months? I've been so busy trying to get Paul I've gone brain-dead. "You're saying it's not possible he used his right hand?" I bluster, trying to pretend I've known this fact all along.

"That's a question," his voice dry, "you might want to ask Dr. Miller."

I could move to strike his answer as being unresponsive, but I don't want to hear his new one; nor do I want to recall Dr. Miller. I can feel my cheeks burning. "Your conclusion," I ask hurriedly, "that there were no other suspects depends, in part, on the truthfulness or correctness of answers given to you by individuals who claim to vouch for the whereabouts of the other plant workers, isn't that so?"

Bonner has to answer that it does, and hopefully it appears that I am preparing the jury for some gigantic revelation down the line, but, in fact, I have nothing to present later but a few minor and irrelevant inconsistencies, if I choose. I get Bonner to admit that he cannot offer any direct evidence of a cash payment or a promise of any kind from Paul Taylor to Doss. Given the other evidence in the case, this hardly seems to matter, but it is all I have. Butterfield will argue that Doss could have been hired by Paul or someone else.

Before I sit down, I decide to test the waters, and ask about Mrs. Ting. "Though Doris Ting discovered her husband's body," I say, "you quickly eliminated her as a suspect, didn't you?"

Bonner says that for a number of reasons he doesn't consider the victim's wife a possibility and tells the jury that her frail condition, her reaction (she was in shock and had to be sedated), and the lack of any physical evidence tying her to the murder ruled her out.

In a few minutes I sit down by Doss and watch Dick get to his feet and walk to the podium. I hope Doss doesn't lean over and ask me if I am getting paid by Butterfield to help him. This is one of the most humiliating moments of my career as a lawyer. Any more of this, and I'll need to go back to social work.

Dick goes after Bonner hard and gets him to admit how little evidence other than the tape the prosecution has against Paul. Bonner is so candid that I begin to suspect he wants the jury to understand that had he been the prosecutor, he wouldn't have charged Paul unless he had gotten Doss to make a deal first. Doubtless, like anyone else, Bonner resents being hung out to dry, and I wish I had been a fly on the wall in his office once it became apparent to him Doss wasn't going to implicate Paul. I watch Paul's face as Dick cross-examines Bonner, and wonder again if, despite everything, he is responsible for this murder. Angela's comment that first day I stopped by her house that Paul could be "ruthless" has stayed with me. In spite of the fact that he isn't as bad as I wanted to make him out to be, I don't trust him and never will.

Though there is no need to put Doris Ting on the stand, Butterfield does it anyway. She looks older than the last time I saw her as she hobbles into the witness chair, and I wonder if Connie even bothered to ask her to try to remember something that would help us. She begins to sob as soon as Butterfield asks her to identify herself for the record, and the loss that she has suffered, if it hasn't before, comes home to the jury. Pausing repeatedly during her testimony to wipe her face with a fistful of tissue, she describes how unusual it was for her husband not to call her or not to answer the phone on Darla's afternoon to volunteer at the school. I look back at Tommy and Connie at the back of the courtroom. Connie has hidden her face in her hands as her mother testifies. For the first time since I've been involved in this case, it seems to be about a man's death, and not my own ego. I look over my shoulder again and see Tommy put his arm around his sister. Mercifully, Butterfield lets Mrs. Ting off the stand as soon as he establishes the time when she went into the plant and found her husband's body. Both Dick and I decline to cross-examine her, an action I assure Doss would hurt more than help.

Butterfield moves through his case smoothly, and by the afternoon he puts on his last witness, Darla Tate, who, in contrast to Doss, has beefed up in the last three months. Already a big woman, Darla now looks like she could start as defensive tackle for her sons' high school team; yet there is still something touching about the way she has tried to get herself dolled up for her testimony. In fact, from the shoulders up, she looks like she has made up for one of those sexy glamour shots that try to make ordinary women into, if not movie stars, at least queens for an afternoon. As my secretary Julia says, Darla has her hair "bouffed up" and is wearing enough makeup to get stuck in if it rains. Gold ball earrings the size of plums hang from her ears; her dress is the color of faded summer grass. Never has a woman tried to look more feminine, I suppose, and failed. Despite the testimony that Butterfield will elicit from her, she can help Doss even as she hurts him, and I hope the women on the jury listen to her even as they mentally pick her apart.

As expected, she talks about the operation of the plant. Had I been Butterfield, I would have called her as one of my first witnesses, but perhaps it makes sense to call her last since she can provide a motive for Doss even if the jury chooses to believe that Paul had nothing to do with Willie's death. She begins to recite her story that she overheard Doss talking about "having gotten the money" while she was in the bathroom but readily admits she doesn't have any idea to whom he was speaking. Butterfield asks if she is sure it was Bledsoe's voice, and she says emphatically that she is "absolutely certain."

In the moment that I see her biceps tense, it occurs to me that Darla has spent a considerable amount of energy pointing me in the wrong direction in this case. First Harrison, the meat inspector, then Jorge Arrazola, and finally Muddy Jessup. Yet she told me right off that she didn't think Doss was capable of murdering Willie. Were these supposed to be wild goose chases? I had rejected the idea of Darla's being a suspect because she had an alibi and, besides, I couldn't imagine a woman taking a knife and slitting her employer's throat. But as I look at her right arm, and see that it may well be as strong as my own, or at least strong enough to slice the carotid artery of an old, unsuspecting man, I have to wonder—why not Darla? She says she was at her sons' private school between two and four, and I know she signed in at the principal's office before two and signed out at 4:30, but what was she actually doing all that time? My mind races to remember. Something about helping to do paperwork in the office. Her story checked out. About a month ago I talked to the office secretary who said that Darla was there the entire time that afternoon. I remember her because she was a thin, intense, almost hyper woman who insisted that I go outside with her while she smoked. Darla, she said, answered the phone and did paperwork. Bonner has also talked to her, according to the file, and everything he has done has checked out, including this conversation. And what would have been her motive? She practically claimed to be in love with Willie. But maybe she wasn't. All I can do now is fish and hope I don't make her too suspicious. Doss nudges me, and I look up at the judge. "Mr. Page?" Johnson asks, for the second time. "Do you wish to examine this witness?"

"Yes, your honor." As I get to my feet, Darla gives me a shy smile as if we are old friends, and I start off by asking her if she remembers telling me that she didn't think Doss was the type to have murdered Willie.

"Doss was a good employee," she volunteers. "I didn't think he would do such a thing. Willie liked him because he was a real hard worker. And Doss had said to me that Willie was a good boss. That's why I was surprised."

"In fact, I believe you said Mr. Ting always treated you very well as an employee."

If Darla is becoming wary, I can't tell it. Immediately, she responds, "I think I told you I was sick almost all one winter, but he told me not to worry about it."

"And right up to his death," I say, casually, "you enjoyed a good working relationship with him, didn't you?"

"Yes, I did," Darla says. "If he thought you worked hard, he'd help out if you needed it. And I appreciated that."

"In fact, Mrs. Tate," I say, in as low-key a manner as possible, "over the last couple of months you've suggested that I investigate two or three other individuals for the murder of Willie Ting, including an individual whom you were pretty sure was stealing money from the plant."

"He was," Darla says, firmly. "I showed you."

"Yes, you did," I say and smile. I pause and pretend I'm looking through my notes. "Now, let's go back to the day of the murder," I murmur. "If the person who murdered Mr. Ting was a worker in the plant, he or she would have known that Tuesday was your day to volunteer in the schools?"

"It wasn't a secret," Darla acknowledges. "I had been doing it for six months. Willie didn't even dock my salary."

"And once you left in the afternoon," I say, "you were gone for the day, isn't that correct?"

"I stay until Mr. Edwards the principal leaves," Darla says, "and that's never before four."

If I am onto something, it is probably much too late to prove it. "And, of course, the day of the murder you followed your normal routine and were at the school the entire time, and whoever murdered Mr. Ting, assuming they were aware you volunteered at the school, could have counted on that, isn't that so?"

"I think so," Darla says. "Like I say, I didn't hide it."

I ask if some of the workers' voices at the plant sound alike.

"Doss and I started the same day five years ago," she says, "and I've talked to him at least once a week. So I'm positive it was him."

I sit down, saying that I would like to recall Darla so she won't be released as a witness. While Dick cross-examines

270

Darla, I turn my head and try to get a glimpse of Connie and Tommy to see if either of them heard anything Darla said they didn't like. Though it is difficult to see her, for an instant I catch sight of Connie, and think I see a puzzled look on her face.

Now that the prosecution's case is at an end, the court recesses, and we go back into Johnson's chambers to go through the routine of asking that the charges against our clients be dismissed.

I make my motion for the record, knowing there isn't a snowball's chance in hell of getting this case dismissed. Then I listen to Dick eloquently argue that Butterfield has put on no evidence against Paul. Oddly enough, this is only the second time I have been back in the judge's chambers, which are mostly bare, since his main office is in Helena. Johnson is quieter and much more passive than I thought he would be, which is the kind of judge lawyers like since he lets you try your case and doesn't take over the questioning. No Judge Ito, he has been so unobtrusive that at times I have hardly noticed him.

While Butterfield makes his response to our motions for dismissal, I muse about Darla Tate. I'd at least like to talk with Connie and Tommy to see what they think of her.

When Butterfield is finished, Johnson leans back in his chair and looks straight at him. "I'm very tempted to grant Mr. Dickerson's motion for a directed verdict and dismiss the charges against his client," he says in a witheringly cold voice. "I find barely sufficient evidence that would allow a jury in good faith to find he had anything to do with the murder of Willie Ting. All the prosecutor has really shown in this case is that the defendant had an ambiguous conversation with the victim in which he mentioned the fact that he would die someday."

Melvin Butterfield looks as if he has been slapped in the face. I was certain that Johnson was in Butterfield's hip pocket. As usual, my assumptions about Bear Creek have been totally false.

We go back out into the courtroom, and Johnson, glancing at the clock on the wall, announces that since it's nearly five o'clock, the court will be in recess for the rest of the day. As soon as his gavel comes down, he leaves the bench and the courtroom quickly empties. I tell Doss that I will be out later to go over his testimony. His only hope now is his credibility. For all I have accomplished, he should have defended himself and saved seven thousand dollars. As the deputy leads Doss away, he hangs his head. I haven't given him any reason to do much else.

From my room at the Bear Creek Inn, I call the Ting residence, and as I hoped, I get Connie and ask, "What has your mother ever said about Darla Tate? Could she have been stealing from the plant?"

Without any hesitation, Connie says, "Mother's said that from time to time workers stole meat. She's never never said anything about Darla, but I'll ask her again."

I tell Connie that I am guessing Darla knew that sooner or later Eddie was going to uncover some major shortages and Darla was trying to blame everything on Muddy Jessup, who, as it turned out, was running too small a scam to account for the losses. "I know this is a long shot," I plead, "but would you ask Eddie to go back to the plant tonight and check the books to see if he can tell whether Darla was cooking the books before your father died? If she was, I think there is a good chance she killed him because he was about to find out she was stealing from him. My guess is that the plant was making so much money he didn't know how much he was losing."

There is a long pause, and I rack my brain trying to think of something to say that will make her help me. It is obvious that I am grasping at straws, but I have been so blinded in this case by my own prejudices that I have begun to use my head only in the last twenty-four hours. Before I can say more, she replies, "Can't she prove she was at the school all that time?"

I think of Mary Kiley, the wiry, nervous woman I talked with outside the school door. I wouldn't have been surprised if she had stuck two cigarettes in her mouth at once. "Maybe, but if it's like any office I've been around, by the middle of the afternoon people get up and do a lot of visiting. Maybe her alibi wasn't there with her the whole time."

"I know what you're going to do, Gideon," Connie says, her voice cold. "You want to get just enough evidence to have the jury doubt your client is guilty. He'll go free and nobody will be charged."

I stare at the ugly green wall across from me. For once, I don't lie. "That's possible," I admit, "but at least you won't have convicted an innocent man."

For a moment Connie does not say anything. Then she says harshly into my ear, "Have you got any other theories?"

One. My assumptions have been wrong so far but I better ask it. "Is there a possibility Darla was in love with your father and got rejected by him?"

Connie laughs sarcastically. "I'll ask my mother that, too."

I hang up and retrieve the now dog-eared file Butterfield gave me and thumb through the statements taken by Bonner until I find the name of Mary Kiley. I read it twice and then decide to go out to her house instead of calling her. In five minutes I pull up at a small frame house on Casey Street only two blocks from the housing project where my distant black relative Mayola Washington presumably still lives. I wonder why I haven't gone by to see her. However, all we have in common is guilt, and I have enough of that.

A child, perhaps ten, her hair in pigtails, comes to the door and regarding me gravely through the screen, yells, "Mama, there's a man out here!"

Within seconds Mary Kiley appears and seeing my face, opens the screen. Though thin as a ballet dancer, she looks okay in a pair of red shorts and a white T-shirt advertising Graceland. "Go on and watch TV, Margie!" she says, shooing her daughter away from her.

"May I talk to you a minute, Mrs. Kiley?" I ask, awkwardly, since she isn't inviting me in. "It's about the trial."

Her lips pucker briefly. "I didn't think you were here to ask me for a date." Without waiting for my reaction, she says, "Let me get my cigarettes."

Presumably, there is no Mr. Kiley. I stand on her stoop and think about Angela. In the last week I have tried hard to block her out of my mind until the trial is over. Was she using me or not? Paul may not be a murderer, but he is a son of a bitch. And yet Angela admitted she was attracted to him. Betrayed Dwight. Do I believe she slept with him to make sure they got a loan? I don't know.

Mrs. Kiley pushes open the screen with a kind of nervous energy that makes me glad I don't have to be around her all the time. "Let's go around to the backyard," she instructs me. "I'd take you through the house to get there, but it looks terrible, and I don't want you talking about me."

"I don't think the judge would find the condition of your house particularly relevant," I say, walking fast to keep up with her. "You've got a cute kid."

"Yeah, I know," she says over her shoulder. "She's so innocent it takes your breath away sometimes."

Away from the school, Mary Kiley seems like a different person, but then most people are when they're not at work. A month ago she was guarded and didn't speak unless asked a question. We sit in two blue and white plastic webbed folding chairs and she lights up an unfiltered Camel with obvious pleasure. "I love these damn things," she says, after taking a long drag. "I hope I die with one in my mouth."

I laugh, and she asks, "Isn't this the second day of the trial?"

I say it is and tell her I came by to check a couple of things she told me before about Darla Tate. "Can you really swear that she was not out of your sight the whole time she was at the school that afternoon?"

Mrs. Kiley blows smoke into the air in the direction of a brown picnic table a few feet to our left. I can see ants crawling on it from where I'm sitting. "So you think she did it, huh?"

"She might have," I say, and summarize briefly why I am sus-

picious. I conclude by saying, "I never considered it a real possibility before, because I didn't think a woman would be cold-
blooded enough to sneak up behind a man and slit his throat."

Mary Kiley narrows her eyes at me as if I couldn't possibly be
so naive. "Have you got the statement I gave to Bonner?" she
asks.

I reach into my briefcase and find the page and hand it to her.
While she reads, I notice her daughter has come to the back
door screen and is staring out at us. She wants to come out but
doesn't want to incur her mother's wrath. I wave at her and she
waves back. She has her mother's dark eyes and small mouth. I
hope she doesn't smoke. Mrs. Kiley looks up at me and says,
"No, I couldn't swear she was there the whole time. When that
prissy sheriff we got came out the first time and questioned me,
it pissed me off. I didn't like him coming out to the school. Hell,
that's why it was built. See, when volunteers are there in the office, it gives me an opportunity to check the halls and the bath-
rooms and the gym to see if anything is going on. A student
who's got study hall that period stays in the principal's office
and answers the phone when he teaches his two higher math
classes. He doesn't have time to blow his nose most days."

"Why didn't you tell me this when I talked to you a month
ago?" I ask, trying to keep the irritation I am feeling out of my
voice.

Mrs. Kiley flips a cigarette under her picnic table. "Because I
thought it was ridiculous for him to think it was her, and you
seemed like you were just kind of going through the motions,
anyway. Besides, everybody said that black man who cut meat
in the plant did it. But thinking about it now, I realize that I
probably wasn't around as much as I made it sound. I could
have been gone as long as thirty minutes. It was the only break
I got."

Going through the motions, that's what I've been doing. I
ask, "Have you seen Darla lately?"

"She called me a couple of weeks ago," Mary Kiley says,
lighting up another cigarette, "and said she had been subpoe-

naed to testify. She asked if I had been. I guess that's what made me a little curious."

I look toward the screen but don't see her daughter. "Would you be willing to testify to what you've told me if the judge lets you?"

Mrs. Kiley stretches unselfconsciously, thrusting her small breasts against Elvis's guitar. "I guess," she says, her face deadpan, "this means we'll be losing a volunteer."

I race out to Brickeys and give Doss a pep talk. "You can convince that jury you didn't do this," I encourage him. He is back in his orange jumpsuit and looks at me through the glass, wanting, I think, to believe me. "Don't look down; don't mumble. When Butterfield questions you, make sure you understand what he is asking. You can say that you don't understand him. . . ."

I leave in an hour. We've gone over his testimony three times. I resist the urge to tell him that I may be able to try to help him for a change. I have no assurance whatsoever that at this late date Johnson will let me call someone who is not on my witness list.

From the Cotton Boll (where I'm almost too late to get anything to eat) Mr. Carpenter lets me call the Ting residence from the counter. Connie answers, and I tell her about my conversation with Mary Kiley. "She's willing to testify, Connie. I think she believes Darla might have killed your father. Darla called her to see if she had been subpoenaed."

"You're going to get him off, aren't you?" Connie says, her voice bitter.

"By itself, this won't be enough," I say, watching McKenzie bring out a dinner salad for me, "unless Darla can be shown to have a motive."

"Well, you should be happy then," she hisses into my ear. "Eddie went back to the plant thirty minutes ago."

This is Tommy's doing, I realize. Perhaps their mother. Connie is too bitter. "Please have him call me if he finds something."

Connie hangs up the phone in my ear without promising me

anything. As I eat a chicken fried steak and mashed potatoes, Mr. Carpenter sits with me and tells me the gossip about the trial. It looks bad for Doss, but Paul never should have been charged. He adds, "Of course, the people who are saying that are the same ones who, if he's convicted, will say they knew from the beginning he was guilty."

I spoon some gravy on the chicken. I could get used to a ten-thousand-calorie-a-day diet. I wonder what people are saying about me but don't dare ask. I don't need to lose any more confidence than I already have. "I guess Paul can run for governor if he's acquitted," I say, reminded of a comment Angela made the first time I saw her.

"Governor?" the old man laughs. "He's too arrogant to be elected dog catcher! It's Dick who should have run for office. He would have made a difference."

The old man doesn't have a clue. A prominent politician hasn't come out of east Arkansas for decades. It's been too bogged down in the politics of race. McKenzie brings out my bill: $6.50. I notice she has written at the bottom "Good Luck!" and drawn a "happy face." I nod vigorously and wink at her. I will need it.

At four in the morning the phone rings, waking me out of a deep sleep. I have dozed off in my clothes. The last time I remember looking at the clock it was one, and I had been in the middle of taking a stab at constructing my closing argument, a futile exercise since I don't know what the evidence will be.

It is Eddie Ting, who sounds exhausted. "All I can tell you," he says, "is that it looks like some receipts where we purchased hogs been altered to make it appear we bought fewer than we did, but it would take an accountant to figure out if anything is wrong. Can you get the judge to delay the trial? I could get my CPA in here and see what's been going on."

I rub my face, knowing a continuance is out of the question. Johnson may not even let Eddie testify. I explain this to him and too tired to think, ask, "How do we know it was Darla and what would she get out of it?"

Eddie responds, "Since she was the bookkeeper, she might have been in on some deal where hogs were being stolen before they were even slaughtered."

This sounds hopeless, but it is all I have. "Will you testify about this tomorrow," I ask, "if the judge lets you?"

"They said I could," Eddie answers wearily, "if I found something suspicious."

I don't have to ask who "they" are. Before I hang up, I ask if he has had any reason to believe Darla was not as wonderful as she has seemed. "In retrospect, doesn't it seem she was trying to head you off by coming up with that stuff on Jessup?"

"I guess it's possible," Eddie says, now cautious.

We talk for a few more minutes and he agrees to meet me at the courthouse with the receipts at seven. I get up, wondering whether Johnson will take me seriously after yesterday's performance. I haven't given anyone so far much of a reason to drag out this trial.

Twenty

"NEITHER OF THESE INDIVIDUALS APPEARS on your witness list, do they, Mr. Page?" Judge Johnson asks, peering over his half-frame glasses. Up close they look as cheap as my own.

I am getting used to this form of inquisition by Johnson. This is obviously his way of making a point. He was not at all happy when I called him at six this morning to ask for a hearing back in chambers before the trial to see if he would permit me to put on witnesses I had not previously disclosed to Butterfield. "No, sir," I say, knowing if I begin to argue now he will interrupt me.

"And you are not saying that you misunderstood the court's cutoff date for disclosing your witnesses, are you? I can ask the stenographer to find your response to me if you wish."

"No, sir," I say, hating Johnson at this moment. What a pedantic asshole.

"And you are not contending," he says, "that neither Mr. Edward Ting nor Mrs. Mary Kiley is a rebuttal witness?"

"No, sir."

"Then what conceivable grounds do you have for them testifying?" he asks, his voice turning into a high whine at the end. "So far as I can tell, the prosecution has been scrupulously fair to your client and has made available to you everything it has

279

had in this case. And now you are attempting to spring surprise witnesses on him."

"The prosecutor has been fair, your honor." I wait for him to nod so I can speak without him cutting me off. Finally he does, and I say, "Your honor, the reason I'd like to call these witnesses is simple justice. It was only yesterday in the middle of Mrs. Tate's testimony that I began to realize that she might be involved in Mr. Ting's murder. If I'm allowed to put Mr. Ting on as a witness, he will show the jury that Darla Tate has falsified receipts in the past year, and Mrs. Kiley will testify that she cannot say that Mrs. Tate was at the school between the hours of two and four on the day Mr. Ting was murdered. Certainly, it would be fair for the prosecutor to have some time to interview these witnesses, and they are waiting outside his office right now to talk with him."

Johnson glares at me as if I am some kind of habitual criminal he has given too many chances already. "Why haven't you investigated the possibility that Mrs. Tate might be involved before now?"

I attempt a feeble smile. I could talk for an hour about how stupid I've been, but I don't think we have the time. "I had, but I didn't find anything. I guess I kind of got suckered, your honor."

"What do you say, Mr. Butterfield?" Johnson says to his supposed friend.

Butterfield, not nearly so ebullient or friendly since yesterday, glares at me and says, "Mr. Page has had almost three months to decide to call these individuals, your honor. If he is allowed to bring witnesses at the last second, you will have prejudiced the state's position by preventing me from having a careful opportunity to prepare my case. The state is entitled to a level playing field."

Johnson, who without his robe looks as slight as a welterweight, frowns at the suggestion he is not being even-handed. "Would your client be prejudiced," he asks Dick, who has been quietly sitting in the corner the entire time, "if I allow these individuals to testify?"

To give himself more time to think, Dick takes off his bifocals and rubs the lenses with a handkerchief. As he does so, it strikes me how easily Darla could have been hired by Paul to murder Willie. No one knows as much about the plant and its employees. In retrospect, Darla made a point to sound bitter toward Paul when I talked to her that first time in her house, but the information she gave me about him and the bank was available from many sources. Of course, at this point I have no way to prove anything.

Jamming his handkerchief in his pocket but continuing to fidget with his glasses, Dick finally answers, "Your honor, I have no choice but to oppose Mr. Page's effort to introduce surprise testimony on what may be the last day of the trial. I don't expect anything either individual may say will prejudice my client, but I'm being forced to make a spur-of-the-moment decision, and so I must object."

I glance at Johnson, who is tapping the tips of his fingers together, and replay what Dick has just said and the way he said it. I am confident he has too much integrity to allow Paul to take the witness stand and lie, but Paul could easily be lying to him, and Dick, no fool, may suspect it. Still, he has a duty to represent him, and the most prudent course of action is to take no chances and wind up the testimony as soon as possible.

Johnson holds his fingers still and says, "A man's life is at stake, and I'm not going to punish him because his lawyer may have overlooked something that possibly may be offered in his defense. Would it not be fair to you, Mr. Butterfield and Mr. Dickerson," he says, "if I allow you an hour to interview these people and then you come back into chambers with Mr. Page, and we'll discuss where to go from there?"

Neither is being given a choice, but Johnson has implied that he might give them a continuance. Both give their assent, and then we all stand as the judge makes a show of consulting his watch. "Please be back here precisely at eight-fifteen."

My face has begun to burn a bit, too, and I get up and follow behind Butterfield out of the judge's chambers to wait for Doss.

Once the door is closed behind us, Melvin says out of the side of his mouth, "And I bet you thought the judge and I were friends. . . ."

Side by side for a moment as we go down the stairs, I have to laugh. I deserve whatever beating I get. I haven't been right about anything since I started on this case. I should have suspected Darla from the beginning, but at the time I wasn't interested. "Well, he's not exactly Mr. Congeniality, is he?"

Even Dick laughs.

I stand by as Butterfield explains to Mary Kiley and Eddie Ting that the judge is allowing him and Dick to interview them. Neither seems surprised, but Mary Kiley, I can tell, needs a cigarette bad. Eddie looks as if he didn't get even an hour's sleep, and she doesn't look much better. It is no fun being a witness. Afterward, I go wait in the courtroom for Doss, who arrives just as Butterfield sticks his head in the door and crooks his finger at me. Upstairs, back in Johnson's chambers, both Dick and Butterfield say they still object to the testimony of persons not previously identified on my witness list, but that if the court lets them testify, neither is asking for a continuance. Butterfield says, "I'm ready to proceed, your honor."

Dick nods. Neither man would say a word to me on our way up the stairs. This could mean one of two things: they aren't worried or they don't want me to have any more time. Johnson shrugs, "Let's get started, then."

Back in the courtroom, I notice that though the spectator section is just as crowded as the last two days, its composition has changed. There are more blacks and fewer whites, which, I interpret, means that they heard there is no evidence against Paul. For the first time, I notice a group of Chinese in the back sitting with the Tings. They may have been here all this time, and I never noticed them. God only knows what they think of the criminal justice system in Bear Creek.

I begin by calling my character witnesses first, and they do well, though Doss's AME minister gets a little carried away.

"Mr. Bledsoe's reputation as a law-abiding nonviolent citizen is as spotless as the son of God's."

I turn and see Butterfield scratching his head as if he might be thinking that Jesus is usually portrayed these days as a revolutionary who set out to overthrow the established order, but he decides to let it go. Now that we've opened up the door on my client's character, Butterfield can attack it, but Doss appears to have led a pretty quiet life, and the prosecutor sits with his hands in his pockets as if this testimony is so much window dressing, which of course it is.

I decide to call Mary Kiley before Eddie Ting and instantly understand why Butterfield was ready to go forward. Instead of the assertive woman who last evening was willing to stick her neck out, today Mary Kiley seems a timid, shy soul who knows she is in trouble for telling the prosecutor one thing and me another. In her own backyard, she projected a strong, almost bitchy, personality; now, she seems like a little girl who will parrot the last person who talked to her. Wearing a white dress that gives her a childlike quality, she has to repeat her name three times before the court reporter can get it down. By the time she sits down, all I have managed to establish is that she isn't certain that Darla was at the school all afternoon.

On direct examination Eddie Ting's testimony is straightforward enough, but as Butterfield begins to wind down, it is clear its usefulness is limited. Paul is motionless while Dick leans forward to hear better. Butterfield is like a giant stork flapping from behind the podium as he follows the time-honored tradition of calling attention to himself and away from the witness on cross-examination. His next-to-last question to Eddie is, "Isn't it a fact that all you have discovered is some receipts for the purchase of hogs from Dixie Farms that appear to have been altered?"

"Yes, sir," Eddie says in a meek voice.

Butterfield drapes himself over the podium. "And you can't positively say who did it or why they did it, can you, Mr. Ting?"

Eddie folds his arms across his chest as if he wishes he hadn't ever made the decision to cross the Mississippi River to come to Arkansas. "No, sir."

Again Dick declines to cross-examine, and I let Eddie step down. The judge has already prevented him from speculating about why the receipts may have been doctored.

"I'd like to recall Darla Tate, your honor," I say, and while we wait for her to come from the witness room, I glance at Paul, but he is like a statue. I look behind the railing for Connie and Tommy. They must be thinking that they have been suckered again. I can't quite see either of them, nor do I really want to.

If Darla has a clue as to why she is being recalled, I can't guess it from her expression. As she enters the courtroom, she is not smiling, but does not appear afraid either. Once again she is wearing a loose, blousy tunic that conceals her biceps. I wish I could make her pull up her sleeves and show the jury her muscles. If Darla doesn't turn out to be the murderer, I will feel like an idiot, not an uncommon emotion for me the last couple of weeks. My face grows hot again as I think how I have allowed myself to be manipulated in this case. "Just a couple of questions, Mrs. Tate," I say, forcing a smile at her as she seats herself.

She nods, now spreading a plastic grin on her own face. I would like to get her to answer before she figures out what is going on, but if she did kill Willie, she will be ready for me. "Mrs. Tate, I'm going to show you some documents which have been identified collectively as defendant's exhibit one," I say, approaching her. "Can you tell the jury what these are?"

Darla squints hard at the sheaf of papers, but I notice her palm and fingers are steady as she takes them from me. She goes through them one by one and announces, "These are receipts from Dixie Farms for hogs."

"Would you look at these closely and tell me if any of the figures on the number of hogs purchased in each one appear to have been altered?"

I have to admit that Darla is either innocent or a cool customer. As if this were a surprise, she says, "You know, they seem to be. For example, this five appears to have been a six, but it looks as if part of it was erased."

I pretend to study the pink copy bearing the Confederate logo of Dixie Farms. "Can you think of a reason why someone would alter these figures?"

Butterfield springs out of his chair. "Objection, your honor. He's asking her to speculate."

Johnson, who has gotten curious and is leaning over to his left to look at the receipts, says, "Overruled."

Tipped off that she doesn't have to answer, Darla says blandly, "I don't know why."

"Well, let me suggest a reason and see if you agree," I say, taking the receipts from her and handing them to Johnson, who helps me out by peering at them. "If somebody wanted to steal some live hogs from the plant and conceal that fact, wouldn't it help to make it appear that the actual number of hogs purchased was different than it truly was?"

Darla doesn't miss a beat. "All you'd have to do to check," she says, shrugging, "is call the person who sold them to you and ask him what his copy says."

"But first you'd have to suspect something was wrong, wouldn't you?"

Darla shrugs. "I suppose so."

I go back to the podium, since Johnson is still going through the papers. "Where do you keep the receipts?"

Darla shifts in her seat for the first time since she has been on the stand. "In a filing cabinet next to my desk."

"Is it kept locked?" I ask.

"No, anybody could have access to the drawer."

I let that answer hang for a few seconds. "I just asked you if it was locked. Did you alter those receipts, Mrs. Tate?"

Darla says, "Absolutely not."

"Your honor, may I come pick up the receipts and show them to the jury?"

Johnson nods, and I come forward and hand them to Ira

Kingston, a white man seated at the end. If he begins to yawn, I'm dead meat.

I turn to Darla and ask, "Are you absolutely certain that you have an alibi for the time Mr. Ting was murdered?"

Darla, indignant now or appearing to be, snaps, "I was at my sons' school volunteering in the office. You can ask the school secretary, Mary Kiley."

I let Darla stew for a moment. "Did you murder Willie Ting because you were involved in some scheme," I ask as dramatically as possible, "to steal meat from the plant and he had found out and was about to fire you?"

"No, I did not!" Darla shouts at me, her bosom heaving under her dress.

"But Mrs. Tate, you did tell me and Eddie Ting a few weeks ago that you had been going through the books and found out that a meat salesman by the name of Muddy Jessup had been stealing from the plant by altering the price sheets?"

"Yes, I did," Darla says, her voice high.

"And you suggested I try to find him, but when I did, it involved only a few hundred dollars, isn't that a fact?"

Darla purses her lips. "That's all we could prove. It may have been more."

"Don't you find it a little strange that you caught the changes in the price sheets but not the changes in the receipts from Dixie Farms?"

"No," she says, angrily, "it never occurred to me to check them."

Knowing I will have to accept whatever answer she gives me, I ask, trying to seem as confident as I can, "Mrs. Tate, do you recall telling me that your sons have worked for Paul Taylor during the last two summers?"

For all Darla knows, they are waiting outside the courtroom to testify. She blinks rapidly, and says, "Sure."

"Just one moment, your honor," I say. Hoping the judge won't stop me, I walk over to Butterfield's table and with my back to her, nod as if I am getting an instruction. Melvin looks at me as if I am crazy.

I come back to the podium and fumble with my papers for a moment before asking, "Now, your sons haven't worked for him since the summertime, is that right?"

Darla has begun ever so slightly to lean back against the witness chair as if she is bracing herself. "That's correct."

My heart pounding, I act as if I am being coy with the next question and mumble it but speak loud enough for her and the jury to hear, "Do you know if they saw Mr. Taylor in January or February of this year?"

Darla cocks her chin slightly, but just for the briefest of instants her eyes track to Paul's table and then back to me. She is taking too long to answer, or I hope she is. "I have no idea."

I smile as if I know the answer and then look back over at Butterfield and nod. He frowns, but I can tell by his eyes that he knows what I am doing. I pause for as long as I dare and then back to Darla and ask, "Mrs. Tate, did Mr. Taylor talk to you about murdering Willie Ting?"

"No!" she answers, shrilly. "He did not!"

I wheel around and make a show of looking at Dick, who is whispering urgently in Paul's ear. I turn back to the judge and say that I have no more questions, and before Dick can get up, I point out that it is almost noon and ask the court to break for the noon recess.

Johnson consults his own watch instead of the clock in the courtroom and says the court will be in recess until one. As soon as the bailiff opens the door that leads into his chambers, I walk quickly to the witness stand before Dick can get to Darla. "If you know what's good for you," I whisper into her left ear, "you'll follow me right now out this courtroom and to my car out back, so we can talk."

Darla looks past me at Paul, who I know is watching her. "He's gonna get off," I continue saying, "and you'll end up in jail."

Darla says nothing, and I head out the door, and go around back to the Blazer, which, like the other thirty or so vehicles sinking into the sweltering asphalt, is now directly in the sun. I climb in and roll down the windows, while the longest minute of my life passes, but I begin to breathe again as Darla comes around the corner. Her face is a mask, but I don't give her time to bullshit me. "Bonner and Butterfield will be coming after you, Darla," I say as soon as she shuts the door. "They're not stupid, and you know it. You've got just enough time to make a deal with Butterfield, but you better do it now. Paul can't be tried again if this case ends today, and you won't have anything to bargain with."

She says nothing, but looks at me with pure hatred in her eyes. "It's Paul who Butterfield wants, not you. He wants to run for office so bad he can taste it, and sending Paul to jail will put him on the map. But you could be the first woman executed in Arkansas if you don't act immediately."

Following her gaze, I turn my head, and sure enough there is Paul, brazen as a whore, standing at the corner of the building waiting to talk to her. "Paul's spent his life sneering at people like you, and if you let him, he'll do it again."

Her temples already beginning to sweat in the heat, she brushes back a lock of wispy gray hair from her forehead. After a moment, she shrugs slightly, and I realize she isn't going to say anything to me. I look back and see that Paul has disappeared. "Wait here, and I'll go tell Butterfield you want to talk to him."

After a long moment, she raises a hand to wipe a tear out of the corner of her right eye. Until this moment, I wasn't certain he was in on it. That is good enough for me. I sprint back into the courthouse to look for Butterfield, whom I find upstairs in his office behind his desk opening a sack lunch, the Arkansas criminal code open before him.

Pushing the sack to one side, he smirks as if he is not at all surprised to see me. I sit down across from him and tell him that Darla is waiting to talk to him in the Blazer.

Melvin looks past me at the closed door behind my chair. "So this case just comes down to good old-fashioned racism, after all, huh?"

I stare at him. He must mean that Mary Kiley lied to the sheriff. "Call it what you want," I say, "but it is obvious she resented the hell out of him and would have tried to protect Adolf Hitler if he had been out there."

As if he has all the time in the world, Butterfield tilts his chair back and asks, "Assuming you're right, what was Tate's motive?"

"Money, probably," I guess. "She didn't say, nor has she admitted anything to me, but she was trying to raise two boys on a secretary's salary. Taylor probably got to know how desperate she was through the boys. He somehow learned she was stealing from the plant and made her an offer she couldn't refuse since Willie was about to find out. The timing for Paul was perfect."

The prosecutor rocks back and forth in his chair with his hands behind his head and thinks. "So your idea is, together this Tate woman and Taylor," he muses, "picked the easiest and the dumbest nigger in the plant to frame?"

I lean forward on my knees. Doss is more decent than dumb, but I won't argue the point. "And *he* picked the dumbest lawyer in the state to represent him," I admit. "I've had my own agenda so long in this case I've been lucky to find the courthouse."

Butterfield abruptly stops rocking and says, "So I've heard."

For a long moment we sit staring at each other. Then, taking a small Sony tape recorder from his desk, Butterfield stands up, his lanky frame uncurling as if it were made of rubber. "Hell," he complains laconically, "I'm not gonna get any lunch."

After nervously gulping down a turkey sandwich and a Coke at a convenience store off the square, I wander around the courthouse hoping to spot Butterfield and Darla. They are not in the Blazer. His office door is shut, but I do not see a light coming from it. I should be sitting with Doss, but we have gone over his story so many times that I can't stay seated. So nervous he can barely speak, Doss is going to make a terrible witness. He will sound guilty, and there is nothing I can do about it.

I walk outside and stand on the front steps. Paul and Dick are nowhere to be seen either. I have looked for Angela, but she has probably walked home, a mere three blocks away, for lunch. I have not talked to her for the last week, and now, I wonder how all of this will affect her. What does she really know? Has she been lying to me all this time? Is she still in love with Paul? I have tried to put her out of my mind, but now it is impossible. What a mistake it was to become involved with her! Now I am hooked. Gloomily, I realize the case is out of my hands. I walk back inside, knowing that if he wants to, on closing argument, Butterfield can brush away the testimony of Eddie Ting and Mary Kiley in two minutes. Darla has admitted nothing, and unless she does, Doss is headed for Cummins, and my anger and stupidity will have helped put him there.

At five minutes after one, Melvin Butterfield is nowhere to be seen, and Judge Johnson, ready to resume the testimony, is fuming. The courtroom is packed to the gills, and I look over at Paul and Dick, who are sitting quietly, giving nothing away by their expressions. Just as the judge orders his bailiff to go look for the prosecutor, Melvin bursts through the side door and Johnson immediately holds him in contempt of court for being late and fines him fifty dollars.

So distracted that he doesn't seem to have heard him, Melvin fidgets with the buttons on his suit coat until Johnson asks him sarcastically if he is finally ready to proceed.

Nervous for the first time since I've known him, Melvin announces, "Your honor, the state moves to dismiss all charges against the defendant Doss Bledsoe!"

I look over at Paul, who grips the table in front of both hands. In the courtroom, the blacks begin to yell and clap, and over the noise, Dick, his face red and angry, gets to his feet and demands a mistrial. Beside me, Doss, a dazed look on his face, tugs at my sleeve. "Does this mean I'm free?"

Johnson bangs his gavel repeatedly and says that the court is in recess and orders the lawyers back into his chambers. I tell Doss it sounds like it to me and that I will be back in a few minutes.

Inside Johnson's chambers, the tension is thick enough to cut with a knife. Dick can hardly contain himself as we arrange ourselves around the judge's table and wait for his court reporter to set up. If looks could kill, I'd be dead as a doornail. Yet I have done nothing unusual or improper except come to my senses. My guess is that Paul has been lying to him all this time, but I may never know the truth. Finally, the judge says formally to the prosecutor, "What exactly is going on, Mr. Butterfield?"

Melvin, his right hand inside his pocket presumably holding his tape recorder, tells the judge, "The state has credible evidence that Doss Bledsoe was being framed by Darla Tate, who has agreed to testify against Mr. Taylor."

I would have loved to have heard that conversation. I can only assume that Darla knew that once the spotlight was going to be on her, the jig was up. Dick, his jaw working furiously, yelps, "The prosecution has already rested its case."

Butterfield, now suddenly relaxed, takes his hand out of his pocket and brings both palms together under his chin. "Any witness can change her story," he says confidently, "on cross-examination."

I sit back and watch Johnson as he irritably drums his fingers on the table in front of him. No judge likes to declare a mistrial, but he knows he may be reversed if he doesn't give Dick an opportunity to prepare a new defense. "I'll grant a motion, Mr. Dickerson, for a mistrial."

Dick nods, but from the expression on his face, he knows Paul's goose is cooked. When we walk back into the courtroom, I give Doss a thumbs-up sign. For the first time since I can remember, a smile splits his face from ear to ear.

After Johnson announces that he has granted a mistrial and that Doss is no longer a defendant in the case, there is another outburst, but Johnson gavels the spectators into silence and explains that the charges against Paul are still outstanding. With his usual dignity, he thanks the jury for its service and allows it to leave the courtroom first.

While they are filing out, Doss touches my arm and whispers, "I didn't think you knew what the hell you were doin', but I guess you did."

I laugh, realizing how incredibly relieved I feel. "It took a while, didn't it?" I kid him.

As I get up to go explain to the Tings what has happened, I hope that Doss will never understand how lucky he has been. Outside, in the hall, I find Tommy and Connie, who, as I expected, is enraged. "Well, you did it, didn't you?" she says, hissing the words and tears streaming down her face. "You got him off!"

I put my finger to my lips and mouth the words, "It was Darla who killed your father; she's going to testify against Paul."

Tommy frowns, but then nods in understanding. "Darla must have lost her nerve," he says to her sister. "If she had kept her mouth shut, they would have gotten away with it."

Connie, looking considerably older today than her forty-nine years, shakes her head. "It's not over. You wait and see. They'll get off somehow."

Not the skeptic his sister is, Tommy shakes my hand and thanks me, and as he does, a photographer from the *Commercial Appeal* out of Memphis snaps our picture. As a reporter comes forward, I wonder if in six months Tommy will have any regrets.

On my way out of town I resist the urge to stop by Angela's.

I did not see her on my way out of the courthouse. There will be time to sort through all of that. I do not trust myself or her enough to talk to her. It is not inconceivable that I could be called as a witness if Paul goes to trial. Right now, I'm just relieved to be leaving Bear Creek in one piece.

Epilogue

CHRISTMAS MORNING I OPEN MY PRESENT from Sarah and smile. *Dad's Own Cook Book.* "Why didn't you give me this seven years ago?" I complain. I glance at the introduction. The author promises not to treat the reader like an idiot, although the book, he promises, is written so an idiot can read and understand it. A book after my own heart. Ever since her mother died, all we've done is open cans and defrost meat and call it cooking.

Sarah, wearing her Banana Republic sweater that I picked out for her, replies. "It's not true," she says, stroking Jessie's muzzle, "that an old dog can't learn some new tricks."

As if on cue, Jessie grabs up a rawhide bone and shakes it proudly. She has finally learned to use the dog door. A runner, not a thinker, but that's okay. Her master doesn't learn very fast either. Sarah grabs up our Polaroid and snaps Jessie's picture. "Jessie, say 'dog biscuit.'"

Hearing her name, Jessie walks over to her. There was a time when I wondered if Amy was going to keep her as a memento.

The phone rings. I take it and wish whoever is calling a politically incorrect "Merry Christmas."

"Mr. Page?"

It is my "little brother," Harold Ritter. Harold is thirteen, black, from the projects, "Needle Park," and has the sweetest smile on a kid I've ever seen. Dan wouldn't let me back out on my promise to join One-on-One. "Harold," I say, "did Santa Claus come last night?"

"Thank you for the watch," he says, dutifully. "What time you comin' by to git me?"

The two of us are going to see the movie *Toy Story*. Sarah will visit her friends. "A little before two," I tell him. At six we are invited over to Angela's for Christmas dinner with her boys. "Wish your mother a Merry Christmas for me."

"Okay," he says solemnly and hangs up.

I put down the phone, wondering if Harold will have a chance to grow up. There is so much gang activity in Blackwell County it is spooky. His mother, who desperately wanted him to be in the One-on-One program, is on welfare. The best thing she could do for Harold is to move to a desert island for the next ten years. Since she can't do that, I'm supposed to take up the slack. Right.

"Dad," Sarah says, as I am about to head out the door a few minutes later to take Jessie over to the park to do her business, "do you think you and Angela will ever get married? You seem to really care about her. I like her, too."

I wonder what my daughter would think about her if she knew as much about Angela as I do. Since she moved over here in September into an apartment close to the river (only about a mile from me as the crow flies), I have unsuccessfully tried to keep my distance from her, but the holidays are always difficult. "This is just dinner."

"Just checking," my daughter says casually. "I can tell she really likes you."

It helps to have your main competition serving a life sentence. Jessie and I cross the street into the park, which, many days, but not this one quite yet, is crisscrossed by mountain bikers, solitary walkers, dogs of all persuasion, and their purported best friends. It is easy going this time of the year, the shrubs and trees having shed their evidence that they had thrived during a long spring and hot summer.

I slip the leash from Jessie's throat. She likes to nose around in the brush but never lets me get too far out of her sight. Sarah has probably told her that I shouldn't be allowed to stray too far from home. Not a bad idea. Bear Creek was, as it turned out, a long way.

Angela. How can I be so attracted to a woman who would have an affair while her husband of thirty years lay dying? I'm not sure if she is a monster or one of the most attractive women I've ever known. If she tells me tonight that she has been lying and is still in love with Paul I won't bat an eye. For all I really know, if Paul hadn't pleaded guilty to first-degree murder in order to be eligible for parole, she might still be living in Bear Creek waiting for the right moment to slip off to the Peabody Hotel in Memphis. Once people lie, you never know if they are telling the truth.

Of course, we all lie, and if not to each other, then to ourselves. All those years I carried a grudge against Paul and his father because I didn't want to admit how screwed up my own family had become. I thought I was so clear-eyed about my past, and I didn't have a clue. Thank God Paul didn't have a trial. His plea agreement let Angela's secrets stay secret. The fortunate thing about guilty pleas is that the real story never comes out. I will always wonder how Paul convinced Darla Tate to actually slit another human being's throat, especially one who had been so good to her. If she hadn't felt so much guilt, she could have pulled it off. Poor Darla. Butterfield has told me that Paul figured out from her boys how desperate she was and began to put the scheme together after Willie turned him down the first time. Her payoff was supposed to be a farm that Paul owned. Instead, she is doing a life sentence as well. According to Butterfield it was to be for her boys, something to pass on. I have wondered if it was my grandfather's property. A nice irony if it was. Land. Sometimes, it seems more of a curse than a blessing in this part of the country.

Jessie spies a squirrel and makes a dash for it, but it scrambles up a tree just in time. What if she had caught it? I've heard it said that it isn't always such a good idea to get the thing you wish for. Except for Eddie, all the Tings are gone forever from Bear Creek. Tommy has returned to D.C., and Mrs. Ting has moved to Memphis to live with Connie. The plant, according to Eddie, has begun to make a profit again. Good for Eddie. Perhaps, because he is younger, and has experienced less rejection, he is more comfortable in a small town than his cousins. Poor Bear Creek. So much tension, so little hope. Of course, that is a white person thinking out loud. Maybe some of the African-American population see it differently.

I squint at my watch. A quarter to eleven. Dan will be coming over for lunch in a few minutes with his new girlfriend, a schoolteacher he met through the personals column in the Little Rock *Free Press*. So much for his dating service. I smile at the thought of my best friend. The idiot is wearing a gold ring in his left ear and looks ridiculous. Some guys can pull it off, but not Dan. When I asked why, he grinned. "It's kind of a fuck-you statement," he admitted. "But it's harmless. I don't wear it to court."

Harmless? As I call Jessie and head back to the house, I think of all the pain I stirred up in Bear Creek. Sometimes, I don't think I am.

About the Author

GRIF STOCKLEY grew up in Marianna, Arkansas, and graduated from Rhodes College in Memphis. For the past twenty-five years, he has been an attorney for the Center for Arkansas Legal Services in Little Rock, which is funded by the federal government to provide representation to indigents in noncriminal cases.